Sarra Manning is an author and journalist. She started her writing career on *Melody Maker*, then spent five years on legendary UK teen mag *J17*, first as a writer then as entertainment editor. Subsequently she edited teen fashion bible *Ellegirl UK* and the BBC's *What To Wear* magazine.

Sarra has written for *ELLE*, *Grazia*, *Red*, *InStyle*, the *Guardian*, the *Mail On Sunday's You* magazine, *Harper's Bazaar*, *Stylist*, *Time Out* and the *Sunday Telegraph's Stella*. Her best-selling young adult novels, which include *Guitar Girl*, *Let's Get Lost*, the *Diary Of A Crush* trilogy and *Nobody's Girl* have been translated into numerous languages.

She has also written two grown-up novels: *Unsticky* and *You Don't Have To Say You Love Me*.

Sarra lives in North London.

T0316099

Also by Sarra Manning

Unsticky
You Don't Have To Say You Love Me

For more information on Sarra Manning and her books,
see her website at www.sarramanning.co.uk

Nine Uses for an

Ex-Boyfriend

Sarra Manning

CORGI BOOKS

TRANSWORLD PUBLISHERS
61–63 Uxbridge Road, London W5 5SA
A Random House Group Company
www.transworldbooks.co.uk

NINE USES FOR AN EX-BOYFRIEND
A CORGI BOOK: 9780552163286

First publication in Great Britain
Corgi edition published 2012

Copyright © Sarra Manning 2012

Sarra Manning has asserted her right under the Copyright, Designs and
Patents Act 1988 to be identified as the author of this work.

This book is a work of fiction and, except in the case of historical fact, any
resemblance to actual persons, living or dead, is purely coincidental.

A CIP catalogue record for this book
is available from the British Library.

This book is sold subject to the condition that it shall not,
by way of trade or otherwise, be lent, resold, hired out,
or otherwise circulated without the publisher's prior
consent in any form of binding or cover other than that
in which it is published and without a similar condition,
including this condition, being imposed on the
subsequent purchaser.

Addresses for companies within
The Penguin Random House Group can be found at:
global.penguinrandomhouse.com

Penguin Random House is committed to a sustainable future for
our business, our readers and our planet. This book is made from
Forest Stewardship Council® certified paper.

MIX
Paper | Supporting
responsible forestry
FSC® C018179

Printed and bound in Great Britain by Clays Ltd, Elcograf S.p.A.
Typeset in Meridien by Falcon Oast Graphic Art Ltd.

4 6 8 10 9 7 5 3

Dedicated to my best friend, Kate Hodges, who was gestating and then giving birth to Dusty and Arthur while I was writing this book. Your finished product totally trumps mine!

Thanks

As ever, I owe huge amounts of gratitude to Gordon and Joanne Shaw, Sarah Bailey, Sophie Wilson and Lesley Lawson for not minding too much when I never returned phone calls or emails. I'd also like to thank my running buddy, Gael Oldfield, and the ladies of Twitter: Sam Baker, Anna Carey, Sarah Franklin and Lucy McCarry for all their support. I'm especially indebted to Ruthie Morgan who very kindly shared her experiences from the primary-school frontline with me and taught me several new ways of telling people off.

Finally, an entirely inadequate thank you to my amazing agent, Karolina Sutton, and Catherine Saunders, Helen Manders and all at Curtis Brown. And to my editor/cheer-leader/provider of tough love, Catherine Cobain, as well as Sarah Roscoe, Madeline Toy, Sophie Wilson (yes, I know, two Sophie Wilsons), and the rest of the team at Transworld.

http://twitter.com/sarramanning

Prologue

It was obvious it wasn't the first time that Hope's boyfriend and her best friend had kissed. It also looked, to the casual observer, as if they usually did more than kiss when they weren't on a clock or running the risk of being discovered.

Hope could hear the wet clash of their mouths and Jack's groans as Susie stroked him, and she didn't know why she was simply standing there when she should have been charging out of the back door and shrieking something along the lines of, *What the hell are you two doing? You utter, utter bastards!*

Jack and Susie were illuminated beautifully in the glare of the sensor light that Jack's dad had fitted on the outside wall to scare off the foxes that kept scavenging through their bins, and Hope had a perfect view of Jack's hand threaded in Susie's glossy treacly brown hair so her beautiful face was upturned, his other hand making strange, contorted shapes under her Catherine Malandrino silk top. If she squinted extra hard she was sure she could even see the tangle of tongues as they kissed as if they were starring in their own porn film.

Jack never kisses me like that any more, Hope thought to herself as she stood on the steps that led from their tiny kitchen to their tiny back garden. Hasn't done for ages and ages. Not since they'd been teenagers snogging furiously in the no-man's-land between their respective houses, ten minutes after Hope's curfew had ended. But Hope would

9

never have shoved her hands down the front of Jack's jeans in those days, as Susie was doing now, and if Jack had tried to touch her breasts *under* her clothes, Hope would have screamed loud enough to wake her parents, if her parents had actually been asleep instead of staying awake until their only daughter was safely tucked up in her single bed.

And still Hope stood there as if her feet had taken root, hands lifted to her mouth to mute any noise she might make. The scent of garlic clinging to her fingers made her stomach heave and oh God . . . Her childhood sweetheart, the boy she'd been with for half her lifetime, her one true love, the man she was meant to be with for ever and ever and ever, amen, was passionately and furiously kissing her best friend.

How could they?

Chapter One

At precisely two on a sunny Saturday afternoon Hope Delafield came to the sudden and shocking realisation that she should never have decided to throw a dinner party.

This epiphany came during her fifth attempt to tie up her lamb roulade without the stuffing oozing out. The same leg of lamb that had meant an hour-and-a-half round trip, up and down several hills, to get to the organic butcher's in Kentish Town. It was only after she'd lugged the lamb and four bottles of Cabernet Sauvignon and Sauvignon Blanc back home in the blistering early-September heat, that Hope realised she'd forgotten to ask the butcher to butterfly the joint and had been forced to retrace her steps.

At least it had been a brief respite and a dose of fresh air for Hope who'd been up since six making double pesto for the roulade filling, a marinade for her scallops starter and soaking brioche in Cointreau for a bread and butter pudding. 'God, I never want to see another pine nut as long as I live,' she proclaimed loudly, but it wasn't loud enough to be heard over the racket of *Red Dead Redemption* and the new Fleet Foxes album. Hope didn't know how Jack could play video games and listen to music at the same time, and she wanted to barge into the living room and yell at him, because the noise was giving her a tension headache.

She even took a step out of the kitchen but stopped herself. She was getting a tension headache because there was double pesto dribbling out of her roulade on to the worktop and even with the back door open their tiny kitchen was stuffy and hot. None of that was Jack's fault and he'd had to work really late the night before and though he thought having a dinner party was a stupid idea, he'd been a really good sport about it, even when Hope had cooked scallops for tea every evening that week as she'd tried to find the right balance between raw and rubbery. It had taken three attempts to get them lightly seared and although there had been a lot of lip-tightening, Jack hadn't said anything, apart from heaping lavish praise on her minted pea purée.

Jack wandered into the kitchen half an hour later as Hope was tentatively poking at the lamb with a wooden spoon as she gave it a quick sear in a frying pan.

'Why the long face, Hopita?' he enquired, leaning over her shoulder so he could peer at the contents of the pan. 'Is it meant to be oozing like that?'

'I don't know!' Hope turned off the gas so she could sink down on the floor, which was liberally scattered with pine nuts, and sit with her back against a cupboard and stretch out her legs. 'I'm this close to going out and getting eight ready meals.'

'You can't do that. You've already blown our entire food budget for the month. We're going to be living on toast and spaghetti hoops as it is,' Jack said wearily, as he prodded the meat with his finger. 'Smells nice though.'

Inspiration suddenly struck. 'Maybe I could baste the joint with the gloop that's oozed out?' Hope mused, hauling herself up as Jack squatted down so that for a moment they were nose to nose and he kissed her forehead, so he couldn't be that mad with her. 'I'm sorry. You were right and I'm never, ever having a dinner party again, even if one day we can afford to live in an actual house with an actual dining room and have the whole thing catered.'

'Do you promise?' Jack asked, taking Hope's sticky,

garlicky, pine-nutty hand and placing it over her heart. 'You have to promise.'

'I promise,' Hope said, wiping her hand off on her T-shirt, which was already smeared with olive oil, butter and jam. 'I mean, I like cooking. Just not when everything has to be perfect and weighed out and . . .'

'You end up using every single dish and utensil that we own,' Jack interrupted, as he rose to full height and surveyed the kitchen, which had pots and pans and cutlery heaped on every surface and even stacked on the two gas rings that Hope wasn't using. 'It's a small kitchen . . .'

'I think you meant to say "poky".' Hope flapped her arms to illustrate said pokiness. Jack could actually stand at the epicentre of their kitchen, stretch out his arms and touch the walls. 'A poky kitchen in a poky basement flat.'

'It's not poky; it's bijou,' Jack argued. 'It's not a basement flat; it's a garden flat. And it's your first step on the property ladder, young lady.'

'The scary thing is that I can't tell whether you sound more like my mum or your mum,' Hope said, picking up her spoon so she could poke her roulade again.

'Well, when they start on the topic of owning your first home they're pretty interchangeable,' Jack said absently as he looked around at the havoc that Hope had wrought. 'You know, if you just tidied up as you went along, then it wouldn't get so chaotic and you could tick off each item on your checklist and you'd feel a lot calmer. I bet you don't even know where the list is.'

Hope knew exactly where the list was. Nowhere, because she'd never got round to making a list. Jack was all about tidying up as he went along and lists and minimalism and sleek, modern lines, and she was about letting things happen in an organic fashion until they all happened at once, like now, and Jack had to force her to write a to-do list, while he started on the washing-up.

Jack was also very anti leaving things on the draining

board instead of drying them with a tea towel and putting them away so the whole process took half an hour, though Hope put up a spirited defence against putting away things that she'd need again in five minutes, until Jack scooped up a handful of sudsy water and flung it at her so the ends of her red hair, which weren't skewered in a bun held together with two HB pencils, were soaked and her T-shirt clung to her breasts.

'Don't you feel better now that you've got a list?' Jack demanded, adroitly fending Hope off as she tried to get in on the dishwater action. 'Like everything's under control?'

'Well, I suppose,' Hope panted, as she tried to duck under Jack's arm. 'The thought of making the list wasn't as bad as the actual making of it, but I'm *drenched*.'

'I know,' Jack said with a leer, reaching up with a wet hand to give her sodden left breast a quick squeeze. 'By the way, nice tits.'

Hope pretended to glare at him but after twenty-six years of knowing her, Jack could spot one of her fake glares at fifty paces so he just grinned as he slyly tweaked her other breast. And even after twenty-six years of knowing him, when Jack was beaming at her like that, Hope was powerless to resist him.

'You'll never get to see them again if you keep doing that,' she told him sternly, because it didn't do Jack any good to know just how potent the power of his smile was.

It was no wonder that Lottie and Nancy from next door, who were ten and twelve respectively, went red in the face and giggly every time they saw Jack. The week before, Jack had been bare-chested as he watered the garden with the hose, and the giggling from the other side of the garden fence had got so shrill and frequent that Hope, who'd been treating her roses for greenfly, had feared for her eardrums.

But if you were a tween, then Jack was all your pre-pubescent fantasies made flesh and living next door. He was tall and slim with thickly lashed blue eyes and a pretty,

14

pouty mouth that wore a perpetual smile. He had a moptop of thick brown hair that was half Beatle, half Justin Bieber, and he dressed just like a teen popstar who'd been given a rock 'n' roll makeover by his stylist: tight jeans that were just loose enough to slip down and show his pert, boxer-shorted arse to the world, Chuck Taylors and skinny T-shirts, which clung lovingly to his chest and proved quite emphatically that he didn't have an ounce of fat anywhere about his person.

Factor in the cool job as art editor on *Skirt* magazine, which meant he could procure tickets for premieres of films featuring sparkling vampires, CDs of the latest boyband and, on one never-to-be-forgotten occasion, tickets for the *X-Factor* final, and it was inevitable that Lottie and Nancy would fall madly and hopelessly in love with Jack, in much the same way that Hope had when she was thirteen and he was fifteen and he'd suddenly stopped being the boy next door and become the measure by which all other boys were judged and found wanting. Back then, though, all that Jack had had in the way of connections was a newspaper round, which meant that he occasionally stole a copy of *J17* for her.

Hope, on the other hand, was a primary-school teacher with red hair, who'd once shouted at Lottie for dashing across the street on her roller skates into the path of a pizza delivery boy on a moped. Even worse, Hope had then frog-marched Lottie back home so she could be shouted at by her mother, Alice, too. Since then Lottie and Nancy had made it perfectly plain that they couldn't understand what the god-like Jack was doing with that 'totally mean ginger girl'.

What he was currently doing was running his eyes down Hope's dinner-party checklist. 'So you've got an hour free now between sealing the roulade and making the mascarpone cream? Shall we sort out the living room?'

Hope nodded unenthusiastically. It was far too hot to be

lugging furniture about, or serving a main course as heavy as lamb roulade with dauphinoise potatoes, for that matter.

'Maybe I should sauté the potatoes instead of baking them with loads of cream,' she pondered out loud. 'Do you think you could get me some more olive oil when you go out?'

Jack groaned. 'This is why you need to be more organised. When you go off road, terrible things always happen, Hopita.'

'No, they don't,' Hope insisted, because this was nothing like the time that she'd run out of caster sugar when she was baking and had improvised by mashing up brown sugar cubes. Or when she'd been learning to knit and hadn't been able to get more of the chunky wool she'd been using so had switched to a fine yarn to give her scarf some texture. 'It's our first dinner party and everything has to be just so.'

'Our *only* dinner party,' Jack reiterated sharply, as if he hadn't been joking earlier. 'We are never doing this again. Not in my lifetime.'

It took them nearly half an hour to tug, shove, lift and heave their futon sofabed (which was uncomfortable both to sit or sleep on) into the bedroom. Hope decided to multi-task and use this time to get Jack on board the dinner-party train. After all, she'd invited his two artboy mates, Otto and Marvin, not just to appease Jack but also as potential cannon fodder for Hope's friends Lauren and Allison, who were both going through a dry spell. Jack had been boringly insistent that they had room for only four guests but Hope had to invite her other friend Susie as a very paltry thank you for buying her a Latitude ticket, even if it did mean that Susie's grumpy boyfriend, Wilson, had to be invited too. And anyway, 'Having a dinner party is grown up and now we own our own home and we have two sets of bed linen and spare towels we should be doing more grown-up things.'

Jack shrugged. 'We don't actually own our own home. It's

jointly owned by our parents, who lent us the deposit, and the Halifax.' He sat down on their bed, which they'd got on Freecycle and which was almost as uncomfortable as the sofabed, and pulled Hope down to sit alongside him. 'Sorry. It's just ... well, it's our last weekend before school starts and you get bogged down with lesson plans and standardised tests. I kinda wanted this weekend to be just the two of us. And now you're mad at me, aren't you?'

'I'm not,' Hope said, though she kind of was, after all the trouble she'd gone to. 'At least I've learned an important life lesson about planning a menu that can be made days in advance and shoved in the freezer.'

'Well, as long as it's been a teachable moment then that's OK.' Jack kissed the top of her head, even as he sighed. 'So, olive oil, and what else have you forgotten? Did you buy a couple of decent bottles of wine that The Pretentious Wanker will deign to drink?'

'He's called Wilson,' Hope said mildly, because Wilson was a pretentious wanker, who only seemed to come with one facial expression, a world-weary sneer. 'The offy was having a four-for-three promotion, so I did get wine but, hmm, I suppose we do need to get something a lot more expensive with a subtle bouquet.'

'And some bottles of fancy imported lager that are teeny tiny and cost three quid each,' Jack said sourly. 'God, he's such a pretentious wanker.'

'Really is,' Hope agreed, pleased that they were finally back in sync, even if it was over the wankerdom of Wilson. 'And if you're popping into Waitrose anyway, can you get some clotted-cream vanilla ice-cream in case my mascarpone curdles in the heat?'

Jack grumbled a little more about the dinner party bankrupting them and how they'd have to live on SupaNoodles for the rest of the month, but Hope ignored him as she added a few more items to the shopping list and sent him off to B&Q with a cheery wave.

Their cunning plan to get around the obstacle of not having a dining table was to buy a wallpaper-pasting table, which they'd return tomorrow in pristine condition. Hope had promised Jack faithfully that she'd put down newspaper under the tablecloth, in case of spillages. Of course they needed eight chairs too, but Jack and Hope would sit on their kitchen stools and Gary the estate agent, who lived in spacious splendour in the rest of the house above them, had promised that they could borrow his four expensive Heal's chairs, though Hope had had to flirt with him for ten very long minutes ('Really? You've doubled your commission in the last six months? Wow! You must be *so* good at selling houses . . .'). He even carried the chairs down the crumbling concrete stairs that led to the basement flat and into the re-purposed living room.

Hope was now meant to go next door, according to her checklist, and borrow two chairs from Alice, Lottie and Nancy's long-suffering mum, but she wasted valuable time following Gary around the flat as he kicked at their skirting boards and advised Hope that she and Jack would 'easily add another ten thou on your resale value if you ripped out the kitchen and put a new one in'. Jack was much better at dealing with Alice anyway as she always wanted to badger Hope about primary-school league tables and whether Nancy had ADD, dyslexia or was just plain lazy.

She was loath to admit it, but having a list made it easier to finish all the preparations, and less than an hour later Hope had nothing left to do in the kitchen until soon before her guests arrived. She couldn't lay a table that didn't exist and so had no choice but to indulge in a long soaky bath, and when Jack still hadn't come home, she even took the time to blow-dry her hair sort of straight.

By now it was after five, Jack had been gone nearly two hours, and Hope's Facebook invites stated quite clearly that pre-dinner drinks would be at seven sharp.

Where are you? she texted him, and it wasn't until she'd

finished putting her make-up on that he texted back, *On my way. Arsenal r playing @ home. Holloway Rd blocked solid.*

'Why didn't you take the back roads then?' Hope muttered to herself, as she applied one last coat of mascara and stepped back to assess her appearance in the mirror glued to the inside of one of the wardrobe doors.

To make up for the rustic, make-do charm of their borrowed table and mismatched chairs, Hope had been going for a look that shrieked effortless glamour, but she wasn't entirely sure she'd succeeded.

She'd started with the shoes; her beloved Stella McCartney leopard-print satin wedges, which had been an unexpected birthday present from Jack – he usually bought her a dress that was at least a size too small and the biggest box of chocolates he could find. The wedges were higher than Hope was used to and so far she hadn't dared to wear them outside, but they went beautifully with her black broderie anglaise maxi dress.

Hope was always grateful that she was the sort of redhead that tanned, or rather freckled until all her freckles mostly joined up to create a tan, and the thin straps of the dress showed off her sun-kissed shoulders. The fabric fell in graceful folds over her pot belly. Hope ran a hand over her tummy, which always made its presence felt during the school holidays. When school broke up, she was always full of plans to visit the gym every day and swim and go on long walks, but the plans usually petered out before the end of the first week in favour of meeting friends for coffee and cake, or lunch, or a cinema outing which involved ice-cream and popcorn. In fact, eating vast quantities of food in a social setting won out over the gym every time, leaving Hope ten pounds heavier at the beginning of term. Although she was hating her midriff right now, she knew that spending seven-hour days wrangling a class of six-year-olds, and going to the gym to alleviate the stress of seven hours spent wrangling a class of six-year-olds, would make the belly fat melt away pretty quickly. Until then it was big knickers and maxi dresses all the way, all the time.

She leaned closer to the mirror to peer critically at her face to make sure that her tinted moisturiser was evening out both freckles and the paler skin in between the freckles and yes, she still loved the creamy-rose shade of the Chanel Rouge Coco Mademoiselle lipstick Jack had got her from a *Skirt* beauty sale. Susie insisted that Hope could get away with a deeper red or even a fuchsia pink on her mouth, which Jack gamely said was a perfect cupid's bow and her oldest brother Matthew used to describe as a cat's bum, but Hope refused.

Her mother had drummed into Hope since she was practically embryonic that she should accentuate her widely spaced blue eyes rather than draw attention to her snub nose and her freckles, which had been the bane of her adolescence. She'd tried everything to get rid of them, from rubbing lemon slices on her face (which had stung like a bitch during her spotty teen years) to green-based foundations and concealers, which she'd never been able to blend in properly and had made her look bilious. Now Hope had learned to love her freckles because it was obvious she was stuck with them, like she was stuck with red hair.

Technically it was auburn. A deep, dark red that wasn't orange and definitely wasn't ginger. It was the kind of red hair that was more Julianne Moore than Sarah Ferguson, or, God forbid, Miranda in the first season of *Sex and the City*. Hope's eyebrows and eyelashes were also the same deep auburn but she'd still been called 'ginger pubes' all the way through school. Even now, Hope could be walking down the street, minding her own business, only to hear someone bellow, 'Oi! Ginger pubes!' from a passing white van, but such was the redhead's lot in life. Hope liked to think that having hair this colour had instilled huge amounts of guts and gumption in her from an early age and, when she wasn't at school, she wore her hair long and loose with pride, even if after half an hour of being long and loose, it was a mass of Medusa-like tangles.

'You'll do,' she told her reflection. 'As long as you don't break your neck on the sticky-up bit of lino in the kitchen.'

Chapter Two

Jack still wasn't back less than an hour before kick-off. Hope grumbled furiously to herself as she consulted Jamie Oliver's recipe for the toasted almonds she was making for pre-dinner nibbles.

But by the time she started concocting a punch from a bottle of fake-Pimm's, a bottle of five-quid vodka from Aldi and two litres of passion fruit juice, Hope was pretending that she was on *Come Dine With Me* and happily talking to an invisible camera.

'. . . and one little tip I have for making a really good punch is to nick a syringe from Janet, the school nurse, so I can inject vodka straight into the strawberries. Gives the punch an added kick,' she babbled, as she chopped up half an elderly cucumber. 'It's also a good way to use up all the fruit that's about to go mushy. I mean, even if it has gone mushy, the alcohol will just disguise the taste and . . .'

There was the sound of a key turning in the lock and she hurried into the hall in time to greet Jack as he staggered through the door, dragging the ersatz dining table behind him.

'There you are!' Hope exclaimed. 'I thought you'd gone to Cornwall to get the clotted-cream ice-cream. People will be here in half an hour!'

'It's not my fault the traffic was gridlocked,' Jack replied angrily. His hair was sticking up as if he'd been clutching at it in frustration at the gridlockedness of the traffic. 'I texted you!'

'That was an hour ago,' Hope reminded him. 'Did you get

lost in a time–space continuum that suddenly opened up on Tollington Road?'

'Yeah, and I managed to get everything that you scribbled down on the fourth shopping list for this bloody dinner party, thanks for asking.'

'You're so late getting back you might just as well not have bothered,' Hope said ungraciously. 'People will be arriving in thirty minutes and you need to get two chairs from Alice next door and have a shower 'cause, quite frankly, you're smelling pretty ripe, and now I have to lay the table when I should be parboiling potatoes and warming my bruschetta.'

'Well, if you'd organised things better then . . .'

'Now's really not the time for a lover's tiff, you two,' said a warm, amused voice from behind Jack, and Hope saw Susie walk through the door clutching two Waitrose carriers and a huge bunch of what might have been flowers or could have been an avant garde art installation. 'Jack saw me coming up the road and gave me a lift, didn't you?'

Jack was still bright-red and furious. 'Sorry about that, Hope. I'm sure that made me at least a whole minute later than I already was.'

Hope wanted to throw herself at Susie with pained little cries but she was too mad with Jack to do anything but say, 'You're early,' in a tight voice.

'Oh dear,' Susie cooed. 'Thought you might need a hand but I can always decamp to the pub across the square if I'll be in the way.'

'God, don't do that,' Hope cried, pushing past Jack to grab Susie by the arm. 'I *need* you.'

'Well, you've got me,' Susie said, dropping the Waitrose bags with a dull thud that made Hope wince because she didn't want olive oil over everything, but then Susie was hugging her hard, the spiky fronds from the bouquet tickling Hope's shoulder blades. 'As it's you, I'll even volunteer my services as your kitchen bitch.'

Hope hugged Susie hard back, until Susie made a small distinct sound of protest. Hope let her go and watched her friend smooth down her peach silk, ruffle-sleeved Catherine Malandrino top, which she was wearing with teeny-tiny cut-off denim shorts and a pair of very strappy, very high gold sandals.

'You look gorgeous,' Hope said, and it wasn't even a compliment but the absolute truth. Susie was small, slim and sleek, from the top of her shiny dark-brown hair, which looked as if she soaked it in keratin every morning, to her perfectly pedicured size-three feet. The bit in between hair and feet was pretty stunning too. Susie was, there was no doubt about this, sultry-looking. Deep brown, sloe-shaped eyes peeped out from behind her fringe, she had a tiny smudge of a nose and full, plush lips that were either pouting or smiling like she'd just heard a really filthy joke.

She also had an olive complexion, a generous helping in the breast department and what her legs lacked in length they made up for in their toned perfection, even though Susie could eat obscene amounts of food and not go near a gym in weeks.

It was hard not to feel less-than when you were in the same room with Susie. And it was also hard not to feel more-than. Hope always felt that she wasn't pretty enough or slim enough or just plain *enough*. When she was with Susie, being five foot, six inches was too tall and being a size twelve was too fat. Right now Hope felt like a gangling Goth in her shapeless black dress. And all that chuff about her redhead pride? Pffft! She was a freckly ginger who . . .

'You're the one who looks gorgeous, Hopey,' Susie interrupted her pity-party. 'How come you always manage to look dreamy and ethereal when I'm sweating like a stuck pig?'

'You need to get your eyes tested,' Hope snorted, as she tried to hide her pleased smile. 'And you couldn't look like a stuck pig if you tried.'

'Well, stuck piglet,' Susie conceded, as Jack brought in two dining-room chairs from next door. 'What needs doing first?'

'The table,' Hope decided. Her voice was getting very squeaky. By her own estimation she was five minutes away from a pre-dinner party meltdown. 'Oh shit, I don't think there's even time to lay the table.'

'Yes, there is,' Susie said firmly, pushing past Hope so she could start grabbing handfuls of cutlery out of the drawer. 'Hopey, find a vase for those weird flowers I got you. I thought they'd be a really cool centrepiece.'

'God, I haven't even thanked you for them!'

'Yeah, well, why don't we leave the grovelling for later and Jack, sweetie, hate to be the one to tell you this, but you stink,' Susie added, as he came into the kitchen and reached up to get glasses down from the cupboard above her head. 'Can you go and have a shower before you asphyxiate us and kill my flowers?'

Jack advanced on Susie with both his arms raised above his head while she giggled and held him back with the bread knife. 'Nothing wrong with a healthy bit of man sweat,' he declared, brandishing his armpits at Susie one final time, then sidestepping past Hope as he stripped off his sweat-soaked T-shirt. 'You look like a Modigliani,' he whispered in Hope's ear, as Susie chattered cheerfully away about how none of their cutlery matched, and it was exactly what she needed to hear.

Not that she did look like a Modigliani – his models were pale and thin and drippy-looking – but it was Jack taking the time to see she was freaking out and calming her down with one of his rare compliments. He wasn't a gushy kind of boyfriend who constantly told Hope that she was awesome so when a compliment did come her way it meant a lot.

'Sorry I'm being such a witch,' she muttered and Jack grinned, and as Susie and Hope finally began to lay the table, Hope could hear him singing 'I Put a Spell on You' in the shower.

'There! That doesn't look too shabby,' Susie said ten minutes later. 'Well, maybe shabby-chic, but you do that whole vintage thing so well. When I try, it just looks like a load of tatty old junk from Oxfam.'

Hope folded her arms and surveyed her temporary dining room and her temporary dining-room table. On top of her red and white polka-dot tablecloth (and it was impossible to tell that last Saturday's *Guardian* was laid out beneath it) were her rose-sprigged placemats, and on top of them were assorted bowls on top of assorted plates, plus cutlery that Hope had found in charity shops and at car-boot sales. At least each setting had a wine glass that was just like the other seven wine glasses but that was only because they'd been in a sale at Habitat.

'It's not sophisticated,' Hope lamented, as she tweaked the strange lemon-like protuberance that was the focal point of Susie's bouquet, 'but it is quirky. And now I know that I can improvise a dining room, I can sign up for *Come Dine With Me*.'

'I'd come dine with you any time,' Susie sniffed the air appreciatively. 'Your whole flat smells of Cointreau and garlic. Right, so what's next?'

Nothing was too much trouble for Susie. She finished making the punch and even though she was wearing a £400 silk top, she was happy to fill a huge B&Q bucket with ice and stick the white wine and beer in it because Hope had run out of fridge space. Susie did draw the line at peeling the potatoes because she'd had her nails done that morning but, still, it was hard for Hope to remember that the first time she'd seen Susie had been at the gym, in full make-up, pedalling sedately on an exercise bike in Stella McCartney for Adidas workout gear and reading *Vogue*, and she'd been intimidated beyond all measure. When Hope went to the gym, she wore saggy leggings, holey T-shirts and scraped her hair back because even the slightest exertion made her drip sweat all over the floor.

Hope would occasionally see Susie in the changing rooms doing her make-up in nothing but an Agent Provocateur thong, so all the other women could admire her lithe body and truly spectacular breasts and make a solemn vow to themselves that they'd either work out harder or stop going to the gym on the same days as Susie. Well, that was how Hope had felt so when she'd signed up for a yoga class and found herself next to Susie it hadn't filled her heart with joy. Especially as Susie could contort herself into the most awkward poses while Hope couldn't even master the basic breathing techniques.

Hope had eventually decided that Susie was a stuck-up cow when she caught her smirking after Hope had fallen out of her Half Moon pose and landed on the floor with a shriek. That was it! No more sneaking admiring glances at Susie as she spent ten minutes blending her eyeshadow in the changing room mirror, no more trying to share a con-spiratorial smile with her when Mr Short-Shorts was doing lunges. Even though Susie barely knew that Hope existed, as far as Hope was concerned, Susie was dead to her.

Then came that fateful yoga class when Hope had set her sights on mastering a shoulder stand if it killed her. She'd just been about to straighten out her legs, when the woman behind her had let out a volley of farts that ricocheted around the studio and Hope had gone crashing to the floor, almost dislocating her collar bone in the process. She'd sprawled on her mat for a second, trying to catch her breath, as the poor woman continued to chuff away. All around her, people were falling out of their poses, all except Susie, whose body, apart from her shaking shoulders, was in a per-fect perpendicular line.

Susie had then gracefully righted herself, caught Hope's eye and wafted her hand in front of her nose. 'Someone shouldn't have had chilli last night,' she'd whispered. Then she'd tentatively sniffed the air. 'My mistake. It was obviously curry.'

After this comment, there had been a deathly silence until the woman finally stopped farting, picked up her yoga mat and practically ran out of the studio. Hope had pursed her lips tight, then risked looking over at Susie again who was now pretending that she'd been suffocated by the fumes and it was . . . GAME OVER. Hope had collapsed back on her mat and put her hand over her mouth but the giggles had leaked out between the cracks of her fingers. Then she'd heard Susie snort and Hope had started to laugh so hard that tears streamed down her cheeks. When Georgie, the yoga instructor, had tried to calm Hope down with a mellifluous but detailed explanation of why yoga made some people fart, Hope had curled up in a crying, shaking, cackling ball of mirth until Susie had yanked her up and hustled her out of the room.

When all Hope had left were a few hiccups, Susie had held out her hand. 'I'm Susie and I can tell this is going to be the start of a beautiful friendship,' she'd said as if she really and absolutely meant it.

And it had turned out to be true. Susie was five years older than Hope, and had all the trimmings and baubles of a sophisticated thirty-something: a high-paid job in PR, a beautifully furnished flat in Highgate, over a hundred pairs of designer shoes, and an actual walk-in wardrobe where she stored all her other designer fripperies. But Hope had quickly discovered that Susie's outside didn't match her inside. Once you got past the sleek glossy exterior, Susie was good people.

She was just as happy downing pints in an old man's boozer on the Holloway Road and finishing up with some spicy hot wings from Chicken Cottage as she was sipping mojitos in Shoreditch House. She'd gone through five iPhones in the eighteen months that Hope had known her; dropping them down toilets, losing them on drunken nights-out and leaving one in a service station on the M60. Susie was also unstintingly generous and had been genuinely devastated when she'd realised that Hope's size-six feet wouldn't fit into any of her size-three statement heels. She even tried to supplement Hope's teacher's salary with free dinners at expensive restaurants on her company credit card.

Hope suspected, and all the evidence indicated, that Susie didn't have a lot of female friends. Not when she looked the way she did and gave off waves and waves of serious attitude. She was rude and crude and used words that would have had Hope's mother itching to wash her mouth out with Fairy Liquid. At times she could even be downright insufferable but blamed it on being raised by a philandering father and an alcoholic mother who'd both had serious boundary issues. Even now, Hope didn't know if that was a joke, but she herself had grown up with three elder brothers who'd loved nothing more than to tease, terrorise and torment her, and she could quell a class of unruly six-year-olds without even raising her voice, so putting Susie in her place when she being obnoxious was hardly a stretch.

Susie was being particularly obnoxious as she watched Hope assemble her brioche bread-and-butter pudding. 'For fuck's sake, why did you invite two teachers?' she whined.

'Piss off! I'm a teacher,' Hope said without rancour.

'Whatever.' Susie pouted. 'If you start sharing wacky anecdotes about your days at teacher-training college, I'm going to kick you under the table.'

'Like you could even reach with your tiny little legs.'

'Why do you think I'm wearing five-inch heels?'

They grinned at each other just as Jack walked back into the kitchen, squeaky-clean, fragrant-fresh, and with a put-upon look on his face. 'OK, what do you want me to do next?'

There actually wasn't anything left to do until the guests arrived, when Hope could whip herself into a state of near hysteria as she tried to simultaneously sear twenty scallops in one pan while frying rounds of black pudding in another.

'Everything's under control,' Hope said proudly.

'It is?' Jack sounded sceptical. 'Are you sure about that?'

'I'm quite sure,' Hope said firmly and a little huffily. 'But if you want to be useful then you could lug that bucket full of ice out of the back door 'cause it's in the way. Oh, and should we put some more wine and beer in there too, do you think?'

Jack smirked like he'd known all along that not everything was under control. Hope wriggled her shoulders in irritation.

'You're doing fine,' Susie said soothingly. 'Everything's going to be perfect and even if it isn't, just get everyone really pissed up and they won't notice if you overcook that lamb thing.'

'It's a roulade,' Hope said, abandoning her pudding to hunt for her list so she could check how long the lamb needed to cook. Should she heat the oven up now? But what if everyone was late and then the oven was too hot and the lamb dried out? Then she'd be stuck with a too-hot oven, which would lead to burnt brioche bread-and-butter pudding and . . . 'Oh, God . . .'

'You need a drink,' Susie and Jack, who'd finished his lugging duties, said in unison.

'I can't,' Hope whimpered. 'I don't dare sear my scallops while I'm under the influence.'

'Hopita, you could sear those scallops blindfolded,' Jack said, snuggling up behind her. 'By Wednesday night your scallops were good enough for *MasterChef*. And who doesn't like black pudding?'

'Well, I don't, because I'm not a dirty Northerner,' Susie hissed, pulling a face at the two people who'd been born and bred just outside Rochdale. 'I'm not eating anything whose main ingredient is blood.'

'I'm going to spit on your scallops,' Hope told her dryly,

nestling back against Jack who obligingly tightened his arms. 'And no minted pea purée for you either.'

'Christ, Jack, give the girl a drink,' Susie drawled. She was leaning back against the kitchen counter, legs tensed, chest stuck out as she gave Hope and Jack a wicked smile. 'In fact, I think we should all have some vodka. Just to get us in the mood.'

'Oh, yeah, and what mood would that be?' Jack drawled back, and Hope realised it was her turn to drawl something vaguely flirtatious but it almost felt as if she was surplus to requirements.

And while she was trying to process that thought, or even decide if the thought needed processing, the doorbell rang. Hope tugged herself free of Jack's arms so she could pat her hair and smooth down her dress and do a complete lap of the kitchen, pausing only to take the scallops out of the fridge.

'Easy, tiger,' Jack said, shaking his head as the doorbell rang again. 'I'll get that, shall I, while you do another circuit?'

Hope took a deep breath. 'I don't know why I'm so nervous,' she said to Susie. 'I mean, I know everyone who's coming and I like them or I wouldn't have invited them, so why am I freaking out?'

'I have no idea,' Susie said, shrugging. 'But you need to stop freaking out because you're getting that blotchy stress rash all over your chest. Not a good look, Hopey.'

There was a distinct possibility that her legs might give way and she'd crumple to the floor, Hope thought, but then the door opened and she could hear Allison and Lauren mocking Jack and the ancient *Death to the Pixies* T-shirt he was wearing, which Hope had neatly mended with red thread because she couldn't find her spool of black cotton.

'Hopey!' Lauren called out, waving to her from the hall. 'Where did you suddenly get a dining room from?'

'Looks fantastic,' Allison added, pushing Jack out of the

way so she could bustle towards the kitchen and throw herself at Hope. 'The offy was having a special on Prosecco so we bought four bottles. Let's get one of them opened. I'm gasping for a drink.'

Susie was already getting glasses, Lauren was presenting Hope with a huge bunch of tulips, and Jack had his hands in his jeans pockets and was looking proudly at Hope as if she might just be a domestic goddess after all.

Everything was going to be all right.

Chapter Three

In all the planning and making of endless lists and scallop dry-runs, Hope had forgotten that a dinner party was still a party and parties were meant to be fun.

Flushed with the success of her perfectly seared scallops and tender lamb roulade (the ends had been a bit dry but she and Jack had had those), Hope sat at one end of the table and allowed herself a small triumphant smile.

For the last two hours she'd been either chained to a hot stove and ministering to pans spitting sizzling olive oil at her, or tending to her guests' every need. She'd made sure their glasses were never less than half full, that Susie had lardons instead of black pudding, and that Otto had a bottle of Heinz ketchup to smother his roulade in, even though she'd wanted to bash him over the head with it.

Hope had barely eaten anything and finally understood why her mother always assumed a martyred air every year at the family Christmas dinner and sat at the table complaining every five minutes, 'Once you've spent hours cooking a meal, you really don't feel like eating it.' Oh yes, Hope now knew that it wasn't just a cunning ruse so Caroline Delafield could spend the rest of the day reclining on the settee watching *The Sound Of Music* and working her way through a box of liqueur chocolates.

It wasn't until Hope had jumped up to stick the pudding in the oven that Lauren had intervened. 'If you make us eat anything else, there will be vomiting,' she'd threatened. 'Sit down, have a glass of wine, 'cause you're lagging seriously behind, and just, y'know, chill.'

So, Hope was chilling. Or, rather, she was able to chill once Jack had put the bread-and-butter pudding in the oven on a very low heat and set the timer. She took a generous gulp of Sauvignon Blanc and surveyed her table, which was attractively lit by just a fraction of the tealights she'd bought in IKEA after Elaine, who taught the Yellow Class, had sworn blind that there were going to be power cuts last winter because the Germans were bogarting all the electricity. Turned out they hadn't and Hope was left with five hundred candles.

To her left Allison was deep in conversation with Marvin, who worked with Jack on the art desk at *Skirt*. The ends of her razor-cut, platinum-blonde bob swung gently as she recalled the infamous X-Acto-knife incident at the secondary school where she taught English. She even pulled back her dress to show Marvin her lilac bra strap and the miniscule mark she should have claimed workers' comp for.

'Was that from the X-Acto knife?' Marvin asked, peering forward to examine it more closely, though his eyes seemed to be firmly fixed on Allison's breasts, which had probably been her intention all along.

'Nah. One of the little bastards threw a chair at me,' Allison recalled with a sniff, as she adjusted her dress and put away her goodies.

Marvin usually looked inscrutable, especially when impressionable young women were throwing themselves at him, which they did frequently because he was absolutely beautiful. Even though Hope was a one-artboy kind of girl, she did have a little crush on Marvin, who was tall and muscular with burnished skin the colour of a bar of chocolate with 70 per cent cocoa solids or Pantone shade 1608C, as he was fond of telling people, which was the kind of lame joke that artboys loved to make. He also had a dirty, flirty way of smiling at you with his tongue curled behind his front teeth, which he was doing now. 'Do you teach in one of those hideous sink schools the *Daily Fail* is always banging on about?'

'Not even!' Allison shook her head vigorously. 'It's one of those swanky-pants Academies, policed by the yummy mummies on the PTA and stuffed full of Xanthes and Saffrons and Orlandos, entitlement oozing from every pore. Vile little sods.'

Hope grinned and looked to her right where Otto, who probably had been a vile little sod when he was at Harrow but had had it kicked out of him at art school, was talking with Lauren about *Mad Men*, the death of the American Dream and post-Capitalist dystopias. Lauren's jaw was set as if she was stifling a thousand yawns, and although Otto was very attractive in an effete, languid way, Hope wasn't surprised when her iPhone beeped. Lauren was a demon touch-texter. Hope surreptitiously looked down at her phone to read: *Christ, rescue me!*

When Hope raised her head, Lauren threw in an imploring look, her pixie-like face scrunched up, lower lip jutting out. She looked alarmingly similar to when they'd first met, on their first day of nursery school, when Lauren was experiencing severe separation anxiety and Hope had just pushed her off the much-coveted red tricycle.

'Great name for a band,' Hope said brightly. 'The Post-Capitalist Dystopias. In fact, I'm pretty sure I saw them playing the second stage at Latitude.'

'You spent the whole weekend trolleyed so I don't think you saw much of anything,' Lauren reminded her wryly, as she ran a hand through her close-cropped brown hair – ever since she and Hope had seen *A Bout de Souffle* at the impressionable age of sixteen, Lauren had decided that gamine would be her USP. 'And you still owe me for my tent, which you wrecked.'

'How on earth did Hope manage to wreck your tent?' Otto sounded incredulous.

'You really don't want to know,' Lauren said, grinning as Hope made zipping motions.

'Oh I do, I really do.'

'Hopey will kill me!'

Lauren and Otto were back on track and Hope could revert to chilling mode and catch up on the drinking; there were at least nine finished bottles waiting to go in the recycling bin. Her eyes skittered down the length of the table, counting the empty plates as she went, until she reached the other end, where Susie and Jack were sitting opposite each other and generally looking like they were having a good time. And at the foot of the table was Wilson, not talking to anyone and generally looking like a man who was scheduled for major surgery the next day.

Hope knew that she should be a good hostess and try to engage Wilson in conversation, but there was a huge expanse of table between them and engaging Wilson in conversation was usually a painful and ultimately futile experience.

He'd only been seeing Susie for the last six months, and Hope wasn't even sure that they were that serious about each other, but she knew that Susie could do so much better. Wilson was entirely lacking in any kind of charisma and he always made Hope feel as if she was an empty-headed, superficial, shallow *girl* who had nothing to say that he would want to hear. He wasn't rude, but Hope always wanted to shiver when he gave her one of those wintry smiles that never reached his steely-grey eyes and, try as she might, she and Wilson had never progressed much further than, 'It's my round, what are you having?' and 'Yeah, it's a bit nippy for this time of year, isn't it?'

Susie was one of her three best friends and Hope wished Wilson was more user-friendly because then they could go out as a foursome a lot more than they did and Jack would have someone to talk boy stuff with while she and Susie debated everything from politics to nail varnishes, but it hadn't worked out like that.

Wilson was a photographer who lived in a converted loft in Kentish Town and used the downstairs space as his studio, where he got paid huge sums of money to shoot advertising campaigns and moody black-and-white shots of the great and good for the Sunday supplements. He drove a vintage Saab and collected vintage cameras and saw the world through a pair of vintage horn-rimmed glasses. He wore his black hair short at the back and swept up into a quiff at the front and was never seen in anything but Dark Wash 501s, snowy-white T-shirts and black V-necks; he and Jack had *nothing* in common, apart from the fact that their respective girlfriends liked spending serious quality time together.

'But what do you see in Wilson?' Hope had once asked Susie during one of their regular let's-bitch-about-our-boyfriends sessions.

Susie had given the matter some serious thought. 'Well, he does have good cheekbones,' she said finally. 'But mostly what I see in him is that he's got a big dick and he knows what to do with it.'

It didn't sound like a compelling enough reason to see Wilson on a regular basis, but it did mean that it was Susie's responsibility to entertain him. Usually she didn't seem to have any problem engaging with Wilson, though most of their conversation consisted of gently taking the piss out of each other, but this evening she'd all but ignored him in favour of talking to Lauren or Jack, and now she was standing up. 'I'm going to have a post-prandial fag in the garden,' she announced. 'Anyone care to join me?'

There was a regretful murmur of dissent. The table was evenly split between those who didn't and those who were currently trying to quit.

'You're all a bunch of lightweights.' Susie sighed, shaking her head. 'After I've topped up my nicotine levels, I'll make a start on the dishes.'

'You don't have to do that,' Hope said half-heartedly. She made a lacklustre attempt at standing up herself, but Susie tutted and flapped her hands at Hope, then at Lauren and Allison who were also making unenthusiastic noises about slapping on the Marigolds.

'You all just sit tight,' Susie insisted firmly. 'It will only take ten minutes and the kitchen is really too small to have four people in there all arguing about who's going to dry.'

It was very sweet of Susie and also very uncharacteristic. She'd already tried to avoid doing anything that might jeopardise her manicure. Wilson certainly seemed to think so. 'Just yell if you run into trouble,' he advised Susie, as she slowly began to squeeze her way out of the room, which involved Marvin and Allison tucking their chairs as close to the table as they possibly could. 'And the green stuff in the bottle by the sink is Fairy Liquid; you'll need some of that.' Hope thought it might have been the first thing he'd said since he'd sat down.

'Very funny,' Susie snapped, as she finally reached the doorway. 'Didn't know you'd invited Oscar Wilde, Hope.'

She left the room grumbling about how smokers were a dying breed, as Jack got to his feet and started gathering up the empty bottles. 'We need more booze,' he said. 'Two bottles of white, one of red. Wilson? I think I've got some more of that Belgian microbrew.'

'Just water. I'm driving. San Pellegrino, if you've got it, thanks,' Wilson said.

Hope realised that as Jack and Susie had left the table, Wilson had no one sitting next to him and she'd have to get up and take Jack's seat so Wilson wouldn't be a total Billy no-mates. She was just glancing down the table to ascertain that yes, Wilson still looked as if he was suffering from a particularly painful bout of lockjaw, when he lifted his eyes from silent contemplation of his pudding spoon and caught her eye.

After a few seconds Hope wished that he'd stop looking at

her because his gaze seemed rather resentful, like he begrudged having to spend the evening eating all the lovely things she'd cooked when he could be polishing his collection of horn-rimmed spectacles or alphabetising his scratchy vinyl records. Both her grandmothers and her mother were insistent that a good hostess made her guests feel welcome and included, no matter what, but it had been a really long day and she had a bread-and-butter pudding in the oven, and Hope's grandmothers and mother would never know that Hope's way of dealing with a difficult dinner guest was by removing herself from the room.

'I'm going to check on pudding,' Hope said loudly, scraping back her chair and standing up. Her voice was perilously high and her face felt as if it was on fire. 'And I'm going to find out why Jack's taking so long to bring us more booze.'

With that, Hope squeezed past Allison and fled from the room without even pausing to pick up any of the dirty dishes.

Chapter Four

BEEEEEEPPPP! BEEEEEEPPPP! BEEEEEEPPPP!

The sound of the oven timer pierced the air and Hope jumped back, just as Jack and Susie tore themselves away from each other.

It was strange that when Hope's world was falling into pieces, tiny, torn pieces that couldn't be stitched back together, she still had the presence of mind to scurry out into the hall so she could re-enter the kitchen and even bang a saucepan lid down on the worktop as if she was in a tearing hurry to turn off the oven before her pudding burnt.

BEEEEEEPPPP! BEEEEEEPPPP! BEEEEEEPPPP!

Hope could hear Susie and Jack talking over the sound of the shrieking alarm but it was impossible to know if they were panicking because they'd seen her jump back from the door, or if they were congratulating themselves for fooling her yet again – and God, just how long had this been going on, anyway?

There were a million thoughts racing through Hope's head, a million fragments that she needed to trace back to their original source but . . .

BEEEEEEPPPP! BEEEEEEPPPP! BEEEEEEPPPP!

'Fuck off!' she screamed at the oven, scrabbling to turn off the timer as she wrenched open the door and yanked out the Pyrex dish.

'Fuck! Fuck! FUCK!' she howled, dropping the dish on

the floor so she could clutch her burnt hand to her mouth. 'Fucking fuck!'

Jack was already rushing in through the back door, closely followed by Susie. 'Hopita! What's up?'

Hope couldn't speak. She just stared at him with eyes widened in pain and horror that had nothing to do with pulling a blisteringly hot dish from an oven without the aid of a glove or even a wadded-up tea towel.

'Shit! Poor baby,' Jack cooed, trying gently to take hold of Hope's arm, but she flinched away. 'You look like you're going to faint.'

Susie had already pushed past him, so she could take the teetering pile of crockery out of the sink and start running the cold tap. 'Come here!' she ordered sharply.

Hope blinked at her. Everything looked strange and frighteningly hyper-real, from the congealed pesto on the worktop to Susie and Jack's concerned faces and the red and white mess of her own hand. Even the hum from the fluorescent strip light sounded deafening.

'Is everything all right in there?' said a voice from the hall and Hope looked over Jack's shoulder to see five anxious faces staring back at her.

'For fuck's sake,' Susie said, grabbing a handful of Hope's dress so she could drag her over to the sink, seize her wrist in a punishing grip and force her hand under the gushing tap.

Instantly the pain became less inner and much more outer and Hope almost welcomed the stinging agony of icy-cold water sluicing against her damaged flesh. The skin on her palm had blistered and bubbled and the sharp waves of pain were beginning to fade into a nagging throb that Hope focused on, matching her breaths to the rhythm of each pulsation, because if she had to think about anything else, what she'd just seen . . . what she'd heard . . . the two of them . . .

'Stop touching me,' she said in a low voice, still firmly

looking down at her hand, because even glimpsing the peach silk of Susie's top out of the corner of her eye made Hope forget that she was trying to be all Zen about her pain and instead long to gouge Susie's heart out with the potato peeler. 'Get off me.'

'You have to promise you'll keep your hand under the tap,' Susie demanded, but she was already letting go so Allison could take her place and rub Hope's back in soothing circles.

'You OK?' she asked Hope softly.

Hope shook her head. 'Alli, everything's so fucked up,' she whispered.

'No, it's all good. Really. The pudding's still intact,' Allison told her cheerfully. 'You'd think the dish would have shattered.'

'It's going to get cold,' Hope said, trying to get away from the sink so she could salvage something from the evening, even if it was just her brioche bread-and-butter pudding. 'I need to put it back in the oven.'

'Where do you think you're going? I'll sort it out,' said Lauren, sifting through the kitchen debris to find the oven gloves, then crouching down to pick up the dish. 'You need to keep your hand under that tap for ten to twenty minutes, then we need to wrap it in clingfilm.'

'Yes, thank you, Florence Nightingale,' Allison snapped, even though her hands were gentle as she continued to rub Hope's back. 'You're not the only one who's a qualified first-aider.'

'Are you sure you're all right, Hopita?' asked Jack, and Hope swivelled round again to see him standing by the back door, next to Susie, and the depth of his deception struck her anew and the pain rose up again and roared.

'Do I fucking look like I'm fucking all right?' she shouted, wrenching away from Allison and the cold water. 'Do I really look like everything in my world is sunshine and rainbows right now?'

Jack reared back but he didn't look guilty. He looked concerned, as if Hope's pain was his pain. 'C'mon, Hopey, stiff upper lip,' he said gently. 'Do you think you need to go to A&E?'

Everyone was looking at her warily, as if they were waiting for another flash of temper, and Hope knew that this wasn't the time or the place. She turned away and stuck her hand back under the tap so she didn't have to look at anyone. 'I'm fine,' Hope insisted, slightly astounded at how steady her voice was. 'It's just the shock that's making me act like a crazy lady.'

There was an almost indecent stampede by some of her guests to leave the scene of the crime, and once Jack and Susie had gone back to the dining room after several more updates on the state of Hope's mental and physical health, only Allison and Lauren lingered. 'You sure you're OK, Hopey?' Allison asked again. 'I mean, you're not usually such a pain wimp.'

'Yeah, you're very stiff of lip,' Lauren added, as Hope finally turned off the tap, cast a cursory look at the raised welts on her hand, which still stung like a swarm of angry wasps had done their worst, and started rooting in the kitchen junk drawer for the clingfilm.

'It's just . . . well . . .' Hope paused. She knew that she could tell Allison and Lauren anything, but this shameful secret was so large that she was scared to give it a voice in case it swallowed her whole. And the thing about best friends, real to-the-death best friends, was that sometimes you had to lie to them and they wouldn't be fooled for a second, but they'd understand. 'I just wanted everything to be perfect and it's not. I've burnt my hand and thrown a hissy fit and everyone thinks I'm a gigantic tool and I'm pretty sure that my brioche bread-and-butter pudding resembles charcoal by now.'

'You silly, silly cow,' Lauren said, and Hope was surrounded on all sides and gathered into a gentle hug that was mindful of her injured hand, as Lauren and Allison murmured soothing words and petted her.

It was established that the pudding was fine. Maybe a little dry, but nothing the mascarpone and the clotted-cream ice-cream couldn't hide. Also, by the guffawing and chink of glasses coming from the former lounge, the getting drunk was back on course, and it was essential 'for someone to have a meltdown at a dinner party, especially the hostess', Allison explained earnestly, as she finished dressing Hope's hand. 'It's the entertainment between courses. It's expected, Hopey, and quite frankly, I've seen better hissy fits than that.'

'Thrown them, more like,' Lauren muttered darkly. Allison gasped in outrage, which Hope knew was faked, but she smiled all the same and it was as if her smile, no matter how frayed at the edges it was, was the cue the other two had been waiting for, because they picked up the pudding and accompaniments and chivvied Hope out of the kitchen.

It took only three steps, not even big steps, to get from the kitchen to the other room, but to Hope it felt as if she was walking the Green Mile. She wasn't sure how she was going to get through the next five minutes, never mind the next hour. She hesitated in the doorway but that was because Allison had to tuck her chair in so she could get through the door.

'Pudding looks amazing,' Marvin said when Hope had resumed her place at the head of the table. She picked up a serving spoon in her uninjured left hand, which was going to make things tricky, but she needed to wrest some control back.

'Do you want me to take over?' Allison asked.

'I'm fine,' Hope insisted.

'Really, it's no trouble. You've had a nasty shock. C'mon, I'll do the slicing.'

'I can manage, Alli, but if you want to be helpful you can pour me a really, really large glass of wine,' Hope told her as she looked down the length of the table. Allison, Lauren, Otto and Marvin were all watching her anxiously but they'd had so much to drink that the concern was making them go cross-eyed, and she couldn't even bring herself to look at Jack and Susie. Instead her gaze rested on Wilson who, to be fair, had got up from the table to make sure that she hadn't been maimed for life, but now that the crisis had been temporarily averted he was more interested in fiddling with his iPhone, which was kind of rude.

Actually, being irritated by Wilson made Hope feel better, or at least feel halfway normal again. Like she was back in her own skin, and it was the push she needed to find the courage to look at Susie and Jack, who at that precise moment were sharing a smile and a raised eyebrow.

That look, that complicit look, was enough to make Hope instantly forget all her honourable intentions of dealing with Susie and Jack at some unspecified time in the future, once she'd become acclimatised to all the horror and hurt and could trust herself not to burst into loud, snotty tears. Also, at this unspecified time in the future there wouldn't be any witnesses to Hope's utter humiliation and despair, but that wasn't right or fair. Why should they get off scot-free?

The serving spoon left Hope's hand before she even realised that she was throwing it in the direction of Jack's head. It was either good or bad that her right hand was out of action and the spoon missed its target. Still, it managed to tear Jack's attention away from Susie so he could stare at Hope with mounting horror.

'I saw the two of you,' she spat out, almost tripping over the words. 'And I know why it took you two hours to get back from Waitrose – you were shagging each other, weren't you?'

There was a terrible hush, as if everyone in the room was holding their breath. All Hope could hear was the pounding of her heart. No one was looking at her, preferring to stare down at their empty bowls, except Wilson. He was looking right at Hope, then at Susie, then at Jack, and back to Hope again. For once Wilson didn't look bored but angry and hurt and betrayed – all the things that Hope was feeling too.

He also seemed surprised, not at Hope's revelation, but with Hope herself, as if she might actually have some hidden depths and he was interested to see how far she was going to take things. Hope shot Wilson an angry, defiant look because if he was a nicer person, a better boyfriend, then Susie wouldn't have to steal other people's almost fiancés. But even as she narrowed her eyes, Hope knew that this wasn't Wilson's fault, and her gaze switched to the top of Jack's bent head. She'd never known silence like this; so thick and charged.

Then Lauren giggled nervously, Allison hissed at her to shut up and the spell was broken.

'I haven't . . .' Jack began automatically, even though it was obvious that he had. That *they* had. 'I went to B&Q and Waitrose, you know I did, and the traffic was a bitch and I really did just meet Susie coming down the road, but we just sat in the car and talked. I swear!'

'I don't believe you,' Hope hissed. 'I saw the way you were kissing. It wasn't even kissing. It was . . . It was . . . You know exactly what it was.'

Susie coughed. 'Look, we'd both had a bit to drink and ended up having a drunken snog. End of,' she said quietly, looking down at her hands, her manicure still in pristine condition because doing the washing-up had been the last thing on her mind when she'd left the table.

There was more to it than that, Hope was sure of it, but she knew what she'd seen, but what if she hadn't seen what she thought she'd seen? Maybe, just maybe, this whole awful, world-shattering nightmare was Susie's idea of a joke, and she'd persuaded Jack to go along with it – and his sense of humour was decidedly suspect. Like, Hope had caught him giggling over repeats of *One Foot in the Grave* on UK Gold on numerous occasions, yet he could remain completely stony-faced when she showed him something on LOLCats, which had made her spit tea down herself. Maybe they hadn't been kissing and groping but just *pretending* to be kissing and groping. Maybe.

Hope actually crossed her fingers behind her back, the skin on her damaged hand tightening painfully, which gave her something real, something tangible to focus on until eventually, reluctantly, Susie raised her head to look at her.

'I'm sorry that you had to see it, though,' she said. There was no bravado, no bluff, she looked genuinely, sickeningly ashamed, which was all the proof that Hope needed, because usually Susie prided herself on having no shame.

'You know what you can do with your "sorry"? You can shove it up your arses,' Hope said, and she walked out of the room because she couldn't stay there and have to look at them, at Jack and Susie, any longer.

Chapter Five

Usually when Hope stormed out of the lounge it was because of a minor disagreement, like Jack refusing to turn off *Grand Theft Auto* so she could watch *Glee* in High Definition, or because he was mocking her for getting all sniffly and teary-eyed while she was watching *Glee* in High Definition. Hope would flounce as far as the bedroom, where she had a secret chocolate stash hidden at the back of her knicker drawer and could watch the show on the crappy TV they'd inherited from Jack's parents.

But this wasn't a minor disagreement. It was The End of Days, and Hope headed for the front door because having to ride out an emotional tsunami in the cramped confines of their flat in front of their closest friends was too much. She needed fresh air to clear her head. If that didn't work, then she needed to find a steep hill, climb it and scream and scream and scream.

Jack appeared in the lounge doorway as Hope fumbled with the latch. 'Hopey . . . Hope. Don't go. Not like this.'

There were so many things wrong with what he was saying that Hope didn't know where to start, so she settled for an indistinct sound that was half growl, half sob, as Jack reached her side.

'Don't. Please don't,' Jack said urgently, right in Hope's ear because he was that close, his long fingers splayed out on the door, just centimetres away from where Hope's hand had stilled on the latch. 'I screwed up, I know that, but if you go now . . . what will everyone think?'

It was interesting, Hope thought to herself in a detached way, that Jack might not want her to leave, would even plead with her to stay, but he wouldn't touch her. He'd known her for every single one of her twenty-six years and he knew better than anyone that once the rage was upon her, when she was this mad, feeling so thoroughly unhinged, that if he touched even the tip of his little finger to her bare arm, she'd punch him.

Hope wished that Jack had the guts to touch her, because, God, she really wanted to punch him. But Jack didn't touch her. In fact, he stepped back as she succeeded in getting her nerveless fingers to open the door. Stumbling out into the night and away from him felt portentous and over-whelming, as if Hope was relinquishing all her rights to him.

'We have to talk,' Jack called out as Hope recovered from her first faltering steps and began to pick up speed, hurrying up the steps and down the front-garden path. 'Running away isn't going to help.'

Hope ignored him as she took a decisive right turn out of the gate and stomped down the street, not in the direction of Holloway Road and the beered-up gangs of teenagers that congregated there on a Saturday night, but cutting through the square on which they lived, and giving a wide berth to the people drinking outside the gastropub, which was the only drinking establishment in the area that wasn't an old man's boozer.

She didn't know how long she'd been walking but after what seemed like hours, Hope realised that her Stella McCartney leopard-print platform wedges were not adapt-ing well to life outside. They hadn't been too painful when Hope was wearing them indoors, but now she had hard pavement underfoot; the shoes were chafing and pinching and generally making their displeasure felt.

The pain was good, or so Hope tried to tell herself. The pain meant that she could still feel, even though the anger had died down and she wasn't feeling much of anything else, apart from lost. It wasn't even a metaphorical lost-ness but an actual 'I don't have a clue where I am and I didn't have the foresight to pick up my iPhone when I stormed out so I can't even use Google Maps to find my way home.' Just the thought of home made Hope's stomach clench, and it was probably better to concentrate on being lost than have to concentrate on all the other shitty stuff that she didn't want to think about.

Hope stood at the junction of three identical roads of Victorian terraced houses, unable to decide which one to take. If she didn't want to go home and she didn't have money or credit cards or phone, then what were her other options?

The wall she sat down on to rest her sore feet was as good a place as any to regroup. It was a still, sticky night. Hope could hear the distant roar of traffic and the low throb of music and conversation all around her. The air was thick with the lingering scent of chargrilled meat as the last-Saturday-of-the-summer-holidays barbecues were all winding down now.

It was terribly unfair that the inhabitants of the neighbouring gardens sounded as if their Saturday nights had been all fun and frolics, when Hope had just had the worst Saturday night of her life. Bar none. No contest. Even the time when she was sixteen and she and Lauren had sneaked off to Leeds to see the White Stripes and she'd had her purse stolen and they'd missed the last train home and had spent the night sitting on a park bench, wide-eyed and terrified that they were either going to be murdered by a beered-up bunch of random homicidal maniacs who might be passing, or murdered by their parents when they finally got home (though more likely grounded for a year). That didn't even come close to the agonies Hope had suffered tonight, and now that she wasn't in forward motion but just sitting there, she had no choice but to start re-living each horrible moment that had revealed all the cracks in her fairly boring but fairly happy little life.

She knew deep in her gut that those kisses, the caresses, the easy way Jack and Susie's bodies fitted together signalled very clearly that something had been going on for quite some time. Hope couldn't believe she'd been oblivious to it. She'd thought that she was the glue that bound Jack and Susie together, and that they'd only tolerated each other because they both wanted Hope in their lives.

'She's kind of vacuous,' was how Jack had described Susie the first time he'd met her. 'She's even more shallow than the fashion and beauty girls at work. I didn't think that was possible.'

Susie hadn't exactly been about to join the Jack fanclub either. 'I get the whole lanky artboy thing, I really do, or I did when I was a teenager,' she'd drawled after her second encounter with Jack, when they'd bumped into her in Islington and the three of them had gone for a quick drink. 'Now I'm into men who are strong enough to pick me up and shag me against the wall, y'know?'

Hope hadn't known because she liked Jack's lankiness, even though he wasn't strong enough to drag her off the sofa when she was hunkered down for the evening with a chick-flick, Kettle Chips and a bottle of rosé. Or maybe it wasn't Jack's puniness that was the issue here, but Hope's fluctuating weight, and how right now she couldn't do the zip up on her favourite pair of skinny jeans. It was Susie who'd decreed that a girl should never have bigger thighs than her lover. Hope stared down at her body masked by the voluminous folds of her black maxi dress and prodded her leg, which wobbled obligingly.

Maybe it was her fault because she'd let herself go, and because she nagged Jack all the time and when she wasn't nagging him, she was driving him to distraction with her messy ways and her blanket refusal to accept responsibility and make decisions. 'I'm responsible for thirty six-year-olds between eight fifty-five and three thirty and I have to make decisions every five minutes,' Hope was fond of saying when Jack tried to get her to commit to pizza toppings or scraping together another £50 a month to put in their joint savings account. 'I'm exhausted with all the responsibility and the decision-making. Why don't you do what you think is best and if I don't agree I'll be sure to let you know?'

She'd taken Jack for granted. Hope shivered, and it might have been with shame, and it might also have been because the humidity was lifting and the night was cooling down.

It was painful to sit on someone's garden wall and calculate all the ways she'd been a terrible girlfriend, but the more Hope thought about it, the more she realised that in other ways she was a superb girlfriend. Jack was incapable of getting out of bed in time for work unless she told him he was going to be late at five-minute intervals as she tried to get ready for school. And because she got home first, she always had dinner ready for him. She read every issue of *Skirt* from cover to cover and could always spot his layouts and praised them to the hilt. She never minded when he stayed late in the office because they were behind schedule . . . though maybe he hadn't had to work late as often as he'd claimed and it had been an excuse to pop round to Susie's beautiful flat, which could have graced the pages of *Elle Decor*, so he could pick her up and shag her against one of her walls, probably the one with the feature wallpaper, which had cost £150 a roll.

Shame was turning back into anger. No matter if she was the worst girlfriend in the world, Jack had made promises to her. Promises that went hand in hand with having both of their names on a title deed, and the understanding that even though Jack hadn't officially asked for her hand in marriage, he was going to soon. Very soon. The sooner the better, particularly as the subject of engagements had become the sorest of sore points lately.

It wasn't just that her mother and Jack's mother brought it up at every opportunity. It wasn't just that they'd been to three weddings in three weekends last April. It wasn't even that the achingly cool, stuck-up couple in the tent next to them at Latitude had been on their honeymoon. Well, it was all of those things, and the way that friends, relatives and acquaintances drove Hope (but never Jack) loopy with their claims that 'You'll be next,' and kept asking her if Jack had popped the question or when he was going to put a ring on it.

It was a fair point, Hope thought, because they'd always been the trailblazers of their social set. The first to go steady. The first couple to get consummated. The first to go away on a minibreak. The first couple to move in together. They were always ahead of the relationship bell curve but now they were getting left behind as the people they'd been at university with were getting married to people they'd only been with for five minutes. Hope and Jack had been dating for thirteen years and now that they owned a flat, getting engaged was the next step. And it was only getting engaged – Hope wasn't even thinking of getting married just yet – but every time she mentioned it to Jack, he pulled a face and muttered things about how people were getting married later these days, according to the latest survey. Or that he couldn't spare the money for a ring when he wanted to upgrade his Mac.

It had all come to a nasty, shouty, flouncy head during their week in Barcelona during the Easter holidays. It was just the two of them and they'd spent lazy mornings on the beach, then when the sun got too fierce they'd retire to their hotel room for a siesta. In the evenings they'd pig out on seafood, tapas and Sangria. It had been wonderful, especially as Jack had kept hinting that he had a special surprise planned for their last night, and Hope had got it into her head that he was going to go down on one knee and present her with a ring. Possibly with a mariachi band serenading the proposal. After all, they'd seen a bride and groom and wedding party pose for pictures outside the cathedral on their second day in Barcelona, and Jack had smiled indulgently and said that Hope would make a beautiful bride. Well, he'd actually said, 'I bet you wouldn't be caught dead in a big old meringue of a wedding dress,' but it had been enough to make Hope's imagination run riot.

So, she was less than pleased when the surprise turned out to be tickets to see one of Jack's favourite bands and they'd had a huge blow-out of a row; Jack had stormed off to see the band on his own and Hope had got drunk in the hotel bar with a gaggle of forty-something divorcees in Barcelona on a girls' weekend.

Jack had come back from the show early and suitably contrite, and the next morning he'd bought her three stackable silver rings for the third finger of her right hand and now they were unofficially pre-engaged, which was a step in the right direction. Except what if Jack and Susie had been getting it on with each other by then, and the whole week that he'd been in Barcelona with Hope, he'd secretly been wishing he was with her best friend?

Jack had taken the thirteen years that they'd been together and thrown them away like they didn't mean anything to him. Like Hope meant nothing to him; and yes, Hope was furious with Susie too, the kind of fury that made her scalp tingle and her skin itch, but she could only deal with being furious with one person at a time, and that person was Jack.

She wasn't sure that she could ever stand to be near him again, and finally she could feel the first wave of grief well up inside her, and after that the lump in her throat, which made swallowing hard, and the prickle in her eye were inevitable. Hope sniffed hard as the first tear slowly trickled down her cheek and she knew it would be the first of many. Although she didn't cry much, she cried *hard*, and she didn't even have any tissues.

She batted away each tear with an impatient hand, but soon they were falling too thick and fast for her to do anything but hiccup and splutter in an effort not to start howling. Even so, a gang of lads walking along the other side of the street bellowed helpfully, 'Cheer up love, it might never happen.'

Hope was scrubbing at her wet face with the hem of her dress, when she became aware of a car inching down the road, its headlights defiantly undipped. She shielded her streaming eyes as the car slowed even further, and if it was some kerb-crawling creep who had mistaken her for a prostitute she was going to get medieval on his perverted arse. Or possibly just keep crying.

Predictably the car came to a halt alongside Hope, and she realised that, with her skirt all rucked up so that she was flashing an indecent amount of fleshy white thigh, she probably did look like a lady of easy virtue. She scrambled off the wall and started to walk briskly along the street because really she didn't have the energy to get medieval on anybody's arse, not even the two people whose arses really deserved it.

The car started up again.

'Hope?' called out a voice that sounded familiar, and when she slanted a glance at the car that looked familiar, too, in a pretentious kind of way.

'Leave me alone,' she said to Wilson, as she squinted through the open car window at him. 'Please, just go away.'

'I've been trawling the back roads of Upper Holloway for over an hour trying to find you,' Wilson sighed, as if Hope's refusal to be found had been deliberate and wilful behaviour on her part. 'Just be a good girl and get in the car.'

'Really, I'm fine,' she gritted her teeth in a smile that felt more manic than likely to reassure Wilson of her calm mental state. 'You don't have to worry about me.'

'Hasn't there been enough drama for one evening, without you wandering the streets without your phone or keys, then ending up raped and left for dead in a skip?'

'This is a perfectly safe area.' Hope snorted derisively.

'Yeah, yeah.' He sighed again. 'Just get in the car.'

'No!'

Wilson didn't even bother to dignify that with a response. He just pressed on the horn for one long, deafeningly loud moment.

'What are you doing?' Hope demanded. 'This is a residential area. You're probably waking up babies and small children.'

This time Wilson let out a volley of toots and when Hope saw the curtains twitch in a nearby house, she shot round the car, yanked open the door and got in.

'There! You happy now?' she snapped, resisting the urge to slam the door shut after her lecture on noise pollution and closing it gently instead. She settled for tugging angrily on the seatbelt as she clipped it into place, but it didn't have the same effect.

'Not even remotely,' Wilson said, as he dropped a carrier bag in Hope's lap. 'Care package from your friend Lauren.'

Hope peered inside the bag to see a cardigan, her phone, her purse and the commuter mug her mother had bought her from a special offer in the *Sunday Express* magazine, which Hope had never used because she'd have felt like a dick getting it out on the bus. She unscrewed the lid and took a cautious sniff. It was full of wine; wine had alcohol in it and alcohol was a famous numbing agent. That was good enough for her.

She took a generous gulp of Sauvignon Blanc and, just like that, she was thinking of the bottle sitting in the bucket full of ice outside the kitchen door, right where Susie and Jack had been eating each other's mouths off each other's faces and, just like that, her eyes started tearing again.

Wilson sighed yet again, and Hope managed both to choke down her sobs and grind her teeth. 'Time for the prodigal girlfriend to go home,' he said, as he started up the car.

Hope wasn't sure which word – 'girlfriend' or 'home' – made her cry just that bit harder. And it was snotty, phlegmy crying, which would have been humiliating at any time, but in front of Wilson, who groped for and then shoved a wad of tissues at her, it was utterly mortifying. 'Home?' she wheezed. 'What happened after I left?'

He didn't answer at first, because he was pulling into the kerb to give way to a car coming in the other direction down the narrow street. 'The Spanish Inquisition, but with more shouting and swearing.'

Hope blew her nose, not even caring at the wet, snotty sound it made. 'Who was doing the shouting and swearing?'

'Your friends, Lauren and Alex—'

'*Allison.*'

'Whatever. They shouted at Susie, who shouted back at them. Then Jack shouted at them for shouting at Susie. Then the black guy shouted at the four of them to stop shouting. A couple of your wine glasses got broken in all the excitement.'

'Then what happened?'

'Susie made a heartfelt but garbled speech about feelings and passion, then Lauren called her a "fucking heartless, two-faced whore" and Susie stormed out.' Wilson paused. 'Then Jack set off in hot pursuit and everyone else decided to go and look for you, but they were all drunk and none of the blokes had any of the girls' mobile numbers, and vice versa, so it wasn't a very successful search mission.'

'So, what? You drew the short straw?' Hope asked rather ungraciously.

'Yeah, something like that,' Wilson replied just as ungraciously. 'And I'm sober and have my own transport.'

'I made a fucking lamb roulade,' Hope said, and she didn't even know why she'd said it but suddenly it was all she could think about. 'Have you any idea how much work is involved in making a lamb roulade, especially when you have to go all the way back down the hill to the butcher's because you've forgotten to ask him to butterfly the joint, and I made pesto from scratch, all so I could make a fucking lamb roulade. And they ruined it. I mean, they didn't ruin the lamb roulade, but they ruined my dinner party.'

'Do you think maybe this is less about your lamb roulade and more about the lamb roulade being a totemic symbol for the state of your relationship?'

Was he fucking kidding her? 'Are you fucking kidding me?'

'It was just a theory.' Wilson shrugged, and Hope noticed for the first time that he'd pulled into the kerb. 'So, shall I take you home?'

Even the abstract thought of home made Hope experience a moment of sheer blind panic. 'Not home,' she mumbled, opening her purse and hunting for her Oyster card. 'Could you maybe drive me to Holloway Road or Archway station, whichever one is nearer?'

Wilson couldn't because, as he smugly pointed out, it was nearly one in the morning and the tube had stopped running.

'OK,' she conceded weakly. 'I can get a nightbus from Holloway Road. It will take me longer to get to South London, but if I call Lauren she won't mind waiting up for me.'

'Fine,' Wilson said, like he didn't care where she went, just as long as she went somewhere.

Chapter Six

They drove in a tense, uncomfortable silence down narrow roads that all looked the same. It wasn't until they drove past Archway station and hit Junction Road that Hope stirred.

'You can just drop me here,' she said.

'I'm driving you into town, so you can get a nightbus to South London,' Wilson said.

'Oh, you don't have to do that.'

'Well, I'm doing it. End of discussion.' Hope had been a teacher for two years and she doubted that even if she stayed a teacher for another thirty, she'd ever be able to get the same note of don't-fuck-with-me-ness in her voice that Wilson had. 'Anyway, how's your hand?'

Hope had completely forgotten about her singed palm. Unbelievably, it was still firmly swathed in clingfilm. She stared down at the raised welt, which throbbed with a fair-to-middling pain, but compared to the pinched agony of her feet in her Stella McCartney wedges, the clenched knot where her stomach usually was, and the hollow feeling in her chest – which may or may not have indicated a broken heart – it was the very least of all her current ouches.

'It's OK, I guess,' she mumbled. 'Doesn't hurt that much.'

Wilson nodded. 'Are you going to keep it wrapped up like that?'

Hope knew the answer to this, she was a trained first-aider after all, but she couldn't even remember what 'ICE' stood for, let alone the proper treatment for superficial burns. 'Hmm, maybe it needs a dressing,' she murmured half to herself. 'So it doesn't get infected. I'll sort it out when I get to Lauren's. She's much better at treating minor injuries than I am.'

That short burst of conversation was followed by another painful silence until they got to Camden and Wilson had to jam on the brakes to avoid mowing down two really drunk teenagers who'd suddenly lurched into the road. Hope was thrown forward and then jerked back by her seatbelt, and just as she was wondering if she'd manage to make it to morning without breaking a rib or getting a mild concussion, Wilson turned down a side road and suddenly stopped the car.

'How could you not know?' he demanded, before the engine had even died. 'Don't tell me that you thought everything was all right?'

'What? No!' Hope shook her head firmly. 'Of course I didn't. Like, why would I?'

'Well, it's not as if they were that discreet about it.' Wilson leaned towards her and Hope shrunk back in her seat because they were in a confined space and Wilson looming at her when he was so angry wasn't doing much for her tattered nerves. 'God, you're either the most unobservant or the most self-involved person I've ever met.'

Hope bristled at the accusation, which was untrue and unfair on both counts. 'I am neither . . . Hang on! What do you mean about them not being discreet? Oh my God, did you know about this? You did, didn't you? You knew!'

'I didn't know for sure,' Wilson said gruffly, but he didn't sound quite so furious. 'I had my suspicions.'

Hope had forgotten that having a conversation with Wilson was like trying to thread a rusty needle with a frayed piece of cotton. 'What kind of suspicions?'

'The usual kind.' When Hope let out a tiny growl of

frustration at his utter inarticulacy, he shifted uncomfortably as if he realised that he had to do better. 'OK, OK. I thought maybe she was seeing someone else, I just didn't think it was your bloke. Well, not until we all went to that thing in Clissold Park.'

Hope frowned as she cast her mind back to that Saturday afternoon a few weeks before when the four of them had gone to a one-day festival in Stoke Newington, all buoyed up with the prospect of not having to camp in a field and with shiny backstage passes on lanyards, courtesy of *Skirt* magazine. As hard as she tried, Hope couldn't remember any instances when she'd caught Jack and Susie exchanging heated glances. Or sloping off together without any explanation and returning a long time later, all hot and flustered.

But then she had spent most of the day getting very merry on the free cocktails supplied by the vodka company sponsoring the backstage hospitality, then queuing for the Portaloos. Still, Hope was sure that if there'd been something going on that day, she'd have noticed it. This was her boyfriend and her best friend they were talking about, after all. Or her ex-best friend and her ex . . . No, she couldn't bear to think of Jack as her ex-anything. Couldn't even form the thought.

'I don't remember them doing anything out of the ordinary,' she insisted weakly. 'Can you be more specific?'

Wilson shrugged. 'She'd send a text on her phone. A split second later, he'd get a text and read it with a smirk on his face. Then he'd text, she'd get a text, smirk, text, smirk, text.'

'But that could have just been a coincidence!'

'It could have been, except it looks like it wasn't. You saw them together. What *did* you see, anyway?'

Although Hope had been trying to convince herself that the heated embrace was a trick of the light and she'd put two and two together and ended up with a number that was way, way greater than four, when she cast her mind back to what she'd seen earlier, she had perfect recall of Susie's hands inside Jack's jeans, his hands on her tits, the hungry slurping sound as they kissed . . . God, it would be etched right into her cerebral cortex until the day she died.

'I saw them kissing,' she said, and she was amazed that her voice sounded so clear and calm. 'And it was the kind of kissing that people do when they're shagging each other but they can't actually shag each other at that particular moment.'

'Right.' Wilson folded his arms. 'You sure you're not just jumping to conclusions? Because I've noticed that you tend to do that.'

'I do *not*!' Hope said indignantly, because she didn't. Apart from the whole engagement-ring fiasco in Barcelona, but that was because Jack had unwittingly led her on. Besides . . . 'Since when were you such an authority on me? You've only ever said about five sentences to me in the whole time I've known you.'

'Well, maybe I might have taken the trouble to get to know you better if you weren't always glaring at me or getting annoyingly drunk and giggly with my girlfriend.'

'I don't giggle,' Hope informed Wilson icily, and the way she was feeling right now, she didn't think she'd ever knowingly giggle ever again. 'Anyway, we're getting wildly off-topic. So, when you had these "suspicions"' – Hope did air-quotes, which, pleasingly, made Wilson wince – 'did you confront Susie about them?'

'Well, no, not then,' Wilson said.

'But you did ask her about them later?'

'I started to ask her but it just turned into an argument about me being half an hour late to pick her up the week before,' Wilson said dryly.

'So you didn't pursue it?' This was even harder than the time Hope had tried to get to the awful truth of who'd let Herbert, the class hamster, out of his cage.

'To be honest, I didn't want to start dragging up stuff if

it meant that all my worst thoughts were confirmed.' Wilson scratched his chin. 'No one but a masochist wants to put themselves in a position where they're likely to get hurt.'

In all her rage and pity and getting really, really annoyed that Wilson was giving her the third-degree like this was all her fault, Hope had been forgetting something – this wasn't just about her. Wilson was also an innocent victim in all this. She reached out to touch Wilson's arm, which made him flinch, but then they'd never touched before. The slight displacement of air when they had leaned in and pursed their lips at a spot approximately five centimetres away from the other's cheek couldn't be classed as touching. But now her hand rested on his arm and stayed there. 'Wilson? Look, I'm sorry.'

He shook his head and pulled his arm away from her. 'You've got nothing to be sorry for. I shouldn't have taken it out on you.'

'No, I mean, I'm sorry that I've made this all about me when you must be feeling pretty cut up about it too.' Hope swallowed past that lump that had taken up residence in her throat again. 'It's just . . . well, I know what you're feeling right now, because I'm feeling it too, and it hurts.'

'It's not the first time I've been in this situation, probably won't be the last,' Wilson said brusquely. 'Still, it's not something you ever get used to, your girlfriend cheating on you. If she is . . . All you actually saw was a kiss. One kiss.'

It wasn't just one kiss. It had been so much more than that. There had been hands in places where they had no right to be and grinding and groping and breathy little gasps and moans. 'Do you really think I'd be this upset if it had just been one kiss?'

'But you did only see them kiss, and Susie said it was just a drunken snog and OK, so maybe they do fancy each other, is that so bad?' Wilson didn't sound like he wanted Hope's opinion but as if he was trying to do damage limitation.

Square away the facts until they seemed a lot less incriminating. 'They fancied each other, they'd both had a skinful, stuff happened and you kicked off, and then Susie kicked off because that's what women do, they love to kick off, and in a few days' time, it will all have blown over, and Jack and Susie probably won't even be able to look at each other. That's what I think, anyway.'

Wilson was a regular chatty Cathy tonight, Hope thought sourly. 'Well, that's not what I think,' she protested. 'You didn't see them. I did, and I know exactly what I saw and it's just about broken my heart.'

The light was dim, but Hope was sure that Wilson had just rolled his eyes. 'If this is the worst thing that's ever happened to you, then you've led a very sheltered life.'

She had led a sheltered life, Hope knew that. Both her parents were still alive and gainfully employed, so there'd always been food, heat and light, and a bit left over for luxuries like trips to the cinema and two weeks on a campsite in Provence every summer. She'd got ten GCSEs, four A-levels, a degree in History and her SCITT with the requisite amounts of revision-related tears but no major angst. She'd dated the boy next door. She'd only ever shagged the boy next door once she was past the age of consent. Then Hope had moved in with the boy next door after university, and bought a flat with the boy next door as soon as she was bringing in her first wage.

At least she'd managed to get out of Lancashire and live in London, when most of the girls she'd been at school with already had kids. Some of them were even on their second marriages, but Wilson was kind of right: Hope didn't just have a sheltered life, it was a very small life, too. 'I'm sorry if my emotional distress is boring the pants off you,' Hope said as she pointedly scooched across the seat so she was almost hugging the car door. 'Maybe if I'd had a succession of crappy relationships, I'd be inured to the pain by now, but

I haven't. And well, it hurts like hell.' Her voice throbbed and broke at the end of the sentence and Hope waited to see if she was going to burst into tears again, but no, she was resolutely dry-eyed as Wilson wriggled where he sat and then coughed a little bit.

'I'm just saying that this is probably something and nothing, and it doesn't help the situation if you're going to completely overreact,' he said in a much gentler voice. 'You need to calm down.'

There was nothing more likely to make Hope start to hiss and bristle than someone telling her to calm down. 'At least I have feelings,' she snarled. 'You're just acting like the whole thing is a minor inconvenience to you. Don't you even care that Susie's been cheating on you?'

'Of course I care!' Wilson would never do anything as uncool as shout but his volume knob was definitely edging towards seven. 'Susie and I might not have been together for twenty bloody years like you and Jack—'

'It's thirteen years, actually. Lots of marriages don't last that long.'

'. . . but I thought we were heading towards something serious, and so if there is more to this than a bit of flirting and one sodding kiss, then, yes, I'm upset about it. But, unlike you, I don't go in for hysterics and hand-wringing.'

'I am not hysterical!' Hope yelled, and she actually flailed on the car seat in a way that would have her squirming when she played this whole sorry scene back at a later date. 'If you're not going to drive me into town, then fine! I can make my own way but I don't have to sit here and listen to you pretend that I've blown this whole thing out of proportion because I'm hysterical and I overreact when you . . .'

'Christ!' Wilson started the car with an angry twist of the ignition key. 'I'll take you into town as long as you promise to just shut the hell up!'

Hope closed her mouth with an audible snap so she could

grind her teeth so furiously that her jaw started to ache, and if she kept that up, she'd be back to wearing a mouth guard at night like she had when she was a teenager and had had far less control on her temper than she did now. Well, not right at this second, but generally she'd learned to control her hissy-fitting by deep breathing. Deep breathing wasn't an option when she was struggling with a veritable tsunami of rage. 'You have no right . . .' she began, her voice murderously low.

'Not another bloody word!'

She settled back into a fulminating silence and for want of anything better to do, like giving Wilson a piece of her mind, Hope delved into the carrier bag and pulled out her phone. She switched it on and yes! There were missed calls. Ten of them. Ten ways for Jack to say he was sorry and make it convincing because she wanted him to be sorry and to promise that it (whatever *it* really was) would never happen again. But when she investigated further, eight of them were from Lauren and Allison, there was one from Marvin and even one from Otto, but nothing from Jack. Except, oh! He'd sent her a text.

R U OK?

And no. No, Hope wasn't OK. Not when he couldn't even take the time to send her a text that contained more than five characters. FIVE!

'I hate him so much right now,' Hope spat out, and she also hated that she had to qualify the statement. That she couldn't just outright hate Jack, but she had to give it a disclaimer. 'I don't even know who he is any more, and I want to blame Susie for all of this, but y'know, when I saw them . . . well, it was obvious that Jack wasn't being forced against his will.'

'I thought we'd decided that we weren't going to talk about this any more.'

'But don't you think we should talk about this?' Hope persisted. 'We're the only two people who *can* talk about it.'

Wilson glanced over at her. 'What part of "shut the hell up" are you having a problem with?'

'You're *horrible!*' Hope ground out, literally ground out because her back molars were now clamped so tightly together it felt as if they'd have to be chiselled apart. 'No wonder Susie has to . . .'

'If you finish that sentence how I think you're going to finish it, then I'm throwing you out of the car *now*, and I won't care that we're in Somers Town and you'll probably get mugged by crackheads.'

There were a million things that Hope still wanted to say but she couldn't say them. Not because she believed Wilson's threats or that she was scared of crackheads (she'd willingly give them her Stella McCartney wedges to flog on eBay). But because she'd reached that knuckle-cracking, limb-stiffening, white-noise place where she was so angry that all she could do now was burst into tears.

It was almost a relief to be crying – not like she'd been crying before, when she'd felt alone and betrayed and sick to the stomach at the thought of Jack and Susie together, but crying because she'd worked herself up into such a temper that all she could do was cry. Unfortunately, angry crying was loud, verging on howling, and Hope knew from bitter experience that her face was scrunched up, wet with tears and livid red, not that she even cared. Her nose started running and she wiped it on the back of her hand and carried on crying, her whole body shaking with sobs – but it didn't make her feel better or less angry, not when she wanted to shout and scream and smash a few glasses or pieces of china.

'Can you stop that racket?' Wilson asked as he drove past University College Hospital and up Gower Street. 'Crying isn't going to help.'

Hope didn't trust herself to speak. She wasn't even sure that any words she could manage to get out would be intelligible, and she couldn't remember the last time she'd really lost it like this. Not since she was at Leeds University and had confronted one of her housemates for letting her sister and her sister's unwashed boyfriend have sex in Hope's bed when she'd gone home for the weekend.

Wilson muttered something under his breath, and then he dared to pat her knee and let his hand rest there. Anyone could have told him that when Hope was crying angry tears, then you should never, ever attempt to touch her, not unless you wanted to get slapped.

Hope smacked his hand off her knee. 'Don't touch me!' she spluttered, her voice clogged with mucus.

'What the fuck is wrong with you?' Wilson demanded. It was a valid question. Hope herself wanted to know what was so wrong with her that Jack and Susie had had to find solace in each other. 'You're meant to teach six-year-olds, not act like one.'

Wilson wasn't helping. He was making everything worse, and some small part of Hope that wasn't subsumed by rage and snot understood that; and the other larger part of her that was currently making all the decisions had come to the conclusion that enough was enough. As Wilson stopped at the traffic lights at Cambridge Circus, she scrabbled for the door handle.

'Now what are you doing, you silly woman?'

Hope succeeded in wrenching the door open. 'I can take it from here,' she sobbed, but they were quieter sobs because she was almost, *almost*, all cried out.

'I'm not letting you wander around Soho in this state,' Wilson said, but he sounded reluctant and Hope couldn't really blame him, which meant that her rationality and reason were beginning to return. 'Just stay where you are.'

But Hope already had the door open and the lights had turned green and Wilson was holding up a stream of traffic, all tooting their horns. Still faintly weeping but mostly hicupping, she scrambled out of the car and stumbled across the road. Wilson shouted something after her but it was swallowed up by the night, and Hope ducked down a side street and stayed there until she was absolutely sure that he wasn't coming after her.

Chapter Seven

Hope spent what was left of the night in Soho. She couldn't face the journey to South London and Lauren's pity and concern that would make her come undone all over again, so she stayed where she was.

Well, first she sat on the stone steps of the Seven Dials monument in Covent Garden but she kept getting harassed by lagered-up men and one lagered-up woman who needed help getting her shoe back on, so eventually Hope hobbled to Bar Italia in Soho. She had to wait an hour for a seat and once she had one, she kept ordering coffees that she didn't drink and paninis that she didn't eat just so she had squatter's rights. An endless stream of clubbers, scene-kids and hipsters, most of them chugging espressos to keep the come-down at bay, was entertaining enough that Hope could sit there and not really have to think about anything.

She didn't know how long she'd been sitting there but her bottom had gone numb and the sight of her fifth cup of cold cappuccino and a congealed panini was starting to make her feel sick. She couldn't stay there for ever, even if she'd wanted to. One of the counter staff had been over to wipe her table down at least ten times in the last half hour, so with a heavy heart and even heavier feet, Hope gathered up her carrier bag and headed out to meet her uncertain future.

It was a glorious day. The sun was already high up in a soft blue sky. A man was walking his schnauzer, a copy of the *Sunday Times* tucked under his arm. Hope checked her phone; it was only a little past seven. She hadn't been up this early on a Sunday since she'd stayed up all of Saturday night at Latitude dancing with Susie.

Hope wished that she didn't have to go home. Ever. Again. She was almost tempted to prolong the inevitable and hunker down in her favourite West End greasy spoon for a fortifying mug of tea and a bacon sandwich, which she might actually eat, but common sense prevailed. Tomorrow was the first inset day of the new school year and she'd promised the deputy head that she'd make her famous chocolate brownies for the infants *v.* juniors staffroom bake-off they had at the beginning of each new term.

The thought of having to do anything oven-related after yesterday's dinner party was almost enough to make Hope cry the first tears of a new day. Instead, she stopped at a Tesco Metro to buy ingredients for the brownies, then stuck out her hand to hail a black cab rather than taking the tube. Her shoes were no less painful than they had been last night and if a black cab had its light on before eight on a Sunday morning, then God obviously wanted her to take it.

Hope stood outside 47 Dunhill Road for long, long moments after the taxi had driven away. If God had really been on her side, he'd have forgotten about gifting Hope with a cab for hire and arranged instead for a handy tornado to pick up the building and its inhabitants and deposit them in a field miles away. But it was still standing there in the middle of the terrace and Hope had no option but to drag herself up the garden path.

As Hope picked her way down the steps that led to the basement flat, she could hear the front door opening and by the time she reached the bottom, Jack was standing there, waiting for her.

His face had been as familiar to her as her own reflection,

but now Hope felt as if it had changed. Something irrevocable had happened in the few hours that she'd been absent.

She didn't know the secret heart of him any more. Wasn't sure that she ever had. And the way he was looking at her, his big blue eyes wide and wary, was shiny and new, too. Maybe he'd changed before now, and she hadn't even noticed because she'd stopped really looking at him and had simply seen the familiar Jack shape with Jack's features, and hadn't bothered to delve any deeper.

They stood there staring at each other, until Hope dropped her eyes to stare at her feet and the chipped nail polish on her big toe because she couldn't bear to look at him any longer.

'You're home . . . I was worried about you,' Jack began brokenly. 'Where have you been?'

'Well, Wilson gave me a lift into town and I spent the night in Bar Italia,' Hope said shortly, as she moved past Jack, all of her tensed in case she accidentally made contact with him in the process. 'Like you even care where I've been.'

'Hopey! Please, don't be like this,' Jack said, touching her shoulder as he followed her into their flat, but letting his hand drop away as soon as he felt the rigid set of her muscles. 'You have to know . . . I never meant to hurt you.'

'Never meant me to find out, you mean,' Hope countered, and she wasn't sure why she was getting in an argument, when all she really wanted to do was demand dates and facts. When did it start? How did it start? Why did it start? Was it my fault? Did I drive you away? Is she better in bed than me? Do you think she's more beautiful than me? Do you love her?

She looked around her. The living room was no longer a dining room, and over Jack's shoulder, Hope could see that the kitchen was back to its usual pristine state. Or rather, it was far more pristine than if she'd been clearing up. Perhaps

72

Lauren and Allison had stayed behind to help or, more likely, given the gleam on the stainless-steel bread bin, Jack had done it. Had he coaxed Susie back after she'd stormed off, and after having sex in Hope's bed, they'd scrubbed down the kitchen together?

Hope decided that the bathroom was her only viable place of retreat. Normally she'd have stripped off on the way, but she didn't want to be naked and vulnerable in front of Jack, especially as he'd compare her body to Susie's, and that was another battle that Hope would lose.

'Are we over?' she asked hoarsely. 'Now that you don't love me any more.'

Jack's aghastness was momentarily gratifying, but only for one very brief moment. 'What? No! Of course we're not over!' He gave her a cowed look, like a dog expecting to have its nose wiped into the area rug that it had just soiled. 'You don't really think I've stopped loving you, do you?'

She hesitated. Because, yes, she did really think that. Didn't want to, but all the evidence suggested that Jack had stopped loving her some time ago and she hadn't even realised it.

'I love you, Hopey,' he said, moving forward to wrap her up in a desperate embrace. 'I never stopped loving you, even when she . . .'

'Don't say it,' Hope begged, but she couldn't not be held by Jack, enveloped in the toasty smell and warmth of him, and not feel all right. One of her hands was creeping up to tug the little tuft of hair at his nape and stroke the back of his neck.

That was the deal with loving someone. When they hurt you, they were the only one who could take the hurt away.

'I never slept with her, I swear,' Jack whispered in her ear. 'It was just one stupid, drunken kiss that I wish I could rewind and erase.'

'That wasn't a one-off kiss,' Hope insisted, but she wasn't struggling to get free, but resting her head on Jack's

73

shoulder as he rubbed her back like he was trying to wind her. 'It looked like you two had kissed countless times, usually without any clothes getting in the way.'

'I don't care what it looked like. It has never happened before and it will never happen again. You have to believe me, Hopey.'

'But why did it happen at all?'

'I don't know!' Jack gave a bitten-off groan. 'I was pissed and Susie and I always have that flirty thing going on, and it was just one of those things you suddenly find yourself doing and you're not sure how or why.'

It didn't even come close to being a good enough excuse and Hope pulled away so she could look Jack in the eye. He looked like her Jack again, pouting slightly, brow knitted in a pleading frown. 'She was my best friend. You didn't just cross a line. You crossed about a hundred lines.'

'I know I did,' Jack said as he grabbed Hope's hands and held them tight like he would never let go, until she yelped in pain as he pressed against the burn on her palm. 'Sorry! It was, like, five minutes of madness that I'll always regret for as long as I live. Please say that you understand.'

Hope wanted to more than anything, except she needed to be certain of one thing. 'You do still love me, don't you?' she begged. 'I know I was a bitch yesterday with all the stress of the dinner party and I know I nag you and that I'm messy and . . .'

'Oh shut up, you stupid cow, of course I love you,' Jack burst out, and it wasn't the nicest way he'd ever said it, but Hope didn't think he'd ever said it with so much feeling. 'I wish I had a time machine and I could go back to last night and make sure that the kiss didn't happen, but I can't. All I can do is keep telling you that I love you until you believe me.'

'I do believe you,' Hope said slowly, and when she sat down on the edge of the bathtub, Jack sank to his knees so he could gaze up at her, and maybe her heart wasn't broken, because it did a little loop-the-loop just from the sight of Jack, with his hair falling into his eyes and his little lopsided smile. 'Are we still unofficially engaged, then?'

Jack gently lifted up Hope's injured hand so he could kiss the three silver rings on her finger. 'God, you don't get rid of me that easily, Hopita,' he said, and now his smile wasn't so lopsided but brighter and sunnier, and it was impossible for Hope not to smile back. 'I will make this up to you. Anything you want, name it, it's yours.'

Hope wouldn't have minded Jack's blessing in moving the three silver rings to the third finger of her left hand, because she really needed that kind of reassurance. But when they went from pre-engaged to properly engaged, she didn't want it to be because they were making up from a fight. And as it was, now she was starting to feel a little foolish that she'd made such a scene about one kiss. *If it had been just one kiss.* But Jack couldn't look at her like that and be lying to her. He just couldn't. She knew him better than that.

'Do you . . . will you promise that you . . . that both of us will never see Susie again? Or Wilson,' she amended hastily, because she never wanted to see his sneery face ever again as long as she lived.

Jack actually sighed in relief. 'Of course. Goes without saying.' He patted Hope's thigh in a consoling manner. 'Was he a total wanker to you?'

'Well, he did come and find me and give me a lift,' she mumbled. 'And he was nice for maybe five minutes, but mostly he was rude, patronising and just unspeakably vile.' Hope was all set to tell Jack that Wilson had accused her of imagining things when she realised that if she believed Jack's version of events, like she really wanted to, then actually she *had* been imagining things. Which meant that Wilson had been right and Hope had been up to her elbows in wrong, but that aside, he'd still spent most of last night being a total bastard. 'I hate him.'

'So, anything else I can do to make it up to you?' Jack asked, because he was obviously already bored with talking about Wilson, which suited Hope just fine.

'You could run me a bath,' Hope said, because she wanted this whole heart-wrenching episode to be done with and for boring, blissful normality to reign in their home once again. She gently pulled herself free from Jack who was still clutching her hands. 'Lots of bubbles, please.'

'Coming right up.' Jack bustled past Hope to get to the taps. 'I'll even go out and get the *Observer* so you can read the magazine while you soak.'

Hope nodded. It was best like this instead of having some painful post-mortem that would make the situation drag on and on. But . . . 'You . . . like, you and her, you haven't? Not ever?'

'How can you even ask me that?' Jack demanded, his aghast face firmly reattached, his hand, which had been whipping up a frenzied froth of L'Occitane Green Tea scented bubbles, stilling.

'How can I not?' She leaned against the sink. 'You have to promise me.'

'I promise you!' Jack said, and he sounded as if he was nearing the very zenith of his contrition. 'And I promise that I'll never see her again. OK?'

'OK,' Hope agreed, because she needed to let this go – even she was getting sick of the clingy desperation in her voice.

'Now can we drop the subject and talk about something else, like me staying to wash your back?' Jack offered with a leer that was a shadow of his usual leer. 'If you wanted.'

Hand-holding and bath-running were all very well, but a quick bout of make-up sex definitely wasn't going to be happening any time soon. It would take at least a week for any lingering Susie DNA to be eradicated from Jack's skin, and though Hope had said the two of them were AOK, saying it and making herself genuinely believe it were two very different things. 'I think I need some alone-time,' she murmured as she stared at their two electric toothbrushes standing neatly side by side.

Within two weeks of moving in together, it had been established that Hope's alone-time was sacrosanct. It either meant that she'd had a hellish day at school or she was between days twenty-three and twenty-eight of her cycle. Or, in worst-case scenarios, she'd had a hellish day *and* her special lady-time was imminent. It was her Get Out Of Jail Free card, and Jack respected Hope's alone-time absolutely because he really didn't like to suffer the spitting, furious consequences if he failed to heed her warning.

Maybe that's why he was nodding in an understanding fashion. 'That's fair enough,' he said, but he still wasn't leaving the bathroom so Hope could wallow in bubbles and self-doubt. 'Hope?'

Her head shot up at the sound of the plaintive, wheedling note in Jack's voice. 'What?' she asked suspiciously.

'Hopey, I know I don't have the right to ask, but you won't tell your mum about this, will you?' Jack screwed his eyes shut. 'Or my mum, come to that,' he added weakly.

'God, no!' It was a relief to be on exactly the same page again. 'You don't deserve that. I don't deserve that. They'll be calling on the hour, every hour, to make sure that we haven't split up.'

Hope and Jack stared at each other in mounting horror.

'I think we can deal with this ourselves without any outside interference,' Hope said firmly, because as hideous as the situation was, their mothers would make it even worse. They'd been best friends and next-door neighbours for twenty-nine years, and had been planning Jack and Hope's nuptials ever since Caroline Delafield's twenty-week scan had told her that after eight years of trying and three sons, she was finally going to have a use for that bottom drawer full of pink babygros and frilly dresses. 'Otherwise our only chance of escape from the maternal jackboot is a joint suicide pact.'

'You bring the pills, I'll get the razor blades,' Jack said.

'Rather have a copy of the *Observer* and some orange juice, please.'

'OK, OK.' Jack held up his hands in surrender. 'I'm going.'

Hope waited until Jack left the bathroom before she bolted the door, stripped off and slowly sank into the scented bath water. Jack always ran the bath slightly too hot and she had to ease herself in.

She ducked her head under the water, then emerged spluttering, hair streaming out behind her. Hope could hear Jack whistling, which always set her teeth on edge, then scoop up his keys and call out a cheery, 'See you in five,' before the front door slammed behind him.

Hope focused on the spot of mildew on the windowsill that no amount of Cillit Bang or vinegar could shift, then stretched out her legs so she could prop her feet up on either side of the taps. She could beat herself up over and over again because Jack had kissed her best friend. Or because if she'd been satisfying him then Jack wouldn't have even contemplated kissing someone else, no matter how drunk he was. Or that he was never going to ask her to marry him if he wanted to have the freedom to kiss other girls.

There were all these 'ors' that she could obsess about or she could just . . . not. She'd told Jack that everything would be fine and they could put the whole sorry mess behind them, and they could.

If they loved each other and they wanted to stay together, grow old together, run the risk of the red-hair gene not being so recessive after all and bringing up a horde of ginger kids, then Hope had to build the world's biggest bridge and get over this. And she had to stop being so argumentative and disorganised, and slobbing out as soon as she got in from work so that when Jack arrived home he was usually met by the less than scintillating sight of Hope in her pyjamas eating cereal straight from the box as she did her lesson plans.

Hope lay there, occasionally and adroitly pulling up the plug with one foot to let the water drain a bit, then adding more hot water, until her fingers and toes were so pruney that they started to hurt. Her head also hurt, but she couldn't tell if it was from sleep deprivation or from chasing all the facts round and round in her head until they made her dizzy.

She was on the verge of hauling herself out of the bath when she heard Jack returning at the same time that her iPhone began to chirp faintly with Blondie's 'Call Me', which was her current ringtone.

'Shall I get that for you?' he called out, and she grunted an affirmative reply as she began to slather on body lotion.

Then her stomach lurched and Hope thought that she might actually throw up, because what if it was Susie phoning to apologise and getting Jack instead of Hope? Hope strained her ears. Jack was talking in a low murmur, not raising his voice, and she was sure that she even heard him chuckle at one point. If it was Susie, he should have hung up by now, and she was all set to charge out of the bathroom and shout at him when Jack suddenly banged on the door.

'How much longer are you going to be in there, anyway?' he complained. 'Someone wants to talk to you.'

Hope yanked a bath sheet off the towel rail. 'Who?' she demanded. 'Who wants to talk to me?'

'Your beloved deputy head wants to remind you to make brownies for tomorrow and, also, if it's not too much trouble, can you make them gluten-free?'

Her suspicions were instantly forgotten as Hope unbolted the door with a scowl on her face. 'No, I can't,' she hissed at Jack, who grinned and handed over her iPhone.

'I'll make coffee,' he said, swatting her on the arse with the *Observer* as he walked away from her and Hope guessed that they were back to normal.

Chapter Eight

When Hope had decided to become a teacher, it wasn't to follow in her parents' footsteps, and it certainly wasn't a grand calling to shape young minds.

Even before she'd acquired her 2.1 degree in History from Leeds University, Hope had had enough sense to know she didn't have the creative skills to become a writer, or any discernible musical ability that meant she could join a band and live out all her rock 'n' roll fantasies. So, between her mother extolling the virtues of teaching, Jack nagging her to come down to London before the ink was dry on her final exam paper, and Lauren suddenly deciding that she wanted to become an educator 'because you get, like, twenty weeks' holiday a year', Hope figured there was no harm in doing a School Centred Initial Teaching Training course while she thought long and hard about what she wanted to do when she grew up.

Hope had trained in a rough inner-city school in Lambeth and spent every night of the first month wondering what the hell she was doing. The children were terrifying, the National Curriculum was daunting, and she doubted her numeracy skills were up to the challenge. Then, during her second month, she had a lightbulb moment as she did some one-to-one reading with a seven-year-old girl called Angel – who had her own lightbulb moment when she suddenly stopped laboriously sounding out syllables and actually began to read, a huge, gappy smile on her face. That was it. Hope had been bitten by the teaching bug and besides, teachers did get a hell of a lot of holidays.

So Hope wasn't entirely despondent about the new school year. It also helped that she could ease into it with two inset days. First, she was briefed about the new curriculum by Dorothy, the deputy head, who looked after the day-to-day running of the infant classes at Balls Pond Primary School, which was known locally as The Bull Pen. Then Hope bitched about the new curriculum with Elaine, who taught the year above hers, the Yellow Class. She also met Marta, who'd just finished her SCITT and would be teaching the tinies in the Red Class, and was in a state of morbid terror after her induction with Dorothy.

Mostly Hope organised her classroom, pinning up all the *Guardian* wall charts of British songbirds, wild flowers and trees that she'd religiously saved during the year, sorting out the detritus of dried-up paint pots and hard brushes in the art corner, and taking custody of four grasshoppers, three goldfish and Herbert, the class hamster, who'd all spent the summer with Saeed, the caretaker.

It was the calm before the storm and, as Wednesday morning approached, Hope could feel herself getting more and more nervous. This was her third year teaching, which was nothing compared to Dorothy, who was approaching her quarter-century, or Elaine, who could remember when inset days were called 'Baker days', and the prospect of thirty six-year-olds staring her down and trying to sniff out her weak spots, of which there were many, filled Hope with dread and uncertainty.

The handover note from Justine, the old Red Class teacher who'd left to follow her Australian boyfriend back to Sydney, wasn't doing much to quell her fears either. She named and shamed the troublemakers, the cry-babies, the incontinent and the two kids 'who've probably got Asperger's or ADD but they both have doting yummy mummies who refuse to believe that their darlings might have been touched with the special stick'.

On the plus side, Hope read on, 'As a class, they'll sell their vital organs for a sticker. If you institute a sticker-reward system that culminates in a gold star and some crap plastic toy from the 99p shop you'll be OK.

'They're also obsessed with Katy Perry, so if they've been really well-behaved, I let them sing "I Kissed a Girl" on Friday afternoons.' It was no surprise Justine had decided to emigrate to Australia after a series of complaints about her unorthodox teaching methods.

By three o'clock on Tuesday afternoon, Hope was done. The art corner was organised, even if its shelves, pots and brushes were still covered in decades' worth of poster paint, glue and glitter. She'd assembled a little chill-out area at the back of the class, with its own desk and two easy chairs, where she and Andy, her new teaching assistant, could do some one-on-one coaching.

Along the big picture windows that took up the far wall Hope had arranged her nature section, where she hoped the grasshoppers and the goldfish would be very happy. Soon the windowsill would be full of Blue Class's attempts to grow watercress on wet tissue paper.

Hope had even made a huge sticker wall chart cum calendar cum merit board, and there were two weeks' worth of lesson plans all neatly collated in her filing cabinet. She'd filled in everybody's names in her register in her best handwriting – though Hope still felt as if she wasn't grown up enough to have ownership of a register – and had written her own name on the whiteboard in block capitals. There wasn't much left to do now but panic.

'You done, Hopey? Fancy a quick pint of Pinot Grigio?'

Panic *or* drink. Hope beamed at Elaine who was standing in the doorway. 'Yes, please,' she agreed eagerly, already picking up her handbag and denim jacket. 'Actually, I fancy a huge glass of rosé, 'cause it's not officially the end of summer until the hordes of ankle-biters descend upon us.'

'Might join you in the pink drink,' Elaine said, as they walked along the corridor, which even after six weeks without any pupils on the premises still smelt of TCP and cheap mince.

They didn't even need to discuss their choice of hostelry but walked round the corner to the Midnight Bell, where most of the teaching staff were already firmly ensconced in the beer garden, the two tables they'd annexed covered in empty glasses and discarded crisp packets.

'We should probably go and make sure Marta is all right.' Hope looked over at the forlorn new recruit, as she and Elaine hovered at the edge of the garden, clutching an ice bucket with a bottle of rosé wedged in it, two glasses and also, in Hope's case, a packet of pork scratchings. 'She's inherited Gurinder,' she added cheerfully because Gurinder, her old classroom assistant, had been a long-suffering, constantly sighing thorn in Hope's side for her first two years at the school. A veteran classroom assistant, Gurinder was always assigned to the newest teacher, and always made it plain that in all her long decades of classroom-assisting, she'd never come across anyone so singularly inept at imparting knowledge. Now she was Marta's problem, but them were the breaks.

'Oh, I'm sure she's fine,' Elaine said airily, marching over to an empty table in the furthest corner of the garden. As Elaine was carrying the bucket of wine, Hope had absolutely no choice but to follow her.

Hope swung her legs over the bench, grabbed the bottle out of the bucket and poured them both a glass. 'So, hey you! How the hell have you been these last few weeks?'

Hope loved Elaine, just a little bit. Even though Elaine was twenty years older than her, they'd instantly clicked on Hope's very first day at The Bull Pen, when she'd timidly walked into the staffroom clutching a Tupperware container full of home-made pecan and toffee tarts. Elaine had demanded the recipe, they'd both realised they shared a passion for home-baking and within ten minutes of talking, had also discovered a mutual love for Victoria Wood, John Hughes films and the odd spliff on a non-school night – after Hope had tried to enquire obliquely about the Council's position on drug-testing teachers.

Now Hope rested her chin on her hands and giggled as Elaine described the 'three weeks of utter bloody hell' that had been her camping trip in the Dordogne with her husband Simon (who'd scored a top-forty hit in the late '80s with his bowl-haircutted, leather-trousered, winkle-picker-wearing indie band but now ran his own recording studio from the bottom of their sprawling garden in Hackney) and her two teenage daughters, who'd spent the entire holiday either throwing monumental strops or sneaking off to smoke, drink and get off with disreputable French boys who drove mopeds at reckless speed.

'And it pissed down with rain most of the time, but I still managed to get bitten by the local mosquito population,' Elaine finished, holding out one tanned arm for Hope's inspection. 'I did buy you some amazing cheese, but it all got eaten by a Japanese poodle-rock band over the weekend.'

'I hope Simon's going to add that to their studio bill.'

'Doubt it. They're paying us in instalments as it is.' Elaine pushed back her fine, Nordic blonde hair, which was just starting to grey at the temples. 'Tell you what, next batch of honey has your name on it.' As well as itinerant rock musicians, Elaine had beehives in her back garden and generally she was Hope's honorary London mum. Much less uptight and judgemental than her Lancashire mum, who could only just about be persuaded to have a glass of wine, never mind a joint heavily laced with THC on a non-school night. And unlike Hope's mother, who regarded teaching as an extension of the endless chore of child-rearing, Elaine, for all her bitching about Dorothy and the 'fucking strait-jacket of the National Curriculum that wants us to turn out a generation of mindless automatons', loved nothing more than taking charge of thirty captive minds and challenging them, nurturing them and making them see the world in a different way.

'So, anyway, enough about me,' Elaine said crisply. 'We haven't really had a chance to talk properly about you.' She'd assumed a more serious expression than her usual mischievous smile and her pale blue eyes were all squinty, which meant she was in perceptive mode. Hope immediately squirmed on the hard wooden bench. Elaine in perceptive mode could be a real pain in the arse.

'Nothing much to say,' Hope demurred, still wriggling uncomfortably. 'I went home for a week, because my dad had taken my baby brother camping, so I had loads of quality time with my mum.'

'And how did that work out for you?'

'Oh, it was just great,' Hope said. 'My mum tried to force me into having my hair combed out and trimmed because she said it was riddled with split ends, and then she spent the rest of the time dropping hints about how she'd like a grandchild before too long.'

'She has grandchildren, doesn't she?'

Hope nodded. 'She has five of them.' Two of her older brothers, Matthew and Luke (and their respective wives), had obliged, but as far as her mother was concerned, being the paternal grandma wasn't a patch on that blissful day when Hope started birthing babies. 'But she says it's not the same when she's only a mother-in-law and the other grandma has first dibs.'

Elaine held a limp hand to her forehead. 'Dear God, I dread the day when one of mine comes home pregnant. Probably be the end of the week, the way those two carry on.' She poured what was left of the bottle of rosé into their glasses. 'So, am I going to have to beat it out of you? What's really up with you? You look like you've had at least three root-canal treatments.'

Did she? Hope had thought that she'd handled the aftermath of the weekend's events with considerable aplomb, and huge amounts of Touche Éclat to hide the effects of the intermittent crying jags and sleepless nights, but apparently her efforts had all been in vain.

'Jack and I have been going through a bit of a rough patch,' Hope said delicately, as if she was the kind of girl who kept her own counsel and didn't blab her deepest, darkest secrets to all and sundry.

Unfortunately, Elaine knew her much better than that because she raised her eyebrows and pursed her lips as she processed that little nugget of information and then nudged Hope's ankle with her toe. 'Do tell.'

Hope told, and Elaine listened avidly, leaning forward so she didn't miss a single word. Hope hadn't planned to over-share to such an alarming degree, but the events of Saturday night had been weighing so heavily on her that it felt as if she couldn't even breathe. Simply telling someone else lightened the load by a few kilograms.

'I can't bear to be inside my own head at the moment,' she admitted to Elaine, when she got to the end of her confession. 'I still can't quite believe Jack when he swears it was just a drunken one-off. But if that is all it was, then I made a complete tit of myself in front of everyone over nothing, and I had a big, fat, ugly cry in front of Wilson who was really scathing and . . . and . . . and I just wish I wasn't still so furious with Jack, but I am!'

'You have every right to be furious with him and to threaten to cut off his willy with your bread knife,' Elaine told her, without the usual twinkle in her eye and as if she was deadly serious about revenge castration. 'Even if it was just a one-time deal, it was still prolonged kissing and groping. And as for that Wilson, he sounds like an utter prick. Anyone who wasn't made of stone would have cried in those circumstances, so I don't know why he had to be so rude to you.'

'Well, I was rude to him too, Elaine. I do feel a bit guilty about that,' Hope admitted.

Elaine sniffed. 'As for Susie, didn't she get the memo that your best friend's boyfriend's dick is completely off-limits? I always thought there was something off about her,' she said darkly, which was a very similar riff to what Lauren and Allison had had to say about Susie, though they'd liked her well enough when the four of them had gone out all those times to drink the bars of central London dry. It had taken them twenty-four hours to get over the initial shock that Susie would violate the first and most important rule of the best-friend code, and now Susie was dead to them. 'Don't get me wrong, she was a real laugh, but strip away the designer clothes and the fake posh accent and all you're left with is a girl with fake boobs who looks like she doesn't wipe her minny after she pees,' had been Allison's savage character assassination of Hope's former friend, while Lauren had announced that from now on she was going to stop secretly calling her 'Shmoozie' and call her 'Floozie' instead.

'You only met her once,' Hope reminded Elaine, and again she wondered why in all her rage at Jack, she still couldn't manage more than annoyance at Susie's actions. OK, she didn't want to go down the same slut-shaming road as Lauren and Allison, but it took two people to drunkenly snog, so really Susie deserved just as much fury as Jack.

'She has a very unfortunate manner,' Elaine said, frowning like she was picturing the time that she'd bumped into Hope and Susie in Wagamama's in Camden, and Susie hadn't looked up from her BlackBerry but had just waved vaguely in Elaine's direction. Then when she had finally finished tweeting, she'd told a very off-colour joke about the Japanese-style fish rolls. 'Yes, she's funny and glamorous and she has a way with her, but I got the impression that there wasn't much to her. All surface, no depth.'

There hadn't been so much as an apologetic text message from Susie, and though she knew that she shouldn't, Hope missed her. Yes, despite the wickedness Susie had wrought, when you spoke to someone at least three times a day, constantly had texts and tweets winging back and forth, and shared pictures of animals in freaky outfits on Facebook, to have them suddenly gone from your life left a huge aching gap that felt as if it could never be filled. Talking of which . . .

'I need to get over myself, don't I?' Hope asked tentatively, because even Lauren and Allison had told her that she only had a week's cooling-off period before she had to let it go once and for all. 'I mean, it was just one measly kiss. Jack swore on all his Beatles vinyl that it was nothing more than that.'

'You've been going out since you were five, right?'

'Well, since I was thirteen, but I've known him all my life.'

Elaine nodded. 'And this is his first misdemeanour?'

'Yeah, apart from the big fight in Barcelona about not getting engaged and the usual minor domestic squabbles. Like, he always yells at me for leaving the fridge door open for longer than ten seconds at a time, and he always breaks into my chocolate stash so that when I go to get an emergency bag of Maltesers, they're all gone. Oh God, and there was this one time that he used an entire tub of my really expensive cleanser to get acrylic paint off his hands. I could have killed him.' Even as she recited this list of Jack's crimes, it occurred to Hope that it was a very short list, and that apart from his recent infidelity, Jack had always been an exemplary boyfriend. 'And he has been really, really sweet the last couple of days,' Hope added. 'Or at least on his very best behaviour.'

It was true. He'd surprised her with breakfast in bed that morning, even though he'd had to get up before eight to present her with two pieces of toast and jam and the least brown banana from the fruit bowl. And he'd come home on Monday night with a huge bouquet of flowers and goodies purloined from the *Skirt* beauty cupboard – it didn't erase the memory of him and Susie, but he was trying to make things all right again.

'Sometimes relationships go through these patches when they're more about tolerating someone and putting up with all their annoying habits,' Elaine mused. 'Other times, the magic and the romance comes back, even though you hadn't even noticed they were missing. When Simon was in the band, he'd disappear off in a transit van for weeks on end, *and* he wore leather trousers, for God's sake.'

'You think he had groupies?'

'I think that I wasn't sitting at home twiddling my thumbs waiting for him to call me from the Newport Pagnell services. If he was out having a good time, then I was going to make bloody sure that I was too,' Elaine said with a rueful smile. 'Which didn't mean I stopped loving him or he stopped loving me, but our relationship went through a phase. A phase when we shagged other people.'

'But you're all right now, though? 'Cause you've talked it through and . . .'

'. . . and he got dropped by his label and stopped touring,' Elaine corrected. 'We had a "don't ask, don't tell" policy, which worked for us then, but now, if he even thought of getting his leg over some other woman, he'd be walking funny for the rest of his life.'

'I should probably give Jack a break,' Hope decided, but she wished that she didn't sound so uncertain. 'I mean, I think we'll be OK, and maybe we needed this to happen to show us that we both need to put a bit more time and effort into our relationship.' Even as she said it, Hope wondered why relationships needed time and effort like lesson plans and redecorating the kitchen, which they'd been talking about ever since they'd bought the flat, but hadn't got much further than picking up paint charts.

'The course of true love never runs smooth, dearie,' Elaine said, picking up the wine bottle and glaring at it as if its emptiness was a deliberate act of wilful behaviour. 'Or love conquers all. Take your pick. I mean, you do love Jack, don't you?'

'Of course I love him. I don't even want to think about what my life would be like without him,' Hope said immediately, and there was no need for Elaine to be giving her the same funny look that she gave Dorothy when she was banging on about STPCDs, SIDPs, PPAs and the many other acronyms that littered her conversation, most of which Elaine and Hope didn't understand. 'So, that's good, right?'

'Of course it's good. And it can't do any harm to buy some new underwear.' Elaine paused delicately, then lowered her voice. 'Nothing crotchless or nippleless though, you wouldn't believe the chafing.'

'Eeewww!' Hope squealed, even as she made a mental note to pop into M&S on the way home. Mopey, self-pitying alone-time was one thing, but maybe they should be having more sexy together-time. Her mind made up, she hauled herself to her feet. 'I need to get going.'

'To the bar?' Elaine asked hopefully, holding up the ice bucket. 'Same again?'

'No, I need to buy tasteful but sexy underwear and get something nice for Jack's tea. Are Marks still doing those dine-in-for-a-tenner promotions?'

'But it's early! It's not even five, and these are our last precious moments of freedom until half-term,' Elaine protested. 'Have one more for the road. One as in bottle, not glass, in case you were wondering.'

Hope wavered. If she glugged down half a bottle of rosé in record time, she could still get to Marks and be at home in her new fancy undies with the smell of something delicious wafting from the oven by the time Jack got back from work. 'Well, I suppose it doesn't matter too much if I have a tiny little hangover tomorrow.'

'Exactly! By the time they've written their names on their folders and told you what they did in the summer holidays, it'll be time to go home,' Elaine said, because she was a terrible enabler – almost as bad as Susie had been, but no, Hope wasn't going to think about Susie any more.

'I suppose another bottle wouldn't hurt.' Hope fished in her handbag for her polka-dot purse. 'But we have to drink it really quickly and we have to ask Marta to join us. She looks like she's about to burst into tears.'

'Oh, she does. Poor little thing.' Elaine sighed. 'Bring her over on your way back from the bar, and I'll also have a bag of salt and vinegar crisps if you're buying.'

Chapter Nine

Three hours later, still damp from a hasty shower, Hope shoved the Ginger, Lime and Coriander Chicken in the oven, with the hasselback potatoes on the lower shelf. She had been planning to get a salad to accompany the main course but as the meal deal included a bottle of wine and a pudding, a salad seemed a lot like shutting the stable door after the horse had bolted.

Tomorrow, once the children were back at school and she could settle into a proper routine, Hope vowed to start eating healthily again and go to the gym regularly to lose the ten pounds she'd put on over the summer. As it was, she'd looked so lumpen in the changing-room mirror that, as well as buying a set of sexy underwear, Hope had bought a matching slip to hide her pot belly and the faint traces of cellulite cascading down the backs of her thighs. Also, starting from tomorrow, she had to stop spending huge sums of money.

Tomorrow and tomorrow and tomorrow . . . it was time to be a grown-up again, Hope thought, as she got down the Russian tea glasses she liked to use as candle holders. They were back to eating dinner in front of the TV, but she could at least set the coffee table and establish a romantic, sexy vibe, because she and Jack, they were *so* having sex tonight. Preferably before ten, because Hope wanted an early night, but having sex would definitely get their relationship back on track.

As Hope arranged her candles on the coffee table and even re-polished the cutlery so it was especially sparkly, she could taste the fear and anticipation at the back of her throat. She couldn't remember ever being this nervous about having sex, apart from their very first time, when she'd gone down to London to visit Jack when he was studying at St Martin's and he'd booked a room in a sweet little bed and breakfast in Bloomsbury so it would be special and romantic.

Hope sighed a little at the memory of Jack hoisting her over his shoulders like a sack of potatoes so he could carry her over the threshold, just as she heard his key turn in the lock.

She hurried out into the hall in time to say, 'You're late,' as soon as he walked through the door. She hadn't meant to sound suspicious or a lot like the proverbial little woman worrying that the dinner would spoil, but that must have been what she sounded like because Jack's face tightened, even as he held up a familiar green carrier bag.

'I always make sure that I have a canvas tote scrunched up in my bag so I don't have to pay five pence for a carrier,' she heard herself say, instead of a husky, 'Hard day at the office, dear?'

Jack dropped the environmentally damaging bag on the floor where something clinked promisingly. 'God, I can't do anything right, can I?'

It was all going wrong before Hope had even had a chance to make things right between them. 'I'm sorry,' she said, padding forward to hug Jack, then losing her nerve at the last moment and gingerly prodding his arm instead. 'I didn't mean to be all confrontational as soon as you got home.' She rolled her eyes. 'I didn't plan on being confrontational at all.'

'I didn't mean to be late,' Jack said a little less sulkily, and he looked so defeated and tired, in a way that had nothing to do with a hard day at the office and everything to do with

Hope shutting him out while she had alone-time, then keeping him up most of the night as she fidgeted, ground her teeth and fretted. 'I thought I'd make us something nice for tea as it's your last few hours of freedom.'

Hope drew a circle on the sea-grass carpet with her toe. 'I had the same idea,' she admitted, and then she placed her hand on her cocked hip, pressed her knees tightly together and stuck her chest out in a pose that a hurried read of *Cosmo* had told her was textbook sexy. If it was, Jack didn't seem to appreciate it, even though Hope had convinced herself that the silvery-grey of the slip was the perfect foil for her hair and made her skin look like alabaster rather than just pasty. 'I even laid the coffee table.'

Jack brushed past her so he could glance at the sensual ambience that Hope had created. 'You should put coasters underneath those candle glasses, otherwise they'll burn rings on the table,' was all he said as Hope glared at the back of his head.

'So, what's for tea, then?' Jack asked, blithely unaware that Hope was giving him the stink-eye. 'Did you get one of those M&S meal deals?'

'Yeah,' Hope muttered, heading back to the kitchen. Once she'd checked on dinner, she might just as well change into her PJs as the new sexy undies had been a total waste of money. 'Some fancy lime and ginger chicken thing and hasselback potatoes, though I'm not sure how a hasselback potato differs from a normal one.'

'Me too,' Jack said, as he followed her. 'Not just about the hasselback potatoes. I got the lime and ginger chicken thing too, but then I got a poncy bagged salad.'

'I *thought* about getting the salad,' Hope exclaimed with more enthusiasm than a salad warranted but at least they were talking, rather than her sniping and Jack getting defensive. 'What did you get for pud?'

'Duh! Chocolate soufflés, of course!'

Hope was already opening the fridge, so she could pull

out her chocolate soufflés. 'Snap! And did you get the Shiraz?'

'I got the rosé, because I know it's your summer drink of choice and it's still officially summer until the hordes of snot-nosed urchins march back into school.'

'I got the Shiraz 'cause I know you prefer red,' Hope said, her smile unforced and genuine for the first time in ever.

They got each other. They were in sync. That was all that really mattered.

'I'm glad our hive mind isn't broken,' Jack said, as he put his arms around her. 'I was kinda worried for a while.'

It was the perfect moment for a kiss, but instead Hope stood on tiptoes so she could rub her nose against Jack's. It was the same silly but affectionate gesture they'd used as teenagers when they'd both been too shy to make the first move that would inevitably lead to a frenzied snogging session.

Hope felt, rather than saw, Jack's smile, and his arms tightened around her momentarily until one hand slid down to cup an arse cheek. 'When you bent down to get the soufflés out of the fridge, I got a flash of a pair of knickers that I don't think I've seen before,' he murmured awkwardly, because he didn't have a suave line in bedroom patter. But Hope didn't mind because neither did she and when Jack did try, he sounded so earnest that it was cute and sexy all at the same time.

'They're new.' Hope looked up at him with her lashes lowered demurely, another move that *Cosmo* had sworn worked better than Viagra. She certainly had Jack's undivided attention, as she pulled down one of the spaghetti straps of her new slip far enough to give him a glimpse of her other new purchase. 'There's a matching bra, too.'

Jack swallowed. 'Right. So is there embroidery on the knickers as well?'

'Well, yeah. It *is* a matching set.'

His hand, which had been absent-mindedly stroking her bum, now made a sneaky foray under her slip so he could smooth down the faux satin on her new undies. 'I'd rather have a show than a tell, if that's all right with you,' Jack said, right before he kissed her.

Hope wound her arms around his neck and kissed him back with every last ounce of fervour she could muster. Which was a lot of ounces. They kissed desperately, tongues delving into each other's mouth for the first time in what felt like weeks – though, surely, it hadn't been that long?

When Jack pulled up her slip, Hope thought that it was time to move this to the bedroom. Then she thought that they should probably call a halt until after dinner because the chicken was just about ready. She even pulled her mouth free from Jack's neck to say exactly that but no words came out, just a surprised squawk as Jack suddenly grasped her around the waist and hauled her up on to the worktop.

The effort of hoisting her on to the counter left Jack red-faced and panting, which wasn't very flattering. Another mood-killer was the worktop, which Hope had just wiped down with a wet cloth while she was waiting for the oven to heat up. Now she could feel her knickers clinging damply to her arse and any frisky, what-the-hell-let's-just-do-it-right-here-right-now feelings she might have had were quickly evaporating.

Jack had other ideas. 'You look so sexy tonight, Hopey,' he declared, stepping nearer the counter and parting her legs so he could stroke his palms along her inner thighs. 'Really, really sexy.'

She didn't feel particularly sexy, sitting in a damp patch with her slip all rucked up so her freckly, wobbly thighs were on display, but Jack was looking at the shimmy of her breasts as Hope wriggled to get more comfortable and she could see his hard cock outlined in denim.

'You look sexy too,' she told him and he did, face flushed, hair rumpled by her fingers, tongue worrying at his bottom lip. 'Kiss me again.'

Hope had been sure that the swoony feeling had gone, but when Jack kissed her, it came rushing back so all she wanted to do was wrap her legs around his hips so she could grind against his cock. She didn't even mind when she heard a tearing sound as Jack pulled her new slip over her head, because the sooner it was off, the sooner he could kiss her again, hands fumbling behind her back as he worked her bra clasp.

Then it was her turn to free him of his worn leather belt and tug his jeans down just enough that she could wrap her hands around his cock. The weight and the length and the curve of him against her fingers was comforting and she didn't want to think about Susie having her hands anywhere near Jack's dick, which was her exclusive property.

She wanted those memories gone. Or at least, Hope wanted new memories to take their place and hot dirty sex in the kitchen was a good place to start. Still clutching hold of Jack's dick, she grabbed one of his hands and hooked it into the waistband of her new knickers. 'I really don't mind if you rip these off me too,' she said.

'How about I just pull them off with great passion?' Jack said, tugging them down as Hope obligingly lifted one bottom cheek then the other.

And they were back on familiar ground – Hope showed him where and how and soon his index finger was gently thrumming her clit and she could go back to jacking him off. Maybe there was something to be said for sitting on the kitchen worktop under the harsh glare of the fluorescent light, because when they weren't stealing clinging, tender kisses from each other, Hope was able to look down and see clearly the effect her fingers were having. Though she wished that she didn't have a pile of takeaway menus and advertising flyers trapped under her left buttock.

'Stop,' Jack muttered, against her mouth, reaching down to still her hand on his wet-tipped cock. 'Stop . . . shall we go to the bedroom?'

He'd taken his hand away from her pussy. Hope yanked it back. 'No, let's do it right here,' she said, scooching right to the edge of the counter.

'You dirty cow.' Jack grinned and even as he lined his cock up and slipped shallowly inside her, he rubbed her nose with his.

It was an awkward angle for Jack, who had to stand on tiptoes and thrust up to compensate for the fact that Hope wasn't level with him, but it worked out just fine for her. He couldn't go that deep but he was going hard and fast and managing to catch her clit every time. Her hands were tight on his hips, directing his every move, and she could hear the slap of their flesh, their ragged gasps and Jack whispering something in her ear, something she couldn't quite make out.

Her hand crept up to tangle in his hair and rub circles on his scalp, and as she pushed forward with her hips she could feel her orgasm rising up, but still just out of reach, so she was biting her lip and whimpering in frustration. If only there was room for her to worm a hand between them.

Jack's voice was getting louder and the words, which had been strung together in one indecipherable clump, suddenly became clear. 'I love you, I love you, I love you, I love you,' he said again and again, like it was a mantra, the magic chant that would wash away all the bad. And maybe it would, because Hope's eyes snapped open, and as the words became a shout she was coming, hands dropping away from Jack to grip the edge of the counter tightly as her legs trapped him deep inside her. He stiffened, his muscles locking and then he was coming too, head dropping down to rest on her breasts, and still all he could say was, 'I love you, I love you, I love you.'

Of course, the Ginger, Lime and Coriander Chicken and

the hasselback potatoes were burnt extra crispy, but the half-hour they had to wait for the second batch of chicken to cook was a small price to pay, even if they had to eat it with the poncy bagged salad.

Chapter Ten

In the space of half an hour on a Wednesday morning, Balls Pond Primary School went from a place of quiet, echoing emptiness to a place where the sound of 210 children's voices became a deafening roar as their new school shoes scuffed the freshly waxed floors.

Hope felt twisted up with nerves as she stood at the door of her classroom wearing a smart grey dress for the first day back – but with a red felt flower corsage pinned to her shoulder to grab the children's attention and let them know that she wasn't a po-faced, no-fun lady who'd scream at them if they made any noise.

Slowly Hope could feel the great big knot in her stomach begin to shrink as she said hello to parents and pupils. The catchment area for the school took in the wide avenues of huge Georgian houses in Canonbury, and Hope smiled until her face ached as she talked to parents who were in the media, or ran successful design consultancies, or worked in the City, but were all committed to the state-school system as long as the local state school continued to do well in the national league tables and be deemed 'outstanding' in the last Ofsted report.

Then there were the other parents who lived in the sprawling council estates behind Essex Road but were equally passionate about the state-school system as they didn't have any other option. But all her pupils' parents, no matter where they lived or how much they earned, shared the same concerns about bullying, numeracy and literacy skills, and why they all had to make allowances for the one child in every class who was allergic to everything from peanuts to Magic Markers.

Back in Whitfield, at the tiny primary school Hope had gone to, where her mother was now headmistress, everyone had been white, everyone had spoken English at home because everybody's family was British, hardly anyone had had free school meals, and every year they'd had a proper Christian Nativity play, with shepherds and wise men and the two prettiest girls in the school slugging it out to see who would be Mary.

Hope knew that things in Whitfield had changed a little, judging by her mother's frequent screeds, which always ended with the words, 'It's political correctness gone mad,' but in the Borough of Islington, it had ever been thus. Blue Class was a glorious mix of Somalian, Polish, Kenyan, Bangladeshi, French, Irish, Israeli, Pakistani, German, Bulgarian, Indian, Croatian, Korean, Australian, Nigerian, Russian, American and Chinese. Every continent but Antarctica was represented. She had two children who were trilingual, five who were bilingual, and one who hadn't spoken a word of English when she'd joined the Red Class the year before. The map of the world that Hope had pinned up on the wall by the door would soon have little stars stuck all over it as each child marked their country of origin.

But now the final tearful mum had left, after telling Hope yet again that little 'Stuart was sounding a bit chesty last night – can you make sure that he keeps his jumper on?' and thirty children were eyeing her warily. Even though Hope had spent each afternoon of the last week of the previous term with them, the summer holidays had been long, and generally six-year-olds had the retention span of fruit flies, so that morning she was back to being an unknown quantity.

For Hope's part, even though she'd memorised their names against their school photos, they all looked the same to her: thirty miniature people wearing identical bottle-green sweatshirts. Apart from Reese who was still crying because she was a girl 'and girls can't be in a Blue Class'.

Hope's nerves had all but gone, though for one final moment, as she looked past their heads to lock eyes with Andy, her new classroom assistant, she felt over-burdened by the responsibility. What if they didn't respect her authority? What if Justine hadn't taught them anything, and they weren't even on nodding terms with the alphabet and numbers one through ten, and couldn't get changed into their PE kits by themselves? What if they left her class at the end of the summer term without being able to write a simple sentence containing a noun, a verb and an adjective? What if her shoddy teaching skills sowed the seeds that ruined them for the rest of their lives and they left school at sixteen with-out any GCSEs and . . . Oh, God, shut up, Hopey, and get your gameface on, she told herself sternly.

She smiled. 'I hope you remember me from last term. I'm Miss Delafield.' To her dentist, her doctor and even her bank manager, Hope was *Ms* Delafield, but pre-pubescents had no truck with titles that drew a polite veil over marital status. 'I have lots of exciting things planned for us this year and I'll tell you all about them after assembly, but first I'm going to start off by wishing you all a good morning.'

Hope didn't even need to prompt them. 'Good morning, Miss Delafield. Good morning, everyone,' came back the chant, and Hope could start to take the register and with any luck remember which name belonged to which child. Then it would be assembly, and by the time they'd had a class discussion about what they'd all done during the summer holidays, it would be morning break and Hope could escape to the staffroom for a much-needed cup of tea and a quick debrief with Marta, who'd been throwing up in the teacher's loos at eight fifteen that morning.

The days seemed to speed by, and Hope felt as if the summer holidays had never happened. Her little collection of stock phrases was back in play and she even found herself saying crossly to Jack one evening, 'If you're talking when I'm talking, then you can't be listening, can you?'

After spending the summer in the company of adults, Hope had forgotten that six-year-olds, as a rule, were much easier to read. They gave Hope a running commentary on everything that was happening in their lives, whether it was last night's *EastEnders* or what their mother had said about Mr Gonzales, the headmaster. They told tales on their classmates with alarming alacrity, and would do anything to bask in Hope's approval or get her attention. It made a nice change when she asked a question and at least fifteen hands shot up and a begging chorus of 'Me! Me! Miss! I know!' rang around the classroom. In a lot of ways, being a teacher was like being a therapist, rockstar and prison guard all rolled into one.

There was only one child that Hope didn't like: Stuart, of chesty-cough fame. His yummy mummy Saskia was convinced that her little darling was a delicate flower with ADD, but it soon transpired that Stuart was the class bully, dispensing Chinese burns and wedgies wherever he saw fit. Plus he always had a ring of encrusted snot under his nose, and it was all Hope could do to disguise her utter loathing of the child, as she repeatedly reminded him, 'Hands are for helping, not hurting.'

Apart from snotty Stuart, this year's Blue Class would do very nicely, Hope decided, after a rousing singalong to 'Single Ladies', which they'd earned by being relatively quiet for the half hour it had taken them to do a spatial-reasoning quiz.

It was three thirty on the Friday of her second week back at school. After saying goodbye to tiny Sorcha (tiny not just because she was six, but because, Hope suspected, she had a growth-hormone deficiency) Hope locked away her laptop, made sure everyone's chair was neatly stacked on the tables, and tried to ignore the feeling of doom in the pit of her stomach. That same feeling of doom she had at going-home time every day because the thought of going home didn't please her.

It wasn't Jack. He was still on his best behaviour. Still buying her flowers and blagging high-end cosmetics and skincare products from the *Skirt* beauty cupboard on her behalf. He'd even made a concerted effort to get up when the second alarm went off, instead of repeatedly hitting the snooze button, so that Hope was forced to interrupt her own frantic morning routine to bully him out of bed.

Hope had also been a paragon of girlfriendly behaviour. Or, rather, she'd been acting like the perfect '50s housewife: having dinner ready as soon as Jack came home, which was bang on seven thirty every night. Before The Susie Incident, Jack had worked late because copy hadn't been filed on time, or there was an emergency with the repro house or the printers. Now he stayed half an hour late to show that he was a team player, then came straight home for a proper cooked tea (no ready meals) with pudding. Hope even made sure that there were always a couple of bottles of Budvar chilling in the fridge.

They'd also been having sex. Lots and lots of sex. It was perfectly nice sex, though its frequency didn't match the ferocity of that time on the fake-granite worktop, though Hope longed for a night off from the sexual gymnastics. But generally, things were back to normal with Jack. Or actually better than normal, because they hadn't had a single argument, not even a little one about whose turn it was to take out the recycling. Still, the thought of going home to cook him dinner and tidy the flat didn't exactly put a spring in Hope's step. For all the sex and all the being solicitous of each other's wellbeing, things weren't right. During the day, Hope was wrapped up in school and trying to coach her class through the two-times table, but when it was just her and Jack and an endless round of 'I don't mind if you want to watch *America's Next Top Model*,' and 'No, it's OK, you can play on the Xbox while I read the *Times Educational Supplement*,' she felt a nagging sense of unease.

Hope was now convinced that all there had ever been between Jack and Susie was some heavy flirting that had got out of hand, and she'd made everything a hundred times worse by turning it into a HUGE THING, when she should have simply laughed it off. So now, when they weren't watching TV or having sex, their conversation was stilted and awkward in a way that it had never been in all the years they'd known each other. It was as if the words they were speaking about menu plans and television-viewing schedules were just inadequate substitutes for all the words that they really wanted to say.

It was no wonder that she didn't want to go home, Hope thought as she trailed miserably down the corridor towards the staffroom. She couldn't even find solace in a quick bottle of wine with Elaine, because she was already on the way to Cornwall for her niece's wedding.

The staffroom was empty as Hope collected a wad of boring-looking memos from her cubbyhole and retrieved her jacket from her locker. Stuffed right at the back was her gym bag, which she'd brought in with her last week when she was full of good intentions to do an hour's workout each night after school. She hadn't even managed to walk home, even though it only took half an hour, and with the school lunches and a home-cooked dinner and pudding every night, the ten pounds she'd put on over the summer were fast becoming a stone.

Hope checked the time. If she got a move on, she could make the five o'clock yoga class. It wasn't an intense cardio workout, but it was best to ease back in gently.

Chapter Eleven

She made it to her gym on the other side of Highbury Corner with ten minutes to spare and had just enough time to squeeze into her yoga bottoms and vest (which had been a lot less snug eight weeks ago) and join the little knot of women waiting outside the main studio.

Hope exchanged smiles and hellos with some of the regulars and was just loudly lamenting the effect that yoga would have on her non-existent abdominal muscles the next morning, after missing so many sessions, when she felt a tap on her shoulder.

She turned round, saw Susie and heard herself say, 'Oh, hi,' because that was her immediate reaction on catching sight of that familiar, sleekly pretty face. Her immediate reaction lasted all of three seconds, then Hope was taking a step back and glaring.

'Hopey . . . God, please don't look at me like that,' Susie said plaintively, even reaching out a hand to touch Hope's arm, then thinking better of it, when Hope made a warning noise in the back of her throat. 'You can't still be mad at me. I've really missed you, and Lauren and Alli aren't talking to me either.'

'What are you doing here?' Hope spat out, not even caring that everyone was staring at them. Usually, pre-class chat consisted of desultory talk about where people had been on holiday, so this was undoubtedly the most exciting thing that had ever happened in the five minutes before yoga class started. 'Have you no shame?'

Susie's face creased in confusion. 'But you know I always duck out of work early on a Friday so I can come to yoga . . . with you,' she added with heavy emphasis. 'Then we go down the pub, because we get pissed quicker after controlling our breathing for an hour.'

'Never mind that,' Hope snapped, hands on her hips to stop them seizing Susie around her neck and throttling her . . . except, even though she was doing her best to whip herself up in a frothing, furious rage, Hope mostly felt sad. She'd wiped Susie out of her life, removed all traces of her. There'd been no goodbye. No last drink. One moment Susie was there, cracking dirty jokes and giving her fashion advice, then she was gone, and for the last two weeks Hope had felt acutely aware that Susie was missing – as if the other woman was a phantom limb, a part of Hope that had had to be amputated due to infection, because even just a drunken kiss with your best mate's boyfriend was the worst possible violation of the girl-code. The only thing worse was if Susie had actually shagged Jack, so Hope was going to be angry with her, even if she had to fake it slightly. 'You have no right to be here when you know that this is my regular yoga class.'

'But you weren't here last week,' Susie protested in a small voice that didn't suit her.

'Maybe I was too upset to come last week, what with you trying to get off with my boyfriend and all.' It was so satisfying to say it out loud, say it to Susie's face, so that the other girl had to confront what she'd done. Maybe that's why Susie looked so scared and unsure, which didn't suit her either. Hope could have done without the audience and the collective gasp, but it was also satisfying to see their condemning looks. 'You have a real nerve showing up like this.'

'Look, why don't we go somewhere else and talk?' Susie suggested, and she actually dared to take hold of Hope's wrist so she could tug her away from the onlookers and the previous class that was now streaming out of the studio.

'No! No!' Hope wrenched her arm free of Susie's hold. 'What the hell have we got to talk about? You knew that Jack was my boyfriend. I mean, what part of "we live together and have been dating for thirteen years" was ambiguous? You knew, and you were meant to be my best friend, but you still went ahead and kissed him, didn't you?'

'I didn't mean for it to happen, Hopey,' said Susie earnestly, and Hope wished that Susie would be flippant and off-hand like she normally was because it would make it much, much easier to hate her. 'Of course I knew you and Jack were together and pre-engaged and all that shit, but I was really drunk and so was he, and you have to admit that you're not that happy with each other. Like, you bitch about him constantly.'

Hope shook her head incredulously. 'It's what friends do! They moan about their boyfriends! You'd know that if you had any other girlfriends – it doesn't mean anything. It certainly doesn't mean that things are so crap between us that you can make a play for him!'

Susie had been taking everything that Hope threw at her, but now her regular, much bolshier nature began to reassert itself. She drew herself up to her full height, which meant that she still had to look up at Hope when she drawled, 'Oh, believe me, I didn't come on to him while he tried to fight me off. It was completely mutual.'

'How . . . how can you stand there and say that to me?' Hope spluttered, absolutely unable to come up with anything better, because Susie's confession wasn't a surprise. It was what Hope had secretly suspected all along, despite Jack's protestations that he'd practically been an innocent bystander who'd slipped and fallen on to Susie's mouth.

'I didn't break you two up,' Susie insisted, her voice softer now that she'd made her point and rendered her opponent powerless and almost incapable of speech. 'You're still together, so stop being such a fucking drama queen about it, OK?'

At least that was something, Hope thought. They hadn't broken up, but their current state of malaise couldn't last for ever either.

Hope snapped out of her funk as a woman pushed past her to try and break the bottleneck that had formed at the door to the yoga studio. Everyone was talking in un-naturally loud voices, their embarrassment tangible, and even their unflappable yoga teacher was proclaiming noisily about turning off the air conditioning and opening the windows so they could work with the sound of birdsong and cars tooting in the background.

It was just Hope and Susie left, then Susie sighed and turned round so she could stomp into the studio . . . except Hope caught hold of the end of Susie's rolled-up yoga mat.

'No,' she said emphatically. 'You tried to take Jack away from me – you're not getting to have our yoga classes too.'

Susie tried to yank her mat out of Hope's clutches but Hope held on tighter. 'Dude, really? It's only fair that I get custody of yoga in the split if you're having Jack.'

'I always had Jack and you . . . you . . . you were just . . . I know you threw yourself at him! He told me!' Hope hissed, though Jack had never said any such thing.

'Oh did he? I bet he left out the part where I didn't have to throw myself very hard,' Susie growled, as she tried to shake Hope off. 'For fuck's sake, let go of my mat.'

'You are *not* ruining yoga for me like you tried to ruin my relationship,' Hope insisted, though really she didn't care that much about yoga, and after two years of attending rather sporadically she still couldn't do a side plank or a one-legged shoulder bridge, but it was a point of principle.

'What did I ruin? You're still together, aren't you? But I'll tell you something for nothing, Hopey: it's not going to be for much long . . .'

'Are you two coming in, or are you going to stay out here

110

and spread your toxic vibes into a room full of people who are trying to concentrate on their alignment and breathing?' It was Georgie, their fifty-something un-flappable yoga instructor, who was looking pretty flapped. 'Are you coming in or taking this somewhere more appropriate?'

'I'm coming in,' they both said in unison, and to Hope's eternal shame, both she and Susie tried to elbow each other out of the way as they fought to get into the studio first.

In the same circumstances, Hope would have put two of her six-year-old pupils in a time-out and she couldn't really blame Georgie for employing the same tactics. She frogmarched them both into the studio, made them place their mats in opposite corners and instructed them to do nothing more than sit cross-legged and focus on their breathing.

It was only after ten minutes that they were both allowed to move on to sun salutes. Hope soon realised that she couldn't even get as far as the plank pose, not when she wanted to leap up from her mat and bash Susie over the head with a bar bell, especially as the other girl was already doing a perfect upward dog.

As soon as they'd finished their cooling-down stretches, Susie was at Hope's side. 'Look, I've been an out-and-out bitch and what I did was beyond wrong,' she said quickly while Hope was still opening and shutting her mouth and unable to make anything come out of it but huffs and puffs of sheer indignation. 'Can't you find a way to forgive me so we can go back to being friends again? Please.'

'How? How are we meant to be friends?' Hope asked incredulously. 'Do you really think that we can go back to how we were before? Like, we'll just go down All Bar One and have a laugh and maybe compare notes on Jack's tech-nique? Do you really think we can do that?'

Susie shook her head impatiently so her glossy dark hair fanned out around her. 'It doesn't have to be like that. I

111

promise I won't see him ever again . . . I mean, I haven't . . . Not since . . .'

Whether she had or she hadn't suddenly didn't seem to matter that much, because Hope was sick of the whole subject. Fed up with feeling sad or angry or guilty, and more usually a gut-churning combination of all three. 'It wouldn't work,' she said. 'Everything's spoiled now. Look, you can have yoga.'

'I don't care about yoga,' Susie insisted, and if Hope didn't know Susie better, she'd have sworn she was on the verge of tears. 'I care about us. Please, Hope, you know I find it hard to make friends with other women.'

No wonder, if you try to steal their boyfriends, Hope thought to herself. 'You can have yoga,' she repeated, turning away as a new class entered the studio. 'You'd probably better go now, I'm staying for step aerobics.'

'You hate step aerobics,' Susie scoffed, but Hope ignored her as she hurried to the corner of the studio to claim a step and drag it to a part of the room where she was guaranteed to get regular cold blasts from the air-conditioning unit.

'Hopey . . . we can't let it end like this.'

Hope stood behind her step and began marching on the spot, staring fixedly at herself in the mirror so she could see Susie shoot her one last exasperated look and her own thighs wobbling. Maybe if her thighs didn't wobble and she lost the extra pounds, then Jack would never so much as look at another girl again – and maybe life wasn't that simple. Because as Susie shut the studio door behind her and the aerobics instructor started up some truly awful thumping dance music, Hope felt like a little piece of her heart was gone for ever. She loved her friends, but Jack had always had the lion's share of her love, demanded the greater part of her time and affection, and when friends had drifted away as some friends did, it hadn't mattered so much and anyway, they were still there on Facebook posting status updates about how hungover they were and showing off their holiday snaps.

But breaking up with Susie was the hardest thing Hope had ever done. The first time she'd ever had to tell someone that there was no room in her life or her heart for them any more. And it was Susie ... Not someone from school or university or work, but a friend she'd chosen solely for herself, someone who got her like hardly anyone else did, except Jack.

Hope scowled at her reflection and began to pump her arms as she jumped on her step, then jumped back down again. What if it wasn't that Jack and Susie understood her better than anyone else? What if Hope wasn't even in the equation and it was Jack and Susie that got each other? What if it hadn't been just a kiss? What if there really had been something going on between them? What if it was still going on?

These were horrible thoughts to have, especially when accompanied by a soundtrack that segued from 'Bad Romance' to 'Toxic'. Hope pumped her arms even harder and made sure she touched her elbow to her knee when they did repeaters, much to the delight of the instructor.

The pain wasn't even a little bit gone after an hour so Hope stayed for kickboxing and when she finally got home just after eight, after walking all the way, she still hurt and could barely feel her legs. The bits of her legs she could still feel ached beyond the telling of it.

Jack was waiting for her at the door with a cross expression on his face. 'Where have you been?' he asked querulously. 'I thought you were making dinner.'

Hope threw her gym bag at his feet by way of reply. 'I do have a life of my own outside school hours, you know. A life that doesn't revolve around having a two-course meal ready for you when you get home. Jesus!'

'But you said you were cooking dinner,' Jack reminded her carefully, not sure how to react to a Hope who was snapping and snarling and completely contravening the rules of their non-aggression pact. 'You actually mentioned the words "beef", "stir" and "fry".'

She had. Jack was right, which was infuriating and way off-message when there were more important things to discuss like, 'I saw Susie earlier,' which Hope flung over her shoulder at Jack as she stomped through to the bedroom so she could peel off her sweat-soaked gym clothes. 'Mutual throwing yourself at each other? *Mutual?*'

'What do you mean, you saw Susie earlier?' Jack asked in a quiet voice. 'I thought we agreed that we wouldn't do that.'

'It was far more important that *you* didn't see her so you wouldn't be tempted to jump her,' Hope said venomously, as she yanked off her yoga pants and hurled them into the corner. 'Apparently you didn't need a whole lot of persuading to stick your tongue down her throat.'

'It wasn't like that,' Jack protested, but he wasn't shouting and Hope would have preferred shouting and maybe even a bit of door-slamming or some crockery-breakage. Something impassioned to reassure her that Susie had been lying and Jack was furious at her lies and plotting to render them asunder.

'Then how was it?' Hope demanded. 'When did it start? How did it start? Who made the first move? Did you stop even for one second to think about me, or our guests who were only five feet away? Did you? DID YOU?'

'Will you give it a rest?' Hope had wanted Jack to shout, but now she had him roaring so loudly that Gary from upstairs banged on his floor. 'You have no right to ask me this stuff!'

'I have every right!'

'No, we got this all sorted out two weeks ago so why the hell are you bringing it up now?'

They were in each other's faces, noses almost touching, but not in a sweet Eskimo kiss. In fact, Hope felt like

114

snapping her teeth together and biting the end of Jack's nose off, Ozzy Osbourne-style. 'But Susie said . . .'

' "Susie said", "Susie said" . . .' Jack mocked back. 'Susie talks utter shite, and we both agreed that we weren't going to see her ever again.'

'It wasn't like I planned it. She was there at the gym, and now she's taken my yoga class away from me too,' Hope gabbled. She hated when Jack did this: took her attack and turned it into a counter-attack and tied her up in conversational knots at the same time. 'What am I meant to do? Stop going to the gym altogether?'

'Well, it would save us fifty quid a month when you only go to yoga about twice a month,' Jack sneered, taking a step back and running a dismissive eye down Hope's body, which was clad only in a sports bra and a pair of shiny black medium-control knickers from Primark. 'I don't know why you even bother.'

'Oh my God! You think I'm fat!' Hope wasn't sure which was worse: Jack and Susie's mutual throwing themselves at each other, or Jack thinking she was a lardarse. They were on a pretty level pegging.

'Whoa! I never said that,' Jack insisted, taking a couple of steps back to get out of range of the laser beams of death that Hope was shooting from her eye sockets. 'But you said that you wouldn't see her any more.'

As Hope remembered it, the main point of their verbal contract had been that *Jack* would never see, speak or have any other contact with Susie ever again, with an additional clause that Wilson would also join the very short list of people that Hope and Jack had solemnly vowed to cut from their lives. Just thinking of how she'd humiliated herself in front of Wilson and of all the other stand-out features of that awful night made Hope dig her heels in, both metaphorically and literally, as she ground her feet into the scratchy sisal flooring. 'At least we both know that if I bump into Susie it's not going to lead to both of us swapping spit within ten seconds,' she shrieked, knowing that her face was as red as her hair and she had a stress rash mottling her chest. At that moment, she couldn't blame Jack for falling for Susie's obvious charms when her own were so severely lacking. 'If I'm such a crap girlfriend then why don't you just break up with me?'

It was a good question that demanded an honest answer and Jack looked at Hope meditatively, as if he could see the cracked heart that beat erratically under her flabby bits and sturdy underwear. Hope was dreading the words that were about to come out of his mouth but at least, finally, it would be the truth.

Her fists clenched at her sides, Hope waited and waited. Jack continued standing there, and then he turned and walked out of the room.

'I do not need this shit,' was all he said before she heard the front door slam shut.

Chapter Twelve

Snapping and sniping at each other was a very stressful way to get through the next week, but it felt a lot more natural to Hope than when they both tried to be on their best behaviour.

For most of that Friday night, Hope had planned to greet Jack with a thin-lipped, bitter 'Nice of you to grace me with your presence,' like she hadn't cared where he'd been, but as it got later and later and then earlier and earlier so that dark became dawn and she was still wide awake and imagining that every noise she could hear on the street outside was Jack coming home, she'd had a change of heart.

Jack had to have been very angry to have stormed off for the whole night. The kind of anger that came from being falsely accused, and if anything was more likely to drive him into another woman's arms, or more specifically Susie's arms, it was going to be Hope herself if she kept on flying into jealous rages.

So when Jack finally reappeared just before lunch on Saturday, Hope already had his favourite coffee and walnut cake baking in the oven, four bottles of Budvar chilling in the fridge, and was full of plans to go to Waitrose to buy lemon sole so they could have posh home-made fish and chips for their tea.

'I'm sorry,' she said, before Jack had even walked through the front door. 'I'm so sorry that I was such a vile, jealous bitch yesterday. And I'm really glad you've come home so I can make it up to you.'

Jack put down his keys on the little shelf by the front door and folded his arms, which stopped Hope in her tracks because they couldn't really hug it out if Jack's arms were folded. 'I am not going to keep having this argument over and over again,' he said sharply. 'I did a stupid thing. I said I was sorry and you forgave me. You *have* to get over this.'

Hope hung her head. 'I just get so mad when I think of you and her together,' she started to explain, but from the grim look on Jack's face he was done with explanations, too. 'You remember how the school-guidance counsellor made me wear an elastic band round my wrist and I had to ping it every time I started to get angry? Maybe I should start wearing one again.'

Of course, when Hope had been fourteen, her hormones and prolonged daily exposure to her mother had meant that she had a very tenuous hold on her temper. She didn't have either of those excuses now, though she did still have a permanent mark on her right wrist from the two years that she'd pinged her elastic band at least twenty times a day. But Jack was nodding in agreement. 'Yeah, well, maybe you should.'

Hope decided that she would seriously think about it, but in the meantime she shot Jack her best, brightest, most beguiling smile. 'I'm baking you a coffee and walnut cake. How about I make some filter coffee and we can sit down and talk?'

'Oh God, do we have to?' Jack groaned, like having coffee, cake and a chat was some kind of ordeal that Hope was forcing on him. 'I've just had lunch, actually, and I've got some freelance work to do so I'm going to hole up in the lounge.'

Jack had holed up in the lounge for the rest of the day and rejected home-made posh fish and chips in favour of a cheese sandwich, which he made himself.

Every time Hope tried to go into the lounge, he sighed and made a big show of rustling his layouts so Hope had no choice but to skulk in the kitchen and the bedroom. Even when Jack finally came to bed at nearly two in the morning and she'd stayed awake so they could have make-up sex, he'd turned out the light before she could snuggle up and rolled on to his side with his back to her. There was something to be said for being a shouter, rather than a sulker. Hope shouted and then, usually, she felt better and could get on with the rest of her life, but when Jack was having a fit of the sullens, it could last weeks.

Still, Hope was sure that Jack's bad mood would melt away when she woke him up on Sunday morning with eggy bread and bacon and another heartfelt apology, but though he ate the eggy bread and the bacon, he cut short her apology with a terse, 'All right, all right. I get it. You're sorry. You don't have to keep saying it.'

'But you don't seem very pleased that I'm sorry,' Hope said.

'Look, Hope, we've been through this before,' Jack said wearily like he hadn't slept for weeks. 'You can't just yell and scream and have temper tantrums and then think that saying sorry cancels it out. You know I don't like confrontations. They make me tense and keyed up and that doesn't go away just because you're done with your snit and you want to be friends again.'

'But it's only 'cause I love you so much, that I get so mad at the thought of you with . . .'

'Oh God! I can't have this conversation with you again,' Jack snapped, scrambling out of bed so he could rifle through the piles of clothes that Hope hadn't got round to putting away. 'Anyway, I'm meeting Marvin in Shoreditch in an hour to have a look round the galleries.'

'I'm going to really, really try to let this whole business die a natural death.' Hope's best, brightest and most beguiling smile was beginning to wane. 'You're right, we should get some fresh air and going to Shoreditch sounds like fun. If you give me five minutes to have another cup of tea, I'll come with you.'

'Look, Hope, we don't have to be joined at the hip.'

'I know,' she said and the effort not to snarl the words almost sapped her of all her strength. As it was, she could actually feel her blood pressure rise as the prickly heat of a stress rash travelled along her chest and down her arms. She was definitely going to hunt for an elastic band in the kitchen junk drawer. 'It's just I've hardly seen you all weekend.'

'And you think that the minute I'm out of your sight, I'm getting up to no good,' Jack added bitterly.

'I don't think that!' Hope insisted, and she stood her ground until Jack raised his eyebrows at her. 'Well, I'm trying really hard not to think that.'

'Well, you have to try harder,' Jack advised, and then he went out and she was alone in the flat and she couldn't help it, she was torturing herself with elaborate, pornographic scenarios of Jack and Susie together and trying to think of a really good reason why she could call Marvin and subtly discover if Jack really was with him, so it was actually a relief when her mother made her weekly Sunday-afternoon call.

Mrs Delafield would have been quite happy to talk to Hope every evening and maybe even for five minutes every morning, but Hope had whittled her down to one Sunday-afternoon call. Yes, she felt guilty for keeping her mother at telephonic arm's length, but as it was, that Sunday call usually lasted up to three hours and always featured a lengthy critique of Hope's lesson and menu plans for the coming week.

That Sunday afternoon, Hope wasn't in the mood to listen to a lecture on how modern primary-school education would benefit greatly from a return to the three Rs, or why soup wasn't a main meal in itself but only a starter, or an *hors d'oeuvre*, as her mother insisted on calling it because she watched too many cookery programmes on the Food Network.

'Soup, salad and maybe a couple of slices of toast is a perfectly decent evening meal,' Hope insisted while they were clocking up their second hour on the phone. 'The world won't end if I forgo having meat, two veg and a starch at every meal.'

'There's absolutely no need to take that tone of voice with me,' her mother said evenly. 'No wonder you're so snippy if you haven't been eating properly. Skipping meals always makes you peevish.'

'I haven't been skipping meals,' Hope said sulkily, except she had, because for the last two nights she hadn't been able to face cooking and then choking down even a bowl of soup when her stomach was tied up in knots. That said, she could always manage a packet of chocolate fingers. 'And that's not why I'm peevish.'

'Oh, is Auntie Flo about to visit?' her mother asked delicately. 'I thought she wasn't due for at least another week.'

There was something very squicky about her mother having such an in-depth knowledge of her menstrual cycle, but Hope knew that she probably marked it out on the calendar in preparation for that happy day when Hope forgot to take her pill and found herself in the family way. She was so desperate for her first Hope-produced grandchild that she wasn't likely to even kick up a fuss if the baby was conceived out of wedlock, though she and Jack's mum, Marge, would march them down the aisle so fast that there'd be no conspicuous baby bump to ruin the wedding photos. During happier times, Jack and Hope had laughed themselves stupid at the very real possibility that their respective mothers had already planned their wedding and had their first-choice caterers, photographers and florists on speed dial, when they'd much prefer to go to Vegas and be married by an Elvis impersonator.

If that was the case, then they were both going to be sorely disappointed. 'No, it's not my special lady-time,' Hope gritted, then she couldn't help sighing, though the sigh was less to do with her mother being annoying and more to do with life in general.

'Well, what's the matter then? You know you can tell me anything. We're more like best friends than mother and daughter, aren't we?'

'Yes, of course we are,' she replied dutifully but with barely any sincerity, and her mother made a little hurt noise, which was usually a precursor to a diatribe about how desperately she'd wanted a daughter and had determinedly set about having a child every eighteen months until she had her longed-for baby girl, and now that baby girl was all grown up and wanted nothing to do with her.

'I always thought that when I had a daughter, we'd be so close. Girls together, confiding in each other, that sort of thing,' her mother predictably began, and as always Hope felt guilty because she wasn't the girly, confiding daughter cum best friend that her mother wanted her to be. And she also felt guilty about taking her bad mood out on her mother, because she wasn't allowed to take it out on Jack any more.

'I'm sorry, I'm being a bitch . . .'

'Language,' her mother chided.

'OK, I'm being a cow,' said Hope, her good intentions to be more confiding and daughterly already under strain. 'It's not PMS and it's not you, it's Jack. We had a row.'

'Oh, Hope,' her mother sighed. 'What have you done now?'

Obviously it would be something that *Hope* had done to cause the row. However much her mother had wanted a daughter, she wanted Jack as a son-in-law even more. Unlike her three older sons, who had spent most of their formative years belching and farting in each other's faces and indulging in ferocious displays of sibling rivalry, Jack had always been smiley and charming and never broke wind in her hearing. That pretty much made him a god in her mother's eyes, and while it would be so satisfying to tell her mother exactly why they'd had a row and pierce her Jack-worshipping bubble a little, Hope's promise to Jack still stood and with good reason. As soon as she let slip that Jack had kissed a girl who wasn't Hope, her mother would race next door, there'd be tears and recriminations, and then both Mrs Delafield and Mrs Benson would break the speed limit to leadfoot it down the motorway and be on Hope's doorstep for a rousing chorus of: 'The shock will kill your grandmothers.' And somehow Hope would get the blame for Jack straying because she didn't iron his shirts, even though generally Jack didn't wear shirts, or because she thought soup constituted an adequate evening meal, or because she wasn't making the best of herself and never blow-dried her hair straight even though it looked much better that way – so who could blame Jack for seeking comfort with another woman?

'I didn't do anything,' Hope said indignantly. 'He did something completely heinous and we've been kind of fighting about it, and then we made up but I was still secretly mad at him, and we had another really big fight and he walked out on Friday evening and stayed out all night and now he's not really speaking to me.'

'What do you mean by heinous?' Caroline Delafield wanted to know.

'You don't need to know that, but he knows, and he has to understand that it's not the kind of thing that I can simply get over in five minutes.'

'Have you been shouting at him?'

'Well, maybe a little bit, but I just get so angry and hurt when I think about the heinous thing, and I do say I'm sorry and I try to make up for the shouting by being really nice,' Hope explained.

Her mother clicked her teeth reprovingly. 'Look, dear,

men have a tendency to be a bit thoughtless and selfish and there's no point in fretting about it. It's just the way they are.'

'Yes, but . . .'

'Even if Jack did do something to tick you off, we both know that when you get riled, your mouth runs away with you. It's the red hair.' She paused to let that revelation sink in, although Hope had sent her many links to articles that stated categorically that there was no correlation between having red hair and a bit of a temper. 'And Lord knows you're stubborn. You never let anything go. You're like a dog with a bone.'

'Wow, that's a really attractive picture you're painting, Mum.' Hope had been sprawled disconsolately on the bed but she managed to rouse herself so she could look at her hair in the mirror on the inner door of her wardrobe. 'Look, Jack did a bad, bad thing and I know he's sorry but I can't seem to move past it.'

'Well, you do need to move past it, and Jack's probably just giving you a wide berth because everyone knows you need a cooling-off period of at least two days when you're angry,' said her mother as if she hadn't heard a single word Hope had said. Or she had, but had chosen to ignore them. 'This will all blow over when you've properly apologised for being such a crosspatch. Why don't you make him something nice for his tea?'

Hope wished that she'd never gone down this well-trodden path with her mother. If she hadn't been a crosspatch before, now she was the crossest patch in Christendom. 'I've said I'm sorry about a hundred times. Quite frankly, *he* should be making *me* something nice for my tea, but he's been so . . .'

'Yes, he's been what?' her mother prompted eagerly and with an icy-cold shudder, Hope realised how close she'd come to blurting out the terrible truth.

'Oh, it doesn't matter . . .'

'Well, if it doesn't matter, then there's no harm in saying you're sorry again, like you really mean it this time. You should never let the sun set on a quarrel and you can't let this silly situation drag on any longer just because you're being obstinate.'

It was like trying to have a conversation with a breeze-block, and Hope made the mistake of telling her mother just that. Which led to another argument and conclusive proof that Hope's red hair was responsible for her sharp tongue and uncontrollable temper. The only way to appease Mrs Delafield and get her off the phone before they ran into a third hour was for Hope to agree that her baby brother, fifteen-year-old Jeremy, could come to stay for half-term. The Delafields and the Bensons wanted to squeeze in a week at the timeshare they co-owned in Corfu but didn't want to drag Jeremy along 'because honestly, we need a week away from him. He's going through that difficult phase that you went through too.' Of course, there was no question of leaving Jeremy home alone to burn the house down or have a party that would be posted on Facebook, with his parents returning home to find the house razed to the ground by marauding teenagers high on Meow-Meow.

By the time Hope rang off, she was emotionally exhausted and hopping mad again. So mad that she had to go for a brisk walk to work off some of the aggression, which took her as far as the Holloway Road to buy a family-sized bag of salt and vinegar crisps and a huge bar of chocolate, and when Jack finally deigned to come home with a Chinese takeaway as a pitifully inadequate peace offering, Hope felt too bilious to eat it.

Jack took Hope's refusal to partake of sweet and sour chicken very badly and they segued seamlessly into the next part of their never-ending row, or maybe it was a new row – Hope couldn't tell any more.

All Hope knew nearly two weeks later was that they still seemed to be locked into a cycle of endless bickering, even though she was trying to be on her very best, most non-confrontational behaviour, which was draining, *and* she had a ring of bruises around her wrist from repeated elastic band-pinging. Jack didn't even appreciate the effort she was making. Not that he was around much to witness her restraint – he'd been working late every night.

Probably this weekend they needed to have some fun and go on a proper date, Hope decided to herself on Friday morning. Commit to a date night every week and book a weekend away somewhere. Then when they were on neutral ground, they could talk about becoming properly engaged. It would make both of them feel more secure.

And then there wasn't time to wonder how she'd broach this controversial topic with Jack because it was five to nine and the school bell was ringing and Blue Class were going on their very first field trip. Hope needed to be clear-headed enough to remember the travel vouchers and make sure that everyone went to the loo before they headed off to the tube, even if they insisted that they didn't need to go. In fact, *especially* if they insisted that they didn't need to go.

Chapter Thirteen

When she'd been planning the class syllabus in the summer holidays, Hope had decided that she needed a theme for the academic year. Preferably a theme that encompassed geography, science, art, history and all the other subjects that weren't maths and English (those were closely supervised by Dorothy so she could be absolutely sure that every pupil in the infant school was exactly where they should be, in line with the Council's guidelines and the national league tables).

Hope had spent most of the summer break failing to come up with a suitable theme. She'd even gone to the British Library for inspiration, and while walking home, she'd taken a wrong turn and stumbled across the Camley Street Natural Park, an honest-to-goodness nature reserve in the industrial wasteland behind King's Cross and St Pancras stations.

It was a tranquil leafy oasis of woodland, meadows and ponds stuffed full of plants, flowers and fungi, geese, ducks and butterflies. Blue Class could learn about the lifecycle that transformed frogspawn into tadpoles into vile, slimy, jumping frogs. They could take photos with the class camera of wild flowers and recreate them out of coloured paper, paint and glue when they were back at school and there were even two resident rabbits, Coco and Merlin, for them to coo over. Best of all, it was only one stop from Highbury and Islington on the Victoria Line.

As she shepherded them through the gates of the park in a slow-moving crocodile with the help of Andy, her classroom assistant, the dreaded Gurinder, on loan for the morning, and three parent volunteers, the excited jabbering of her class was validation enough. Hope knew that some of them had whopping great gardens and weekly deliveries of an Abel & Cole box full of seasonal vegetables, but a good half of them lived in grim blocks of flats and their only brush with nature came from a few withered trees breaking up the relentless grey concrete.

They stopped at the visitors' centre to meet their guide, a cheerful girl with dreadlocks, who took them down the meandering path that circled the ponds and pointed out rare species of fungi, kingfishers and a bat box. Each new discovery was greeted with rapturous oohs and aahs and lots of hands shooting up to ask questions.

Once the guided tour was over, Hope split them into supervised groups of six, gave each group a worksheet to complete and shooed them away so she could sit on a bench and quickly scribble down notes for their next visit. That was the plan, but it was such a gorgeous day for early October, neither summer nor autumn, but somewhere in between, with the sun high in the sky and only the faintest of breezes stirring the reeds and rushes, that Hope put down her pad so she could tilt her face towards the sun and bask a little in its warm glow. She usually applied sunblock like a fiend but on the other hand, she didn't want to end up with a vitamin D deficiency.

Hope could hear birds warbling and her class shrieking and yelling and generally sounding like they were so overstimulated that it was going to be hell to get them through the next chapter of their Key Stage Two Numeracy workbooks that afternoon. Hope sighed. She'd deal with that then. Maybe dangle the promise of a rare gold star for the whole class if they worked in total silence and . . .

'Hey, stranger,' said a deep voice, and someone sat down next to her on the bench. 'Haven't seen you for a while.'

It wasn't some random bloke trying to hit on her, as Hope had first suspected. It was someone far worse. Hope opened her eyes so she could shoot Wilson a wary, anxious look.

'Oh, hi,' she muttered, hand raised to smooth back her hair in a nervous gesture, until she realised that it was neatly braided and pinned up. Hope could feel her face heating up in embarrassment even as she twisted her lips in a vague approximation of a smile. For the life of her she couldn't think what to say next – or at least something that wouldn't hark back to the unhappy circumstances of their last meeting.

Wilson sat back and crossed his legs as if he planned to stay there and not say anything for quite a while. Hope looked around wildly for salvation in the form of a stray six-year-old who looked as if they might be about to fall into a pond, but they were all diligently examining leaves and fighting over who got to hold the worksheet, damn them.

'So, how's the hand?'

Hope seized on this conversational gambit gratefully and held up the appendage in question. 'It's much better, thanks,' she said, turning up her palm so Wilson could see the shiny pink scar that itched slightly when she thought about it. 'And you, you're all right?'

Wilson dipped his head. 'Yup.'

She could feel him looking at her as she stared fixedly ahead, not just because she was reliving her abject mortification all over again, but also because the whole tiny-child-falling-into-pond scenario was a distinct possibility.

'You look different,' Wilson continued, echoing Hope's thoughts and confirming her suspicions that his mind was playing back to their last fraught, high-volume, tear-soaked and, oh God, snot-dripping encounter. 'All buttoned up. Are you wearing your teacher's hat? Are those children yours?'

'Only between eight fifty-five and three thirty,' Hope told him, allowing herself to relax slightly because she did have thirty chaperones. Thirty-five, if she included assistants and volunteers, Hope amended, as she caught Gurinder's disapproving eye. 'We're doing this year-long project on "The World Around Us" and they have a really good education programme set up here. It dovetails really nicely with Key Stage Two in the National Curriculum.'

'Right, yeah, sure it does.' Wilson was staring again. She prayed that it wasn't because he was remembering the last time he'd seen her, when she was blotchy and red-faced like a laboratory bunny in the custody of a major pharmaceuticals company. It was probably because he'd always seen her in mufti before and now Hope was wearing one of her school uniforms: black Gap curvy-fit trousers, a filmy black and white polka-dot blouse and a red cardigan that Jack's nan had knitted for her and which her mother insisted clashed with her hair. A pair of black Converses completed her ensemble, which was meant to be smart without being too smart. Practical but not boring, unlike Wilson who was wearing his usual uniform of dark wash Levis, white T-shirt and black v-neck, accessorised with an old-fashioned camera hanging from a strap round his neck.

'This one of your usual haunts, then?' Hope asked, horrified to discover that the words that came out of her mouth sounded biting and sarcastic. 'I mean, this is quite a hidden little spot, isn't it?'

'Yeah. I'm shooting just down the road and thought I'd take a walk while they finish building the set,' Wilson offered. 'Hard to believe we're in the middle of London.'

'Right.' Hope scanned the pond again for any sinking six-year-olds. 'So . . .'

'So . . .'

'Like . . .' Hope took a deep breath. 'About that night, well . . .'

'Well, emotions were running high.'

Hope seized on that in the same way that she hoped one of her pupils would grab hold of a lifebelt if they did fall in the pond. 'Right! And there was alcohol, lots of it, and it was all very upsetting and intense, and I'd been completely stressed out before the party even started.' She stopped again because she was gabbling like an utter fool and there was the faintest hint of a smile playing around Wilson's mouth. 'What I'm trying to say is that I said stuff and you said stuff, like, we both said stuff we shouldn't have said, and the situation that we found ourselves in didn't bring out the best in either of us, and I'm not really sure how to deal with you sitting next to me when I thought I'd never see you again.' One day explorers would discover a land where everyone spoke in run-on sentences and Hope would move there and the inhabitants of that land would make her their queen, Hope thought to herself as she tried to catch her breath.

'Oh, so that's why you unfriended me on Facebook,' Wilson finished for her. 'Don't mention it. I completely understand.'

'Well, Jack and I agreed that we wouldn't have any contact with you and Susie again,' Hope explained.

Wilson's eyebrows shot up. 'So, you and Jack are still together, then?'

There was no reason for him to sound quite so amazed. 'Of course we are! We've been together all this time and that thing with Susie . . . you were right, it was just a kiss. And yes, I acted like a gigantic tool and made a ginormous deal about it, when really it was a very tiny deal.' Her voice was shrill and desperate as if she wasn't just trying to convince Wilson but herself as well. 'Obviously Jack and I have some stuff that we need to work through.'

'Obviously.' Wilson cleared his throat. 'Funny. You didn't really strike me as that . . . well, never mind.'

'That *what*?'

Wilson gave her a cool look. 'That stupid or that gullible.'

'Look, I told you, Jack and I have been together for over thirteen years and you don't just throw away that kind of commitment because of a . . . a . . . kiss,' Hope exclaimed, trying to run her fingers through her tightly constricted hair again. 'OK, a kiss and some light flirting.' Wilson opened his mouth to say something, but Hope rushed on because she didn't want yet another debate about that night. She was sick of talking about it. 'Anyway, are you and Susie still together?'

Wilson shrugged. 'Off and on. More off than on.'

'So, if I hadn't unfriended you on Facebook, I'd have seen that your relationship status was set to "It's complicated"?' Hope asked in an attempt at some levity.

'I think we're at that stage in breaking up when we're just having one long row interspersed with bouts of make-up sex, y'know?'

Hope didn't know, as she'd never broken up with anyone before. It sounded exhausting and also needlessly dramatic. Either you were broken up or you weren't. Whenever Lauren and Allison were going through the death throes of a relationship, she always longed to tell them that it would be a lot quicker and a lot less painful to stop weeping and wailing and endlessly analysing every single look, line and misdemeanour and just cut the boy who'd done them wrong out of their lives. End of. Obviously she'd never actually acted on that impulse but instead had been there with tissues and ice-cream and an endless litany of 'It's his loss and anyway, you were far, far too good for him.'

'Well, I'm sorry to hear that,' she said to Wilson, who didn't look like he needed tissues, ice-cream or her platitudes.

'If I tell you something, will you listen and process it,

132

and not go flying off the deep end like you usually do, right?'

Nothing was more guaranteed to get Hope all riled up than someone telling her *not* to get riled up. She surreptitiously pinged her elastic band and took a deep breath. 'I'll try,' she agreed unenthusiastically.

'Good enough, I suppose,' Wilson said with a shrug. 'OK, right.' He was twisting his hands together nervously, those long fingers rubbing against each other. 'Susie's all cut up about you and about me and blah blah, but mostly she wants to talk about Jack and how they're "in the grip of something more powerful than doing the right thing".' Wilson's top lip curled. 'That's a direct quote, by the way. There's another woman who loves to over-dramatise.'

'It's simply not true,' Hope said furiously, because kissing was one thing, one very horrible, deceitful thing, but the suggestion that they might be in the thrall of an over-whelming passion, and actually having sex, was more than she could bear to deal with. It was far easier to just deny everything. 'Jack would never do that to me. He said it was just one kiss. He's promised that it will never happen again and he loves me – and Susie, well, she can just fuck off!'

'Eloquently put, as usual.'

'Why do you always have to be such a knob . . . ?' Hope shut her mouth with an audible snap as a small hand tugged on her cardigan sleeve.

'Miss! Miss!' said Sorcha urgently as Hope turned to look at the tiniest member of Blue Class in horror. How much had she heard? 'Miss!'

'What's the matter, Sorcha?' Hope asked, trying to modulate her voice from screechy to calm and in control.

'It's Stuart,' Sorcha said indignantly, hands on hips. 'He's all up in my business, Miss.'

The storm had passed and, miracle of miracles, Wilson was actually smiling indulgently because Sorcha was flaxen-haired and blue-eyed and looked like she'd been booked from Central Casting in response to a plea for a whey-faced moppet. Hope was made of stronger stuff. 'I don't know what that means,' she lied, though Wilson had been all up in her business not two minutes ago. 'You need to use your words.'

Sorcha's eyes crossed as she tried to come up with another explanation. 'He was shouting right in my face,' she revealed. As far as Blue Class were concerned, hurting puppies and kittens, being up yourself and shouting right in someone's face were crimes of pure evil. 'He grabbed the worksheet even though Andy said it was my turn to hold it, and he wouldn't give it back, and then he said he was going to push me in the pond. He was totally disrespecting me, Miss.'

'Right, let's go and sort this out,' Hope said briskly, as she got to her feet. Sorcha grabbed hold of her cardigan sleeve again so she could tug Hope in the direction of horrible Stuart. Hope turned her head to fling a goodbye at Wilson but he was standing up too.

She could feel his eyes on her back as she let herself be dragged over to the little group of children who were watching Andy tell Stuart off.

'Everything all right here?' Hope asked because she didn't want to step on Andy's toes, even if she did feel that sometimes his approach to discipline was a bit too touchy-feely to be truly effective.

'I think some of us are finding the concept of working together a bit challenging,' was the woolly answer Hope got. Andy was an idealistic Philosophy graduate who'd just returned from three years' volunteer work in Cambodia. Now he was trying to make a difference in Islington. There were times when Hope wished he'd go and make a difference somewhere else but at least he wasn't Gurinder, who was bearing down on them with a grim look on her face.

Hope chose Timothy, quiet studious Timothy who'd

already written the Latin names for five different plants on the disputed worksheet, to get an impartial take on what had happened. What had happened was a lot of shoving and shouting and 'then Stuart threw the worksheet on the ground in a fit of pick . . .'

'Pique,' Hope corrected gently.

'And it's all muddy. It was very hard to make my hand-writing especially neat without a desk to rest on and now it's ruined,' Timothy finished on an anguished wail. 'Will I still get a sticker for correctly identifying a marsh warbler when Andy thought it was a reed warbler?'

'I think this is a good time to remind everyone' – Hope glared pointedly at Stuart who stared back at her defiantly – 'that as well as giving out stickers, I can also take them away.'

From the shock that greeted her words, it was apparent that Blue Class hadn't been aware of this. 'And I also want to remind you that we're supposed to be coming back to Camley Street throughout the year so we can learn how the different seasons affect the world around us.' Hope paused, because all of Blue Class was now assembled in a semi-circle around her and she could do a quick sweep of their anxious faces. 'I'm not sure they'll let us come back if you can't behave like big boys and girls instead of a pack of savages.'

There was nothing more to be said. Hope wasn't going to haul Stuart up in front of everyone, but they would definitely be having words once they were back at school. She contented herself with pulling a pack of tissues from her handbag and thrusting one at him. 'You need to blow your nose, Stuart,' she told him crisply. 'Now, has anyone got any questions?'

Hope was anticipating questions about nature that hope-fully she'd be able to answer because she'd swotted up the night before, or that someone would want clarification on her sticker position, but instead there was a giggle from the back and Javan's hand shot up.

Inwardly Hope groaned because although she spent a lot of time telling Javan to stop mucking about, his gap-toothed grin and twinkling eyes always made her melt a little. Give it another ten years and he'd be leaving a string of broken hearts all along Upper Street and the Essex Road.

'Miss! Miss! Is that your boyfriend, Miss?' Javan demanded, nudging Sirhan and Luca, his co-conspirators, who were giggling wildly.

Completely blind-sided, Hope suddenly realised that Wilson was still there, standing behind her, and a source of much interest to Blue Class. 'No . . . no, he's not,' she gasped, and this was no way to maintain authority.

Javan's eyes widened dramatically. 'Is he a stranger, Miss? 'Cause it's wrong to talk to strangers.'

Hope nodded. 'Yes it is, very wrong.' There was nothing else for it but to usher Wilson forward. It was like trying to move concrete, but served him right for sticking around when he wasn't wanted. 'This is my friend, Wilson. What do we say when we meet a new person?'

'Good morning, Wilson,' Blue Class parroted back.

Wilson grunted something and stared down at his black brogues.

'Miss! Miss! What's that around his neck?' Luca asked, and to Hope's surprise, Wilson stepped forward.

'It's a camera,' he said, his voice strained. 'I take pictures for my job.'

'But you can take pictures on your phone,' someone pointed out, and Wilson agreed that you could and just as Hope expected him to launch into some long-winded monologue about double exposures and auto-focus, he squatted down so he was on the children's level, rather than looming over them, and gave them a brief and concise description of what his camera did, although he did wince when lots of grubby fingers thrust forward when he removed the lens cap.

Then he herded them together for several class photos,

with Hope smiling stiffly at the centre, and even took some action shots of Javan, Sirhan and Luca pretending to fall into the lake.

'Can we take some photos with Coco and Merlin?' Sorcha begged, but they had half an hour left to get back to school before lunch, so Hope shook her head and began to corral her charges.

'Everyone find a partner and line up in twos,' she ordered. 'Do you want to miss lunch?'

'Can't we go Burger King, Miss?' Javan asked, and winked at Hope when she clonked him on the head with the worksheets.

Then, clutching hold of Sorcha and Timothy (getting to hold Hope's hand was serious social real estate), Hope brought up the rear of the straggly crocodile that marched through the park.

Wilson fell into step beside them and for once the smile that Hope shot him was entirely genuine. 'Don't suppose you fancy a job as a classroom assistant, do you?' she asked.

Wilson grinned back, looking ten years younger and about a million times more approachable. 'I have lots of nieces and nephews,' he explained. 'In fact, my oldest nephew, Alfie, is currently my assistant's assistant. It's why I ducked out of the studio before I could kill him.'

Sorcha and Timothy were having a heated debate about why they always had fish and chips for lunch on Friday, so Hope felt as if she could talk freely. 'My fifteen-year-old brother's coming up for half-term,' she said with a shudder. 'It's going to be tough. He only talks in fluent grunt.'

'Ah, Alfie's moved on from grunting to fluent sneering.' Wilson shook his head. 'Left school with one GCSE but thinks he knows everything.'

'Jeremy doesn't know anything. Seriously, he thought the Crimea War happened between the Great War and the Second World War and he got really narked when I told him it didn't.' Hope pulled a face. 'Maybe I should take him to the Imperial War Museum while he's in London.'

It was time to cross a road, which usually took at least ten minutes. Luckily, Gurinder, clad in a fluoro-yellow safety vest, was taking no nonsense from any heavy-goods vehicles that thought they had right of way.

Wilson touched Hope lightly on the arm. 'I'll stick the photos in the post once I get them developed,' he said, then checked to make sure that Sorcha and Timothy were engrossed in their Green Cross Code. 'About the other stuff . . . well, you need to have a serious talk with your boy.'

All she'd been doing was having serious talks with her boy, and they never ended well. 'It's all good, I trust Jack,' Hope protested. 'If you believe everything Susie says, then you're an idiot, and don't call Jack a boy, it's so patronising.' She wished that she'd never bumped into Wilson because he was dragging up everything that she'd been trying not to think about.

'Hey, don't shoot the messenger.'

'You were the one who said that I always jump to conclusions and overreact,' Hope reminded him. 'And now when everything is almost back to normal, you're stirring things up.'

'I'm not stirring, I'm giving you a bit of friendly advice because this Pollyanna routine doesn't suit you,' Wilson said, and it was so typical of him to end on a sarcastic note. 'But, fine, if you want to bury your head in the sand, go ahead.'

'Look, I'm sorry if you and *her* are having problems but that's between the two of you. It has nothing to do with Jack and me. I trust Jack and if he says that it's . . .'

'This whole conversation is getting old. If you don't want to listen when someone is trying to help, then more fool you.' Every word was another constricting band around Hope's chest. 'Look, I'll see you around.'

'Yeah, well, I've really got to go.' Hope summoned up a smile that was so weak it needed its own life-support system. 'Thanks for being so great with the kids.'

Then Gurinder was barking that it was time to cross the road without any dawdling and with a firm grip on Sorcha and Timothy, Hope was able to scurry across without a backward glance.

Chapter Fourteen

Hope spent most of her lunch-hour rehearsing what she'd say to Jack when she got home that evening. Or when he got home, after yet another stint of working late or whatever the hell it was that he was doing. Despite all her good intentions to employ a stealthy, softly-softly approach, Hope was sure she'd start screaming, 'Are you still seeing that skank?' within thirty seconds of Jack walking through the door.

And Hope wasn't sure she wanted to know if Jack was still seeing that skank. People always said that the truth hurt, but this particular truth would destroy her. It would mean that not only was Jack having sex with someone who wasn't her, but he was doing it behind her back, and that meant that he wasn't just cheating, he was lying and betraying everything that he and Hope had. She couldn't even fathom why Jack could behave like that, and the reason she kept coming back to, again and again, was that it had to have started *after* the kiss and she'd driven Jack to it with all her ranting and raving. Maybe Jack had figured that if he was getting so much aggro for something he hadn't done, then he might just as well go ahead and do it.

Of course, there was another option. That Jack was steadfast and true and when he said that there was nothing going on, it was because there wasn't. Just because Susie claimed to be in love with Jack, didn't mean that Jack was in love with her. Instead of wasting all this time and effort on suspicions that were entirely unfounded, Hope should be focusing on the unassailable fact that Jack loved her and her love for him was without limit. Maybe she should lead with that before any other kind of discussion on their current relationship issues.

Hope was still pondering how best to approach the subject when she was cornered by Dorothy at the end of the day and asked if she'd take charge of the infant school's contribution to the Winter Pageant. Though it was less of a question and more of a direct order.

'Can't Elaine do it?' Hope blurted out. 'Or Marta?'

'Elaine's done it for the last five years and strictly *entre nous*, I think her ideas are getting a little stale. Time for some fresh blood,' Dorothy insisted stoutly, her iron-grey bob swinging in agitation. 'Marta can just about handle a very basic lesson plan right now. Extra-curricular duties will send her over the edge.'

'But it's only two months away and I'm knee-deep in Harvest Festival stuff as it is,' Hope countered, with a giddy thrill as she realised that she was actually standing up to Dorothy for once and hey, the world hadn't ended and Dorothy wasn't threatening her with disciplinary action.

'You've got lots of time,' Dorothy said airily. 'I'm sure lots of parents will help out and I've signed you up for a two-day drama workshop during half-term. The Governors have very kindly approved the course fees.'

'But . . .'

'No need to worry about Christmas and Kwanzaa; the junior school will cover that. You will need to at least acknowledge Chanukah.' Dorothy smiled vaguely. 'Get them to sing a song about it or something.'

'Chanukah?' Hope repeated. 'But I don't know anything about Chanukah. I don't even know anybody Jewish!'

Dorothy shrugged. 'Can't you look it up online?' She fixed Hope with a stern look. 'Fortune favours the brave and the Governors favour staff who go the extra mile. Remember, there's no "I" in team!'

This new development meant there was no point going home with all guns blazing. Not when she'd have to wheedle and nag Jack to take time off work to supervise Jeremy who couldn't be left on his own in London for two days. Once Mrs Delafield had let him and his best friend go to Manchester for the day and they'd ended up in Hull. Besides, if she had it out with Jack and it didn't go well, they could hardly have Jeremy to stay while they were acting out scenes from *Who's Afraid of Virginia Woolf*?

As it was, Jack was home at a very respectable seven thirty to find Hope freshly showered after her step aerobics class and waiting for him with a nervous smile. 'Hey,' she said.

'Hey,' he said back, his own smile just as tentative. 'What's up?'

This was *not* going to be Hope's cue to start an interrogation, the likes of which hadn't been seen since the days of the Nuremberg Trials. Instead she got up from the computer where she'd been reading up on Chanukah so she could swing her arms nervously. 'Do you fancy catching the bus up to Muswell Hill and getting fish and chips at Toff's?'

Jack's relief was palpable. Hope could have sworn he lost an inch in height as all the tension left his body. 'Cool,' he said, twirling his keys around. 'You ready to go now?'

After haddock and chips at arguably the best chippy in London, they walked off the stodge by staggering down the steep hill towards Crouch End, which had much nicer, more gentrified pubs than Holloway. They found a quiet corner in the Queen's, a cavernous Victorian pub full of nooks and crannies, and decided to kick it old skool by drinking bottles of cider – but posh artisan cider, rather than the Woodpecker of their youth. Hope was determined to keep the conversation light, and even now, when she wasn't sure that Jack was being entirely truthful with her, she could still make him laugh as she told him about the morning at

Camley Street Natural Park and how Blue Class would sell their mothers for a sticker.

She didn't tell Jack about Wilson's guest appearance, or how she felt sick every time she thought about the conversation they'd had, which was another facet of this new splintered phase in their relationship. They used to tell each other everything – she knew far more about the annoying quirks of InDesign that any non-design person should know – but talking about Wilson would inevitably lead to talking about Susie, which would even more inevitably lead to a row.

As Hope went to the bar to get the next round, she saw Jack whip out his phone and start tapping away furiously, but when she got back to their table, he tucked it away and looked up at her with the sweet, disarming smile that was her favourite out of all his smiles. It made Hope feel as if she was Jack's reason for living and as she sat down, he took her hand in his and traced his finger along her heartline.

'Things have been really weird with us these last couple of weeks, Hopita Bonita,' he said softly. 'Where did you go? I missed you.'

'I don't know.' Hope took a sip of her cider. 'Where did *you* go?'

'I was right here all the time,' Jack said, lowering his head to kiss the spot that his fingers had just stroked.

'It didn't feel like it,' Hope admitted, trapping Jack's hand between hers. 'I wish . . . we are going to be all right, aren't we? I mean, I've been trying so hard to get us back on track but I think I'm making a complete hash of it. I don't know what to do to make us better.'

'You don't have to do anything.' Jack smiled wryly. 'Well, you could not try so hard. You're either snarling or going all Stepford Wife on me. It'd be easier if you could find a point in the middle and stay there.'

'I hate that there's this atmosphere between us all the time, and I know I open my mouth and make it worse by

143

being mean and generally behaving like a grade-A bitch,' Hope said. 'And believe me, I don't like hearing myself act like that any more than you do, but Jack, please be straight with me, do I have a reason to act like that?'

'No, no!' Jack assured her, squeezing her hand so tight that Hope had to resist the urge to wince. 'I love you. That hasn't changed and it never will, I swear.'

'Do you really love me?' Hope begged, even though she loathed getting stuck in the role of the needy girlfriend. She liked to think that she had more stones than that.

'I love you more than my Pantone book. And I love you more than Helvetica. And I even love you more than my signed copy of The Beatles' *Rubber Soul* on vinyl, though that's a pretty close call.'

'I still reckon it's not their actual signatures,' Hope said, a glint in her eyes that hadn't been there for a while. 'I mean, if it was, it would have been up for auction at Sotheby's, not in a Sue Ryder shop in Leeds.'

'Shut it!' Jack snapped, but he leaned in to kiss her forehead. 'Honestly, Hopey, I love you and everything will be all right, I promise. OK?'

Hope could tell when Jack was lying. It wasn't anything he did, like scratching his nose or avoiding her gaze. It was more of a gut feeling, in the same way that she could spot a six-year-old who needed to go to the loo or she could tell that her mother was going to ring at the exact moment she'd sat down with a mug of tea and *heat* magazine. That was why she knew that Jack was telling the absolute truth and she could nod and smile and say, 'OK.' And just 'OK' wouldn't do. 'I love you too, you know,' Hope said and she meant it more than she ever had before. This time she tried to say it with feeling because she did love Jack. Loved his smile and his sulky face. Loved the smell of him, the feel of him. Loved that he was her best friend as well as her lover. Loved that he doggedly persisted in calling her 'Hopita Bonita' even though it was the lamest nickname ever. Loved that he tidied up after her, without too much complaining. Loved the way he balled his fists like a baby when he slept. Still loved him despite the fact that there were dark days when she wasn't sure if she trusted him any more.

Neither of them said anything. Jack looked at Hope and Hope looked right back at him. And there was an unspoken question on his face, which she tried to answer in the sweep of her lashes and the curve of her smile and the dogged, determined devotion she was sure was oozing from her every pore.

Then Jack raised his bottle of cider and the spell was broken. 'So, just between us, there had to be a moment this morning when you looked around to make sure there weren't any witnesses and thought about pushing snotty Stuart into the pond and holding his head under the water with your foot. Right?'

'Of course not,' Hope gasped, ratcheting up the fake indignation because she wanted them to get back to that place where they teased each other mercilessly. 'Though if someone else from Blue Class had thrown him in I'd have turned a blind eye.'

'You black-hearted wench,' Jack sniffed. 'I've a good mind to report you to the Board of Governors.'

'Yeah, right after I tell the head of human resources that you leaked that story about the Keira Knightley cover shoot to Holy Moly,' Hope rapped back, and Jack, who had still been holding her hand, now dropped it so he could dig her in the ribs to make her squeal, and Hope let herself believe that they were going to be all right.

And maybe they were. It wasn't like those first frantic days of non-stop sexual acrobatics after Hope had caught Jack and Susie together. And it wasn't like the last fortnight of open hostility.

It was more like they used to be. They bitched and moaned at each other, but it was bitching and moaning because Hope had used the last of the milk then put the empty carton back in the fridge, or Jack had decided to re-shelve their books according to genre *before* he alphabetised them and Hope couldn't find her copy of *French Women Don't Get Fat*.

Hope only cooked tea when she could be bothered and Jack didn't come home at seven thirty every night, but at least he called to say that he was going to be late. And they had sex and sometimes they talked about having sex but ended up watching *True Blood* instead.

It was how they used to be. Kind of predictable and a little bit boring, but after the last month, Hope was a little bit in love with kind of predictable and a little bit boring.

Jack had agreed to take two days off work during half-term to babysit Jeremy and take him to the IMAX cinema and a *Doctor Who* exhibition. Hope had got through the Harvest Festival with only five tins of marrowfat peas to be donated to the poor and needy of the borough (last year it had been *nine*) and a minor spat with one of the Trustafarian mothers who couldn't understand why the poor and needy didn't want the five elderly courgettes that had been left over from her weekly Ocado delivery, even if they were organic.

Perhaps it had been going too well, and when a large manila envelope, with her name written on it in a vaguely familiar hand, turned up by recorded delivery it was actually a timely reminder that there were still hairline cracks in Hope and Jack's version of normal.

Hope gingerly opened the envelope as if she suspected there might be anthrax inside, and not several contact sheets and six large glossy photographs. Hope fanned out the black-and-white images; there were group shots of her class beaming gummily; two adorable pictures of Sorcha and Timothy crouching down to study some plants; a shot of Javan pretending to jump into the pond with Sirhan and Luça grabbing on to his arms; and a photo of her sitting on the bench.

As far as Hope could remember she'd been studiously scribbling in her notebook, but Wilson had snapped her staring pensively into the middle distance, eyes cloudy, mouth set in a tight thin line. She looked sulky as anything and at least ten years older.

There was also a handwritten sheet of paper with Wilson's scrawl on it. He'd once admitted, under duress and much baiting from Susie, that he had to write in block capitals to ensure that people could decipher a single word.

HOPE,
HEREWITH PHOTOS FROM CAMLEY STREET NATURAL
PARK. I PRINTED UP THE ONES I PREFERRED, BUT HAVE
INCLUDED THE CONTACT SHEETS SO YOU CAN PICK
OUT YOUR FAVOURITES TOO. LET ME KNOW WHICH
PRINTS YOU'D LIKE.
HOPE ALL ELSE IS GOOD WITH YOU.
REGARDS,
WILSON

Considering that their every encounter went from show-down to stand-off within five minutes, it was actually a sweet (if stilted) note, but it still sent Hope into a tailspin.

When it had just been her and Jack trying to move forward it was all right. Better than all right. But now Wilson's note reminded Hope of why she and Jack were trying to move forward in the first place.

Hope stuffed the envelope in her tote bag to take to school with her. It was time that she left for work, except Jack was still in bed and refusing to get up. There was nothing new about this; it simply meant that Hope would leave the house late, run to catch the bus, then run all the way to school from the bus stop and arrive hot and sweaty just before the bell rang with no time to gather herself or her lesson plans.

She stuck her head round the bedroom door to see a lump under the duvet, just the top of Jack's head visible.

'Come on,' she wheedled. 'It's time to get up or you'll be late and you've already made me late. *Again.*'

There was an indistinct grunt, which Hope correctly translated as, 'Just five more minutes and then I'll get up, I swear.'

Except five minutes would pass, then he'd want another five minutes, and now that Wilson's presence by way of the Royal Mail had watered the seeds of doubt and suspicion in Hope's mind, she didn't feel inclined to indulge Jack.

'This is your five-second warning,' Hope said firmly. 'I'm counting to five and then I'm going to work.'

This time the grunt sounded plaintive, which meant that Jack was mumbling something about having to have worked late the night before. Or had he? Maybe working late really meant sucking face with Susie. Or even one of the impossibly pretty girls from *Skirt*'s fashion department.

Just the mental image *that* conjured up was enough to make Hope bite out, 'Onetwothreefourfive!' super quickly, which was against the rules of counting up to five, but then Jack hadn't cared about the rules when he kissed Susie.

She'd gone over to the dark side once more, and as Jack hadn't stirred, despite fair warning, he could be late for work and suffer the consequences. Though as he was one of only three straight men in the *Skirt* office and all the female staff doted on him, the consequences were never that dire.

'I'm going,' Hope said. 'Hope you manage to get to work before lunchtime.'

Jack obviously thought this was just an empty threat because he barely, stirred and Hope was just about to make good on it when she caught sight of Jack's iPhone charging on top of the chest of drawers. They were always mixing up each other's iPhones, especially since they were both encased in identical black-rubber cases. Jack had bought Hope her case, after two incidents of Hope dropping her iPhone on unyielding surfaces and shattering the glass.

Which had actually been very sweet of him, and how was Hope repaying him now?

By stealthily padding back into the room to carefully unplug his phone so she could stash it in the pocket of her denim jacket, that's how. Even as she was doing it, Hope was repulsed by her actions – but not repulsed enough to put Jack's phone back where she found it.

But she had to know once and for all if Jack really had seen the error of his ways. Yes, she could just ask him, but he'd swear blind he was innocent and then they'd have another row about her trust issues. So, really, this was the only choice she had.

Chapter Fifteen

Even though it was a dead weight in her jacket pocket, Hope couldn't bring herself to take out the phone and start scrolling through Jack's text messages and emails. It went against everything she believed in. She was meant to be a role model to her pupils, not a lowdown dirty sneak who invaded other people's privacy. Just thinking about sliding the lock on Jack's phone made her feel bilious, so bilious that Hope was resolved to rush home at lunchtime, shove the phone under the pile of clothes that also lived on top of the chest of drawers and pretend the whole shameful episode had never happened.

Hope was a lot of things, and she'd discovered a side of herself that she didn't much like during the last few weeks, but she wasn't going to let herself become *that* girl, she decided.

Her mind made up, she waited until after she'd taken the register to call Blue Class up in groups of five to show them Wilson's photos so they could choose which pictures they wanted to stick on their nature wall.

It all got a little heated. Blue Class refused to grasp the concept that a free vote was the cornerstone of democracy, and Hope was just about to invoke her right as *ipso facto* Head of State to cast the deciding vote when Mr Gonzales, the headmaster, walked into the classroom.

Usually Mr Gonzales was only seen at morning assembly, although he and snotty Stuart were much better acquainted, but occasionally he did a sweep of the school. He said it was because he missed the thrill of grass-roots teaching, but Hope and Elaine suspected that he longed to catch his staff mucking about on Facebook while their class watched a DVD.

As it was, Hope was horrified when he strolled in, but quickly realised that she couldn't look a gift-horse headmaster in the mouth. 'This is what happens when you can't behave,' she told Blue Class. 'You've been making so much noise that Mr Gonzales could hear you all the way over in the junior school.'

Blue Class had never been so quiet, all sitting behind their desks, bottom lips quivering, eyes like saucers. Mr Gonzales, who was in his forties, eschewed suit and tie in favour of chinos and open-necked plaid shirts, and liked to refer to himself as 'an originator as well as an educator' on the school's website.

He came to stand by Hope's desk and smiled encouragingly at the class. 'Well, what's got you all so excited?' He pointed at Luca. 'What has Ms Delafield been teaching you this morning?'

Luca bit his lip and scrunched up his face with the effort of remembering exactly what Hope had been saying in a dull roar. 'We was gonna choose the photos for our nature wall but then we argued and Miss started talking about demer . . . demokassy and me and Javan said it wasn't fair that our picture didn't get chose and Miss said that life wasn't fair and . . .'

'Yes, I think Mr Gonzales gets the general drift,' Hope said quickly, even though Mr Gonzales' eyebrows were up around his hairline. There was nothing for it but to launch into a hurried explanation of their first visit to Camley Street Natural Park, making sure that she asked the more articulate members of the class to chime in on the chorus.

Mr Gonzales leafed through the contact sheets and even shared a wry smile with Hope as he looked at the shots of

Javan, Sirhan and Luca mugging for the camera. 'Do you know what I think?' he asked Blue Class, who clearly didn't have a freaking clue. 'I think these pictures would look very good on the wall outside my office. Would you like to make a big display all about your class project?'

Again, Blue Class were silent and unable to speak to Mr Gonzales unless he specifically pointed at one of them and asked Hope who they were.

'That's very exciting, isn't it?' Hope said brightly. 'We can include some of our nature samples, and we're all getting much better at colouring *inside* the lines.'

After a brief yet agonising pep talk about how pleased Mr Gonzales was that Hope was on board with the Winter Pageant, he left the room. There were thirty seconds of utter silence, then Blue Class erupted into noisy squeals. Hope was just threatening them with dire sticker consequences when there was a knock at the classroom door.

'That's probably Mr Gonzales coming back to say that he can't have a special display outside his office from such noisy children,' Hope told them, almost believing it herself as she saw Kathryn, Mr Gonzales' PA, beckoning to her urgently.

'I'm very sorry, Hope,' she said in a stage whisper. 'Can you call your boyfriend on his office number? Family emergency.'

The words struck terror into Hope's heart. Her father's mother was getting very doddery, and Caroline Delafield was always claiming that it was only a matter of time before she broke a hip and promptly died from shock. 'I don't have any cover,' she hissed, looking over her shoulder. Andy volunteered at a centre for adults with learning difficulties on alternate Fridays.

Now it was Kathryn's turn to look terrified. 'Well, I suppose I could stand in for five minutes.' She peered round the door. 'I wouldn't have to teach them, would I?'

Hope shook her head. 'Just stand there and look friendly,

but don't engage with them and don't let them smell your fear,' Hope said, leading Kathryn into the classroom. 'Mrs MacDonald is going to keep an eye on you while you do some quiet reading.'

Hope grabbed her phone and fairly galloped for the staffroom, her mind racing with awful possibilities. Maybe the family emergency was about Jack's paternal grand-mother who'd been suffering with dementia for years, in which case it would still be terrible, but a blessed relief. And his other grandmother had had a double mastectomy last year.

The parents would have to cancel their trip to Corfu, and instead of picking up Jeremy from Euston tomorrow, she and Jack would probably be driving to Lancashire. Oh! She'd have to cancel the two-day drama workshop. Dorothy was going to explode with rage if they refused to refund the course fees, but a death in the family took precedent over learning dramatic techniques for the under-eights.

By the time Hope was shutting the staffroom door behind her, mentally she was already in Lancashire making salmon paste and cucumber sandwiches for the wake. 'My God, are you OK?' she asked as soon as Jack answered the phone. 'Is it your Granny Thwaites? I thought she was looking really frail last time we saw her.'

'No, she's fine,' Jack replied. 'It's just that . . .'

'Christ! It's not my grandma, is it? I was meant to call her on the weekend and . . .'

'No,' Jack said sharply to cut Hope off before she began castigating herself for being a neglectful granddaughter. 'No one's died.'

Hope still didn't dare to relax. 'Has someone broken a hip, then?'

Jack sighed in exasperation. 'No! I only said it was a family emergency so they'd get you out of class and you could turn your phone back on.'

'Well, this had better be bloody good,' Hope snapped,

because really death was about the only acceptable reason for having her dragged out of class.

'Don't be like that, Hopey, I wouldn't have called if it wasn't important. It's just . . . did you see my phone before you left this morning? And oh, thanks for waking me. I didn't get to work until after eleven.'

Hope gasped with relief and a little bit of indignation too. 'Oh, please!' she scoffed. 'I woke you up about fifteen times and each time you hit "snooze" and went back to sleep. I do have a job to get to myself, thank you very much.'

'Yeah, yeah. My phone, have you seen it? I'm sure I left it charging on the chest of drawers but it wasn't there this morning. I looked in the drawers, I even pulled the whole thing out to see if it had fallen down the back. I've tried ringing it, but no one picks up, so I wondered if you'd mistaken it for yours and it might be in your bag.' Jack took a deep breath. 'Like, if you have got it, I can send a bike for it.' He took a deeper breath. 'No need to turn it on or anything, just pop it in a jiffy bag and I'll have a courier come and collect it within the hour.'

Shame had swept away Hope's relief and she'd been all set to feign surprise and admit to *inadvertently* taking Jack's phone. But the longer Jack talked, or gibbered in panic, to be more precise, the less shame she felt. In fact, her worst fears were being confirmed, and she was almost inclined to give in to his demands to hand the phone over to a courier without checking its contents first. Almost. But the sound of Jack practically hyperventilating wasn't the kind of proof that would stand up in a court of law or in the middle of a blazing row.

'I don't think I've got your phone,' she heard herself say as coolly as a cucumber chilling in a fridge on a hot summer's day. 'If I do find it in my bag, I'll let you know.'

It was only a slight greying of the truth – Hope would definitely let Jack know that she had his phone if she found anything on it that shouldn't be there. Yup, he'd be the very first to know.

'Would you?' Jack didn't sound at all comforted by the thought. 'And like I said, there's no need to open it if there's, like, missed calls or texts or anything. I mean, it was just me trying to locate the bloody thing.'

'Look, I have to go. I have thirty young minds ripe for moulding,' Hope said. 'I'm sure your phone will turn up. Maybe it's in your jeans pocket.'

'But I'm wearing the same jeans I had on yesterday!' Jack growled, but Hope didn't want to listen any longer so she hung up on him.

There was another mad gallop down the corridor to get back to Blue Class, who weren't quietly reading if the sound of excited chatter was anything to go by. She certainly wasn't going to rifle through Jack's phone when they were meant to be having another bash at the two-times table.

Hope still wasn't even entirely sure that she was going to rifle through Jack's phone at all – it was so low. She'd never even read Lauren's diary when they shared a room for a year at university, and she'd known that Lauren kept it hidden under the mattress.

Her resolve held all the way through lunch, helped by the fact that she went to Wetherspoon's with Elaine and Marta, who had got over her nerves and was now happy to bitch about Dorothy and Gurinder and dish the dirt on her more annoying parents. But even as Hope listened to a convoluted story about a helicopter mummy who was mounting a one-woman campaign to have the class work-sheets printed on bio-degradable paper, she had one sweaty hand clutched around Jack's phone.

Eventually Hope could bear it no longer. 'I nicked Jack's phone this morning,' she blurted out, before Marta could get to the end of her story. 'I don't know why, but I have an idea that he might still be seeing Susie and there'll be some incriminating texts on it.'

Elaine gave a long, low whistle. 'Really? I thought things were back to normal.'

'I thought they were, too,' Hope said. 'But then he had me hauled out of class to ask me if I'd seen his phone, and he was so panic-stricken that for a moment I thought he'd actually stopped breathing.'

Marta had already heard all about Hope's relationship woes. 'My sister suspected that her boyfriend had another Facebook account so she waited until he went to the loo, but was still logged in, and guess what?'

'What?'

'He had *three* other Facebook accounts and he was using them to hook up with other women,' Marta announced with some relish. 'It was obvious, really. He had a monobrow. Never trust a man with a monobrow.'

'Jack doesn't have a monobrow,' Hope groused.

'Yeah, but he's already kinda cheated on you once. Or once that you know about,' Marta added, and Hope had definitely liked her more when she spent most of the break and lunchtimes in a state of abject terror. 'You have every right to check up on him.'

Hope turned pleading eyes on Elaine who was looking distinctly disapproving. 'What do you think I should do?'

'Eavesdroppers never hear any good of themselves,' she said, even though this wasn't technically eavesdropping. Then she shrugged. 'But if it was me, I probably would, then I'd wish I hadn't.'

'You're a lot of help,' Hope complained as she rested the phone on her palm. 'Maybe one of you could look for me, and if there is bad stuff on it, you could just summarise. Without too much detail, unless there are details I should know about, and then you . . .'

'Oh, for God's sake,' Elaine snapped, snatching the phone from Hope. 'I'll look after this, and you come and find me at three thirty when I expect you to have made a decision one way or another.'

It was a good plan, so Hope could concentrate on the afternoon lessons, but her mind was still distracted, and Blue Class were restless as they hadn't accrued enough stickers to qualify for half an hour of Golden Time at the end of the day, when they'd sit on the carpet and have the story of their choice read to them before finishing the week with a rousing song.

'You still need another ten stickers,' Hope told them, because she hadn't planned anything for the last half hour of school and was as desperate for Golden Time as they were. 'How might you earn them?'

'We could get them for sitting on our chairs properly?' piped up a voice from the back of the class.

Hope shook her head. 'You should be sitting on your chairs properly anyway. What areas do we need to work on?'

They spent some time practising queuing up in single file and walking quietly down the corridor, but failed miserably. Things were looking grim, and a couple of the more highly strung girls even started crying at the prospect of missing Golden Time. Eventually inspiration struck, and Hope set them to tidying up the nature wall, the little class library, the stationery cupboard and the art corner, which they did quietly and intently, so she could then issue them with ten more class stars and they could have Golden Time. Six-year-olds were so malleable, Hope thought, as Blue Class charged into the playground for afternoon break. Maybe she should have had Jack on a sticker-reward programme, it would have simpled things up so much.

Hope avoided the staffroom and Marta and Elaine's knowing looks at break, but after a read-through of *The Gruffalo*, with a lot of class participation, and a medley of Motown hits, which Blue Class had been learning with the music teacher, there was no putting it off any longer.

'Give me the phone,' Hope demanded of Elaine, who was still tidying up her classroom. 'Give it to me. *Now*.'

'Are you sure?' Elaine asked doubtfully. She took the phone from her bag and offered it to Hope, who grabbed it and then did nothing but stare down at the silent but potentially deadly device encased in black rubber. Since when had Apple started to manufacture Pandora's boxes?

'Do you really want to do this?' Elaine asked again, though given Hope's grim, resolute expression it was obviously a rhetorical question.

'How can I not?' Hope shook her head. 'I'm a terrible, terrible person, but if Jack's doing what I think he might be doing, then he's much worse than I am. All this time he's been lying to me. How could he do that?'

'You still don't know that he *is* doing anything. Look, let's go down the Midnight Bell, order a vat of wine, and I'll be there if you want to have a little peek, just to set your mind at ease.'

It sounded good, or the vat of wine did at any rate, but Hope preferred that there shouldn't be any witnesses if and when her world crumbled to nothing more than a pile of dust. 'Except I'm meeting Lauren and Allison in town tonight for cheap cocktails so I'd better hold off until then,' she said, turning away to make her escape, but Elaine's hand on her shoulder stilled her.

'Prepare for the worst, hope for the best,' she advised. 'I'm *sure* it was just that one-off kiss. That's not so bad, is it?'

'Yeah, you're probably right,' Hope agreed, and with every single fibre of her being she hoped that her sneaky, shameful behaviour would confirm only that she was sneaky and shameful and nothing else. 'Anyway, I'd better go. Have a nice half-term.'

'You too, sweetie. Hope the drama workshop isn't the same ninth circle of hell that it was when I did it,' Elaine said cheerfully, though she'd been careful not to share that little fact with Hope until now. 'Give me a call and let me know how things turn out. Oh, and maybe Jeremy can hang out with Lola and Abby later on in the week – he doesn't sound like the sort of boy who might impregnate them while my back's turned.'

'God, no!' Hope said, genuinely grinning as she thought of Jeremy coming face to face with Lola and Abby, who both looked at least twenty-five and were usually caked in badly applied make-up and poured into skintight jeans and teeny tops from which their burgeoning bosoms always threatened to break free. They'd eat him alive.

Chapter Sixteen

As soon as she got home, before she'd even taken off her jacket or put her keys down, Hope was pulling out Jack's phone, staring at its John Lennon wallpaper, and then unlocking it.

Even doing that felt like the worst thing in the world. Rooting around on Jack's phone went against everything Hope believed in, and in the same position, if Jack, or anyone, invaded her privacy she'd be furious, and rightly so. She couldn't do this, Hope decided, glancing down at the screen, which happened to show Jack's recent text messages . . . and there was Susie's name, and all of a sudden Jack's right to privacy didn't seem to matter any more. Not when he was texting Susie, even though he'd sworn six weeks before, on his life and his mother's life and his Beatles vinyl, that he wouldn't be in contact with Susie ever again. That was it. All the proof that Hope needed, but she was still scrolling up the screen so she could read all the messages that Susie and Jack had sent and received.

The first message was dated the night before at ten thirty, just before Jack had come home from working late. *Love you. Love fucking you. Wish I hadn't had to go. Talk to you tomorrow. Jack x*

It was everything Hope had feared. Everything, and more, and so much worse, and for one crazy, tip-tilting second, she was relieved. Relieved to know that she'd been right all along, although being right had never, ever felt so wrong.

She hadn't been going crazy, and she hadn't been creating drama for the sake of it. It was more than one kiss. It wasn't even just sex, which would have been horrific enough, they were having a love affair. They were *in love*.

Hope put her hand on her heart to check if it was still working, as she tried to scroll through the stream of text messages. Some of them were pornographic – things they'd done, things they wanted to do, things they wanted to repeat – but the words that hurt like sharp knives, tearing into her guts, were the tender ones. The *I love you*'s. The *I miss you*'s. The *I'm going crazy not knowing when I'm going to see you again*'s.

Hope sank to the hall floor. She couldn't bear to load the earlier texts, so she started to read the emails, tracing the affair back to the email Jack had sent Susie the week before Hope's birthday last May:

```
Hey Susie Q
Help a mate out with a huge favour. Want to
get Hope something really cool for her
birthday and not something that she says she
likes, then goes through my pockets looking
for the receipt an hour later.

She's pored over the Grazia shoe supplement
three times in the last day and keeps sighing
and looking at me pointedly, but she always
moans that she can't do heels. Or should I get
her a bag? Obviously something from Topshop
isn't going to cut it, but can I get her a
statement pair of shoes or bag for less than
£200?

Are you free for a lunchtime shopping trip
sometime this week?
Laters, taters
Jack
```

161

There was much emailing back and forth about dates, with links to netaporter.com and talk of discount cards that Jack could sweet-talk from the fashion girls at work.

Then, one lunchtime shopping date and Hope's pair of Stella McCartney wedge sandals later, there was an email from Susie:

```
Oh, Jacky boy
Shit! What have we done? All I can think about
is how it would destroy Hopey if she knew, but
how much I want to do it again.
  Still sore and I've got a carpet burn on my
back, which smarts like fuck, but God, it was
so good.
  We're going straight to hell for this,
aren't we?
Love, Susie
```

May? *May? MAY?* It was almost the end of October now. Jack had been fucking Susie for over five months, ever since Hope and Jack had got back from not getting officially engaged in Barcelona.

Not just fucking Susie but lying to Hope for every single day of those just over five months. There was absolutely no comfort knowing that this was something Jack had done of his own free will, and that it wasn't Hope's wild mood-swings and erratic behaviour since The Kiss that had hurled him into Susie's arms. No, there was absolutely no comfort in that at all.

Hope only skimmed the rest of the emails as far as August, which were all variations on the themes of 'we're terrible people', 'oh poor Hopey', 'you're the best fuck I've ever had'. After August, well ... What did it really matter? They'd been found out, and whatever the emails revealed about their thoughts on being found out, they'd still continued to do exactly what they wanted, no matter how much it would hurt Hope.

The sheer scale of Jack's betrayal struck Hope anew. He'd looked her right in the eye on numerous occasions and had sworn on the lives of his loved ones that nothing had happened, and all that time . . . Hope had never known that Jack could lie so well, but it was obvious that she didn't know Jack at all.

This was the man she was going to spend the rest of her life with. The man she referred to as 'my better half', and even though she always said it with a smirk, Hope had meant it. The Jack she'd known was kind and funny and sweet and yes, he was handsome, but it was the kind and the funny and the sweet bits of him that she loved most of all. But all her love and devotion obviously didn't mean anything to Jack. If they had, then how could he? *How could he?*

He never texted Hope even once a day to say that he loved her, unless they were in the middle of a fight. And he'd never, ever texted Hope to let her know that she was the best fuck that he'd ever had and he was hard just thinking about her. Not ever.

Just to torment herself a little more, Hope had a quick look at Jack's photos, then wished she hadn't when she saw a snap of Susie lolling stark-naked on her expensive Heal's bed with the padded-leather headboard, glistening pink and wet, her legs wide apart. She was a perfect pornographic priestess, whereas Hope wouldn't even let Jack take a picture of her in a swimsuit.

The thirteen years they'd been together counted for nothing when compared to Susie and all her charms – Hope couldn't begin to compete.

She got up from the floor, and it was good that she hadn't taken her jacket off and still had her handbag strap looped around her wrist. It meant that she didn't have to waste any time, but could head straight out of the door. Normally for a night out with Lauren and Allison – hopping between any number of bars that did cheap cocktails and ending up in a nightclub, the tackier the better – Hope would spend a couple of hours getting ready. Even going to the trouble of straightening her hair, and doing her make-up properly, rather than just applying a dash of mascara and a quick smear of tinted lip-gloss. But now Hope didn't even care that she was still in her work-rumpled clothes, with felt-tip stains on her floral blouse, and that her hair was scraped back in a severe bun as she hadn't had time to wash it that morning because she'd wasted valuable minutes trying to rouse Jack from sleep.

Even thinking his name sent a shooting stab of pain to the base of Hope's skull. She was going to fucking kill him. And then she might fucking kill herself because it was the only way she could think of not to feel like *this*.

With murder on her mind, Hope didn't bother with the Piccadilly Line but stuck out her hand the minute she hit Holloway Road and saw a cab with its light on. It was late in the afternoon and there was little traffic going into town. The taxi pulled up outside the Magnum Media building a scant twenty minutes later. Hope stuffed a £20 note in the driver's hand and insisted that he could keep the £7.40 change because she couldn't wait the vital ten seconds for him to count out the money.

Then she marched into the chrome and marble lobby, up to the reception desk, and said that she had an urgent delivery for Jack Benson on *Skirt* magazine. The receptionist dialled Jack's extension even as she directed Hope to the lifts.

She could see Jack waiting as the lift doors opened on the fourth floor. For one moment he looked utterly flummoxed to see Hope standing there – he even did a swift double-take before he smiled. Hope wanted to smack it right off his face.

'This is a nice surprise,' he said cheerfully. 'I thought you were meeting up with Lauren and Alli for a night of hard drinking.'

'I am,' Hope said, and she marvelled that she could sound reasonably sane. 'I found your phone.'

Jack allowed himself one small sigh of relief then tensed up. 'Oh, really? Where was it?'

'Well, you were right, it *was* charging on the chest of drawers this morning when I took it and put it in my bag,' Hope said without even a flicker of guilt because she'd got over *that* a couple of hours ago.

'Right.' Jack nodded. The tips of his ears were so red they looked as if they might start smoking. 'So, did you mistake it for yours?'

'No, I knew it was yours.' Hope struck a pensive pose, one hip jutting out, a finger on her chin. 'It was a moment of madness because I was still convinced there was something going on between you and Susie, and I had to know one way or another. I've spent most of the day wrestling with my conscience.'

Jack was almost dancing on the spot, unsure if he should back away or move closer to snatch his phone as Hope pulled it out of her pocket. 'But you didn't look through my phone, did you?' he asked shakily. Hope could see his fear and uncertainty, but then he shook his head. 'Of course you didn't, because you always do the right thing.'

Hope held up the phone. 'Guess again, *Jacky boy*,' she snarled as she hurled it on the floor, which was covered in the same marble tiles as the downstairs reception area. Jack gave a bellow of rage – or was it panic? – as the phone landed and it was too soon to assess any damage, especially as Hope was now stomping on it. She wasn't wearing her Converses today but her Doc Marten brogues that Jack always said made her look like a lesbian or a policewoman. Or a lesbian policewoman. But Hope was really appreciating how the thick rubber soles could inflict maximum hurt on an iPhone. The glass and innards had shattered into tiny pieces, though, frustratingly, the stainless-steel backing was merely buckled, even after Hope had jumped up and down on it repeatedly.

For weeks now, every time she'd got mad at Jack or suspicious of Jack she'd told herself she was acting like a crazy woman, but now she *was* acting like a crazy woman, and in front of a small horrified gaggle of *Skirt* employees gathered by the big double doors that led to the magazine's offices. In fact, Hope didn't know why acting like a crazy woman got such a bad press when it felt *so* good.

'There!' she said, kicking what was left of the phone over to where Jack stood, his arms limp, his mouth hanging open in disbelief. 'You can have it back now.'

'You had no right,' Jack mumbled when he finally regained the power of speech. 'No right . . .'

'I had every fucking right!' Hope shouted. 'You said it was over. In fact, you said nothing had ever happened. You *promised* you'd never, ever contact her again, and all the time, you were fucking each other. For months! You've been fucking her, and cheating and lying to me. You've looked me right in the eye and lied to me. *To me!*'

Jack opened his mouth, then closed it again when he heard a gasp and a few shocked giggles coming from his colleagues in the corner. He stepped over the high-tech mess that used to be his iPhone to grab Hope by the arm and tug her down the corridor.

'Get off me!' she spat out, pulling her arm free so she could swing it back and smack him, with one loud vicious crack against his left cheek. Jack barely reacted, because suddenly he had Hope in an artboy version of a Vulcan death-grip, and he yanked her, squirming and wriggling and telling him that he was a 'fucking bastard', into a little kitchen, which smelt of gone-off milk and microwaved food, and slammed the door shut.

It was just the two of them in a stinky, confined space. They were both breathing hard and everything about Jack that Hope had loved – his thick, brown hair that she always wanted to run her fingers through, his guileless blue eyes, the planes and angles of his face, even the gangliness of his limbs – she now hated. She could hardly bear to look at him.

'Why?' she demanded. 'Why didn't you dump me when you first started fucking each other, or when I caught you together? You obviously had no intention of giving up Susie, so why didn't you give me up instead?'

'Because I fucking love you!' Jack shouted, as if it was obvious. 'I love you, all right?'

'No, it's not all right,' Hope hurled back at him. 'You were hedging your bets, weren't you? Because Susie has a low boredom threshold and you wanted to make sure that good old Hope was still waiting in the wings. Have you any idea how that makes me feel?'

'You don't understand . . . you don't know what I've been going through.' Jack stopped as soon as he realised how extremely lame that sounded, or it might have been the inelegant snorting noise Hope was making.

'It's not just about me though, is it? What about Wilson? It was obvious that neither of you gave a toss about his feelings either.'

Now it was Jack's turn to scoff. 'Since when do *you* give a toss about Wilson?'

'Since Wilson knows exactly what I'm going through,' Hope told him, though that wasn't strictly true. Wilson had had a much clearer grasp of the depths of Jack and Susie's deception than Hope, and he'd tried to warn her, but she'd refused to listen. But now the battle lines were drawn. Jack and Susie on one side, Hope and Wilson on the other. In fact, Wilson was like a kindred spirit, but his relationship with Susie barely counted as a relationship compared to the thirteen years Hope and Jack had racked up. So, there was no way that Wilson could ever feel as destroyed as Hope did. It just wasn't possible. 'Jesus, how could you do this? Did you never stop to think that what you were doing was wrong and that people were going to get hurt?' Hope wrapped her arms tightly around herself. 'You're . . . you're *vile*!'

'Yeah? And what does that make you?' Jack asked belligerently, though he had absolutely nothing to be belligerent about because . . .

'Yes? So, I nag you a bit and sometimes I can be a bitch, but if that was really bothering you, you could have ended it,' Hope said thickly. 'You had options that didn't involve fucking my best friend behind my back.'

'I'm not talking about that. I'm talking about you going through my phone, even when I asked you not to . . .'

Hope knew what Jack was doing. Attack was the best form of defence, after all. And he was right, up to a point. 'That's bullshit and you know it. Stop trying to dodge the issue – this is not about your bloody phone.'

'And then you come to my office and show me up in front of the people I work with,' Jack continued, hands tensed as they clutched the draining board behind him. He was whipping up his anger bit by bit, but it couldn't hold a candle to Hope's fury. She didn't know how she'd managed to restrain herself from smacking him again.

'I don't care about the people you work with,' Hope burst out. 'I don't care what they think of me. And I really, really don't care that they might realise you're not the loveable cheeky chappy that you pretend to be.'

'Look, I'm not going to talk about any of this with you until you can start acting like a calm, rational human being,' Jack insisted once he realised that his attempts to deflect her attention away from his crimes weren't working.

'I don't give a fuck about being calm and rational!' Hope screamed, but her voice broke on the last defiant syllable.

'You want to know why I've been seeing Susie?' Jack asked her. 'You really want to know?'

They were flinging words at each other now, not even bothering to check their tempers or remember that hateful things said in the heat of battle couldn't be unsaid.

'Go on, enlighten me,' Hope choked around the sobs that were welling up. 'Tell me why you decided to break my heart.'

'Because she's not on my case 24/7, that's why,' Jack said brutally. 'She doesn't moan at me about going to IKEA and throwing stupid pretentious dinner parties, or nag and nag about everything from getting up on time to changing lightbulbs . . .'

'I have vertigo . . .'

'Whatever. You've become so boring, Hopey. Like you're a middle-aged woman trapped in a twenty-something body. In fact, you're pretty much turning into your mother.'

Hope could only stare at Jack in horror. Her temper was fizzling away because there wasn't room for anything other than the icy-cold realisation that the reason Jack had been fucking Susie, mad, impulsive, couldn't-give-a-damn Susie, was simple. Susie wasn't her and he was sick to death of her.

But Jack wasn't done yet. 'And since you really want to know, I'll tell you something else about Susie – she's actually fun to be around, in and out of bed. At least she doesn't try to schedule when we have sex and then lie back like a sack of potatoes and think about lesson plans. And she doesn't go on and on and on about wanting to get bloody married!'

Jack had finally finished hammering the last nail in the coffin that contained the bloated corpse that was their relationship, if his triumphant self-satisfied smile was any indication. 'So there!' it seemed to say. 'How do you like that?'

The longer Hope stood there, arms still wrapped around her torso, silent and pinch-faced, the more his smile began to fade. 'Right,' she managed to say. 'Right. Well. I guess that's that, then.'

'Yeah, it is,' Jack said, but now his bravado sounded false. 'And don't expect me to turn up a few days from now and beg your forgiveness. It's not going to happen.'

'OK, yeah. That's probably for the best because I never want to see you again,' Hope told him, and God, she wished that she meant it, but it wasn't true. She wasn't Jack. And she couldn't just stop loving him, even now. She'd always loved him and she wasn't capable of *not* loving him.

Chapter Seventeen

Thirteen hours later, Hope was woken by the impatient beep of her phone. She groaned, groped for the offending piece of machinery and knocked over a glass, a couple of books and a tub of hand cream.

Sitting up was an ordeal in itself. It felt as if the world was pitching forward and about to fling her off the edge. This wasn't just a hangover courtesy of several pitchers of Margaritas and the tequila shots that the guys on the next table had kept buying Hope in a vain attempt to cheer her up. It was a hangover made worse by the fact that she'd cried for five hours straight and had leeched every last drop of moisture out of her body via her tearducts, before the alcohol could even start to dehydrate her.

After leaving Jack's office, Hope had walked up Oxford Street, bawling her eyes out with every step, but had still managed to be on time to meet Lauren and Allison outside the Salsa Bar on Charing Cross Road.

She'd crumpled into their arms and their big girls' night out had descended into every break-up cliché in the book. Lauren had gone to the Ladies and brought back a huge, industrial-sized roll of toilet tissue for Hope to mop her eyes with as she'd spluttered and choked her way through the saga of the iPhone and her ignominious role in it.

Somewhere around the end of the second jug of Margaritas, Hope had moved on to a snotty, tear-soaked account of her final showdown with Jack in *Skirt's* malodorous kitchen, and by the time they were making major inroads into the fourth jug and the first round of tequila shots had been sent over, Hope was verging on hysterical as she tried to come to terms with her new single status.

'That's it. I'll never find another boyfriend because I'm boring and fat and ginger and I'm shit in bed,' she'd sobbed, tearing off another wad of loo roll so she could blow her nose. 'I'm unloveable.'

Lauren and Allison had been the stuff of legends. Hope had seen the pair of them through countless boyfriend-related traumas and even though she'd completely ruined their night out, they'd hugged her and wiped her face and said supportive things like, 'He's a fucking bastard and you're well shot of him. He's probably riddled with disgusting STIs by now.'

And, 'Of course you're not a bad person for taking his iPhone and going through his stuff. Wanker left you no choice. Honestly, Hopey, any girl with half a braincell would have done the exact same thing.'

They'd even travelled to Holloway with her, held her hair back while she puked into a bin outside Argos and seen her safely home, before catching a ruinously expensive minicab back to South London. 'It's no trouble,' they'd kept saying each time Hope apologised. 'It's what friends are for. And remember to prop your pillows up so you don't choke on your own vomit and die in the night.'

Hope wished that she *had* died in the night and then she wouldn't have had to wake up with a splitting headache, sore ribs and a sandpaper throat from all the throwing-up and crying. And those ailments barely registered compared to the sucking chest wound where her heart used to be. She burrowed under the duvet to warm up her cold and clammy skin as she stuck one hand out to hunt for her phone.

It was probably either Lauren or Allison phoning to check up on her and remind her to put all of Jack's stuff into bin bags and throw them into the nearest skip. Then she was meant to call a locksmith to make sure he could never come home again. They'd both been very clear about that.

But just when Hope thought that life couldn't get any worse, she saw that it wasn't a missed call from Lauren or Allison but a text from her mother: *Just put Jeremy on the London train. Arrives at Euston at 10.10 a.m. Must be there to pick him up. Dread to think what trouble he'll get into if you're late. Love Mum (and Dad)*

It was all the motivation Hope needed to sit upright, although she wished she hadn't. 'Oh, shit, shit, *shit*!' she exclaimed, as she flung back the duvet, placed two very shaky feet on the floor and staggered to the bathroom, clinging on to the wall and pieces of furniture as she went.

A stinging-hot shower and hairwash didn't make her feel remotely better. Neither did a mug of tea and three ibuprofen. In fact swallowing anything made Hope feel as if she was about to die, and then she remembered what had happened yesterday and decided that something in her was already dead anyway.

Instead of getting dressed, she got back into bed and curled herself into a small miserable ball at the thought of all the days that would make up the rest of her life, and how she'd spend them without Jack. Then she wondered how she could still love him after everything he'd done. Maybe loving him, despite all his many faults and shortcomings, was preferable to being alone. The most time she'd ever spent on her own was maybe forty-eight hours, and usually it was just the journey to and from school and the two hours before Jack came home.

How did single people manage without anyone to talk to or share the washing-up with? They couldn't all live in flat-shares, so some of them must have to spend serious time on their own. Not Hope's brand of alone-time when she took lots of hot baths and ate chocolate, but days upon days of alone-time because they had no other choice. How was she going to get through the next week without even the distraction of teaching?

Another text message from her mother was a salient reminder that she wasn't going to be alone. *Why haven't you replied to my last text message? Have you left for the station? Best to get there early, just in case. Love Mum (and Dad)*

It was nine thirty. Hope had only forty minutes. She got dressed in what she could find on the floor, which were jeans, a green T-shirt, which was speckled with poster paint, and her red cardigan – and yes, the whole ensemble clashed and she wasn't wearing a bra and she'd gone back to bed with damp hair so it was sticking up in all directions, but it would have to do.

The lack of bra meant that Hope couldn't run to the tube but she arrived at Euston only five minutes after Jeremy's train, which surely wasn't late enough for him to have already been spirited away by white-slave traders.

He hadn't been. He was sitting on a huge rucksack in the middle of the concourse, looking utterly miserable. Welcome to my world, Hope thought as she plastered a smile on her face and hurried towards him.

Jeremy had gone emo since she'd seen him briefly last Easter, except he was too ruddy-faced for the guyliner and his thighs were far too beefy for skinny jeans, which might have been why the crotch was somewhere around his knees as he stood up. He'd also grown at least six inches in as many months and towered over Hope.

'You're late,' he grumbled, shying away as Hope tried to hug him.

'Only five minutes,' she said, as she settled for squeezing his arm instead. 'Did you have a good journey? It's *so* good to see you! We're going to have so much *fun*!'

Jeremy pulled a face. 'I didn't want to come. Mum made me. I could have stayed home and been responsible and not wrecked the house. 'Sides, my best mate is having a party and everyone's going, except me.'

Hope wasn't sure how she was going to get through seven days of Jeremy's adolescent, high-school melodrama. 'You think you've got problems?' she wanted to scream at him. 'I'll give you problems!'

But then again, Mrs Delafield had obviously woken him up at the merest sliver of dawn to catch the seven o'clock train and emo teenagers needed a lot of sleep, so he couldn't really be blamed.

'Yeah, but you get to spend the week in London,' she reasoned, gesturing at him to pick up his backpack because there was no way in hell that she was carrying it. 'That's pretty cool, and we'll take loads of photos for you to post on Facebook and they'll all be dead jealous.'

'Yeah, whatever.' Jeremy sniffed. 'So, can we go to the skate shop in Covent Garden and then get some sushi?'

At the mention of sushi, Hope gagged, though she tried to pretend it was a cough. 'Why don't we go home and dump your stuff first?' she suggested brightly. 'I haven't been shopping because I don't know what you like to eat, so we should probably hit up Morrisons at some stage.'

Jeremy's scowl kicked up a notch. 'I can go to Morrisons in Rochdale!'

'OK, we'll go to Waitrose then,' Hope said and by now her smile and her temper were wearing pretty thin.

Thankfully, a brief trip on the tube was a welcome distraction. Jeremy refused to sit down or indicate in any way that he and Hope were together, even though it was too soon for him to have mastered the art of standing up and not holding on to anything.

At least when they got to Holloway the eclectic mix of bookies, greasy spoons, dodgy pubs and shops selling discount toiletries, household items and tacky clothing met with Jeremy's approval. When you lived in a small village outside Rochdale and the most thrilling event in the local calendar was the monthly Youth Club disco, the Holloway Road was positively exotic.

Jeremy's happiness didn't last long. As soon as he walked through the door of the flat, his face screwed up. 'It's really small. I didn't think it would be this small,' he complained, because he had no freaking idea about London property prices and how the cost of this 'really small' flat would have bought Hope and Jack a three-bedroomed house back North. And talk of the devil. 'Where's Jack?'

Hope stared at him, her mind racing. 'Well, he's not here. Um, he's working this weekend and we decided it'd be best if he stayed at a friend's while you were down. I mean, you're right. The flat is *really* small.'

It was obvious she was lying. Obvious unless you were a self-obsessed teenager who hero-worshipped your sister's cool boyfriend who had a cool job on a cool magazine and hooked you up with cool bands that your friends had never heard of, and you didn't want to believe that the object of your affections didn't want to spend time with you. 'But I thought I'd get to hang out with him.' Jeremy threw down his backpack in a fit of ruddy-cheeked pique. 'It's the only reason I agreed to stay with you.'

'I think Mum would see it differently,' Hope snapped, because God, she did not need this. 'You know, Jerry, you might actually enjoy yourself if you stopped making such a concerted effort to pick holes in everything.'

'Jez.'

'Jez what?'

'Jez, that's my name. No one calls me Jerry. Old men are called Jerry.'

Their mother had called Jeremy – sorry, Jez – 'Jerry' repeatedly during her phone call the previous Sunday, but Hope decided not to share that. 'Jez?' She tested out the word. It didn't suit him at all. 'OK, Jez. You're here for a week. Might as well make the best of it.'

'So, when's Jack coming back then?'

'Not sure,' Hope said. 'You get settled in and I'll ring him.'

Once Jeremy was settled with a cup of tea and a mound

of toast and jam, Hope cloistered herself in the bedroom to ring Jack. Except, it was hard to ring someone whose phone had been smashed to pieces less than twenty-four hours ago.

She had to settle for ringing round Jack's friends, who claimed to have no knowledge of his whereabouts, but the sheer hostility and disapproval in their voices made it painfully obvious that they knew *exactly* where he was and were Team Jack all the way. Only Otto was a little more forthcoming.

'But you smashed his iPhone, Hopey,' he explained tremulously. 'I mean, was there really any need to do that?'

'It was a heat-of-the-moment thing,' Hope said through gritted teeth, because as far as she knew iPhones were replaceable, hearts weren't. 'Compared to what Jack's done to me, I think he got off pretty lightly, don't you? I mean, I'm in bloody pieces over wh—'

'Yes, well, don't want to get into that. Conflict of interest, you know?'

Hope ground her teeth harder. 'Where is he?' she asked baldly. 'If you know that I smashed his iPhone then you must have spoken to him recently, and you also know what I'm capable of doing to *you*, if you insist on withholding information.'

'I think he's staying with a friend.'

'Which friend?'

'You know which friend,' Otto muttered unwillingly. 'And don't say you heard it from me.'

Of course Jack was staying with Susie. Why sleep on a friend's sofa, when he could sleep with Susie and have wild, experimental sex on tap?

Even though she'd deleted Susie's number from her phone, Hope's fingers tapped over the right keys in the right order without her even having to think about it. If she *had* stopped to think about it, then the very last thing she'd want to do was to call Susie. So far, all her rage had been focused on Jack, but Hope was sure that she still had vast, untapped pools of rage ready to unleash in Susie's direction once she got her second wind.

Susie obviously hadn't deleted Hope from her phone because she answered warily, as if Hope's name had flashed up and given her a nasty fright.

'Is he there?' Hope demanded, ignoring Susie's 'Hello?' because she wasn't ringing for a chat. 'I need to talk to him.'

She heard Susie's sharp intake of breath. 'Hang on.' Hope strained her ears to catch the muffled conversation, but she couldn't make out even a single word, unless the word was fllggpmhwrt. 'I'm sorry, he can't come to the phone right now,' Susie eventually said, like she was a secretary refusing to put an irate caller through to her boss. 'Is there a message?'

'You've got to be kidding me!' Hope snapped. 'Put him on the line.'

There was another indecipherable exchange of words. 'He says he doesn't want to speak to you,' Susie relayed. Hope felt a momentary flash of embarrassment that Susie had been put in the untenable position of piggy-in-the-middle. Then again, it was the *very* least that Susie deserved.

'Tell him that Jeremy's down for the week and that he promised he'd take him out on Monday and Tuesday,' Hope said tightly. 'I need to know if he's going to turn up or if he's going to break that promise as well and let down my baby brother who actually seems to be looking forward to spending time with him.'

Hope wasn't very good at emotional blackmail, especially when it had to be passed through a very partial third party, but she waited while Susie passed on the message.

'He says he'll come round tomorrow before lunch to see Jeremy.' Susie paused. 'Um, like, maybe it would be best if you weren't there.'

'As if I even want to see him.' It was a pity that Hope couldn't turn her love off like a stopcock, because Jack was doing everything he could to make her hate him. 'Believe me, the moment he turns up, I'll be out of the door.'

'You know, it won't always be like this,' Susie said. 'I get that it's all come as a bit of a shock, but I did try to warn you, Hopey. When you've calmed down, there's no reason why we can't all just chillax and be cool.'

'There's every reason. There're about a million reasons,' Hope spluttered and she actually had to stop spluttering and do a quick mental review of the facts at hand to see if she was being completely unreasonable, given the circumstances. No, she was being entirely reasonable. Some would even commend Hope for her restraint. Yes, she'd trashed an iPhone and slapped Jack around the face, but when they'd been doing their teacher training, Lauren had got up close and very personal with one of the tutors and then keyed his car once she found out that he was also up close and personal with half a dozen other wannabe teachers. Even Elaine in her wilder, rock 'n' roll days had smashed Simon's vintage Les Paul guitar and had climbed up on stage at a gig in Aylesbury to kick him in the nuts when one of his groupies looked like she was becoming a permanent fixture.

Hope realised that she was still on the phone because she could hear Susie squawking at her something about how . . . 'this is difficult for everyone, Hopey. Bet you anything that one day – OK, maybe a really long time from now – we'll go out for a drink and laugh about all this.'

There were no words. Or there *were* words, but every single one of them carried a Parental Advisory warning, so Hope pinged the elastic band, which she'd started wearing again only thirty minutes earlier so she wouldn't be tempted to shout at her whiny little brother, hung up, then wandered back into the living room where Jeremy was sitting on the sofa, still wearing his army jacket and a truculent expression.

'Just spoken to Jack,' she said, managing not to flinch as

she said his name. 'He'll be round tomorrow. So, anyway, shall we go and get the food shopping done?'

'I want to go to the skate shop in Covent Garden.'

'You can do that with Jack,' Hope said firmly. 'Shall we make a list before we hit the shops or shall we just kick it freestyle?'

'I didn't get up at six this morning to come to London so I could go to a supermarket,' he huffed. 'I can go to Covent Garden by myself.'

'Over my dead body will you go by yourself!'

'But I looked it up in the *A to Z*!' Jeremy pulled out of his rucksack a battered, yellowing *A to Z* that looked very familiar. The same *A to Z* that Hope had pored over as a teenager, tracing the main thoroughfares of Camden Town that she'd read about in the *NME*, and vowing that one day she'd live on one of those hallowed streets. Of course now Camden Town was a mere husk of what it used to be; the market sold dodgy tie-dyed T-shirts, bootleg concert DVDs and hideous hippie jewellery, and the Stables markets, which at least had some decent vintage stalls, were being torn down to make way for a massive shopping centre. Besides which . . .

'That *A to Z* is so old that it's missing at least four underground lines and I don't know how many streets,' Hope told Jeremy. 'Mum and Dad bought it when they came down to London for the Silver Jubilee. Matthew had only just been born!'

Jeremy stuck out his chin in that familiar dogged Delafield way, one of the traits which all five children had inherited from their mother (which also included an irrational hatred of hedgehogs and the inability to digest smoked mackerel). 'But the Piccadilly Line is still there and if I get the tube at Holloway Road I don't even have to change lines. I checked, and I know exactly where to go after that, and I won't talk to anyone I don't know, apart from the staff in the skate shop because I want to get a new set of wheels and maybe some decals. And I promised my friends I'd go and I'd take pictures – and if I don't, they'll think I'm a lying twat. Please, Hope, don't be so boring. You're acting just like Mum!'

Jeremy was making a very compelling argument, *and* he was talking to her using whole sentences with prepositions and active verbs, which was a welcome relief. Also, Hope was nothing like Mrs Delafield. 'But what about the time you ended up in Hull?'

'Four words: rail replacement bus service!' he practically shouted.

'Oh, well, yeah, that explains everything,' Hope agreed. 'Are you sure you know where to go after you come out of the tube?'

'Yes! I go straight ahead, down Neal Street until I find Shorts Gardens on my left, then I come to a shop selling stinky cheese and there's a little alley and that's where the skate shop is.' Jeremy had obviously memorised the directions, and it was a much better set of directions than Hope would have given him.

'You have to take the *A to Z* with you. And phone me when you get there. Then phone me when you're at Holloway Road tube station and I'll come and meet you.' She was struck by a sudden inspiration. 'This'll be our little secret. No need to tell Mum about this.'

It was a miracle, but Jeremy was smiling. At her. So even with the badly crimped hair and cack-handed application of guyliner he looked a lot like the winsome toddler that Hope had had no time for when she'd been a surly, belligerent teenager herself. 'Thanks, Hopey, you're the best big sister ever. Now can you go and put a bra on?'

Chapter Eighteen

Hope saw Jeremy to the tube, then set off for Morrisons with a list of his favourite foods, which consisted of potato-based snacks, meat pies and biscuits. She even allowed herself a reason to feel cheery – maybe having Jeremy around for the week might even be fun, once he realised that Hope wasn't a younger version of their mother, but actually his cool elder sister.

Hope had been eleven when Jeremy was born and it was a moot point who was more shocked; her or her forty-four-year-old mother who thought she was going through an early menopause. How completely gross to be at the same primary school where her mother was deputy head and for everyone to know that her parents still had sex. Urgh!

No wonder Hope had been such a stroppy teenager, listening to angry girl guitar bands and screaming at the annoying little brother who followed her around like a puppy and put his sticky hands all over her stuff. By the time she'd grown out of her stroppy stage (though her mother swore that she still hadn't) and Jeremy had grown out of smearing chocolate over her CDs and magazines, Hope had left to go to university, and they'd never had the chance to develop a proper relationship. And, poor sod, he'd had eight years of being alone with Mum and Dad with no siblings to ease the burden. Hope had often hated having three older brothers, especially when they ganged up on her for being a girl, but at least she'd *had* a ready-made gang and, as an added bonus, she'd always got preferential treatment from their parents because she *was* the only girl.

As she walked back from the shops, laden down with junk food and a few token vegetables, Hope allowed herself a little fantasy of Jeremy studying for his degree in London. They'd go to art galleries and plays together and he'd introduce her to his girlfriends, who'd look up to her as the voice of womanly experience.

'Hopey's not just my cool, older sister,' Jeremy would say at one of Hope's well-attended, gastronomically daring dinner parties, Hope thought to herself as she opened the front door. 'She's my best friend.'

Except what Jeremy should actually have been saying right then was, 'I'm at Covent Garden tube station, heading due north towards Shorts Gardens.'

Hope dropped the shopping on the kitchen floor and rooted for her iPhone. There were no missed calls or text messages, and when she tried to call Jeremy, his phone went straight to voicemail. He couldn't still be on the tube. Not unless the whole skate-shop thing was a cunning ruse and he was really en route to Heathrow Airport where he'd board the first plane to New York and never be heard from again.

There was nothing to do but sweat it out. Hope unpacked the shopping, tidied up, stuck a wash on and even vacuumed. Then there was nothing to do but pace her miniscule square-footage and imagine all the awful things that could have happened to Jeremy. Worse, she'd have to tell her mother that she'd lost him, and he'd last been seen happily climbing into a white transit van belonging to four suicide bombers.

Two long hours later, during which Hope had aged at least ten years, Jeremy rang. 'Where the hell are you?' Hope shrieked. 'I've been worried sick!'

There was a bit of heavy breathing at the other end of the line, then a pitiful, 'Don't shout at me, but I'm in East Ham.'

'East Ham?' Hope shouted. 'How did you get to bloody East Ham?'

There was a garbled explanation about the Piccadilly Line being suspended at King's Cross for engineering works and how the Hammersmith and City Line had led Jeremy astray by pretending to be the Circle Line but the upshot of it was Hope growling, 'Stay right where you are. Don't even twitch a bloody eyelash – I'm coming to get you.'

It took Hope nearly two hours to get to East Ham. She used the time to work on the skin-stripping telling-off she'd give Jeremy, but when she finally reached her destination the sight of him huddled miserably at the station entrance, his guyliner smudged like there'd been a few tears shed, had her biting her tongue and pinging her elastic band.

They travelled back in silence and when they got home, Jeremy said he was tired and wanted to go to bed. Hope left him curled up on the sofa under the patchwork quilt, a much-loved present from some of the mums of last year's Blue Class.

It was only eight o'clock, which was far too early to go to bed on a Saturday night, but it had been twenty-four of some of the most hideous hours of her life and Hope couldn't wait to get into bed with a well-thumbed Jilly Cooper and a packet of chocolate digestives.

Jeremy was very subdued the next day. He barely had any appetite for breakfast and didn't notice how jumpy Hope was.

'I'll probably go out for a walk when Jack gets here,' she said, after many moments of mental rehearsal. 'Give you two a chance to catch up without me getting in the way.'

But Jeremy was back to merely grunting. The only reason that Hope knew he wasn't completely catatonic was because he'd managed to fire up the Xbox and was giving some horribly violent shoot-'em-up game his full attention.

Having Jeremy around made Hope feel like a stranger in

her own home, or maybe it was the expectation of Jack's arrival. She wasn't sure what time he was going to show up, which meant she couldn't settle to anything.

Jack was still a no-show at eleven when Hope, still in pyjama bottoms, an old Kenickie T-shirt and, in deference to Jeremy, a bra, was slumped over the kitchen counter, mindlessly eating handfuls of Rice Krispies straight from the box and reading the bumf from the drama workshop for the twentieth time. Then she heard his key in the lock.

Hope had already decided that she wasn't going to get angry with Jack. There was no point. It didn't make her feel the least bit better. It didn't make Jack even the least bit contrite, and then she stayed angry for the next forty-eight hours and the only way to squash it down was with huge amounts of chocolate.

She straightened up, tried to arrange her face into a neutral expression and resolved to stay calm and detached.

Jack didn't even look in her direction, but disappeared into the lounge where the sounds of gunfire were suddenly paused. Whatever he had to say to Jeremy didn't last long, certainly not long enough for Hope to finish getting changed. She was struggling to do up her most forgiving pair of jeans, the ones she wore when she was suffering from pre-menstrual bloat, when Jack walked into the bedroom.

It was hard to stay calm and detached with your muffin top on display and your breasts spilling over the cups of a bra that had been through the wash too many times. Especially when the sight of Jack made her catch her breath. He had the ability to do that to her sometimes, when the sight of him caught Hope unawares and it was as if she was seeing his beauty for the first time all over again.

Unlike Hope, whose pain and suffering were written all over her face and emphasised by the dark circles under her eyes, the stress spots and the puffy cheeks where at least half of the week's extra calories were lodged, Jack looked as if he didn't have a care in the world. He'd had his hair cut shorter, which accentuated the clean, delicate lines of his face, and was wearing a pair of slim-cut trousers, a navy-blue shirt that Hope hadn't seen before and his old denim jacket, which Hope had seen before. She'd even sewed up the holes on the elbow, but the overall effect was stylish in an urban, Hoxton-ish kind of way. It felt as if they were a million worlds apart.

Jack didn't say anything right away and, flustered, Hope snatched up one of her Breton tops, which she pulled on before she remembered that horizontal stripes were not her friends these days.

'It's OK,' she said, as she sat down to pull on socks. 'I'll clear out so you and Jeremy can have a proper chat. It's just I didn't know what time you were coming round.'

'You might have told him that if he was going to play on the Xbox to put the games back in their cases once he was finished,' Jack spat out as he reached up to grab a holdall from the top of the wardrobe, and dislodged a laundry bag full of Hope's old clothes. 'Oh, Christ, Hope, can't you ever throw anything away?'

'I might be able to get into those again one day,' Hope said, scooping up the size-ten Topshop bodycon dress, which she'd only been able to wear for the halcyon week when she'd got food poisoning very soon after a bout of swine flu.

'Yeah, right,' Jack sneered. 'If you say so.'

'Wow! That's kind of mean,' Hope said to Jack's back as he began packing clothes neatly into his bag. 'Can we try and be civil to each other?'

'You weren't civil to me on Friday, were you?' Jack still sounded bullish, but then he turned round and looked at her. Hope was proud of herself for standing there and look-ing right back at him calmly. She didn't even have to ping her elastic band. As she stood there and Jack could see that she was really trying and not about to make any sudden movements with concealed weapons, Hope watched the fight go out of him. 'Yeah, you're right, we should try and be grown-ups about this.'

Hope nodded. 'So, what's going on, then? Are you moving in with Susie . . . permanently?' She had to swallow round the last word, and it hung in the air like an invisible barrier between them.

'Well, I can hardly stay here with you. That's not an option, is it?'

Hope looked up at the ceiling as if she might find inspiration there. 'If you were unhappy with me, you should have said something ages ago, not started an affair with my best friend because you were too chickenshit to end it any other way.'

Jack closed his eyes like he'd suddenly been struck. 'You don't understand,' he said tightly. 'This thing, it's not about you and me. It's about me and Susie.'

Now it was Hope's turn to close her eyes. 'But you and her aren't a for-ever kind of deal. I mean, Jack, we can't be *over*. Not like this.' She sank back down on the bed. 'We've been together for thirteen years and . . .'

'I know! I fucking *know*. Do you think I don't know that? Do you think that doesn't keep me up at night?' Jack now started stuffing clothes into his bag furiously, without any of his usual fussy precision. 'Thirteen years, when it really comes down to it, doesn't mean anything. It's just a bloody long amount of time.'

'It means *everything*. And don't *I* mean something?' Despite all her good intentions and the way that Jack's anguish was tugging at her heart – even though he had no right to act like he was suffering too – Hope could feel the anger bubbling up. 'God, you haven't even said you're sorry!'

'Well, of course I'm sorry!' Jack said, like it was obvious when it really, really wasn't. 'It goes without saying.'

'No, it doesn't. You should have at least, at the very least, said you were sorry. Are you sorry? Are you?' Hope didn't know why she was getting so riled up about saying sorry, when Jack's failure to say sorry was the most minor of all his crimes.

'How can you even ask me that?' Jack demanded and he sounded as if he was also losing his grip on behaving like a calm, reasonable adult. 'I might not have said those exact words but . . .'

'Well, you should have, because they're fucking important words,' Hope snapped and she was never going to get over this, because she'd never be able to bury the hurt deep enough, it would always be lurking just below the surface, ready to rise to the top and scream out its pain. 'You should have said sorry for fucking her and lying, God, you've lied so much . . . You're disgusting!'

Jack threw his phone charger across the room. 'I did a disgusting thing, that doesn't make me a disgusting person,' he shouted back. 'You ever thought that maybe if everything was good between us I wouldn't have even looked twice at Susie? But things haven't been good for ages, and that's just as much your fault as it is mine. Maybe more, because you're the one with this pathological need to get engaged and you use sex as a bargaining tool and then there's the way you . . .'

Hope sank down on to the bed and clapped her hands over her ears because she couldn't bear to listen to this. It was all her worst fears realised. She let Jack's words become white noise, a static, chaotic screeching in her head, and it took her some time to realise that Jeremy was standing in the bedroom doorway, his mouth open, and she shook her head just in time to hear him roar at Jack, 'Don't you dare talk to my sister like that!'

Then he charged at Jack with an angry bellow, while all Hope could do was stare in frozen horror, until Jeremy tripped over the laundry basket she'd left in the middle of the floor and the moment shifted from high-octane drama to slapstick, as Jeremy windmilled his arms and pedalled his legs in an effort to stay upright.

At least it made Jack come to his senses. He grabbed Jeremy before he could hit the floor, then looped an arm round his shoulders and tried to ruffle his hair as the younger boy struggled away. 'It's all right, Budly,' Jack said gently, a shadow passing over his face when Jeremy refused to look at him. 'Sometimes Hopey and I fight. It's not the end of the world.'

'I *heard* you.' Jeremy looked over at Hope, who tried to smile, tried to show that it wasn't the end of the world, not exactly, but she obviously didn't succeed because Jeremy turned back to Jack with an ugly scowl on his face. 'You're a fucking bastard!' He said it quickly and bravely, like it was the very worst thing he could ever think of calling someone. It probably was, and this time the ache Hope felt was for her little brother, because she had a horrible feeling that he'd just come of age right there in her bedroom. His hero had come crashing down off his pedestal, and even if he'd only suspected it before, he now knew that grown-ups were shitty and mean and not worthy of his adulation.

'It's OK, Jerry,' Hope said, standing up so she could give him a hug. 'It's all going to be fine.'

It wasn't going to be fine. Jeremy was hugging her back for one thing.

Jack tried again. 'Let's go down the park and have a kick-about, Budly.'

Jeremy stiffened in Hope's arms and turned round so quickly that he almost fell over again. 'I'm not five!' he said scathingly. 'Stop calling me that stupid nickname, and I hate football and I hate you and I don't want to go anywhere with you ever again, so just fu . . . just go away!'

'You'll probably feel better for some fresh air,' Hope said, because this wasn't about her (that was certainly becoming a general and overriding theme), this was about Jack and Jeremy.

'I hate fresh air too!' Jeremy shouted. 'I hate everything!'

Hope wouldn't have believed it was possible, but she and

Jack shared an exasperated eye-roll, and being so in tune with him, if only for a brief moment, felt bittersweet. Actually, more bitter than sweet.

'Maybe you should go?' Hope suggested hesitantly to Jack with an apologetic smile. 'And Jeremy will see you tomorrow. You could go to the skate shop and then the IMAX, and isn't there a sushi place on the South Bank?'

Jack played along. 'Yeah, there is. We could go there for lunch.'

'No, we couldn't, because I'm not going anywhere with you,' Jeremy said belligerently. 'I know what you did and you're trying to make out that it's all Hopey's fault. She's right, you're *disgusting*.'

'Look, Budly, it's not as simple as that,' Jack said and his voice wasn't gentle any more, but strained, like he was barely managing to control his anger. 'You'll understand when you're a bit older.'

Yeah, you'll understand that adults do really terrible things and then refuse to accept any responsibility for them, Hope wanted to say, but instead she smiled tightly.

Jeremy wasn't buying it either. 'No,' he said, shaking his head violently. 'No. I thought you were cool, really cool, and you're not. You're crap.'

There was no point in arguing with Jeremy when he had his cob on. It was like trying to wade through treacle in gumboots. Jack had obviously reached the same conclusion. 'Fine, whatever,' he snarled as he zipped up his holdall. 'I don't fucking need this.'

'Don't take it out on him,' Hope warned in a low voice, because it worked both ways. If she had to choose between placating Jeremy and placating Jack, then Jeremy was going to win every time. And not just because Jack was doing his utmost to make Hope hate him. Jeremy was her baby brother and he held great sway with her mother, too. There was no contest.

Hope made a subtle shooing motion to Jeremy but he

stayed where he was, arms folded, like he was her body-guard and was going to stay right where he was in case Jack turned nasty. Or nastier.

'This will all be fine,' Hope said, mostly to puncture a hole in the tense, thick atmosphere, rather than because she believed it any more. 'You'll see.'

'No, Hopey, it's not going to be fine,' Jack barked, hoisting up his bag with a vicious movement. 'I only really came round to get some stuff, and you know what, Budly, I've got better things to do with my days off than babysitting you.'

He bumped shoulders with Hope on his way out of the room, Jeremy standing aside to let him pass, and Hope realised she was holding her breath and she couldn't exhale until she heard the front door slam shut behind him. Then she let out the breath she was holding and turned round so she wouldn't have to see the look on Jeremy's face.

She nearly screamed when she felt Jeremy's arms awkwardly wrap around her, while trying to avoid touching her boobs. 'There, there,' he said gruffly. 'You're better off without him.'

It was so like something that her father would say – in fact, Hope was sure that her father had said something very similar when she'd been sacked from her first Saturday job in the local chemist for daydreaming and trying out the nail-varnish testers when she should have been working – that she stifled a giggle.

Jeremy must have thought it was a stifled sob and decided to redouble his efforts. One heavy hand landed on her head and attempted to stroke Hope's hair, which was tangled and knotty, because Hope's second-day hair was always tangled and knotty, and his fingers got stuck. The other arm continued to clasp her, but it felt less like a hug and more like the Heimlich manoeuvre.

This time Hope did laugh and Jeremy tensed up. 'You're not hysterical, are you?' he asked fearfully.

'No, no,' Hope assured him. 'I'm fine. Really I am.'

Then she burst into tears.

Jeremy had no idea what to do with a sobbing female once he'd exhausted the awkward hugging and hair-stroking, but he tried his best.

As Hope curled up in a forlorn heap on her bed, hiccupping and spluttering in a futile attempt to choke back the sobs, Jeremy disappeared into the kitchen and returned half an hour later with a mug of very sweet, very milky tea, some chargrilled toast and half a bar of cooking chocolate.

It was very sweet and just made Hope cry harder.

Eventually she was able to stumble to the lounge and curl up on the sofa where Jeremy brought her a pint glass full of white wine, because he really had no idea about these sorts of things.

Or maybe he had exactly the right idea because when the glass was half empty (Hope was definitely in a glass-half-empty mindset), she did feel a bit better.

'I'm sorry about all that,' she said to Jeremy, who was sitting next to her, watching *Extreme Makeover Home Edition* without a murmur of complaint. 'I'm sure we'll work our way through it.'

Jeremy made an indistinct sound, not his usual grunt, but something wordless that seemed to convey his deep scepticism that Jack and Hope would work their way through it.

Hope ploughed on regardless. 'If you want to hang out with him tomorrow and Tuesday, I'm sure he'd love that. I know he said that he didn't want to, but he was just angry. Not with you, with me,' she added.

'I don't,' Jeremy said baldly. 'Not after what he said and, like, the things he's done. Y'know, the cheating and stuff.'

He must have heard every single shouted word, Hope thought to herself, as she struggled to appear calm. 'You don't need to worry about that and if you don't want to hang with Jack, well, I'll take you out. I'll phone up the drama-workshop people and pretend I've got flu.'

Jeremy looked utterly scandalised, like he thought only Jack had the monopoly on duplicitous behaviour. 'You can't do that. You said it was important and the school was making you go.' He swallowed manfully. 'It's all right, Hopey. I can just stay here and play on the Xbox.'

Poor, poor Jeremy. Packed off to London under extreme duress and now confined to quarters. 'What if I find some other people to take you out?'

'I'm not some little kid!'

'I know you're not,' Hope said quickly, patting one plump knee, then snatching her hand away because it was hard to know where Jeremy's personal-space boundaries started and finished. 'But you can't stay indoors for two days solid playing *Warcraft III*, and I do know some cool people, FYI.'

'If you say so,' Jeremy huffed, but then he nudged her with his elbow and Hope realised that was meant to be a joke.

Though once she was in the kitchen scrolling through her contact numbers it was painfully obvious that the number of cool people she knew who would be happy to ferry Jeremy around town was limited. All artboys were obviously out of bounds as they were Jack's friends. Elaine, Simon and their two tearaway teen daughters were camping in Devon. Allison was willing to take him but she could only do two hours on Tuesday morning, when he could tag along with her to a craft fair at Olympia, and Hope didn't think that either of them would enjoy themselves. Lauren had gone back to Whitfield to see her parents, and it transpired that Jack had prior claim on all their other cool friends because he'd met them first.

Hope had hit the W section of her contacts when she saw Wilson's number, though she could have sworn she'd deleted him from her phone. Actually, she couldn't even remember putting his number into her phone in the first place, but there it was, and hadn't Wilson mentioned that he was also closely acquainted with a grunting teenage boy?

Hope's finger hovered. Did she really have the balls to phone him up and throw herself on his tender mercy, when his mercy was usually the absolute opposite of tender?

The sounds of ancient warcraft were clearly audible from the lounge and anything had to be better than Jeremy cooped up indoors playing violent computer games, and Wilson could say no if he wanted to, and well, it was worth the longest of long shots . . .

Wilson answered just as Hope thought the call was going to roll to voicemail and she'd have to leave a garbled message.

Still, his 'Hello? Hope?' sounded surprised and a little forbidding.

'Hi,' she squeaked. 'Is this a bad time?'

It wasn't, or Wilson said it wasn't, though it sounded like a football match was going on in the background.

'I called to thank you for the photos,' Hope said, although she really hadn't, much to her shame. She should have phoned to thank him for sending the photos anyway. After half-term, she'd have to remember to get Blue Class to make Wilson a thank-you card. 'The kids were really excited and they've chosen their favourites, and they're going to be part of a special nature display on the headmaster's notice board.'

'Good,' Wilson said. 'Email me the numbers from the contact sheets, I'll get them printed up for you. Probably end of the week. Is that all right?'

'Well, it's half-term, so no rush.' Hope bit her lip and tried to rehearse what she needed to ask in the three seconds before Wilson said:

'Great. So anything else . . . ?'

He was usually hard to talk to, but even worse on the phone. 'So . . . you know you said that your nephew worked with you . . . ?'

'I'd hardly call it "work". More like flounces about and argues with me every time I ask him to do something,' Wilson said dryly. 'Fancy taking him off my hands for an afternoon? Not sure you can motivate him with the promise of stickers, but it might work with lager and crisps.'

Hope picked up a flyer for the posh pizza place that she only ordered from just after payday. Once this call was over, she was so treating herself to a huge Quattro Formaggi thin crust with extra toppings.

'I think I might have mentioned it, but I actually have a surly teenager of my own for this week,' she began cautiously. 'My little brother, Jeremy, and he's not so much surly as fifteen and angst-ridden.' She hoped that Jeremy couldn't hear her pithy summing-up of his character. 'And the thing is, he was going to spend tomorrow and Tuesday with Jack, except that's kind of not really going to happen now.'

'Oh, why not?' Wilson asked in surprise.

'We decided to spend some time apart.' It hurt to even say that much, like a nagging toothache that she'd only just got under control, then forgotten about, and bitten on something hard so the raw throb was rearing up all over again. 'Well, it's complicated, and I don't want to bore you with all the details.'

'And this surly younger brother can't be left unattended?'

Hope was so grateful that Wilson didn't probe the subject of her and Jack any further that she immediately launched into a long account of Jeremy's disastrous trip to Covent Garden, which was a little disloyal of her, especially as, 'He's not that surly. Not all the time, and he can also be really sweet, and I've been roped into this two-day drama work-shop, and I wondered if maybe your nephew could show him round town or something,' she finished weakly, because why would Wilson's nephew want to get stuck playing guide for some kid he didn't know when he was meant to be working, and what was it about Wilson that made Hope yammer and yammer until she felt short of breath?

'I need Alfie at the studio Monday and Tuesday,' Wilson said, and he didn't even sound the slightest bit apologetic, but why should he? 'Doing a big two-day shoot for one of the Sunday supplements and he needs to shift his scrawny arse and do some work for once.'

'Well, I figured it was worth a try,' Hope said brightly, though she felt distinctly un-bright. 'And really, thanks again for the photos.'

She was all set to ring off and ask Jeremy if he'd like to come to the drama workshop with her, if she paid him fifty quid to sit quietly in the corner with a book, when Wilson coughed. 'This shoot I'm doing ... it's ten new bands recreating classic shots of old bands, like The Beatles on the zebra crossing outside Abbey Road Studios, and that Who shot with Pete Townshend in the Union Jack jacket.'

'That sounds like a lot to get through,' Hope said politely. 'No wonder you need Alfie around.'

'The thing is, I could probably do with an extra pair of hands. Is your brother any good at making tea?'

Hope thought back to the milky abomination Jeremy had presented her with a couple of hours ago. 'He's a champion tea-brewer.'

'It's an early start. He has to be at the studio at eight sharp, and if he doesn't get in my way and doesn't annoy me by asking anyone for their autograph, I might have him back on Tuesday, too.'

'He'll be as good as gold, I promise,' Hope assured Wilson fervently. 'Thank you so much. He said he'd be all right here but I don't think it's healthy for him to spend so much time playing computer games, and he's had a pretty rotten time in London so far. It'll mean . . .'

'Just as long as you're not sticking me with a younger version of Alfie,' Wilson warned her. 'And I've never heard of half of these bands and Alfie just sneered when he saw the list, so maybe – Jeremy, is it?'

'Jez,' Hope said firmly.

'Well, maybe he can fill in some of the blanks for me.'

Wilson made Hope write down a list of the bands, and she promised that Jeremy would be on his absolute best behaviour and if he wasn't, she'd come and pick him up immediately. Then the football-match background noise increased in intensity and volume and Wilson said he had to go.

'Thanks again,' Hope bleated inadequately. 'You've been so kind with the photos and now this . . . You have to let me make it up to you.'

'You don't have to do that,' Wilson said rather stiffly. 'I'm sure you'd do the same for me.'

Hope wasn't too sure about that. Unless Wilson knew a six-year-old who was having trouble tying their shoelaces or needed help with their two-times table. Once she'd rung off, she decided that if Jeremy didn't make a complete nuisance of himself and Wilson didn't put the fear of God into him, then maybe she'd invite Wilson and Alfie round for dinner on Friday night, as a little farewell send-off for Jeremy. Then she remembered what had happened the last time she threw a dinner party and shuddered. Taking them out for a curry would work just as well.

Chapter Nineteen

Getting Jeremy up at six thirty was almost as bad as trying to get Jack up for eight o'clock. Though Jack never spent ages in the bathroom applying eyeliner and using almost an entire tube of Hope's Frizz-Ease serum on his hair.

Hope had ironed his favourite black T-shirt, which was identical to all his other black T-shirts, and though he'd done a very undignified jig when Hope had told him about Wilson's offer and shown him the list of bands, this morning he was sullen and jumpy. He'd even told Hope to 'piss off' when she tried to make him eat some breakfast before they left the house to make the journey to Kentish Town.

Sitting uncomfortably between a joiner's yard and a shabby office complex that looked as if it hadn't had a paint job since the 1970s was a five-storey, red-brick building with huge lead-glass windows and an engraved keystone over the heavy metal door giving the year of construction as 1897. Wilson's studio was on the fourth floor. Although it was ten to eight and Jeremy wanted to lurk for ten minutes, 'because we can't turn up on time. It's so lame,' Hope ignored him and pressed the buzzer. As they climbed up the stairs, Jeremy's face was ashen rather than ruddy. 'It's very exciting,' she told him. 'Making tea for all those bands.'

'Whatever.'

'And think of the bragging rights when you go back to school next week,' she insisted, as they reached the fourth floor.

'Like, anyone will even believe me!' Jeremy snapped, as they stepped through the open door into the studio, which was a huge stark white space. One wall was almost entirely made up of windows so the studio was full of natural light. It was also full of activity.

There were several scruffy young men manhandling lights, ladders and huge cable spools. Caterers were assembling a substantial breakfast buffet on a trestle table, and beyond them in an alcove that led to a small dressing room was a bevy of girls unpacking clothes and arranging them on rails.

'I thought it was just going to be this Wilson bloke and that Alfie.' Jeremy turned accusing eyes on his sister. 'You never said there'd be so many people.'

'I didn't know myself.' Hope looked around the cavernous space and tried to spot Wilson when a tall, lanky youth detached himself from the throng and loped over.

'Jez, right?' he grunted. 'Alfie. We're about to hang the backdrop. It's white. Are your hands clean?'

They were spotless because Hope had stood over Jeremy and made him go to town with a bar of soap and a nail-brush, so Jeremy grunted in the affirmative and trotted off with Alfie without even a backward glance at Hope or a goodbye. Now Hope knew what it felt like to be one of those mothers who couldn't let go on the first day of the school year.

'Ring and let me know how you're getting on,' she called after Jeremy, who finally turned round and gave her a positively demonic glare.

Hope didn't hear from Jeremy for the rest of the day, so she supposed that he was getting on all right. Or else he wasn't getting on and had already been fired and was too scared to tell her.

She eventually got a text from him at six: *working l8. W wll drv me back 2 urs*. Instead of occupying her alone-time by crying or phoning Jack and begging him to come home,

Hope did her workshop homework and wrote a short dramatic scene that would make full use of thirty six-year-olds but not tax their tiny brains. Then she did have a little cry when she retrieved a pair of Jack's socks that had ended up under the bed. But before the little cry could upgrade to a big ugly cry she dutifully called both her grandmas for a catch-up, but mostly listened to them complain about their various ailments and by then it was eight o'clock and Jeremy still wasn't home and hadn't replied to the seven text messages she'd sent him.

There was nothing to do but try Jack's mobile, which insisted 'this number is temporarily unavailable'. Then she called his work extension to see if he was still at the office, but he wasn't, and Hope even contemplated calling Susie to see if he was there, though she didn't know what she wanted to say to him. Didn't know what she could say to him that would make him change his mind. There wasn't much else Hope could do except let the pain roll over her, but then Lauren called to see how she was holding up. 'I'm barely holding up,' Hope told her but it took another hour to describe in detail all the ways that she was barely holding up and when Lauren finally rang off Hope realised it was half past nine. She was just about to put on her shoes so she could drive down to the studio to retrieve Jeremy and give Wilson a stern lecture on child-labour laws, when there was a ring on the bell.

As she opened the door she heard a car horn beep and saw Wilson drive away but she was more interested in the blissed-out expression on Jeremy's face. He hadn't looked that happy since Christmas 1998 when he'd received all four Teletubbies and a blue tricycle with a bell.

'How did it go?' she asked, as she shut the door behind him.

'It was a-maaa-zing,' came the reply. 'It was, like, the most awesome day of my whole entire life. God, I've got so much to tell you!'

Jeremy talked for over an hour, pausing only to demolish a packet of Penguins and drink two mugs of tea. He'd spent the day fetching and carrying and lugging, had learned all about light meters and Coloramas, and he'd hung out with five bands 'and they weren't at all up themselves'. And despite Wilson's ban on Jeremy having his photo taken in close proximity to any musician, Jeremy showed Hope a fistful of Polaroids of him snuggling up to all five bands, all taken by Wilson as he supposedly tested out the lighting.

It was all 'Wilson says' and 'Alfie thinks', and there wasn't a murmur of protest when it got to eleven and Hope told Jeremy to go to bed because he had another six a.m. start the next day. On the contrary, there was a spontaneous hug and an effusive, 'Thanks for setting this up, Hopey. You're the best sister ever.'

The next morning when she dropped Jeremy off, minus guyliner and hair products because 'Alfie says that girls aren't into all that', Hope did see Wilson. Or at least she assumed it was Wilson because it looked *exactly* like him, but the man in question was simultaneously checking something on a MacBook, fiddling with something that Hope thought might be a light meter, and chatting away to three people, *and* he had a broad smile on his face. It was most disconcerting, but Hope had never seen Wilson in his natural habitat before, only in social situations when he seemed entirely ill at ease. The ear-to-ear grin and relaxed stance suited him a lot better, Hope decided – he looked almost friendly. She wondered whether she should go and say hello but then they were waylaid by the famous Alfie, who spirited Jeremy off to find an extra ladder, and Hope felt like she couldn't just march over to Wilson when he was obviously busy.

At least it meant that Hope could attend the second day of the drama workshop with a lighter heart and a less distracted head. Though she wouldn't admit it to Dorothy, when she was inevitably grilled about it the following Monday morning, it had been very useful.

Hope had learned that it didn't matter what she got the Red Class to do because they'd muck it up anyway but they'd look so cute while they were mucking it up that no one would care. The attendees had also shared tips on how to rope reluctant parents into making costumes and helping out backstage, had had a two-hour pub lunch, which was light on the lunch and heavy on the alcohol, and when they'd got back to the stuffy conference room in Marble Arch, they'd taken turns brainstorming each other's drama crises.

Hope was a lot happier (or less panic-stricken, in her current emotional state, happier was pushing it) about the Winter Pageant, now she had plans to make Yellow Class tell the story of Chanukah through the medium of song and force nine of them to become a human menorah.

Even better, two of the other workshoppers, Michael and Elise, were from a school in Newham, and they'd made plans to all meet up in a couple of weeks' time. After all, Hope had a vacancy on the friend front and neither Michael nor Elise, who were a couple, seemed like the type who'd run off with Hope's boyfriend. Hope couldn't bear to think about whether she still had a boyfriend but if, no, *when* Jack came back to her, it would be good if all her friends were so reliable that she'd never have to worry about leaving Jack alone in a room with them.

'We should get together for a drink. Bring your mob along,' Michael had said when they all finally piled out of the conference room and stood out on the street, gratefully breathing in huge lungfuls of fresh air. It was starting to get properly cold now, with that crisp, pre-frost nip in the air that always made Hope feel excited because it promised Halloween sweets, fireworks and three-week Christmas holidays. 'We can swap war stories.'

Hope was planning to go home and make Jeremy a proper tea so he wouldn't tell Mrs Delafield that he'd been surviving on a diet of toast, pizza, crisps and chocolate, because he *so* would – their mother would winkle the information out of him in five minutes – when she got a text:

Just fnshing up. Pls com & get me. Can i go 2 gig wiv Alfie on Fri? Pls! Pls!

Hope sighed and set off to catch the C2 from Oxford Circus. When she got to Wilson's studio, it was still a hive of activity but it was like a rewind of the hustle and bustle of yesterday morning. There was still the same crew of lanky young men in skinny T-shirts and sloppy jeans, but this time they were dismantling the lighting rigs, rolling up the backdrops and hefting huge flight cases down the stairs. The caterers were collecting empty plates and dirty cups from the trestle table and the stylists were packing away outfits in garment bags.

Hope stood uncertainly by the door, not wanting to get in anyone's way, as she tried to spot Jeremy. Then she saw him standing on the top rung of a ladder doing something with a screwdriver and the room swung wildly around her. She had such bad vertigo that even going down a flight of stairs or looking up at a tall building gave her a headrush and a nauseous feeling, but Jeremy was obviously made of stronger stuff.

She hurried over, all ready to start clucking at him to come down RIGHT NOW before he broke his neck, but before she could get there and clutch hold of Jeremy's leg to save him, she was intercepted by Wilson.

Hope blinked at him unsteadily because he was still smiling and it was slightly unsettling. 'All right?' he enquired cheerfully by way of greeting, which was even more unsettling.

'I'm fine,' Hope said distractedly, turning her attention back to Jeremy, who'd now seen her and was waving happily, when he should have been concentrating on not falling from a great height. 'Is it safe up there? Don't you think he should probably come down? Like, now.'

Wilson glanced over. 'He's been up and down ladders all day. Got a head for heights.'

'I can't even climb on a chair to change a lightbulb or hang a pair of curtains. I start hyperventilating and crying actual tears,' Hope admitted. 'Are you sure he's OK?'

'Don't fuss. He's fine.' Wilson nodded. 'Jerry's a good kid, and because Alfie wanted to be top dog, he got off his lazy arse and behaved himself. It all worked out really well,' he added in a tone of mild incredulity, as if he'd doubted that it would work out at all.

Hope took a while to process this. 'Jerry?' she queried. 'He's back to calling himself Jerry now? Right. I'll have to remember that.'

Wilson grinned and Hope thought that it was a pity that he kept this sunny, smiley version of himself so carefully hidden. 'When I really want to piss off Alfie, I call him Alfred in front of everyone. Works every time.' He touched Hope lightly on the arm. 'There was money in the shoot budget for another assistant so I slipped Jerry a few quid.'

'That's really nice of you, but he's had such a good time, I think he wouldn't have minded paying you.'

The grin disappeared and Wilson shifted uncomfortably. 'I gave him two hundred.'

'Two hundred! I thought we were in the grip of the worst recession since the 1930s!' Hope exclaimed. 'I'm going to charge him rent.'

This time they grinned at each other and it lasted ten companionable seconds before things reverted back to their more usual awkward state.

'Look . . .'

'So . . .'

'You go first . . .'

'Sorry, you were saying . . .'

Wilson gestured with his arm to indicate that Hope had the floor. 'I just wanted to thank you for letting Jeremy spend the last couple of days here. He was having such a rotten time and it's really cheered him up.'

'Don't mention it. Like I said, the kid was a big help.'

Be that as it may, and Hope doubted that Jeremy's tea- and toast-making abilities had passed muster, reparations needed to be made.

'Well, I *am* grateful and it needs mentioning,' she insisted. 'And we, Jeremy and I – well, would you and Alfie have tea with us on Friday?'

The frown on Wilson's face was much more familiar than the grinning and the smiling. 'Tea as in dinner?'

Hope nodded. She'd lived down South for five years now, but dinner would always be tea, as far as she was concerned.

The frown deepened. 'Are you having another dinner party?'

'No! Not ever, ever again.' Hope winced. 'I was thinking I could take us all out for a curry on Friday evening if you're not too busy. Alfie as well.'

'We can't,' said a plaintive voice behind her. 'There's a gig. I texted you.'

'You were very short on details,' Hope said, relieved that Jeremy was back on solid ground, even if he was being exceedingly whiny. 'What gig? Where? What time does it end?'

Two of the bands that Wilson had shot were playing Friday night at the Forum, at the other end of Kentish Town. Alfie and Jeremy were on the guest list, there was talk of backstage passes and an unprompted promise that Jeremy would steer clear of the moshpit.

It was a scenario that would have had her mother going into conniptions at the thought of her baby going to a rock concert in the company of a boy with a pierced nose, two tattoos and jeans slung so low that Hope could see his red pants. She was on the verge of refusing to give permission when she thought back to her own teens and how she'd never bothered to ask her parents if she could go into town to see a band. She'd just pretend that she was going to a sleepover and change on the bus into town while getting absolutely hammered on lime-flavoured Bacardi Breezers. Ah, life had been much simpler back then.

And hadn't her mother also said that she trusted Hope to use her better judgement if Jeremy wanted to do something liable to cause him bodily harm? To use her better judgement and establish clear-cut boundaries? 'Well, I don't know,' Hope mused, mostly because it made Jeremy pull an imploring face that made him look like about five. 'No after-show, no stage-diving and absolutely no alcohol. I repeat, *no* alcohol.'

Jeremy's face drooped down to his shoes, then he gave a double-take. 'I can go? Really? You mean it? Is there a catch? There has to be a catch.'

'No alcohol,' Hope repeated sternly.

'Cool,' Alfie said, hands in the pockets of his jeans. 'We can be, like, straight-edge for one night.'

Jeremy was happy. Alfie appeared to be happy and Wilson had yet to be thanked adequately. She could still invite Wilson to dinner on Friday night while Jeremy was getting up to all sorts of no good at the Forum, but the thought of sitting opposite him in a restaurant, shoved into the bit with all the other couples out for a romantic evening, seemed to shriek 'date'. And they'd have to talk to each other for at least ninety minutes, maybe even a couple of hours.

'We're going out on Friday,' Hope announced in such a squeaky voice that all three of them looked at her strangely. 'To the skate shop in Covent Garden, then I said we'd go to the South Bank and walk down to Tate Modern to see that exhibition with the porcelain sunflower seeds. If you two would like to come as well,' she added, looking first at Alfie and then Wilson so it was clear which two she meant.

Wilson looked at Alfie who shrugged, then Alfie looked at Wilson who shrugged, then turned to Hope. 'That would be fine.'

It was all settled, and time to get Jeremy home and force him to eat a hot, nutritionally balanced meal. 'Great. Well, we'll see you on Friday. Say, eleven at Covent Garden tube?'

There was more shrugging and nodding before Wilson agreed, and just as Hope thought she was free and clear, Wilson smiled. 'You and I might as well go out for our tea, while Alfie and Jerry are at the gig absolutely not drinking alcohol.'

Chapter Twenty

Hope had worried that the two days when it was just her and Jeremy would be awkward, and he'd revert back to being sulky and grunting a lot, but he actually turned out to be really good company.

On the Wednesday they went into town so Jeremy could spend his wages before their mother made him put the money in his savings account. He wanted a new pair of non-skinny jeans because 'Alfie says that even his dad has got a pair of skinny jeans,' he wanted to get his hair cut in the trendy barber's in Soho where Alfie went, and he wanted to go to Forbidden Planet to load up on *Doctor Who* collectibles. Hope felt as if she was getting to know the real Jeremy. Not the annoying toddler, or the spoilt younger brother, or even the whiny teenager, but the person he was slowly becoming who was kind and clever and so funny that he made Hope spit beer all over the table when they went for dim sum in Chinatown and he kept doing sly impressions of their surly waiter.

Thursday was bright and sunny, if nippy, and on a sudden impulse that was carefully nurtured by Jeremy over breakfast, Hope decided to drive to Brighton, even though she hated driving and she particularly hated driving on the motorway.

They poked around the North Laines, where Jeremy spent what was left of his wages on a red military jacket with piping and epaulettes, even though Hope begged him not to. And because they'd driven down and she didn't have to lug stuff back on the train, she could buy more mis-matched crockery, a stack of books and two black vintage dresses, one she could fit into and one she'd be able to fit into once she lost the extra poundage. Which was going to be a long time coming because she and Jeremy shared a bag of hot doughnuts dipped in sugar at the entrance to the Palace Pier, and after they'd been on all the rides twice, they sat on the beach, huddled together for warmth, and ate haddock and chips liberally doused with vinegar.

Then it was back home, stopping en route to pick up chocolate, crisps, red wine for Hope and full-fat coke for Jeremy, so they didn't have to move from the sofa while they watched a double bill of *Superbad* and *Napoleon Dynamite*.

Yes, they'd had a great time and were fast becoming firm friends, but every night when Jeremy was tucked up on the sofa and Hope was alone in her own bed, which still smelt of Jack because she hadn't had time to do a wash, she felt as if she'd been hurled at great speed into the very pits of despair. She couldn't even cry because the walls in the flat were gossamer thin. Instead, Hope would spend the night completely submerged under the duvet, fingers sometimes wedged in her mouth if she felt as if she was about to start sobbing. The secret was to lie very, very still and focus only on the sound of her own ragged breaths and nothing else, because if Hope's attention wavered or she forgot for just one second what she was trying to forget and stretched out her legs or rolled over, she'd have five blissful seconds of feeling all right and feeling normal, then she'd wonder why Jack wasn't curled up next to her and she'd have to remember why he wasn't there and have to experience the pain all over again.

The pain never hurt any less. In fact, it seemed to hurt more, and the only way to squash it down was to get out of bed and pad quietly to the kitchen and make herself a huge cheese and crisp sandwich, which she'd wash down with a large glass of wine.

It was no wonder, then, that on Friday morning Hope was suffering from several nights of sleep deprivation and was having something of a wardrobe dilemma. It was freezing cold, the day was going to feature a lot of walking along the Thames with an icy river breeze tangling up her hair, culminating in a dinner non-date with Wilson, *and* she couldn't fit into any of her clothes that had a waistband. Hope meditatively contemplated her muffin top, which had now been upgraded to a spare tyre, then surveyed her tired selection of school-holiday clothes. It was all very uninspiring and Jeremy hammering on the bedroom door and bellowing, 'We're going to be late!' at five-minute intervals wasn't helping much.

In the end, Hope pulled on her trusty black support-leggings, a fine-knit mossy-green shirt dress with long sleeves and a chunky black coatigan, and rummaged under her bed for hat, scarf and gloves in the plastic crate where she'd packed away all her cold-weather gear. Finally she emerged for Jeremy's impatient inspection. 'You look like a bruise,' he said.

'Yeah? Well, Sergeant Pepper's Lonely Hearts' Club Band called and they want their stupid red jacket back,' Hope snapped as she checked she had her Oyster card.

Jeremy didn't storm from hall to lounge in a huff like he'd have done at the beginning of the week. Instead he gave Hope another once-over, then frowned. 'So, girls in London are *still* wearing Uggs? Right. OK. What*ever.*'

She knew when she was beaten. 'Oh, piss off,' Hope said to a grinning Jeremy, as she pushed him towards the front door.

Being dragged around a skate shop, then having to stand and watch as Jeremy fell off his board in the little skate park on the South Bank wasn't something that Hope was particularly looking forward to. She also didn't know how she was going to get through the day with Wilson being all sneery and perceptive when she wasn't firing on even one cylinder. Her legs felt as if they were made of rubber, her jaw ached from the constant teeth-grinding and her hands were clammy inside her woollen gloves as she and Jeremy fought their way to the ticket barrier and then emerged from Covent Garden station in a tight press of people.

'It's so busy,' Jeremy said, then gave a joyous yelp. 'There's Alfie!'

Hope looked over and yes, there was Alfie, in a bright-red hoodie the same shade as Jeremy's jacket so they'd be easy to spot if they wandered off, along with two girls, in skimpy T-shirts, tight black skirts that could have doubled as belts, fishnet tights and Converses, who'd turned looking non-chalant into an artform. And finally, raising a hand in greeting, was Wilson, wearing dark-blue 501s, a black jumper and black leather jacket, and still managing to look less bruise-like than Hope.

The four of them were standing outside Oasis, clutching cups of coffee, as Jeremy bounded over, followed more slowly by Hope. She felt completely out of her depth, like a proper stuffy grown-up compared to the four teenagers (it turned out that Belle and Lucy were sixteen and eighteen respectively and nieces of Wilson and cousins of Alfie). She had more in common with him than she did with them, Hope thought, as Jeremy was welcomed into the fold and she was left to fall into step with Wilson, as they crossed over Long Acre and slowly walked down Neal Street, accosted by *Big Issue* sellers, chuggers and touters from the local hairdressing salons who all wanted to know where Hope got her hair cut.

She pulled her hat down over her hair that hadn't seen the touch of a professional hairdresser in well over a year and tried to think of something to say to Wilson. 'So, is this your sum total of nieces and nephews?'

He shook his head. 'I left the London-based under-sixteens at home.'

What with four full siblings, two half-siblings and five step-siblings, Wilson had nearly twenty-three (his half-sister Louise was due to give birth any day) nieces and nephews scattered from London to Preston and all points in between.

It was amazing that Wilson came from such a large family yet remained so taciturn. Maybe he'd never been able to get a word in edgeways, Hope mused as the pair of them were banished from the tiny skate shop ('Hopey, you're just getting in the way and asking stupid questions') and had to sit shivering outside in Neal's Yard drinking excellent coffee from the Monmouth Coffee shop just around the corner.

Then it was a slow walk through Covent Garden to the Strand and across the Thames on Jubilee Bridge. The South Bank was heaving with people: gangs of kids on half-term, tourists wrapped up warmly as they took pictures of each other by the sculptures, lunchtime joggers weaving through the crowd and people braving the cold to sit at the tables outside the restaurants beneath the Royal Festival Hall.

There was some problem with adjusting the new wheels on Jeremy's skateboard, which Wilson helped with, so Hope was left with Belle and Lucy who asked what she did for a living and then shied away in horror when she confessed the awful truth. In the end she left the five of them to it while she browsed the second-hand book stall, picking up a pristine Winston Churchill biography, which would make an excellent Christmas present for her dad, and a copy of *The Velveteen Rabbit* for Blue Class's book corner. Then force of habit made her pick up a book about The Beatles, which she knew Jack didn't have. Hope hesitated, then slotted the book back into place, and as she did it she shivered in a way that had nothing to do with the wind whipping past her, but because that small gesture seemed to prove that their relationship was dead.

It was one of those fatal thoughts that she didn't want to think, so Hope deliberately and ruthlessly pushed it away as she reached for the new Jilly Cooper. Comfort eating wasn't doing her any favours so maybe comfort reading would be kinder to her waistline.

As she was about to pay, Hope spotted a Diane Arbus biography, about whom she knew practically nothing except that she was an American photographer who'd taken gloomy but beautiful black-and-white pictures of odd-looking people. She could give it to Jeremy to give to Wilson to say thank you for going absolutely above and beyond what could possibly be termed as doing someone a favour.

Hope glanced over her shoulder. Alfie and Jeremy were finally on their skateboards. Jeremy was surprisingly adept at twisting and turning and flipping off the end of ramps and slopes without falling off. It was rather lovely to see him take such absolute delight in what he was doing, and Hope was glad to see Wilson snapping away at the pair of them on a small fiddly-looking digital camera.

Belle and Lucy were nowhere to be seen, and Hope was surplus to requirements so she drifted over to the river's edge and gazed out over the water. To her left was the London Eye and past that the Houses of Parliament, and to her right, the City skyline: St Paul's Cathedral, the NatWest Tower, the Gherkin and other buildings that were familiar to her, even if she couldn't name them. It was a view that never failed to stir her, the old in harmony with the new, the city evolving and growing and changing before her eyes. Hope still didn't really think of London as home, but when she came down to the river, she felt as if she was part of London, even as she was humbled by it at the same time.

Just looking at the cityscape and the backdrop of blue skies and fluffy clouds that looked as if they'd been painted on was making big, sad emotions well up in Hope. Emotions that made her swipe a gloved hand under her eyes to mop up tears that she couldn't blame on the wind. She almost screamed when she felt a hand on her shoulder, but it was just Wilson who gave her one of his patented squinty-eyed, penetrating looks but didn't say anything other than that their four teenage charges wanted to get sushi for lunch.

The day dragged on and on and on. There were a few moments of light relief, like Jeremy coming to the swift realisation that he *hated* sushi apart from the crispy salmon skin and despatching Hope to Pret A Manger to buy him a sandwich. She also had to bite her lip many times to suppress the giggles because Jeremy, Alfie, Belle and Lucy's conversation consisted of one of them suddenly announcing, 'Ha! Simon Cowell!' or, 'Urgh! Legwarmers!' or even, 'Cupcakes are so sad,' and then they'd all make sneery comments about the item in question. The four of them were getting on famously, which was more than could be said for Hope and Wilson.

Hope had never known him so monosyllabic. Not even the first few times that she'd met him when he'd been her newish friend's new boyfriend and Susie had already said that she didn't think he was a keeper. What with the strain of making forced conversation, the constant threat of tears because of the stupid book about The Beatles and the wind smacking her in the face as they walked down to Tate Modern, browsed through Borough Market, then ended up at the Design Museum, Hope felt as if steel bands were slowly crushing her skull. Her head throbbed in time with every step she took and when they got to London Bridge tube it was only six o'clock. The gig didn't start until eight, so it would be hours before Hope could go home and not sleep, perchance to dream.

Jeremy was adamant that they had time to go to Oxford Street so he could visit Niketown and take photos for the kids back home, and Belle and Lucy wanted to go to 'Topshop and Urban Outfitters and we might as well go to American Apparel while we're there'. It was all Hope could do not to sink down on to the pavement and refuse to take another step.

'Well, you need to have some tea before the gig,' she murmured weakly.

'Yeah, but we don't need to be there the minute the doors open,' Alfie said scathingly. 'And the first support band suck.'

'Yeah, they really suck,' Belle and Lucy said in unison, while Jeremy nodded in agreement.

'Shut up,' Wilson suddenly growled at the four of them. 'Just about had enough of you lot.'

'Yeah, but . . .'

'Shut it, Alfred,' Wilson said in a way that sent shivers down Hope's spine but Alfie just grinned slyly, as if he was used to having his God-given name snarled at him like that. Wilson pulled out his wallet and handed his nephew a couple of twenty-pound notes. 'Go to bloody Oxford Street, then use this money to get some dinner, and I want receipts and change.'

'Why?'

'Because I want proof that you didn't spend the money on tacky shit and pick and mix.'

'We *so* wouldn't do that,' Lucy breathed, but Hope knew she *so* would. It was exactly what she used to do whenever she'd got slipped a tenner by an unsuspecting grandparent.

Hope reached for her own purse and put another twenty pounds in the kitty. 'For pudding and soft drinks,' she said with a significant glare that made the steel bands tighten. She wanted to weep tears of unrestrained joy as the four of them trooped into the tube station – until she realised that she and Wilson were the last two standing. Or drooping, in her case.

'Shall we get a taxi?' Wilson asked, already hailing a black cab.

Hope thought about putting up a fight because she'd been spending money like she had a huge trust fund to fall back on, but her head and feet were killing her, and in the end it was easier just to say, 'Thank you,' when Wilson held the door open for her, and sink gratefully on to the seat.

Hope pulled off her hat and rubbed her forehead, as Wilson sat down beside her.

'I told him to go to Kentish Town,' he said. 'Unless you'd rather go home and I could pick Jeremy up later and drop him off?'

Hope thought about spending hours in her empty flat with not much else to do but unleash the onslaught of tears that had been threatening all day. And Wilson had already done her so many favours and she needed to man up, get over herself, take some ibuprofen and treat him to a slap-up meal. Or at least a curry and a couple of bottles of beer.

'Kentish Town is fine,' she said, and it was meant to come out firmly but her voice wavered and she had to swallow hard. 'Though we've got *hours* before they need picking up.'

Wilson stared straight ahead. 'Fancy coming back to mine for a cup of tea?'

No, because that would be weird. Very weird, but it was *still* better than being home alone. 'Tea sounds fine too,' Hope said, and she sat there, her muscles stiff and tense as she tried to think of something else to say.

It took a while. Finally she managed, 'Well, they all seemed to get on, didn't they? Like, they really bonded over slagging off stuff, don't you think?'

'You don't have to talk,' Wilson said. His lips twisted as Hope cringed. 'I mean, the silence won't kill us, and you look like you've got a headache.' He lightly touched the spot between her eyebrows where the pain had centred. 'You've had a little furrow there for the last hour.'

Wilson's hand moved up to cover her forehead. Hope didn't think she was running a temperature but the feel of his cool fingers on her head was kind of soothing, or maybe it was the small, unexpected pleasure of someone being concerned about her. 'I just need some painkillers,' she muttered. 'I have some in my bag, but I can't take them dry.'

She was no good at silence, never had been, but at least

Wilson's hand was back on his lap. The concern had been nice but it had also made her even more likely to start weeping. Hope shut her eyes and leaned her head back and let the steady put-put-put of the engine lull her into a gentle doze that was only disturbed when they had to stop at a red light or went over a speed bump.

Wilson wouldn't let Hope pay for the cab. He even went as far as batting her hand away when she proffered a crumpled ten-pound note. There was nothing else to do but follow him through the door of his building, up the stairs and through the dark studio.

He paused at the bottom of the iron spiral staircase that led up to his apartment. 'I'm just going to nick some milk out of the fridge in the studio kitchen, but you go up, you know the way.'

Hope did know the way from her only previous visit, which had been to pick up Susie en route for a night drinking martinis and dancing at the Hideaway in Tufnell Park. Then she'd only had a vague impression of metal joists and industrial light fittings, as Susie had hopped about on one foot in her underwear, squawking because the strap had broken on her favourite pair of sandals.

Upstairs was similar to downstairs: a vast expanse of white walls, big windows and knotted, untreated floorboards, with a galleried bedroom up a small flight of slatted stairs. There was a galley kitchen running along the back wall and a brushed-steel dining table with matching chairs around it, but Wilson, coming up the spiral stairs with a carton of milk, was gesturing in the direction of a huge leather Chesterfield. It was a weathered tan colour and so big that two people could have lain on it quite happily, but Hope perched uncomfortably at one end and looked over with some trepidation at Wilson who was already in the kitchen and busy with the tea-making.

Hope watched surreptitiously as Wilson filled the kettle and got down mugs, humming a jaunty tune as he worked.

He was being really nice, or rather he hadn't said anything sarcastic for at least an hour, and it was very discomfiting.

As she heard the whistle of the kettle (why couldn't Wilson have a regular plug-in kettle like a normal person?) Hope was composed enough to be able to look at her surroundings in more detail.

On the wall opposite her were three poster-sized, tinted photos of sights that were instantly familiar to her: Blackpool Tower all lit up, the retro '50s ice-cream van from Morecambe which bore the legend *Everyday is Like Sundae*, and Southport Pier. All three photographs made her think of those long childhood summers of day trips to the seaside and fighting with her brothers as they made huge sandcastle cities with their own complex drainage systems, then driving home to Whitfield, sleepy from too much sun and ice-cream. God, life had been so much simpler when all Hope had worried about was trying to mastermind the downfall of her three older, bossier brothers, Adrian, Luke and Matthew.

Hope was just remembering the time they'd buried her up to her neck in sand for *hours* and told their parents that she had run away, only confessing to their crime once the police had been called, when Wilson emerged from the kitchen with a laden tray.

Hope struggled upright from her despondent slump to accept a steaming mug of tea with a muttered 'Thanks'. Wilson sat down right next to her, not saying anything as she took two ibuprofen – normally Hope hated Wilson's silence because he wielded it like a weapon, but right now it was such a relief not to have to talk.

Maybe that was why when she finished her mug of perfectly brewed tea, Hope found herself struggling not to let her head loll on to Wilson's shoulder. Her eyes would drift shut and she'd tune out, only to come back to full consciousness a few seconds later.

She struggled to stay awake, blinking her gritty eyes

furiously, and caught sight of her bulging tote bag perched on the floor. 'I got you something,' she said, and she realised that they'd been sitting in silence for at least twenty minutes. 'To say thank you.'

'We've been through this,' Wilson sighed, leaning forward to put down his empty mug. 'You don't *need* to say thank you for anything.'

'Well, I want to and I saw this' – Hope pulled out the Diane Arbus book – 'and I thought you might like it.'

Wilson opened his mouth, probably to make a stuffy speech about how she had no reason to be beholden to him, so Hope just shoved the book at him so he had no choice but to take it. He glanced down at the cover and a slow smile crept over his face. It was a warm, unguarded smile that Hope had never seen from him before.

'Thank you,' he said simply. 'This has been on my Amazon wishlist for ages.'

That wasn't so difficult, was it? Hope was tempted to say but for once she managed to hold her tongue. She settled back against the cushions with a contented little sigh as Wilson began to flick through the book.

Chapter Twenty-one

She must have dozed off again, because Hope only woke up when the pillow she was snoozing on shifted and someone patted her shoulder.

'If we want to get something to eat before we pick up the awful foursome, we should probably get going,' Wilson said, as Hope's head shot up from where it had been resting on, as she now realised, his chest.

Face flushed, she put a cautious hand to her hair, which felt alarmingly tendril-like. During the day, if it wasn't tightly contained, her hair attracted tangles like ball bearings to a magnet.

To mask her confusion and to gauge exactly how bird's-nesty her hair had got, Hope fished her make-up bag out of her tote and hunted for her pocket mirror. As she suspected, it looked as if someone had plugged her into the national grid and a big, ugly spot was getting ready to hatch on her chin. All this stress was making her lose her looks.

'So, are you hungry?' Wilson prompted.

'Yeah, I could eat,' Hope said casually, when actually it had been at least five hours since she'd last stuffed food into her mouth and she was close to starving. 'Do you still fancy a curry?'

Wilson did and after Hope had retired to the bathroom to heap concealer on her nascent zit, they walked along Kentish Town Road to the Bengal Lancer. It was an Indian restaurant that had spurned the need for red flock wallpaper and big brass vases full of plastic flowers like the curry houses of Rochdale and, indeed, the Holloway Road, in favour of a slick, white minimalist interior. Wilson was obviously a regular as he was greeted cheerily by the staff and they were led to his 'usual table', which was almost by the window but not quite, which suited Hope just fine as she hated eating in full view of anyone who happened to be walking past, especially if that someone was a gang of teenagers.

She was also relieved that the menu wasn't as sleek and minimalist as the restaurant's interior. On the contrary, it was full of dear and familiar spicy friends. Hope and Wilson quickly established that they could both do hot, and ordered accordingly. Soon they were both happily munching away on poppadoms heaped with mango chutney.

They'd reached the lull between courses and the conversation had faded out. They couldn't spend the duration of the meal in silence. Or Hope couldn't, at any rate. 'How did you get into photography?' she asked. 'Was it something you've always wanted to do?'

Wilson pulled a face. 'I will talk under my own steam if you let me.'

'I know that,' Hope said, although all evidence pointed to the contrary. 'But I'm genuinely interested in how you knew that photography was your true calling. I just went into teaching because my parents were teachers and I didn't have a clue what to do with my life.'

'But you like teaching, don't you?' Wilson gestured at the last poppadom and Hope didn't need telling twice. 'You seemed to have Blue Class under firm control, anyway.'

'It's very easy to get six-year-olds to bend to my will.' Hope fixed him with her most teacherly gaze, the one she pulled out when she wanted absolute silence from Blue Class and wasn't getting it. 'Anyway, that's enough about me, I thought we were talking about you.'

'Well, I didn't have a lightbulb moment that I wanted to

take pictures for a living, and I didn't see *Blow-Up* at an impressionable age and think that being a photographer was a passport to orgies with models and the like . . .' Wilson seemed to run out of steam and fidgeted unhappily as the waiter came to remove their poppadom debris.

They both ordered more beer and Wilson seemed to think they were done talking about him, because he refused to look Hope in the eye and instead stared fixedly out of the window. His face was bright red, and though Hope felt sorry that bringing Wilson out of his shell was obviously such an ordeal for him, she was now determined to get to the truth.

'So, no eureka moment or desire to emulate David Bailey . . .' she persisted. 'Come on, don't leave me in suspense.'

Wilson looked around the restaurant for inspiration, or at least the waiter coming with their main course, but when help wasn't at hand, he reluctantly turned to Hope. 'My step-dad's best mate was a photographer,' he said, face now redder even than Hope's when she'd run the bath too hot. 'Nothing fancy, just weddings, christenings, family portraits, stuff like that.'

'And he took you under his wing?'

He shook his head. 'I wasn't very good with people when I was younger.' Every word sounded as if it was being dragged out of him with the assistance of a waterboard and an electrical current. 'The school said it was Social Anxiety Disorder. My mam reckoned I was just shy so she persuaded Mike to let me tag along on some jobs. Thought it would bring me out of myself, having to interact with new people.'

Well, that explained Wilson's gruffness and why he took so long to warm up, Hope decided as the waiter placed a dazzling selection of piping-hot, aromatic dishes in front of them.

'I suppose if you can handle doing wedding photography, then you can handle anything,' she said. 'Even taking pictures in the middle of a warzone. When my oldest brother got married, there was a punch-up in the car park between my next-oldest brother and one of the bride's cousins. I thought my mum was going to kill both of them.'

Wilson grinned, and there was a natural pause in the conversation as they passed dishes back and forth and realised they'd over-estimated how hot they could take their food when they'd ordered the Kalapuri chicken. Once all the toing and froing was over, Wilson went back to the subject in hand, though Hope had thought that she'd have to nag to get him talking again.

'I realised that I loved framing shots and seeing people on their happiest days and I liked pottering away in the dark-room, *and* it got my mam off my back, which was an added bonus.'

'I hear you,' Hope muttered darkly.

From assisting with bouncing babies and blushing brides, Wilson started doing the odd Golden Wedding party himself, then began building up a portfolio by shooting any band who played a gig in Preston. Then he started freelancing for the local papers and London-based music magazines. 'I began a photography degree at Manchester School of Art but halfway through my second year, I was offered a staff job at the *NME* and I jacked it in. My mam had something to say about that, too,' he added with a grin, and even waggled his eyebrows for good measure.

'I guess when you're photographing people either they're the centre of attention or your camera is.' Hope heard what she'd just blurted out and tried to backtrack. 'I mean, I'm not saying that you still have Social Anxiety Disorder. Of course you don't.'

'I know you think I'm bloody-minded, I think I am too, but it's like . . .' Wilson took a ruminative swig from his bottle of Cobra beer. 'It's like when you listen to a recording of your own voice and it makes you cringe . . . Before I say something, I hear myself saying it and then I decide to just shut the fuck up instead. And when I do say stuff, it usually comes out wrong.'

There! Hope knew it wasn't Wilson's fault that he was so horribly blunt and to the point.

'Except when I do say something, can't see any use in faffing about and taking ages not to say what I really mean,' Wilson continued. 'I'm allergic to bullshit.'

'Are you like that with everyone?' Hope asked, but what she really meant was, *So you're not just like that with me, are you?*

'Obviously not with everyone. Family, mates, girlfriends.' Wilson put down his knife and fork. 'Takes me a while to warm to people. And vice versa. Guess you and I must be pretty toasty by now if I'm telling you.'

'I guess we must be,' Hope agreed, ridiculously pleased that Wilson had confided in her, even if it was because she'd badgered him until he'd spilled his secrets.

There wasn't much left in the bowls, but Hope scraped out the residue of the tandoori sauce with the last piece of naan bread, because Wilson had pushed his plate away and obviously didn't intend to eat any more. Hope wished that she had the same kind of restraint.

'So, what's going on with you?' Wilson asked, when there was finally no more food left for Hope to eat, which was just as well as it felt as if she might split the seams of her support leggings.

She shrugged. 'Nothing much. Back to school on Monday, worse luck!'

'I mean, what's with you and Jack?' Wilson clarified. 'Can't be too good if he wasn't around to help out with Jerry.'

'He had to work,' Hope snapped reflexively, then stopped. What was the point of pretending? Wilson pretty much knew what had happened – God, did he ever know! If it wasn't for him, then she'd never have stolen Jack's phone, and that one act of madness led to the fact that it was Friday night and she was out with Wilson on a non-date, even if the waiters kept shooting them approving smiles. Hope decided to try again. 'No, he didn't have to work. You were right. He's still seeing Susie. Or rather, they've been having a full-on affair for months, though I had to steal his phone to discover that because he sure as hell wasn't going to tell me. And then I confronted him about it and smashed his phone and now he's moved out. So, well, that's what's up with me and Jack.'

The horrible lump-in-the-throat, ache-in-the-heart, throb-in-the-tear-ducts feelings from before swept over Hope again. She also felt like she was going to throw up from a surfeit of curry.

Wilson rested his elbows on the table. 'So where is Jack, if he's not at your place?'

Hope stared down at her hands. She had sticky yellow sauce on her fingers, which she started to lick off absent-mindedly, until she realised how disgusting that was and wiped them on a napkin instead. 'Well, he's with Susie,' she said. 'And until I know what he wants to do, until we have a chance to talk about it properly, I'm stuck in this holding pattern.'

'He's with Susie – I think it's pretty clear what he wants to do,' Wilson said, and Social Anxiety Disorder nothing, it was such a savage summation of the wretched days and the sleepless nights Hope had endured, that she flinched. 'Anyway, why does it have to be his decision? Can't you make up your own mind?'

'Of course I can! It's just not so cut and dried,' Hope explained, because she didn't want it to be cut and dried. She wanted some ambiguity and doubt behind Jack's sudden and swift departure, because then he might still come back to her.

'Listen, Hope, can I be brutally frank with you?'

Hope summoned up the ghost of a smile. 'Um, when are you *not* brutally frank with me?'

Wilson dipped his head in acknowledgment of this truth, then his expression grew serious. 'Speaking as someone who's been both dumped and dumper, I'm going to give you the benefit of my years of experience.'

It was nice that Wilson was giving her advice, like they were friends. And in a strange way, a really strange way, they were, Hope thought to herself. They'd been thrown together by the circumstance that was their partners screwing each other and at least Hope had someone to share the pain with. Except, she just needed to clear up one point. 'Well, Jack hasn't dumped me,' she explained. Yes, he was with Susie right now, but that was because she and Jack were going through a bad patch. True, it was the worst bad patch since records began, but nobody had actually dumped anyone . . . yet. 'And when he comes home, we are going to have to seriously . . .'

'He fucked Susie,' Wilson said rather gently, all things considered. 'He's still fucking Susie. Q E fucking D.'

'You know that thing you do when you think about what you're going to say, then you decide not to say it? That would work just fine for me.' Hope put her head in her hands, even though her hair would end up reeking of mango chutney and tandoori sauce until she washed it. 'We were both angry. We both said things that we shouldn't have, but once we've both calmed down, then I'm sure Jack will see that he's making a terrible mistake.'

'And what if he doesn't? Then it's down to you to start dealing with it and the longer you put it off, the longer you're going to feel like shit.' Wilson smiled ruefully. 'Bet you preferred me when I only talked in monosyllables.'

'Kind of,' Hope admitted with a rueful smile of her own. 'This decision . . . it's a no-going-back sort of decision and when I try to think about going forward, I can't imagine a life without him. He's just always been *there* and I don't know how to be on my own. Oh God, I don't want to be on my own.'

'There's nothing wrong with being on your own for a while. Give yourself time to regroup, figure out what your next move is going to be,' Wilson advised her, and he made it seem so reasonable, so easy, so manageable. 'You have to decide what *you* want, what's going to be best for you.'

'All I want is to not feel like this,' Hope exclaimed. 'It . . . I just feel awful all the time, like I've got really bad flu, and I always thought that when people talked about heartache, they were just being metaphorical, but my heart really does ache.' She rested her hand over the damaged organ and looked at Wilson who should have been rolling his eyes but instead was nodding.

'Yeah, that's what it feels like when you lose someone that you love.'

Hope shook her head impatiently. 'This isn't just some "break-up".' She did angry air-quotes. 'We were . . . we've been going out for thirteen years. That's longer than a lot of marriages.'

'Yeah, and people get divorced after decades of marriage and they still manage to function on their own. I've heard stories of divorcees who are seen laughing, and there's also talk that some of them actually find new partners and get married again.' Wilson pursed his lips. 'Though those are unsubstantiated rumours.'

'I've just told you how shit I feel and you think it's OK to take the piss out of me?' She brushed back her hair so Wilson could get the full horror of the dark shadows under her eyes. 'I'm not going to get over this anytime soon because Jack and I aren't over, and anyway you don't have a clue what I'm going through.'

'Oh, I think I have some idea, seeing how Jack is currently shagging my ex-girlfriend and yes, Susie and I didn't have some big, serious thing but it still feels like shit when you're rejected by someone,' Wilson told her in a low voice. 'Just like it felt like shit all the other times I was in a relationship that ended, even when I was the one who ended it. You don't have the monopoly on feeling like this.'

'I know I don't,' Hope admitted. 'But feeling like this is so new and hideous and I'm scared I'm always going to feel like this. I won't, will I?'

'Course you won't,' Wilson assured her stoutly. 'You'll have bad times, real lows, when it seems like there's no point in . . .'

'I'm kind of up to speed on that part. Can you skip to the bit where it starts to get better?' Hope begged.

'But it doesn't just get better, not until you've done every-thing you can think of to take the pain away, whether it's necking handfuls of class As, or becoming best mates with a bottle of Scotch, or healing the hurt by finding a fuck-buddy.' Wilson shrugged, then looked over to see if he had Hope's full attention, which he did. Her rapt attention.

'So, like, are you sleeping with other women?' she asked, because Wilson wouldn't have brought it up if it wasn't a suitable topic for discussion. 'But it's hardly been any time at all since you and Susie split up.'

'Well, we were on the outs ever since your infamous dinner party, and we were pretty much over when I last saw you – which was, what, two weeks ago?'

Hope nodded.

'But we took so long to break up, what with all the drama and her running to Jack every five minutes, that I'd already done the whisky-drinking and the chewing-the-carpet thing,' Wilson said with a wry smile like it was funny but he didn't sound that amused. 'And I have an arrangement with a couple of girl mates if we're currently single. So, yeah, I'm hooking up with my friend Juliet, who was fed up with me being more dour and Northern than I normally am.'

It might work for Wilson, but Hope couldn't approve of him having another girl to warm his sheets within a fortnight. It just wasn't appropriate. You had to give your-self time to grieve. 'Well, I would never do that,' she said censoriously. 'I mean, I appreciate the advice from someone

228

who's been there but, really, I would never do *that*.'

Now Hope was thinking about Wilson doing *that*, she just couldn't help it, and he was the one who'd brought it up. She remembered Susie telling her that not only was Wilson well-endowed but that 'he's always up for it. Always, Hopey. Behind that surly, fifties-throwback exterior is a sex machine.'

Then Hope had giggled and pulled a disgusted face, but now she was looking prim, mainly so she didn't look intrigued. She no longer thought of Wilson as simply a pretentious wanker; he did have actual layers, kind, funny, surprisingly sweet layers, but she didn't want to think of him in that way. 'The thing is,' she continued, because now Wilson had lapsed into silence and was giving her the keen stare of old. 'The thing is, I'm just not ready to move on. This business with Susie will burn itself out and until that happens I'm not ready to start thinking about what my options are.'

'You haven't listened to a single word I've been saying. You really need to grow a pair,' Wilson told Hope sharply. 'You're not going to find any answers at the bottom of the biscuit tin or a tub of ice-cream . . .'

'So I've been comfort eating? This is about the only time in a girl's life that she's actually allowed to stuff her face with junk food,' Hope protested, uncomfortably aware that she'd easily eaten almost twice as much food as Wilson.

'And is it making you feel better?' Wilson enquired, after he'd asked the waiter for the bill.

Hope shook her head sadly.

'Course it isn't. It's food, not a magic eight ball.'

They'd been getting on so well. Hope had started to think that she knew what made Wilson tick, and that the one good thing to come out of the horrific ordeal was their friendship. Well, sod that. If she wanted someone to kick her when she was down, Hope could always call her mother.

When the bill was presented on a little silver dish, she put down her debit card with great force. 'I'm getting this,' she hissed. 'To say thank you.'

'We'll go halves.' Wilson was already pulling his wallet from his pocket.

'No, we will bloody not.' Hope actually slapped his hand away, then followed it up with some ferocious glaring, which made Wilson look more bemused than anything else.

'Maybe I shouldn't have mentioned that you'd put on weight but you're a pretty . . .'

'Oh my God! Why are you still mentioning it, then?' The waiter handed Hope the card reader but she was so upset that it took her three attempts to pay, and by then it was too late to do anything about keying in a 50 per cent tip. The service had been good, but not *that* good. 'I know I'm eating too much, and I know it's not the answer, especially when Jack waltzes in with his fancy new clothes and his fancy new haircut, and he's been with Susie who's slim and beautiful and I look like a spotty, ginger pig . . .'

'You do go on, don't you?' Wilson pushed back his chair and stood up. 'Stop whining and do something about it. Send him packing, go on a diet, just do *something*.'

Hope marched out of the restaurant, without even bothering to see if Wilson was behind her. The truth really hurt, but what was a little more hurt on top of all her current agonies? None of this was her fault and, quite frankly, there had been times over the last six weeks when a bag of Kettle Chips and a box of Ferrero Rocher had been her only friends.

Wilson caught up with her in mere seconds. Hope could sense him looking at her, but she forced her features to remain absolutely boot-faced. It was barely a five-minute walk to the Forum, where they'd have to wait in the cold for at least half an hour for Jeremy to emerge.

In the normal way, Hope would have suggested they go for a quick drink, but she'd rather stand about, freezing her bits off, than sit around another small table with Wilson while he doled out some home truths that she really didn't want to hear. What Wilson was saying made perfect sense, of course it did, but if Hope changed the locks and donated all of Jack's belongings to Oxfam and asked Gary from upstairs to value their flat and put it on the market, she wasn't just moving on, she was making it impossible for her and Jack to work through this. Because he might have said things when he was angry and upset, but things that were said in anger weren't always true, and Jack might still come back and they could salvage their relationship. They could move on together.

Deep in thought, Hope marched up the street and only came to a halt when it was time to cross over the road that led to the big industrial estate that sprawled out behind the high street. Wilson stopped too, then suddenly took her arm and began to pull her down a road where there was nothing more exciting than factories and lock-ups and a Royal Mail sorting office.

'You're going totally the wrong way,' Hope insisted, trying and failing to tug her arm free. 'How long have you lived in Kentish Town, anyway? *Everyone* knows where the Forum is.'

'Shut up,' Wilson said, then he yanked her into a dark gully between two squat office blocks and kissed her.

Hope's initial reaction was to struggle and flap her hands against Wilson's shoulders.

Her second reaction was to kiss him back, because as soon as she felt his mouth on hers, her brain kicked in with the message that this was a really good kiss and she'd be mad to end it by slapping Wilson's face in a fit of maidenly outrage. So Hope stopped trying to hit him and let him press his body against her, curved her arms around him and savoured the pleasure of kissing and being kissed. It wasn't just that she needed to feel as if she was still desirable and any pair of lips would do; it was solely about Wilson's lips and how he had one hand around her waist and the other cupping the side of her face, his fingers gentle as he kissed her hard.

Then his hand bypassed knitted coat and shirt dress, and when Hope made an approving sound and arched closer, Wilson stroked the slope of her breast, which was spilling over a bra that was at least one cup size too small, and rubbed his thumb against one tightly budded nipple.

Hope gasped, not just because his hand was cold, but because it wasn't enough. She wanted Wilson's hands everywhere, wanted to do more than arch against his hard body, wanted that body on top of her, wanted the hard cock she could feel against her hip inside her. But they were on the outskirts of an industrial estate on a freezing-cold night and yanking down her constricting leggings for a quick knee-trembler . . . it shouldn't be like that. Not that Hope was sure that *it* was a good idea but God, she hadn't wanted someone this badly since . . .

Before she could go to that dark place where Jack was always centre-stage, Hope lifted her hand so she could stroke the back of Wilson's neck and gently tugged his plump earlobe between her teeth. He tweaked her nipple in revenge and kissed her with even more ferocity, and just as Hope was re-thinking her position on knee-tremblers, he pulled away.

It wasn't a regroup. It was 'time to pick up our respective teens'.

Hope adjusted her clothing so she wasn't flashing her breasts to the world and adjusted the belt on her coatigan a little more tightly than was strictly necessary.

'So what was *that* about?' she asked, as they started walking back towards the high street.

Wilson didn't answer at first, then he gave her a swift, wicked grin. 'Just giving you some options,' he said.

Chapter Twenty-two

What a difference a week made. It was Saturday morning and Hope was back at Euston station, her mother texting every five minutes to check what time Jeremy's train left, and what time it would arrive in Rochdale, and did he still have his ticket, and Hope really needed to get him some food for the journey because it was far too expensive to buy anything from the buffet car.

'I swear I'm this close to giving my phone to the first beggar I see,' she said to Jeremy, as they sat in Caffè Nero drinking cappuccinos because his train didn't leave for another half hour and there was still plenty of time to get him a sandwich and crisps.

Jeremy grinned. 'Maybe I shouldn't have had my hair cut. Now she's going to be able to tell I'm listening to my iPod rather than to her.'

'You *haven't*?' Hope looked at him aghast while secretly wishing that iPods had been around when she was Jeremy's age, and she could have used the same tactics whenever her mother had pencilled in a little chat about the birds and bees and how 'you'll get a terrible infection if you let a boy touch you in your special place when he hasn't washed his hands'.

'Maybe I have and maybe I haven't,' Jeremy stated and they had a quick tussle with their elbows until Hope reached up to ruffle his shorn head.

'I know it sucked to start, but did you have a good week?' she asked.

'It's been the best week *ever*,' Jeremy said gravely. 'Even the bits that sucked, 'cause if I had hung out with Jack then I wouldn't have met Wilson and Alfie and three of my favourite bands and well, I wouldn't have got to hang out with you, like properly spend time with you.' He looked horrified as Hope's bottom lip wobbled. 'I mean, you're all right when you're not crying in public and embarrassing me.'

'I am not crying,' Hope said indignantly. 'And you're all right too. You can come and stay any time. *Mi casa es tu casa,* and all that.'

'But it won't be your *casa* for much longer, will it?' Jeremy stated plainly, like it was an irrefutable fact. 'Like, now that Jack's moved out, you'll have to find your own place.'

'Well, it's not as simple as that,' Hope began, then she stopped because actually it was that simple. Jack had moved out. It didn't get much more simple than that, no matter that the way she felt about it was messy and confused. 'You can come and stay with me wherever I'm living,' Hope hastily amended, then looked at Jeremy from under her lashes.

'What?' he asked, instantly suspicious. 'I know that look.'

'What look?'

'The look you used to give me when I was little and you were about to force me into a dress and make me sing and dance for your friends,' Jeremy reminded Hope, who flushed with shame. She really had been a little beast, although Jeremy's performance of 'Like a Prayer' had always been a show-stopper, and it explained why he was probably the only teenage boy in Whitfield to experiment with eyeliner and crimping irons. 'You want me to do something that I probably don't want to do.'

'It's nothing, except, well, I'd really appreciate it if you didn't mention to Mum or Marge what's going on with us,' Hope said imploringly, even squeezing Jeremy's arm meaningfully so he could be in no doubt that this was a heartfelt request. 'Not until I'm absolutely sure what's going on . . .'

'No! Hopey, I can't! She even asked me to look out for signs that you and Jack might finally be getting officially engaged and she'll interrogate me, you know she will, and I'll start twitching, and she'll badger me and won't let it go until I've told her everything.' Jeremy flailed his hands in agitation and managed to knock over his cappuccino.

Hope was not impressed. 'Why can't you just lie?' she demanded. 'God, what is wrong with you?'

Jeremy remained resolute. 'I'm a crap liar. It's probably because you left home before you could give me any pointers.'

'True,' Hope conceded, as she jumped down from her stool. 'Come on, we'd better go. I need to get you a sandwich from M&S so you don't expire from hunger on the train.'

They gathered up their stuff, Hope sent Jeremy back for his skateboard, which he'd left under their table, and when he turned up in M&S he had a sly smile on his face. Now it was her turn to look suspicious. 'What?'

'Nothing,' he said innocently as he selected a BLT sarnie. 'It's just, well, if you throw in a large bag of chilli-flavoured crisps and a tub of chocolate mini-rolls, I swear your secret will be safe with me.'

'You utter little shit!' Hope exclaimed. 'After all I've done for you.'

Jeremy looked completely unrepentant. 'What can I say? I learned from the best.'

With Jeremy on the Rochdale train, Jack still MIA, and Lauren cancelling their plans to go out that evening because she was going on a date with the bloke she'd been eyeing up on the bus into work for *months*, Hope had no choice but to start putting her house in order.

Well, she did have a choice but it involved sacking out on the sofa with a packet of chocolate digestives and all the episodes of *Glee* that had mounted up on the SKY box, but what would that really accomplish? Nothing but a chocolate hangover.

Wilson had been right last night. She couldn't just drift along, waiting for Jack to make up his mind. It was painfully obvious that Jack's future plans didn't include Hope. So the first thing she did was to empty out the kitchen cupboards and the fridge and the secret hidey place at the back of her knicker drawer where she stashed her emergency chocolate bars. Hope held back one bag of Lindt truffle balls just in case she relapsed, but stuffed the rest in two carrier bags and took them to her neighbours.

'Haven't seen Jack around much lately,' Alice from next door said, her eyes gleaming inquisitively. 'Away on a work trip, is he?'

'He's moved out,' Hope said baldly, because part of admitting it to herself was admitting it to other people. 'You must have heard the rows.'

Alice nodded sympathetically. She and her husband, Robert, were always going at it in a spectacular fashion, too. Hope could set her watch by the argument they had at ten to six every Sunday about whose turn it was to persuade their daughters that they needed to have an early night.

'Anyway, I thought Lottie and Nancy might be able to munch their way through this lot,' Hope continued, handing over her calorific contraband and giving a little start as Alice took the bags and gave Hope's hand a quick squeeze at the same time.

'I'm here if you ever want to talk,' she said. 'In that brief window of time on a Saturday morning when the girls are at ballet and Robert's kicking a ball around with his mates and pretending that he's David Beckham.' She sniffed. 'I admire you, you know, having the guts to get out before you're in too deep.'

'Well, it's not quite like that.' Hope started edging towards the door. She was touched by Alice's concern, but her own relationship woes were about all she could handle, without having to listen to anyone else's. 'But, anyway, yes, we should totally get together for a coffee.'

'The girls are going to be upset if you move out,' Alice called after Hope as she hurried down the path. 'They love Jack so much!'

The obvious thing to do after ridding the flat of junk food was head to the gym, even though Hope had great difficulty in squeezing herself into a racer-back sports bra and finding a pair of tracksuit bottoms that didn't make her arse look like two wobbly blancmanges encased in black lycra. She jogged to the gym and once there, she forced herself to pick all the machines that were placed in front of mirrors for added motivation. Looking at her red sweaty face and seeing her flesh jiggling about was a salient lesson that just because she'd done some exercise, it didn't mean that she had free rein to order a Chinese takeaway when she got home.

After a quick shower and a mushroom omelette, because three elderly mushrooms appeared to be the only vegetables in the fridge, Hope steeled herself for the next part of her plan.

It was hard. Simply walking into their bedroom felt as if she was crossing a minefield. Hope's courage almost deserted her, because it was all very well making plans, but the next item on the agenda was to dismantle their life together on her own because Jack wasn't there. And why wasn't he there? Because he was already busy making a new life for himself.

Hope sat down on the bed, a roll of heavy-duty black bin bags in her lap, and thought about the only feasible option that she had. It was Wilson. Wilson kissing her and touching her and making her want him so badly that even now, almost twenty-four hours later, she could still feel the ghost echo of that need that had clawed up inside her and made her press and rub and writhe against him.

But was that an option or was it just lust? Was it wanting to be wanted by somebody, by *anybody*, to make her feel better because Jack didn't want her any more? Hope sat there and thought about it – thought about going out with Wilson or being in a relationship with him – but all she could imagine was a couple of hours of fairly laboured conversation before they had sex. Sex with Wilson and his big dick that had got rave reviews from Susie. Hope was sure that if she ever found herself having sex with Wilson, then Susie would be all that she would think about.

Did Susie think about Hope when she was fucking Jack, or had she got past that now to regard Jack as her own personal property, rather than something she'd borrowed without asking first? Hope sighed because there was no point in torturing herself with these hypothetical questions. It was easier to just have a plan and stick to it, she thought, as she forced herself to get off the bed and move purposefully towards the chest of drawers.

She started off with Jack's socks and underwear. It was hard to get emotional about packing away fifteen pairs of black socks and countless grey and black boxer shorts. The T-shirts were much harder. There was the Pantone T-shirt she'd bought him in a pop-up Gap store when they'd gone to New York for the weekend to celebrate Jack's twenty-fifth birthday. It was Pantone shade 14-0848, which was exactly the same shade of blue as Jack's eyes. And the black Beatles T-shirt with the apple logo that Jack had been wearing on the day they moved in to the flat, and stuffed right at the back of the drawer was the greying, faded, holey Coldplay T-shirt that she'd taken off Jack and slept in the night they'd had sex for the first time in the little B&B in Bloomsbury, even though Jack now pretended that he'd never liked Coldplay.

They weren't clothes, they were memories and Hope was

folding each one and packing it away, stopping occasionally to gulp away tears. She had an almost-cry when she carefully packed away the really expensive Marc Jacobs suit he'd bought (with a borrowed discount card from the *Skirt* fashion department) last summer because they'd had four weddings, one christening, his grandparents' fiftieth-anniversary party and a ball to go to. Jack had looked so sleek and handsome every time he wore it, Hope remembered sadly as she reverently placed it between sheets of crêpe paper, which were left over from last year's Blue Class art project.

Once the clothes were in bin bags, the rest was relatively easy. Hope was determined not to be one of those clingy ex-girlfriends who caused a scene about who owned what, and technically they'd bought some of the CDs and DVDs together or from their joint account, but whatever. Jack could have the CDs, they'd all been ripped to iTunes anyway, and he could have a lot of the DVDs as well. In fact, Hope could finally admit to herself that she didn't find *Monty Python* the least bit funny, and she didn't care if she never saw any of the *Star Wars* films ever again.

It was past one o'clock when Hope finished. She dragged all the bags into the hall and now the bedroom looked bare and unfinished – a bit like her current emotional state. The clocks were going back that night so she could have stayed up a while longer to clear the bathroom of Jack's vast array of expensive grooming products, but instead she went to bed and slept better than she had done in weeks.

Hope did have a little cry when she woke up the next morning and remembered why the bedroom was looking a lot less like a jumble sale, with all her clothes neatly tidied away thanks to the extra drawer space.

There was no point in moping around the flat, so she set out for the local farmers' market to buy organic, home-grown vegetables and absolutely no organic, home-grown cakes. Hope always felt as if winter officially started once the clocks had gone back, and winter meant putting the flannel sheets on the bed and making soup. There'd been a recipe for pumpkin soup in last week's *Observer*, and her body was yearning for some vegetable nourishment after weeks of stuffing down sugar, grease and carbohydrates.

The soup was simmering on the hob when Hope sat down at the kitchen counter with a hardback A4 notebook that she'd bought on the way back from the market. It was the notebook that would contain 'The Plans For The Rest Of My Life', or at least for the next six months.

If she wrote them down, then the facts were indisputable.

1. Jack doesn't love me any more.
2. Jack is not my lover or my boyfriend, or my unofficial fiancé.
3. Jack is my ex-boyfriend.
4. Jack is shagging Susie.
5. Jack is shacking up with Susie.
6. I can't afford the mortgage on my own.
7. Jack never liked this flat anyway, and even if he could afford the mortgage on his own, he wouldn't want to live here.
8. Ergo [Hope wasn't entirely sure what ergo meant, but it seemed like the right word to use] we need to put this flat up for sale.
9. There are many, many things wrong with this flat that need to be put right before I can even think about calling an estate agent.

Hope chewed ruminatively on the end of her pen and wondered if she should ask Gary from upstairs for some advice, but she wasn't up to him kicking her skirting boards again, and wanting to know what had happened between her and Jack. Besides, he was leery enough without knowing that Hope would soon be on the market along with 'a bijou garden flat, beautifully maintained by its current occupiers. Perfect first-time buy.'

Hope didn't even want to know the sheer extent of the home improvements that needed to be done, but like so many other things in her life, they couldn't be avoided. And it was only making a list – it wasn't as if she needed to immediately drive to B&Q to buy grouting and nails and twenty pots of very cheap white paint.

She started with the bathroom because it was the smallest room in the house and the one that needed the least amount of work. They'd had the whole room redone soon after they'd moved in, when it became evident that there was some major leakage going on behind the washbasin. From there, Hope did an inventory in the bedroom, lounge and hall, and then returned to the kitchen to catalogue that room's many faults, from dodgy electrics to torn lino to the broken carousel in the corner cupboard.

It took five pages to list all the wrongs that needed to be made right, but some of them were just little things that anyone could do. Anyone who wasn't Hope, who didn't even know how to put music on her iPod because Jack had always done it for her, and her extreme vertigo meant that anything involving stepladders was also out. Still, she reasoned, as she got up to give the soup a poke and a stir, she could wield a mean paintbrush and possibly she might be able to hammer in some nails under close supervision.

The soup tasted heavenly after Hope added a little more nutmeg, and she was just cutting a slice of the sourdough bread she'd also bought at the farmers' market when the front door opened and Jack walked in.

Everything in Hope's body, from sphincter to fists to throat, clenched. Jack first stood where he was and looked around like he wasn't sure of his bearings. It was the oddest thing, but it seemed to Hope that he didn't belong in their flat any more, and he certainly didn't belong in their kitchen, which was where he was currently headed.

Last night in her great packing purge she'd wrapped all of Jack's Alessi kitchen gadgets and stark-white china in newspaper, then placed them in a cardboard box, which was now perched on a stool. ' "Jack's kitchen stuff" ', he read out loud, then gestured at the pile of black bin bags in the hall. 'Can see you've been busy, then.'

He sounded belligerent, like he was still sore about the iPhone and a bunch of other things he didn't have any right to be sore about, because he was the one who was breaking up their once-happy home.

Hope put down the bread knife, because after the iPhone incident she didn't want Jack to think she was still harbouring violent thoughts, and folded her arms. 'I'm so sick of fighting with you,' she said, cocking her head to look at him, trying to strip away the thunderous expression and the hip new clothes. Somewhere underneath that hostile exterior was the ghost of the boy she used to know. 'We're, both of us, better than that.'

Jack nodded. 'I just came to get more of my stuff,' he said in a less confrontational way. 'Didn't think it would be all packed up and waiting for me.'

'It wasn't meant to be a declaration of war,' Hope explained, picking up the bread knife again so she could saw away at the loaf, though her appetite had deserted her. 'I had to do *something* to make myself accept the situation, something that wasn't eating ice-cream and moping.'

He had the grace to squirm a little. 'So, how have you been?' he asked. 'Were things OK with Jeremy? I felt bad about ducking out on him like that, but he was so aggro and it didn't seem like he wanted to spend quality time with me.' Jack scratched his chin. 'Or any other sort of time, come to that.'

'Everything was fine. He ended up having a really great week.' Hope didn't want Jack to get off that easily, because making Jeremy suffer for Jack's sins might have been his most nefarious deed to date, but she didn't have the emotional reserves for another argument. Not when she was trying so hard to make plans and move forward.

'And I've been fine too. Or I'm getting there, at least.'

Hope didn't know what to say next. She couldn't ask Jack where he'd been, or how he'd been, because he'd been with Susie and Susie made him much happier than she could, and it was hard to understand how you could know someone all your life, think that you knew everything about them, then one Sunday they'd be standing in the kitchen of the flat that you both owned and seem like a total stranger.

'I'll sort Jerry out a goodie bag from work,' Jack said, as he frowned at the mound of pumpkin debris still heaped on the chopping board, but if he didn't live here any more then he didn't have the right to nag her about tidying up as she cooked. 'What are you making?'

Hope gestured at the big pan on the stove. 'Pumpkin soup. You can have a bowl, if you like,' she offered magnanimously. 'I added a teensy bit of cumin and nutmeg to give it a bit of welly.'

Jack was already getting down a bowl. 'You're so predictable, Hopey,' he said with his back to her, as he rooted through the cutlery drawer, which had degenerated into chaos in his absence, to find a spoon. 'You always make soup the day that the clocks go back. I bet you even put the flannel sheets on the bed.'

'Well, it's winter now, and why do you have to start picking on me within five minutes of walking through the door?' Hope saw that she was brandishing the bread knife in what could be misconstrued as a threatening manner, and put it down again. 'I told you, I don't want to fight, so you can either stay and have a bowl of soup or you can, well, like, leave.' She said it calmly and reasonably without shouting or whining and it was impossible to know which one of them was more shocked.

It was probably Jack, because he narrowed his eyes as if he suspected that Hope had devised some new subtle way to exact revenge on him.

'Are you going to have some soup? It's not like I've spat in it or anything,' Hope said dryly.

Jack slowly nodded. 'It smells good,' he conceded, with a tiny shrug. 'Well, I guess I could stay for a spot of lunch, if you don't mind.'

'Of course I don't,' Hope said, and she wondered why this careful, cautious politeness was more painful than when they were screaming at each other. She carefully ladled out a bowl of soup and even grated some fresh nutmeg to sit prettily on the surface. 'Help yourself to bread.'

It felt just like how they used to be: Jack happily eating something she'd cooked and making appreciative noises while he did so. Even looking up and smiling at Hope as she half-heartedly began to clear up the mess she'd made. She was just wiping down the worktop with a damp piece of kitchen roll and ignoring Jack, who was telling her to use the sponge cloths they'd bought expressly for that purpose, when her phone rang.

Hope glanced at the wall clock and her heart sank before she'd even looked at the name that was flashing up on her phone.

It was quarter past two. It was her mother, who wasn't meant to be calling for another fifteen minutes.

Hope pulled a face as she picked up her phone. 'Hi, Mum,' she said brightly. 'Did you have a nice week away? What was the weather like?'

'Rained every day until the morning we left,' came the glum reply. 'Your father and Roger couldn't play golf so they kept getting under our feet.'

'Oh dear,' Hope cooed, glancing over at Jack, who was leafing through her DIY of Doom lists and looking completely pole-axed at the sheer amount of work that had to be done before they could go their separate ways. He looked as if he might start to cry, which did Hope's already bruised ego the world of good. 'So did Jerry get back OK?'

He had, though her mother had a very dim view of his

new haircut and the fact that her express approval hadn't been obtained before Hope had taken him to the barber's.

'Mum,' Hope groaned. 'His hair looks much better now there's much less of it. Please don't give him a hard time. We had a lovely week together.'

She grimaced at Jack and expected him to grimace back at her, because it was what they did during these Sunday-afternoon calls, but he was still reading her list with a face like boiled suet.

'Well, the week wasn't that lovely, was it?' her mother said acidly and before Hope's stomach could begin to churn, she got down to business. 'He told me about you and Jack. Really, Hope, what have you done?'

'I haven't done anything!' she insisted weakly, and she should have prepared better for this, because it was inevitable. Hope was amazed that Jeremy had managed to hold out for a whole twenty-four hours.

'Because you do nag him a lot. Marge and I remarked on it last time we saw you both, and you do have that temper.'

'So, it must be my fault,' Hope hissed down the phone. 'Just like I suppose it was my fault that Jack decided to shag my best friend behind my back for months. Yeah, I can see that *that* was all my fault!'

Her mother was beyond words; all she could do was gasp in shock as Hope steeled herself to shoot Jack a defiant look, because why the hell should she have to keep his sordid little secret for him? But the defiance slipped away because when she actually looked at Jack, he was sitting there *crying*. His face was all crumpled up and red, and tears were streaming down his cheeks and when he saw her looking he buried his head in his hands, his shoulders shaking.

Hope took no pleasure from Jack's pain. The only other time she'd seen him cry was when he was seventeen and Bucky, the Benson family collie, had to be put down.

'There are difficult phases in every relationship,' her mother was saying rather unbelievably as Jack's phone started to ring. 'But sometimes they can bring a couple closer together.'

He scrubbed his face with the sleeve of his new, expensive-looking black jumper, gulped back a sob and answered his phone. 'Hello, Mum.'

Of course it was his mum. Because it had been three minutes since Jeremy's bombshell made Hope's mum call early, and three minutes was the time it took for Marge Benson to leave the Delafields' house, hurry next door, relay the terrible news to Jack's dad that everyone's favourite couple was on the rocks, then call her son to find out exactly what had been going on. Jeremy might have spilled the beans, but he obviously hadn't told them why Hopey and Jack were no longer together and, again, Hope took no satisfaction from hearing Jack mutter fiercely, 'Look, it wasn't like that. I've been . . . well, I've been seeing someone else.'

Her mother was still jawing on, her tone verging on hectoring '. . . Obviously, Jack's done a terrible thing, but Jerry says that you've put on weight and sometimes you don't even wear a bra when you go out. What kind of message does that send out? It says that you've let yourself go. Of course Jack is going to stray if you've stopped making an effort . . .'

'Thanks for the support, Mum. Do you have even the slightest idea of what I've been going through?'

Jack got to his feet and stumbled to the bedroom, shutting the door behind him so he could speak to his mother in privacy, though Hope was sure that he wasn't getting such a hard time. Not Jack, their beloved only child who shot sunbeams out of his arse.

'Hope, you know that we love you to pieces,' her mother said, and it seemed to Hope, as if often did, that this alleged love was in spite of the way she'd turned out rather than being completely unconditional. 'I'm just saying it takes two people to make a relationship, and two people to break one up.'

'Yes, and those two people would be Jack and my former best friend. Oh, I'm forgetting that none of this is Jack's fault; I drove him away because I'm a fat bitch who doesn't wear a bra.'

'There is no talking to you when you're in one of your moods,' her mother rapped back. 'Obviously this hasn't been easy for you, but it's been quite a bolt out of the blue for us, too.'

'The thing is that really it's got nothing to do with you,' Hope said, even though it had *everything* to do with her parents and Jack's parents and their grandparents and, when she stopped to think about it, probably the whole of Whitfield had a vested interest in their relationship.

Her mother seemed to think so. 'It has everything to do with us and if you can't sort out this mess, the shock is going to kill your grandma.'

'Mum, please . . .'

'You'll have to come home so we can talk about this properly,' her mother stated implacably. 'Can you get a few days off if you explain that there's a family emergency?'

'Not a chance in hell,' Hope said equally firmly.

'Well, you'll have to get the train down on Friday after school. I must say, I thought you'd be more upset than this. You sound almost flippant.'

'I am *not* flippant, and believe me, I've been plenty upset about this. I've cried myself to sleep more nights than I can remember, and the reason I'm so bloody lardy is because I've been stuffing down chocolate like it's going out of fashion,' Hope admitted, and she was on the verge of tears now, but they were angry tears because she was so furious with her mother she'd almost lost the power of speech. 'I am in pieces right now.'

'Oh, Hopey, poor old thing, don't cry. I'm sure that Jack never meant to hurt you. He loves you,' her mother said, and at least now she sounded like Hope's emotional wellbeing was her number-one priority. 'Look, sweetie, please come down for the weekend for some proper TLC.'

Usually Mrs Delafield was more about tough love, rather than TLC. 'I don't know,' ventured Hope. 'There's so much to do here. Like, if we're going to sell the flat . . .' She trailed off as her mother took another sharp intake of breath.

'I think it's far too soon to be thinking about that kind of thing,' she said, once she'd got over the fright that Hope had given her. 'If you get the fast train, you can be here by seven, and I'll pick you up from the station. We can have a nice girly weekend, just you, me and Marge.'

There was absolutely no point in arguing. Hope knew her mother would drive up to London if she had to, but . . . 'What about if I persuaded Jack to come home with me and we drove up on Saturday?'

'No need for that.' Her mother gave a shrill laugh. 'Dad and Roger are going to drive down to London and spend some time with Jack, and we'll get this whole horrible business squared away.'

For one brief, blissful moment, Hope dared to believe that with some heavy-handed parental intervention, the whole horrible business *could* get squared away, but there were Jack's worldly goods encased in black bin bags in the hall and her list for the rest of her life sitting on the kitchen counter, and there was nothing to be squared away. It was all fucked up and over.

'I don't think that's going to happen, Mum,' she whispered. 'How can he still love me if he's doing that with *her*?'

'Stop being so silly. Jack obviously adores you. We'll talk about it over the weekend,' her mother said in a slightly manic voice. 'Now, be sure to let me know what train you'll be getting, though you should probably be able to make the four o'clock train out of Euston if you don't dawdle. I've got to go, I have some bread proving.'

'Fine. OK. Whatever.' Hope guessed that her mother had achieved all she wanted from their phone call. 'I'll email you the train times, though all the talking in the world isn't going to change what's happened.'

'Oh, and don't keep sounding so negative, Hopey. You need to have a can-do attitude. This will all blow over, I'm sure of it, and that reminds me, I'll make you an appointment to have your hair done on Saturday afternoon. Jeremy said your hair was mostly tangles, so we'll get Mandy to give you a comb-out. I'll remind you to take a couple of ibuprofen before we leave for the salon.'

As Hope rang off, Jack emerged from the bedroom and they shared a strained smile. 'So I hope you didn't have any exciting plans for next weekend,' he said sheepishly.

'By exciting plans, did you mean being frogmarched to Hair by Mandy to have a comb-out on Saturday afternoon?' Hope asked peevishly.

Jack winced. 'Ouch.'

He sat back down on the stool and dipped a finger in his bowl of soup. 'This is barely lukewarm now.'

'I'll heat it up again.' Hope poured the contents back into the big pan, which was still on a low simmer, and stirred. 'So, did you actually agree to our two dads coming up for the weekend?'

'I tried to say no several times but Mum doesn't understand that word.'

Hope attempted another smile. 'You never know, it might work.' And just like that, just from looking at Jack sitting in their kitchen with her, in their home, where he truly belonged, all Hope's plans for the future, and her good intentions to move on with her life were gone. Out of the window. Because, really? They weren't what she wanted from her life. Jack was what she wanted, which was why she couldn't help herself from going over to him so she could wrap her arms around him and kiss the top of his head, and Jack was letting her, so that was a good sign, right? 'I still love you,' she whispered in his ear. 'Have you really stopped loving me?'

'I'll always love you,' he said, and he bent his head so he could kiss her knuckles. 'But this thing with Susie . . . it's like we can't get enough of each other. Sometimes I feel like I'm drowning in her.' Jack stopped and looked imploringly up at her as if he didn't have the right words to describe this supposed thrall that Susie had wrapped him in, and that maybe Hope could help him out.

Hope didn't feel inclined to lend her assistance, and even though Jack's face was right in front of her, she stared pointedly at a spot over his left shoulder where they'd tried unsuccessfully to hang the kitchen clock and made a mess instead. She needed to add it to the list. 'Is it just a sex thing, then?' she muttered, when Jack pinched her waist.

'I've never felt like this before,' Jack said, and Hope didn't know why he felt the need to tell her this, or why he thought she'd be interested, but when she tried to disentangle herself, he clung to her like she was the last lifebelt on the *Titanic*. 'I keep thinking it will burn itself out. It has to.'

'And you expect me to wait for you to get it out of your system?' Hope asked a little bitterly, even though she suspected that if Jack asked her to, she would wait. And to think that usually people described Hope as feisty. All her feisty seemed to have upped and left. 'Because Susie's all fiery-hot and I'm like, tepid.'

'It's not like that.' Jack glared at her as if she was deliberately not getting a clue. 'Susie's like a really spicy Thai meal and you, well, you're pumpkin soup or shepherd's pie or . . . or . . . freshly baked bread.'

Hope tore herself out of Jack's arms so she could put some distance between them. 'My God! Do you go out of your way to think of the most hateful things to say to me?'

'Don't you get it though, Hopey? Thai food is amazing and, like, if you go to Thailand you eat it every day . . .'

'You've never fucking been to fucking Thailand!'

'But say that I had, and when I got home I thought I'd want to go back to eating freshly baked bread and shepherd's pie, but it didn't happen.' Jack ran long fingers through his hair but it was too short now and he gave up with a frustrated groan. 'I know I'm behaving like a complete tosser. If it's any consolation, I hate myself for it.'

'Well, no, it isn't,' Hope said brusquely, and she turned her back on Jack, which he took as his cue to get off the stool and try and put his arms around her again. 'Can you stop mauling me, please?'

'I'm trying here, Hope! Could you at least meet me halfway?'

Well, try harder because it doesn't look like you're trying at all! she almost said. 'If your mum hadn't called, you'd have eaten your bowl of soup and taken some more of your stuff and gone back to Susie's,' Hope pointed out, and she thought she should be given some credit for hardly raising her voice. 'I was starting to think that maybe you were having regrets, but nothing has changed at all. You've just had an attack of conscience.'

'I'm just trying to explain why I've acted the way I have,' Jack said, and he sounded as if he really meant it. 'And I'm trying to tell you that I don't think it will do any good for the dads to come down to talk some sense into me. Otto and Marvin have already tried and failed.'

Hope felt compelled to turn round. 'Really? I thought they hated me for daring to smash a sacred phone manufactured by Apple?' She flushed. 'Did you have to buy a new one or did you manage to claim it back on the insurance?'

'I had to buy a new one, but it's really not that big a deal,' Jack said. 'And of course Otto and Marvin don't hate you. They both said that I was lucky that you only took it out on my iPhone.'

'Oh. So much for "bros before hos", eh?'

'Hope, honestly, I don't see the point of our parents staging an intervention,' Jack said earnestly. 'You have to admit our relationship has been broken for ages and there isn't a way to fix this, to fix us.'

Hope would admit no such thing, and as she understood it, there were lots of ways to fix them: Jack could stop seeing Susie, forswear Thai food, exercise a bit of bloody restraint and stop being led by his dick. She didn't say that, but was sure that the sour expression on her face said it for her. 'Well, if you're not even going to try, then I don't see why I have to be the one to go back to Whitfield and you get to stay in London,' she said. 'Don't you think you've put me through enough without a two-pronged attack from both our mums?'

'But you've got to get a comb-out at Hair by Mandy.' Jack grinned, and Hope also wanted to tell him that they weren't in a joking place, not at all, and that the agony she was going to go through on Saturday afternoon (and actually for the entire weekend and for the foreseeable future) was no laughing matter.

'I don't know how you can act like this is funny,' she said. 'That I'm not important. That what we had doesn't matter to you.'

'I don't think like that. Not at all.'

'Because I love you. I can't stop loving you, despite how much you've hurt me, and if you end this with her, I'll take you back. No questions. No judgement. I'll take you back. Please, Jack.' Hope didn't even care that all her pride was gone and she was giving Jack all her love and devotion, with absolutely no guarantee that he'd return them.

'Please, Hopey, don't,' he said gently. 'In the long run, getting rid of me will be the best thing you've ever done.' He tried out a winsome grin on her, the kind of grin that even two weeks ago still had the power to make Hope's foolish heart melt. 'Look, if we end this now, before things get really ugly . . .'

'Things already *are* really ugly,' Hope said, because, lists aside, Jack had left misery and chaos in his wake and if this was only just the beginning . . .

'If we end this now and don't let ourselves get dragged

down into more fighting and scoring points off each other, then we can still be friends,' Jack said hopefully. 'We'll laugh about this one day.'

'Yeah, I think I'll just about die from laughing.'

'Look, it's only a weekend.' Jack raised his eyebrows. 'You break the bad news to the mums, and I'll do the dads.'

'But why do you get to decide that it's over and I have no say in it?' Hope asked, and she could feel her face wanting to collapse in on itself, as she forced the tears back. 'What would have happened if I hadn't gone through your phone? Would you still be pretending that we were OK?'

'I wanted to tell you, but well . . .' Jack looked down at his hands, in preference to looking at Hope's frozen face. 'It's not easy to tell someone, to tell *you*, that it is over. Please try to understand, Hopey, I *do* love you, but it isn't enough any more.'

'It's enough for me,' she whispered, but her voice was so low that Jack obviously didn't hear her.

'We'll talk properly once we've told our parents,' he said, picking up his spoon. 'So, do you reckon that the soup has heated up by now?'

Chapter Twenty-three

As soon as Hope stepped on to the platform at Rochdale station, she could feel herself regressing to her truculent fifteen-year-old self as she slouched towards her mother with a sullen expression on her face.

'Goodness, Jerry was right. You *have* put on weight,' was her mother's cheery greeting, and Hope wondered if her mother had regressed to the hectoring martinet of her teen years, until she remembered that her mother had always been like that. She'd probably been born like that.

As they drove towards the village of Whitfield, where Hope had grown up and where her parents still lived in the same house, she could sense her mother looking at her meaningfully as if she suspected that Hope's defiant pout was a flimsy façade, and that with a little prodding she'd break down and cry. It was a theory that Hope didn't want to put to the test. Not when she'd already cried herself to sleep every night that week.

Instead she shot her mother a meaningful look of her own. 'You look like you managed to catch the sun while you were away,' she commented. 'It suits you.'

'Well, I'm not sure how. Did I mention that it rained the entire time that we were there?' Caroline Delafield angled a glance at herself in the windscreen mirror and allowed herself a small smile of quiet satisfaction. Despite giving birth to four strapping sons and one heffalump of a daughter, she'd clung on to her trim figure with grim determination, and though she didn't have the delicate prettiness of Jack's mother, Marge, she prided herself on always being immaculately groomed.

Caroline Delafield got up six every morning so she could wash and blow-dry her ash-blonde hair into regimental smoothness, never went anywhere without a little tinted moisturiser and a sweep of mascara framing her cornflower-blue eyes, and did not possess a pair of jeans. Or a pair of trainers. Or any clothing with a pattern or picture. As soon as she got home from a hard day's headmistressing, Mrs Delafield changed out of her smart slacks and coordinated blouse and cardigan into casual slacks and a casual top, or sometimes if the weather was warm she really let rip and put on a T-shirt.

Now she cast a disapproving eye over Hope's jeans and green and black stripy T-shirt worn over a long-sleeved black top. 'Please tell me you didn't wear that to school today.'

''Fraid so,' Hope said, looking down at her outfit. 'We were making a nature display and there was no point wearing anything smart if I was going to get glue or leaf mould on it.'

'And the school doesn't mind you wearing trainers?'

'They're plimsolls.' At least the green flash on her Dunlops coordinated with her top. 'Sometimes Mr Gonzales wears trainers too, Mum.'

Her mother actually harrumphed, glanced over at Hope one last time and sighed. 'You really shouldn't wear horizontal stripes when you've piled on a few extra pounds, dear.'

Hope understood why her mother gave her such a hard time and she sympathised, up to a point, but it didn't make it any easier to deal with, especially in the cramped confines of her mother's Ford Focus when she'd forgotten to slip an elastic band on her wrist to ping when her mother was goading her to the very edge of her temper. If things had gone according to her strict plan, Caroline Delafield wouldn't have needed four attempts to make a perfect daughter, one who'd delight in shopping trips and cake-baking sessions, who'd come to her mother for advice on boys and how to apply foundation correctly, a daughter who'd also be a best friend and a source of maternal pride. Instead she'd had son after son after son, so when Hope had finally arrived, all her dreams and expectations for a daughter, of delightful pink clothes and girly toys – after six years of blue, grey and khaki and Lego – had all rested on Hope.

There was no way that any girl, let alone Hope, could have lived up to such high ideals. And Hope was far more interested in winning the approval of her three rambunctious, girl-hating older brothers than in baking fairy cakes with her mother, and she'd preferred Tonka toys and digging for worms over Barbie dolls and ballet classes. Though this evening she could tell from her mother's compressed lips that she was pissed off with her, Hope knew that she'd never reach the same levels of wrath as the time when she'd been expelled from Brownies for being a disruptive influence.

Hope wished that she and her mother had a better relationship than the sniping, passive-aggressive behaviour they always fell into. It was very easy to make her mother happy, though most of the time Hope didn't even bother to try.

'Hey, Mum,' she said, as her mother expertly parallel-parked the car next to her father's Volvo. 'You said we were going to have a girly weekend, so why don't we order a takeaway, open a bottle of wine and watch a soppy movie? Just the two of us?'

That was usually the magic incantation that made her mother dare to believe that she was finally getting the daughter she wanted. 'We can't,' her mother said flatly, unclipping her seatbelt. 'Marge is bringing round dinner so we can thrash out this silly argument you've had with Jack.'

'Mum, don't you think we should keep Marge out of this for now?' Hope asked as she got out of the car. 'It's a bit of a delicate situation, her son cheating on me, y'know.'

'Marge is family,' her mother insisted. 'She's as horrified as I am, and anyway, she said she was making lasagne, though you'd probably be better off with a salad.'

Hope was sent upstairs to freshen up. The Delafields lived in a solidly built stone house, formerly the old vicarage, on the outskirts of the village. Behind the house were rolling open fields and beyond those, the Pennines. On a cold early-November night, there should have been something warm and comforting about being back in her childhood home, but as Hope opened the door of her bedroom, right next to her parents' room, and was assaulted by the lingering smell of the Bodyshop's White Musk perfume, she felt as confused and as uncertain as she had been when she was a teenager and these same four walls had been her sanctuary – apart from the times her mother had blatantly ignored the huge 'KEEP THE HELL OUT!!!!!!!' sign on the door and barged in without knocking. There were still Kenickie and *Amélie* posters on the wall. Her old textbooks were still neatly arranged on the shelves, and even the cuddly toys that she'd never played with were amassed on the bed. It was reassuring yet depressing at the same time.

Hope pulled off the derided stripy top and dug out an old black jumper, which she hoped was slimming enough that her mother would relent and let her have some lasagne. Well, she was going to have lasagne whether her mother approved or not, but she'd prefer to eat it without a running commentary about how many calories she was wolfing down, and wasn't it odd that she stored the fat in her face like a hamster?

The doorbell rang at eight on the dot. Hope raced down the stairs to get to the front door before her mother could bustle out of the kitchen.

Marge, at least, looked pleased to see her. 'Darling girl,

you look beautiful,' she said, as she stepped into the hall. 'I would hug you if I wasn't carrying a very hot, very heavy baking dish.'

Her mother and Marge were so in sync that instead of saying hello, they launched back into a conversation about the trouble the vicar was having finding someone to re-flaunch his chimney stack, which Hope supposed they'd started earlier in the day. She sat at the huge kitchen table, with Charlton, their enormous tabby cat, purring on her lap as she stroked him under his chin, and watched her mother and Marge work quickly and seamlessly to gather up crockery, cutlery and glasses.

Marge was tiny, dark and elegant with almost Asiatic features, but although she appeared to float ethereally through life in loose-fitting linen accessorised with chunky silver jewellery, she was a pillar of the community. As well as working as a part-time receptionist at the doctor's surgery, she was chairwoman of the Parish Council, headed up the volunteer services at the local hospital and was also heavily involved with the Rotary Club, the Historical Society and the events committee at the Golf Club. Hope's mother was no slouch in the local do-gooding stakes, but compared to Marge, she was a total slacker.

After they'd finished discussing the novel they were reading for their book club, Marge finally came and sat down next to Hope so she could hold her hand and tell her how pleased she was to see her. Hope wondered, as she often did, if her life would have turned out better if Marge had been her mum, instead of just her honorary auntie from next door. If *she'd* have turned out better.

While her mother made a salad and garlic bread, which she'd already forbidden Hope from eating, all she got from Marge was sympathy and a huge glass of Cabernet Sauvignon. 'You're pretty and you're smart and you're funny,' she said to Hope. 'I honestly think he's taken complete leave of his senses.'

'Hope is far from perfect,' her mother remarked, then realised that she was being exceedingly harsh, even for her. 'But you do have a kind heart.'

Coming from Caroline Delafield, this was quite the ringing endorsement, and Hope let herself relax and even took a huge helping of salad to please her mother, but the warm fuzzies only lasted the short time it took to dish up the lasagne. Then, before Hope could get the first forkful into her mouth, they attacked, without warning, and left Hope completely blind-sided.

'What you have to understand about men of Jack's age, dear, is that they go through these phases,' her mother said. 'It doesn't mean anything.'

'He's just having a last-minute panic,' Marge added helpfully. 'Men don't crave commitment in the same way that women do. Don't get me wrong, they settle into it eventually, but not as easily as us girls.'

They went on and on and on and although they didn't use the phrase 'sowing his wild oats', they might just as well have done.

'But what about love?' Hope asked, pushing away the food that she suddenly had no appetite for. 'If he loved me, really loved me, then he wouldn't want to be with anybody else but me.'

'He does really love you,' Marge said earnestly. 'But that can be very scary in itself and sometimes the easy option looks more appealing. This girl . . . this Susie, she sounds appalling.'

'She was Hope's friend,' her mother reminded Marge, like if Hope had been more discerning in her choice of friends, then all of this could have been avoided. It was something Hope had thought herself, but how like her mother to bring it up.

'And affairs don't last,' Marge offered weakly. 'What you and Jack have is the real thing. This could make your relationship stronger.'

Hope shook her head. 'It hasn't . . .' She took a deep breath because neither of them wanted to hear what she was about to say but they *needed* to hear it all the same. 'The thing is, Jack doesn't love me. He loves Susie. He says he wants to be with her, he doesn't want to be with me, and nothing that anyone can say will make him change his mind. God knows, I've tried.'

She'd finally succeeded in getting the pair of them to listen, really listen, to what she was saying and had shocked them into silence as an added bonus. Then in direct contravention of her mother's rule that you only ever had one glass of wine, then saved the rest of the bottle for another day, she poured herself another glass of Cabernet Sauvignon. 'I'm sorry, Marge, I'm sorry, Mum, but it's not like Jack and I haven't discussed this. We have.'

Marge and Caroline shared a brief, panicked look. 'Well, no, that's where you're wrong because if Jack didn't love you, then why would he agree to Roger and Bill going down to London to talk to him?' Marge cried in desperation. 'He loves you, Hope. He was *sobbing*!'

Hope put her head in her hands. 'I don't want to talk about this any more. We're just going round in circles.' She forced herself to look her mother in the eye, but bottled out at the last second. 'You said we could thrash this out but, can't you see, you're just flogging a dead horse?'

Her mother flapped her hands dismissively. 'Nonsense! Jack just needs a gentle nudge in the right direction.'

'He needs to be reminded of where his priorities lie,' Marge chimed in, and Hope steeled herself for a completely inappropriate pep talk about putting the spice back into their sex life, and if they started talking about buying some raunchy underwear and taking striptease lessons, she was going to run screaming out into the night. Or hitch a ride to the station, she really was.

'. . . time to think about having a baby . . .'

Hope's head shot up. 'Say *what*?'

'Obviously you'll have to stay in London at that school to qualify for your maternity benefit, which is a shame, because the health service is much better here,' Caroline Delafield said with a sniff. 'Then once you've had the baby, you can both come home. You'll want to have another child quite soon, nothing worse than an only child, then you can go back to work once they're both at nursery. I can easily find you a teaching job. I do have rather a lot of sway with the local education authority. There might even be a position at my school. That would be nice, us working together, wouldn't it?'

Hope was appalled. If this was their cunning plan, then she'd totally wasted the price of a return train ticket. She did want babies, of course she did, but *years* from now. And she didn't want babies with a man who was in love with another woman. And Christ, she never wanted her mother as her boss. Just kill her now. 'I'd take Jack back in a heartbeat, he knows that I would, but I'm not going to trick him into staying with me, by getting pregnant!'

'Well, you want to get married to Jack, don't you?' her mother demanded. 'Remember that barney you had when you thought he was going to propose in Spain? Well, having a baby is practically the same as getting married.'

'It's *nothing* like getting married, Mum!'

Marge patted Hope's hand. 'But Jack wants to be with you, he's just confused right now, and I know it's not very fashionable to say this, but biologically this is the best time for you to start a family.'

'But there's tons of stuff I want to do, and I'm only twenty-six, and Gurinder at work had her kids when she was in her late thirties.'

That stopped them in their baby-making tracks. All thoughts of Hope and Jack's rapprochement were forgotten as they began to harangue her about all the birth defects that Hope's hypothetical children would have if she left it too late. 'Do you know what the medical term is for women who have babies after thirty-five?' her mother shouted, her face red. *'Geriatric* mothers. Do you want to be a geriatric mother?'

'You were forty-five when you had Jerry, so just stop it!' Hope shouted back. 'I mean it! When you said that we could find a solution to this *fucking* nightmare, I actually dared to hope that you meant it, but all you have is some bullshit scheme that's not going to bring me and Jack back together. It's just about you trying to micro-manage our bloody lives like you have done for the last twenty years! I don't even know if I really did want to get married, or if it was because you banged on about it so much that I went along with it just to get you to shut up!'

'Hope Louise Delafield! I won't be spoken to like that!' Caroline Delafield banged her fist on the table so hard that her wine glass bounced off the edge and shattered on the slate-tile floor. 'Now look what you've done!'

'Fine! I'm going!'

Hope got up, flounced out of the kitchen, flounced back to apologise to Marge, then stomped up the stairs to her room. Flinging herself on her lonely single bed seemed like the right thing to do – she really was channelling her not-so-inner teen.

Jack, as ever, had definitely got the better of the deal. The three of them had probably gone down the pub and were talking about football. Then in the five minutes before they left on Sunday morning, her dad or Roger would say, 'We're relying on you to do the right thing, son.' Jack always got off easy.

Hope could remember lying on this bed when she was thirteen and thinking about Jack then too. But in those days it was hatching plan after plan to get him to stop seeing her as his friend who just happened to be a girl, and to start seeing her as a potential girlfriend. She'd stuffed her trainer bra with cottonwool balls, which had given her very fake, very lumpy boobs. And she'd stood shivering on the sidelines of a muddy, waterlogged field, cheering until her throat was hoarse, when Jack had played football for the local youth team. When that hadn't worked, she'd doled out huge amounts of icy disdain in Jack's direction in time-honoured 'treat 'em mean to keep 'em keen' tradition, which Lauren and *Sugar* magazine swore would work where everything else had failed.

She must have done something right because then there'd been that night Jack was walking her home from the once-a-month Youth Club disco, which he always did because her mum had asked him to and he did live next door, when he'd suddenly coughed nervously and asked if he could kiss her.

Hope could still remember every single detail of that first close-mouthed, bumped-nose kiss. It had been unexpected and utterly thrilling but also scary to have Jack's lips on hers, and she hadn't known what to do with her mouth or how to breathe or if she'd freak out if he used tongue. No other kiss ever could compete with that first kiss and all the months and months of desperate yearning that had preceded it.

But then there was that other kiss. A kiss that she never expected, because she'd imagined that the only man who'd ever kiss her for the rest of her life was Jack. Jack's first kiss had filled Hope full of longing but when Wilson had kissed her exactly one week ago, it had triggered a deep, dark lust that Hope hadn't known she was capable of feeling. Kisses could change your life, or at least change the direction that your life was going.

But Wilson was just . . . just the sexual equivalent of a couple of ibuprofen, and she had to stop transferring or displacing, or whatever the hell it was that she was doing. Hope hung off the edge of the bed so she could yank open one of the divan drawers and pull out a pink shoebox covered in Take That and Hello Kitty stickers.

Hope dumped the contents on her duvet and sifted

through photos of teenage parties, daytrips to Blackpool, nights out at the indie disco in Oldham. She could still conjure up the smell of Elnett and singed hair as she got ready at Lauren's house, swigging from Diet-Coke bottles filled up with Malibu and pineapple juice. They'd meet up with the rest of their little gang to get the bus into town, and she'd sit on the back seat with Jack, snogging. Once Jack had left for university, there were the weekends in London. Hope would swear blind to her mother that she'd have her own room in Jack's shared house when in reality they'd spend the whole time shagging, in between the shopping and drinking. She'd been so happy back then, really happy in a way that you could only be when you were a teenager and you were in love, and in every photo that anyone took of you, his arms were around you and you were both gazing at the camera with goofy grins and red pupils.

They hadn't been that kind of happy for a long, long time, but maybe that stopped when you had a mortgage and credit cards and full-time jobs. It was the kind of happiness that came from being young and completely free from any kind of responsibility. They could still be happy, Hope was sure of that, but it was more of a quiet contentedness than that wild exuberant rush that had always made Hope shiver with anticipation when she'd been on the London-bound train.

But how could you have quiet contentment with some-one when every time that he said he was working late, you immediately suspected that he was with another woman? Or you had to stop yourself from poring over his Facebook account to see if he was getting wall messages from women that he'd sworn he would never have any contact with? Or if every time he bought you flowers or a tub of ice-cream, you assumed it was to assuage his guilty conscience because he'd been doing something with someone who wasn't you?

Once the trust was gone, you weren't left with much to base a relationship on, Hope thought as she stuffed the photos back in the box and shoved it out of sight. And if your other half didn't want to be your other half, then you didn't even have a relationship.

When her mother gently tapped on the door and opened it, Hope was in bed, squeezed into a pair of old pyjamas, listening to a Britpop mix CD Jack had made her on her battered old Discman.

Hope immediately tensed up and prayed that her mother would go against type, just this once, and not comment on how crying had left her eyes puffy and red. She unhooked her headphones as her mother came into the room and sat down on the edge of the bed. 'Oh Hopey,' she said, her voice a lot gentler than Hope had expected. 'I know you think I'm too hard on you, but I just want you to be happy.'

'I know,' Hope said, as she let her mother stroke the lump that was her thigh. 'But we never seem to agree on what would make me happy.'

Caroline Delafield sighed. 'It's just that I can't wait for you to give me a grandchild. A little granddaughter with Jack's hair and your eyes.'

'But you already have five grandchildren,' Hope pointed out. 'Two of which are granddaughters.'

'Yes, but it's different when it's your daughter, rather than your daughter-in-law,' her mother said, and it was odd to be having a conversation together with no back-biting, no raised voices, even if the subject matter was making Hope die a little. 'You know what they say.'

'No, what do *they* say?'

'That you have a daughter for life. You have a son until he gets married.' Her mother was obviously on her way to bed as she'd taken off her make-up and her hair was tied back in a scrunchie. She looked older and a lot more tired than she usually did, and Hope felt moved to lean forward and give her a quick hug, even brush her lips against her mother's cheek.

'I'm sorry about this, Mum,' she murmured. 'And if there

is a way out of this situation that doesn't involve us break-ing up or me getting up the duff . . .'

'Hopey! That's a revolting expression!'

'Getting pregnant, then,' Hope amended hastily, nudging her mother with her foot and teasing a brief smile from her. 'I'm just saying, I'm willing to put the effort in if Jack will too but . . . it's just . . . It's like he's changed so much and I can't trust a single word he says any more.'

Her mother shot off the bed like she'd suddenly remem-bered an urgent load of laundry that she just had to do. 'I'm sure that's not the case. He's always been very reliable in the past.'

'Mum, he's changed, and I don't feel like I know the new Jack or, well, if I even like him that much.'

The conversation had taken a sharp turn into territory where her mother didn't want to go because she was scurrying for the safety of the landing. 'It's late and you've had a lot to drink and we'll talk about this tomorrow,' she said, as she flicked off the main light, without even asking Hope if she was ready to turn in for the night.

Chapter Twenty-four

Caroline Delafield stayed absolutely true to her word and she did talk about it the next morning. She talked about Jack and Hope and her plans for their future at lunch too, and came with Hope to the hairdresser's so she could carp on about property prices and the standard of living in the Greater Manchester area, which were much lower and much higher respectively than they were in London.

She only paused before the Great Comb-Out began, when Hope mooted the possibility of cutting a good ten inches off so she'd end up with a jawline bob that wouldn't need combing out.

'But you've got such lovely, long hair,' her mother exclaimed. 'Or it would be if you ran a brush through it occasionally, and really you don't have the bone structure to go that short.'

Then the tugging and pulling commenced and all Hope could do was say, 'Ouch!' and 'Christ!' and 'Can you stop for a second?' She wasn't sure if she was talking to Mandy and her wide-toothed comb, or to her mother who was *still* talking babies, but this time about the future progeny of Prince William and the former Kate Middleton and how she hoped they wouldn't inherit their looks from the Windsor side of the family.

It was no wonder that Hope ended Saturday afternoon with a killer headache and zero possibility of being left alone to sleep it off when her mother had plans for them to reorganise the linen cupboard together. Hope knew she couldn't take much more.

As soon as Jeremy came back from his friend's house, she persuaded him to come with her to Oldham to see a film. Persuade was perhaps not the right word. Hope pleaded, begged, cajoled, threatened and reminded him at five-minute intervals that he was responsible for her current predicament by opening his fat mouth and landing her in it.

'God, did you take nagging lessons from Mum?' he spat in disgust before he capitulated, and Hope was so mad at him for even daring to suggest such a heinous thing, that she forced him to see a rom-com and pay for his own popcorn.

On Sunday morning, Hope stayed in bed for as long as she dared, which was hard when her mother was pointedly vacuuming right outside her bedroom door for a good twenty minutes until Hope gave in to the inevitable and got out of bed to face the second performance of the music.

At least Jeremy was there to diffuse the tension with his endless demands for help with his coursework and more toast. Then her dad phoned, which necessitated her mother shutting herself in the conservatory with the phone and refusing to tell Hope how the London arm of the peace talks was going.

'Never mind that,' her mother said briskly, as she shut the Sunday supplement that Hope was trying to read. 'No time for that either. Go and get washed and dressed, so we can go over to Matthew and Kathy's for lunch. She'll need help with the prep – apparently she's still got post-natal depression,' she added sceptically. 'We never had that in my day.'

It was the next phase of her mother's evil masterplan. Her oldest brother and his wife had recently had their third child, her brother Luke and his wife, Lisa, were turning up with their two children, and the only reason her brother Adrian and Hope's favourite sister-in-law, Tanya, weren't coming was because they didn't have any children so had the time, money and energy to jet off on a last-minute mini-break to Brussels.

As soon as they walked through the door, three-month-old Gretchen was dumped in Hope's arms and actually she didn't mind at all. Gretchen was warm, smiley and felt wonderfully solid and comforting as Hope obediently sniffed the top of her head, which smelt of Johnson's Baby Shampoo. What she did mind was her mother watching her like a hawk, eyes narrowed, as if she could see right through to Hope's uterus, which should have been clenched in longing. It wasn't, and when Hope followed Kathy into the kitchen to help with making lunch, her sister-in-law wasn't exactly the poster girl for procreation either.

'Gretchen's so adorable. Don't you just want to cuddle her all day long?' Hope remarked as she peeled potatoes, because she could totally appreciate other people's babies, even though she didn't want one of her own in nine months' time, and she could never really think of what to say to Kathy, because she collected little china cats and had a framed photo of Michael Bublé on the hall wall.

'It never sleeps,' Kathy said through gritted teeth, pushing back her lank hair, which hadn't been highlighted in months, so Hope could see her red-rimmed bloodshot eyes. 'It just never bloody sleeps so, no, I don't want to cuddle her all bloody day long, I just want to get an hour's uninterrupted sleep.'

'Oh dear,' Hope said helplessly, glancing through the serving hatch into the lounge where her eighteen-month-old niece, Kirsten, and three-year-old nephew, Alex, were pummelling her brother Matthew as he tried to programme the SKY box. 'Still, it's nice that the three of them are so close in age.'

'Are you fucking joking? Three children under the age of four? It's like I'm stuck in a nightmare that I can't wake up from because I never get to bloody sleep.' Kathy sounded too manic to even cry, and Hope was beyond relieved when

Lisa, Luke's wife, came into the kitchen with her two sons clinging to her skirt. They demanded to know if Hope had bought them a present, and when she pulled out the Ben 10 toys she'd bought them, it turned out they already had them and she 'was a stupidhead' and 'smelt of wee-wee'. Being an aunt was different to being a teacher, and Hope didn't really feel as if she was in a position to put them on a time-out or deprive them of stickers. Not that Lisa paid them any attention. She and Kathy were having a horrific conversation about episiotomy scars and mastitis and how it was 'a load of bloody bollocks that putting a cabbage leaf in your bra helps'.

By the time lunch was finally served, Hope was contemplating having her tubes tied the moment she got back to London. She was also seriously considering upping the limit on her overdraft, so she could fly off somewhere sunny instead of coming home for Christmas, because all five of her nieces and nephews had perfected a piercing squeal when confronted with anything they didn't like, such as broccoli or her mother telling them to use their indoor voices, and the lingering headache from yesterday's comb-out was threatening to upgrade to a migraine.

Then Jack walked into the room just as Kathy had refused to serve her any pudding because 'your Mum says you're trying to lose weight'. Hope had to rub her eyes because she was obviously hallucinating. It couldn't be Jack, because Jack was in London with her dad and Roger. She shook her pounding head and yes, it was Jack, smiling nervously around the assembled guests as he tried to fend off the attentions of Alex, Hope's youngest nephew, who was intent on punching him in the testicles.

'What are you doing here?' Hope gasped, standing up so she could hustle Jack out of the room, away from beady eyes. The beadiest eyes of all belonged to her mother, who looked as if she might just explode from sheer, smug satisfaction.

'Thought you might fancy a lift home,' Jack said, as she pulled him into the downstairs cloakroom, which was the only place where they would be sure of some privacy. 'Also thought you might fancy being rescued.'

'Yes. God, yes!' Hope didn't think she'd ever been so relieved to see anyone in her life. But as Jack kissed the top of her head and gave her a quick but fervent hug, she realised that she was actually pleased to see *Jack*, which was unexpected and confusing. 'It's been awful, increasing in awfulness every hour. How did things go with you?'

Jack moved his head from side to side as he considered the question. 'It wasn't exactly fun,' he said at last. 'Mostly we talked about football, and then we went to B&Q, and then we went down the pub to talk about football again, and they told me that I was a bloody idiot every five minutes. I mean, I'm approximating, but you get the idea. Your hair looks nice. Smooth. Guess the comb-out was worth it.'

Hope touched her hair, which was still relatively tangle-free, primarily because her mother had insisted that she sleep with a silk scarf tied around her head. 'It was agony, but not as agonising as Kathy's episiotomy scar, which is still stinging every time she pees, FYI.'

'What the actual fuck?'

'Can we go home? Now? Please?' Hope begged, clutching the front of Jack's denim jacket in her fists, even though she'd been determined not to cling and whine the next time she saw him.

'Am I allowed a cup of tea and something to eat first?' Jack asked, unlocking the cloakroom door, and he kept his arm around her shoulders as they walked back into the dining room, though Hope didn't know if that was some indication of how he felt about her or whether he was keeping up appearances.

They stayed long enough for Jack to wolf down a plate of roast beef with all the trimmings and two helpings of apple pie and cream because *he* didn't need to lose any weight. Hope tried to talk to her dad but after a brief discussion about the National Curriculum, he turned to Luke and Matthew for a riveting chat about the trouble they'd had coming off the M6 at the Croft Interchange, especially with Jack in convoy behind them.

Caroline Delafield had been so desperate for a daughter that when Hope had arrived, she'd made it clear to her husband that she'd given him three sons to do manly stuff with, and that Hope was all hers. Hope knew that her father loved her, that was a given, but he couldn't talk to her about anything other than the weather, her job, his job and what he should buy his wife for her birthday, Christmas and their anniversary. It had become more noticeable since Hope got older, but it might also have had something to do with the fact that neither of them had recovered from the three unhappy years when he'd taught her geography at secondary school. To this day, Hope still broke out in a cold sweat at the mere mention of tectonic plates or glaciers.

As visits back to the loving bosom of her family went, this one had been pretty horrific, Hope decided, as Jack began to make noises about them heading off to beat the traffic.

'Hopey needs to go home and get her stuff,' her mother said. 'We'll come with you and have a proper chat.'

Hope wanted to drop to the floor and beat her feet and fists on Matthew and Kathy's worsted carpet, in much the same way as Kirsten was currently doing. 'But Mum . . .'

'You've had Hopey all weekend, Caroline, don't you think it's my turn?' Jack asked with that cheeky grin that made her mother sigh happily and say to her father as soon as they were out of the door, 'I don't know what Hope thinks she's playing at. She'll never do better than Jack, and that's a fact.'

Finally, after a protracted goodbye and enforced kissing of squirming young relatives who'd rather not have been kissed, it was just the two of them. They drove to her parents' house to get Hope's weekend bag in silence. Not a tense silence, because they were listening to the Manics on the iPod, but once they got back in the car, Jack turned down the volume.

'So . . . ?' he said. 'What happened?'

'My mum thinks that you're just freaking out about being tied down to me for the rest of your life, and that you're making up for never having the opportunity to sow your wild oats,' Hope said, as if it was that simple and the last few weeks of hurt could all be explained in a way that completely exonerated Jack from causing all those weeks of hurt. 'In conclusion, she thinks I should get pregnant, either with or without your agreement, and that will be the answer to everything.'

Jack raised his eyebrows. 'Right. Wow. Suppose I should have seen that one coming. I guess my mum was in complete agreement?'

'Yup, they were singing from the same hymn sheet, running things up the same flagpole, looking at the same blips on the radar screen,' Hope said. 'And by the way, I'm not in complete agreement and I am NOT getting pregnant.'

'Well, thank God for that,' Jack said with great fervour and, of course, that made Hope seethe a little. She was off babies after seeing the Delafield genes replicated that afternoon, but she wanted Jack to want to have a baby with her. Maybe. One Day.

'So, how did you and the dads leave things, then?' Hope asked tentatively, because she didn't know what she wanted the answer to be.

'Bottom line was, and this is a direct quote, I "need to shit or get off the pot".' Jack shot her a wry glance as Hope made gagging noises. 'We all agreed that I was a daft fool, and we also agreed that I still loved you, and our two dads, who drink pints of bitter and play golf and call their wives "the little ladies" without any irony, think we should have couples counselling.'

It was just as well that Hope wasn't driving, as she'd have ploughed into the central reservation. 'What? They said that? They want us to see a relationship counsellor?'

'They even said they'd pay for it.' Jack paused. 'I said I'd think about it.'

Hope folded her arms and slunk down in the seat so her chin was resting on her chest. 'You did?'

'I didn't say I would for sure. I said that it was worth considering,' Jack said, and boy, he really wasn't giving her any false expectations.

After the baby-hatching madness, Hope had almost convinced herself that their end was nigh, and that neither set of parents was going to come up with a sensible solution that didn't involve huge amounts of emotional blackmail. But it turned out she'd been wrong, because actually counselling wasn't a bad idea at all. On the contrary, it was a very good idea and, even better, it didn't involve her uterus. That said, she felt a tiny flicker of something in the pit of her stomach and she realised it was a little flame of hope. Hope that she might have a future that didn't involve trying to get used to the idea that they were over, making to-do lists and grieving. True, Jack didn't seem entirely on board with the idea, but at least she had something to work with now.

'Well, it's definitely worth considering,' Hope said slowly, so she didn't spook Jack. 'I mean, if we talked things over with an impartial third party they might help us to resolve some of our issues.' She angled a sideways glance at Jack who was staring straight in front of him at the road ahead. 'How long would this counselling take?'

'I don't know. A few weeks, a couple of months, something like that.'

'We've been together for thirteen years . . .'

'Oh, Hope, please don't start,' Jack groaned, but he put his hand on her knee. 'Don't give me that speech again.'

'It's not *that* speech. Well, it's a variation on that speech,'

Hope insisted through gritted teeth, and she made mental note that she needed to find an elastic band when they stopped at the next service station because she wanted to get back to London without once shouting, screaming or in any way losing her temper. 'We've been together for thirteen years and all I'm asking, Jack, is that you give us a few weeks, say to the end of the year, to come to counselling with me and see if we can get through this. That's not much to ask, is it?'

'When you put it like that, it's not.' Jack sighed. 'But counselling isn't some amazing cure-all, though. You need to be realistic about it.'

'Why? Are you saying that you don't love me any more?' Hope bit her lip hard to stop the tears from falling.

'I *do* love you, but it seems like I always end up going back to her,' Jack said, and Hope got why he was saying it – because he was trying to be straight with her and he didn't want her to jump to conclusions and start picturing an engagement ring, or worse, her wedding dress, a bouquet and centrepieces – but it still hurt. Didn't mean she was going to back down without using every weapon in her arsenal, though.

'Or you could say that you *always* end up coming back to me,' she pointed out. 'Because you do love me and I love you, even after all the shit you've put me through, I still love you. I still want to be with you and I think we're worth saving.'

'I want to think that we're worth saving, too,' Jack said in a small voice, and Hope waited for the inevitable 'but' and when it didn't come, she decided to press her advantage.

'Then, come on, Jack! Let's do this! You've given me thirteen mostly wonderful years, all I'm asking for is another few weeks, and if the counselling works and we get back to what we were, then that's a good thing, isn't it? And if it doesn't, I'll let you go, even though it will half kill me, and you can go to Susie if you really think she'll make you happy.' She let out a huge breath. 'Really, for you, this is win/win.'

'Well, OK, yeah, you're right.' Jack still had his hand on Hope's knee and he squeezed her thigh. 'It can't hurt, can it?'

'Do you want to try that once more with feeling, Jack?' she asked archly. 'This doesn't stand a chance of working if you're just coming along for the ride and you're not prepared to put any effort into it.'

Hope was pushing him, but she didn't know if she was pushing him too far or not enough. There seemed to be a very fine line between the two, but Jack wasn't getting defensive; rather, he was nodding like he actually agreed with her. 'Sorry, I know I'm not likely to get much sympathy but I'm just so confused. It's like I don't know what's going on in my own head any more and, for the record, I haven't liked myself very much these last few months. It's been a total headfuck, if you must know.'

Good, was the first thought that popped into Hope's head, but she ruthlessly thrust it away. 'Is that so?' She tried with all her might to make her voice sound noncommittal, but she wasn't entirely sure that she'd succeeded.

'There are things I can't tell you because it's not fair to start going on about the person I've been seeing behind your back, but for every moment that I've been really happy with Susie there were hours when I was in hell over what I was doing to you.' Jack's hand on her knee tightened again. 'It's important that you know that. And do you know what my worst moment was?'

'Was it when I found out for real and we had that fight in the *Skirt* kitchen?'

Jack shook his head. 'Truthfully? I was just relieved that it was finally out in the open.' At least he had the grace to look thoroughly ashamed. 'It was reading that list you wrote,' he said. 'It was like a punch in the gut, if you must know. That's why I started blubbing.'

Hope rolled her eyes. 'You're saying that having counselling and staying with me is preferable to all that DIY we have to do so we can put the flat on the market? Really? *Really?*'

'Fuck off, Hopey! I'm talking about the other list, where you wrote that I didn't love you any more and that I was your ex-boyfriend, like they were items that you'd already checked off. To know that that was what you were thinking . . . that that was what I'd put you through . . . I already *told* you, this thing with Susie, I've never felt like this about anyone but I still have feelings for you, Hope. Big, important feelings.'

'But the sex is better with her?' Hope asked, even though as soon as the words had left her mouth she regretted them.

'Not better, but different,' Jack said tactfully. 'Maybe we might be able to get our mojo back with the guidance of a trained professional.'

But surely, if they loved each other, then they shouldn't need tips and leaflets and advice on how to put the lead back in their pencils, Hope thought to herself. 'I want this to work so much, I've never wanted anything so badly,' she confessed. 'But if you're just doing this to get our parents off your back or because you feel guilty then . . .'

'Look, I said I'll give it a go, Hopey,' Jack was beginning to sound really exasperated. 'We've got another six weeks or so until Christmas and we'll have some counselling and then I'll make a decision. I can't give you any more than that right now, I wish I could, but I can't. But I promise you, I will take it seriously.'

It was more than Hope had dared to dream. And now that Jack was finally opening up to her, she couldn't embark on an intensive course of couples therapy without being as honest as him. She owed him that and God, she couldn't live with the guilt for much longer.

'I have to tell you something,' she said in a voice so

strained that she could hardly choke out the words. 'It might change the way you feel.'

Jack tensed up. 'What?'

Hope exhaled slowly. 'Well, it's just, in the interests of full disclosure I have to be completely truthful with you. And you have every right to be mad at me but . . .'

'For fuck's sake, Hopey, just tell me!'

'I kissed Wilson!' That wasn't how she'd meant to deliver the news; shrieking it into existence without any back story, and Jack took his eyes off the road to stare at her in horror in a way that Hope wished he wouldn't when they were gunning down the fast lane of the M62. 'Keep your eyes on the road!'

'What do you mean, you kissed Wilson?' he rapped, pressing down hard on the horn to beep at someone who'd dared to beep at them when they'd swerved between lanes.

'Well, I've seen him around a bit,' Hope explained like that made it all right. 'Then he helped out with Jeremy last week, gave him a couple of days of work, and I took him out to dinner to say thank you and well, we ended up kissing.'

'So it was just a thank-you kiss?' Jack asked, and Hope could hear the relief, hear the 'nothing to see here, move along', and it would be so easy to go along with that version of events but if she wanted to be honest, then she had to be really honest.

'Actually,' she said, 'it was more of a snog. Mutual snogging. I can't deny it, Jack, it was good to have someone kiss me like they really meant it, and at the time, I really enjoyed it.'

Which wasn't strictly true. Every time she recalled the kiss, and there had been plenty of times over the last week, when she treated herself to a slow-motion action replay, Hope could feel her insides curling up with lust until guilt made them promptly uncurl.

'Oh, Hopita, has it really been that long since I kissed you? Like, kissed you properly?'

It had been ages. Hope couldn't even remember how long it had been but that had been the last thing on her mind when she'd been pressing into Wilson's hands as he stroked her breast, arching up against him, shuddering with need every time his tongue dipped into her mouth. 'I'm sorry,' she said and 'sorry' was such a stupid, inadequate thing to say.

Jack patted her knee again, then kept his hand on her leg. She rested her hand on top of his. 'It's OK,' he said, and after expecting shouting and maybe a little swearing, his calm acceptance was a little anti-climactic and rather disappointing. If he loved her, then it shouldn't be OK that she'd been kissing someone else.

'It's not OK. It's not even a little bit OK.'

'I get it,' Jack said. 'You were mad at me, and Wilson, it's obvious that he wanted to get back at me and Susie. She said that Wilson was obsessed with her, kept phoning her and begging her to take him back.'

Hope had to bite down hard on her lip because one of the things she definitely didn't miss about Susie was the way she'd insisted that damn near every man she encountered was obsessed with her. 'Way to make it obvious,' she'd sneer if someone with a penis dared to stand too close to her in Caffè Nero. Or, 'God, he wants me,' she'd complain in a long-suffering tone if a man bumped into her while they were walking along the street. And yes, it had kind of been a running joke with them but then again, it kind of hadn't.

'Well, it wasn't quite like that from what I heard,' Hope said. 'I mean, does Wilson strike you as the type to beg anyone to do anything *ever*?' Hope thought about leaving it there before she said something bitchy, but God, she wasn't a saint. 'Just so you know, there was overlap. Quite a bit of it. She was breaking up with Wilson, which seemed to involve a lot of sex, even while she was shagging you. It's a tricky one.'

The moment that she said it, Hope knew she shouldn't

have, even though it had to be said, and Jack was shooting her a look, the look he always gave her when she was drunk and behaving like a complete tool, or she was kicking off about something that didn't really warrant a kicking-off when he was trying to work or watch something on TV. It was a look that very clearly said, 'Tread carefully, because you're *this* close to sleeping on the sofa tonight.'

'It was messy, Hope. Everyone got hurt,' he said thinly. 'Of course there was going to be fallout and . . . overlap.'

'I wasn't overlapping with Wilson. It was just one kiss and you were staying round at Susie's then anyway and it wasn't like . . .'

'Well, it's not important now, and, well, I won't see Susie while we're having a bash at this counselling,' Jack said, with a little expectant glance as if he wanted Hope to lavish praise on him. 'That shows some commitment, doesn't it?'

'Yeah, well, the last time you said you wouldn't see Susie wasn't such a rousing success, was it?' She actually smacked her hand against her forehead in an attempt to smack some sense into her brain. 'I'm sorry! I don't mean to keep being so, y'know . . .'

'Bitchy?' Jack suggested.

'Yes, bitchy, but I'm angry with you, Jack. Doesn't mean I don't love you, but I'm really, really mad at you,' Hope admitted, not that it was breaking news. 'But well, I won't see Wilson again if you don't want me to. Not that there's anything between us. We're sort of friends now, but friends that argue a lot.'

'And friends that kiss?' Jack still wasn't sounding bothered about it. Curious and intrigued, but not as if he was about to storm round to Wilson's loft and ask him to step outside.

'I think he was just trying to prove a point. It didn't mean anything to him,' Hope said, though she wasn't sure if that was true.

Jack seemed convinced, though. 'Look, I'm fine with you

seeing him, because I trust you. And if this works out then maybe you'll start trusting me again, too.'

'Anyway, this counsellor person, do you have any idea how to find one?' Hope asked, more to change the subject than anything else, because the subject was making her feel very uncomfortable. 'Shall we Google it?'

'I think Max, our Editor at Large, is in therapy . . . he spends a lot of time in LA . . . I could ask him.' Jack pinched her thigh. 'But I'm not seeing anyone who has a framed quote from *Jonathan Livingston Seagull* on their office wall, agreed?'

'Hell, yeah, it's agreed. And if anything in their office is made from raffia, batik or bark, then we're leaving right away.'

'Ditto for dreamcatchers hanging up in the window, and if they have a special talking stick that you have to hold if you want to speak.'

'And a big box of tissues in a prominent position on the coffee table that's been made from re-purposed driftwood,' Hope added, and this time when she caught Jack's eye, they both grinned.

It was good to know that they were still in complete agreement about some things, even if it was their absolute dealbreakers for choosing a counsellor who might be able to save them from themselves.

Chapter Twenty-five

The counsellor they eventually found, through Jack's colleague Max, didn't have any touchy-feely hippie paraphernalia in her practice rooms, apart from 'a metric arseload of pictures of her cat', and when Hope phoned to book their first appointment, she didn't issue forth a great stream of psychobabble, but sounded brisk and business-like. Though that may have been more to do with the way she insisted that they pay for six sessions up front.

Their first appointment was booked for the following Friday, and they'd both agreed that Jack wouldn't move back in unless it was all right with their counsellor. As it was, Hope wasn't entirely sure that it was OK with her. About the only good thing to come out of living apart was that she'd got used to having the flat to herself, and the extra drawer space. Besides, she didn't think that Jack should just shuttle from Susie to her and start counselling without any pause for reflection. After much stonewalling on Jack's part, instead of staying with Susie for one last, shag-filled hurrah, he went back to sleeping on Otto's sofa. He even sent Hope photos of him in residence, holding up Otto's clock as proof that he was where he said he was.

Not believing a single word that came out of Jack's mouth was another thing Hope had got used to, as well as spending half her waking hours imagining him and Susie wrapped around each other in coital ecstasy. And having angry confrontational rows with him in her head, where she made Jack rue the very day he was born. But she wanted to get back to that place where she missed him like mad when she got home from school and spent the next two hours waiting for the sound of his key. How just seeing his face, his smile, when he walked through the door made her forget the lousy day she'd had at work, or getting rained on at the bus stop. How she spent her day thinking about all the things she'd tell Jack while they were eating dinner, everything from how annoying Dorothy had been in a staff meeting to Blue Class's theories on where electricity came from. Of course she missed the sex, but a relationship wasn't so much about the sex, it was about the other stuff: the quiet moments and the jokey moments and those lovely moments when they'd cuddle up on the sofa, her feet in Jack's lap, as they drank wine and talked all the way through the film they were meant to be watching.

That was what it was about. That was why Hope had to get over her rage and her hurt, and use all her powers of persuasion to make Jack realise that he belonged with her. Not that Lauren or Allison agreed with her.

'You're mad taking him back,' they'd both said, loudly and frequently, when they'd met up for Mexican food and Margaritas bigger than their heads on Tuesday evening.

Lauren had finished her lecture on 'Women Who Love Too Much', and how Hope had no right to call herself a feminist if she stayed with a man who failed to treat her like the goddess she was, with her favourite Oprah-ism. 'He cheat, he beat, he hit the street,' she announced, even though Hope made it clear that Jack had never, ever beaten her.

Hope prayed that their counsellor wouldn't condemn her for being a doormat, because she wasn't. She wasn't being passive, she was fighting for what she believed in, but if the counsellor wanted to condemn Jack a little bit for being a two-timing, lying bastard, then that would be all right.

In the end it was easier not to worry about Jack or counselling until Friday evening, especially as Blue Class were about to tackle the ten-times table and she needed to start planning the infant school's contribution to the Winter Pageant.

Red Class were going to do a dramatic re-enactment of 'Jingle Bells'. Yellow Class were down for the Chanukah portion of the evening; they would sing 'The Dreidel Song' and also form a human menorah, while the best reader in the class recited the nail-biting story of how the Maccabees only had enough oil left to keep the eternal flame in the Temple alight for one more day, though miraculously it lasted the eight days it took them to get some more con-secrated oil. 'It's obviously a metaphor for the energy crisis. Maybe we can tie it into a moral message about how it's better to walk your children to school, instead of blocking up the road in your gigantic, petrol-guzzling SUV,' Elaine had blithely commented, until Hope had pointed out that the oil in question was actually olive oil.

Against her better judgement, Hope had also given in to her class's pleas to be allowed to do a choreographed medley of Lady Gaga hits. They'd even promised to forgo their Friday afternoon Golden Time in favour of rehearsing, as well as making more of an effort to walk quietly to and from assembly, so Hope didn't really feel as if she could say no.

Hope did want to say no, however, when she was cornered in the staffroom on Wednesday morning by Dorothy and Mr Gonzales. They were both wearing ingratiating smiles, which meant they weren't going to tell her off because Stuart had managed to get into the girls' toi-lets again, but they were going to try and make her do something that she didn't want to do.

'Oh my God, I've been *so* busy with the Winter Pageant,' Hope bleated, before either of them could speak. 'Really, really busy. And Blue Class are struggling to grasp the concept of the ten-times table. I hardly have a moment to call my own.'

'Yes, about the Winter Pageant,' Dorothy said, with a teeth-baring smile which always made Hope think of a shark wearing lipstick. 'What shall we do about photographs?'

Hope shrugged. 'Are we not letting the parents use cameras in the school hall, then?' she asked in bemusement. ''Cause I have to say, if that's the case, I think there'll be outright mutiny, maybe even letters to the *Ham & High*.'

'Official photographs,' Mr Gonzales clarified, rocking back on his Hush Puppies. 'What about the guy who took the pictures of Blue Class on their field trip?'

Out of the corner of her eye, Hope could see Elaine taking tremendous pleasure in the fact that this was now Hope's problem. She even had the nerve to wipe imaginary sweat off her brow. Hope vowed to exact revenge at a later date by telling Yellow Class that Elaine particularly appreciated gifts of lavender bath salts for Christmas.

She turned her attention back to Mr Gonzales. 'The thing is that he's always very busy taking photos for *Rolling Stone* and the *Observer* . . .'

'Perfect,' Dorothy exclaimed. 'Last year, Elaine got one of her daughters' friends to take the photos, and he was more used to shooting pictures for his Facebook profile.'

'I'm sure he'd be willing to help his local community,' Mr Gonzales said optimistically. 'It is Christmas, after all, and the children and their parents will be so disappointed if we don't have some high-resolution images to put on the school website, which can be downloaded for a small fee.'

'Which will in turn benefit the school. Budget cuts,' Dorothy added darkly. 'We really do need a new projector.'

'But Wilson lives in the Borough of Camden, not Islington, so he's not a part of our community,' Hope countered weakly. 'And he's probably already booked up.'

'So, you'll ask him, then?' Mr Gonzales decreed, allowing

himself to give Hope's arm a quick squeeze that in no way could be misconstrued as inappropriate touching. 'I do like a team player.'

Even though Jack had been annoyingly blasé about Wilson being on the periphery of Hope's life, she'd already made the decision that she couldn't have anything more to do with him. It went against the whole spirit of being committed to couples counselling, and as for being in close proximity to Wilson? Well, it was just too confusing, with the way he'd be so sweet one minute, then destroy her entire belief-system the next. As for the kissing – Hope didn't want to be put in a position where there might be more kissing, because Jack was the only person she really wanted to be kissing. The Wilson Kiss had to be consigned to history and only pulled out and dusted off on those days when she needed some validation.

So, there was no way she was phoning Wilson, even with a harmless business proposition. No way. Nuh-huh. Not going to happen. She'd tell Mr Gonzales and Dorothy that Wilson had had to decline their kind offer, and that was that.

Mind you, there was nothing to stop Wilson phoning *her*, which he did that evening when Hope was eating toast and resolutely not phoning *him*.

Hope nearly slid off the kitchen stool, and for a moment she contemplated letting the call roll over to voicemail, but curiosity got the better of her and she answered with a nervous, 'Hi?'

'You've been avoiding me,' Wilson said, instead of a more cordial *Hi, how are you?* 'Is that because the rumours are true and you and Jack are having another crack at domestic bliss?'

'By rumours, do you mean that you've spoken to Susie?' Hope asked. 'So, are you and her having another crack at the let's-be-friends thing?'

'More like the let's-be-friends as long as you don't keep

jawing on and crying about the bloke you were fucking when you were meant to be seeing me,' Wilson said dryly.

Interesting. Very interesting. So Jack was following orders. That was a very good sign. 'OK. Right. And, no, I haven't been avoiding you,' she lied, though she hadn't known that she and Wilson were now meant to be in that place where they called each other up for little chats. 'I was summoned home for the weekend, and I've been working late on the infant school's contribution to the Winter Pageant, which is sucking the soul right out of me. I've been lumbered with Chanukah. And also a dance routine to the hits of Lady Gaga.'

Wilson laughed at that because, really, who wouldn't, and just as Hope allowed herself to relax and wonder why she'd been so nervous about calling him, he made a tiny impatient sound. 'So, don't dodge the question. You and Jack, on or off?'

'Please don't . . .'

'It's a reasonable question.'

Hope looked up at the kitchen ceiling in supplication. How a splodge of grease had got up there, she didn't know. And as she always talked too much when she was having a conversation with Wilson, she found herself launching into a garbled, over-share-y account of the weekend peace summit, and adding, 'So he's not moved back in or anything like that, but we're going to our first counselling session on Friday evening. I mean, it's got to be worth a shot, hasn't it?'

'I don't know, has it?'

Hope decided that attack was the best form of defence, or had to be better than falling back on the old standby of holding up her thirteen years with Jack as a badge of honour that she didn't want to tarnish. 'Anyway, let's not get into all that,' she said quickly. 'Why are you calling me? Did you want *me* to call *you*, then?'

'I just thought that after the other week, you'd know that you could call me up if you were feeling lonely,' Wilson said.

He sounded cagey, and Hope wasn't sure if he meant calling him up so she could share her sadness and he'd then tell her to buck up, and/or because he thought that now they'd kissed, they could move on to being fuck-buddies.

'Well, er, I didn't know that,' she mumbled, and there was no reason for her face to be so red that it felt like it did the time she'd spent an entire August day on the beach at Blackpool without sunblock when she was fifteen. 'So, why did you call?'

'To thank you for the card I got from Blue Class last Saturday,' Wilson said, and now he sounded more amused than anything else. 'I have to ask, is that a colony of dragons on the front?'

'No, it's not!' Hope said indignantly, confusion forgotten as she sprang to the defence of Blue Class and their artistic prowess. 'All the kids drew a self-portrait. They don't look anything like dragons!'

Last week during their arts and crafts afternoon, Hope had got the class to make Wilson a huge A3-sized card to say thank you for the photos. Then she'd given it to Kathryn, Mr Gonzales' assistant, to post and had promptly forgotten about it amid all the dread of going to Whitfield and getting her head around the prospect of couples counselling.

'My mistake. But their lettering is excellent.'

Hope beamed. 'It is, isn't it?' Then something occurred to her. 'You're totally taking the piss, aren't you?'

'Well, a little bit,' Wilson agreed. 'But I stuck it up in the studio kitchen and even Alfie dropped his sneer long enough to mutter something about how sweet it was.'

There was a little lull in the conversation, not as awkward as their lulls usually were, but Hope still felt dutybound to fill it up and, anyway, Wilson had called her so she might just as well fulfil her contractual obligations to the Borough of Islington. 'Actually, I was going to call you. Would you believe I need to ask you a massive, humongous favour? Again?'

'I'd believe it only too easily.'

'Sorry, there are forces at work here that are far greater than my embarrassment at having to throw myself on your good graces.'

'I don't know, you throwing yourself at me sounds like it might be fun.' Wilson was flirting with her, which gave credence to her theory that maybe he thought he could add her to his list of female friends who were up for a bit of discreet fun when they were in between partners. The thought filled Hope with panic and maybe a little bit of regret, because she still felt short of breath every time she remembered their kiss. And, despite trying not to, she'd been remembering it a lot. Still, Hope reasoned to herself, Wilson wasn't the sort of man who flirted with abandon, so despite the fact that she was totally off-limits, he must fancy her a little bit. It was futile fancying, but her ego welcomed it.

'If I threw myself at you, then you'd probably end up in A&E with a slipped disc,' Hope said, prodding her muffin top, which was still spilling over the waistband of her black trousers though maybe not spilling quite as much as it had been. 'You don't have to say yes – I wouldn't say yes if I were you – but I'm going to ask you anyway . . .'

'Not over the phone. If you're going to exploit my good nature *again*, then at least have the decency to buy me a drink and ask me to my face,' Wilson said quickly and a little breathlessly, like he didn't want to give Hope an opportunity to interrupt him with her protests.

Still, she was going to give it the old college try. 'But that's not fa—'

'Eight o'clock tomorrow night at the York & Albany on Parkway. That's my final offer,' Wilson said. Then he had the nerve to hang up.

Hope knew that she could simply not turn up and then cobble together a story for Dorothy and Mr Gonzales that Wilson had refused to photograph the Balls Pond Primary

School's Winter Pageant during one of the busiest times of the year for absolutely no money. But then again, Wilson might want to do it, though 'want' was probably too strong a word. Maybe he needed pictures of grubby-faced children in home-made costumes pretending that they were trying out for *Britain's Got Talent*. Stranger things had happened.

But the next evening, as Hope rushed to the gym to burn as many calories as she could in one hour, then rushed home to shower and change, she knew that the only reason she was going to meet Wilson was because she wanted to. In twenty-four hours' time, she'd be getting ready to see the relationship counsellor to embark on a new and improved chapter in the *Book of Jack and Hope,* so this was her last night of freedom. Well, not freedom. It wasn't as if Jack was the proverbial ball and chain, but there would be hard work involved. Hope was a bit vague on the details of what this hard work might involve, but she imagined a lot of intense talking about their future, and maybe they'd have to play some trust-building games, though she didn't fancy the idea of falling backwards and hoping that Jack would catch her.

But tonight Hope didn't have to work at all. She was going out to drink and flirt with a man who'd made no secret of the fact that he found her attractive and that if the circumstances were different, he'd probably want to have sex with her. More than once, and not just because there was nothing on telly and he'd completed all the levels on *Call of Duty: Black Ops*. She wasn't hedging her bets. This wasn't about making sure that Wilson was there as back-up in case Jack didn't make it through even the first counselling session – it was just a little bit of light-hearted fun and she did *need* to ask Wilson about the Winter Pageant photographs.

As she was getting ready to leave, though, she succumbed to a last-minute fit of nerves or pangs of conscience; she couldn't tell the difference. *Going for a quick drink with Wilson to talk about photographs for the Winter Pageant*, she texted Jack. *Is that OK? Hope xxx*

Jack texted her back ten minutes later: *Cool. I'm working late on looks for the next cover shoot with Max & Celia. Honest! Jack x* He'd even attached a picture of Max, *Skirt*'s Editor at Large, and Celia, one of the fashion team, pointing at a clock and grinning. Hope knew that Jack was only trying to lighten things up, but she didn't see anything remotely funny about the way he hadn't been where he said he'd been for months and months. And she didn't appreciate the way his colleagues were in on the joke either. It was only because she liked Celia and they'd bonded about being red-heads at several *Skirt* parties that Hope wasn't instantly suspicious that she and Jack were getting up to no good in the fashion cupboard. As it was, she was only a little bit suspicious, and that made it easy to decide that yes, she was going to go and meet Wilson for a drink and, God damn it, she was going to enjoy herself.

Hope even thrilled to the slight edge of nerves that made her jiggle from foot to foot as she looked through her wardrobe. Since Jeremy's visit, not a single piece of chocolate or deep-fried anything had passed between her lips, and on the days when she couldn't get to the gym, Hope tried to walk to and from work. She was too chicken to get on the scales, but her spare tyre seemed to be shrinking back down to a more manageable pot belly, and she could still get into her favourite winter dress – a black, empire-cut wool dress that ended mid-thigh – and thank God for black opaque tights, which hid a multitude of wobbly sins, and her black leather knee-high boots, which were unbearable to walk in until her toes went numb.

Inevitably the comb-out had only lasted a scant forty-eight hours, so Hope gathered her wild curls into a loose plait, then sat down to do her make-up with proper brushes, and blended eyeshadow and applied lip-liner and lipstick. The finished effect was spoiled somewhat by hat, gloves, scarf and the old faux-leopard fur coat that had been ratty when Hope first bought it eight years ago with her first student-loan cheque, and now looked as if it had a bad case of mange.

She had just enough time to hobble down to the Holloway Road to catch the bus to Camden, the slight edge of nerves now upgraded to a full-on wibble.

Chapter Twenty-six

The York & Albany was situated in a beautiful John Nash building opposite Regent's Park, and was a one-stop shop for fancypants organic living, featuring a hotel, two restaurants, a gourmet-food shop and the bar that Wilson had summoned her to. Even at the best of times, Hope hated meeting people in bars, because her mother always said that girls who went into licensed establishments on their own ran the risk of everyone thinking that they were prostitutes.

Hope was sure that the clientele of the York & Albany would think no such thing, ratty fur coat notwithstanding. They were too cool to do more than flick an eyelid in her general direction. The room was dominated by a huge, steel-topped bar with a dazzling array of bottles lined up behind it. She decided against one of the plush velvet bar stools in favour of a sofa tucked away in the corner so she could rubberneck the diners going in and out of the Angela Hartnett-helmed restaurant.

She'd barely had time to look at the menu when Wilson walked in. His concession to winter dressing was a bright-red cashmere scarf tucked into a leather jacket, which he began to unwind before catching sight of Hope.

'You made it, then?' he said, as he sat down beside her. She could feel the cold air still clinging to him, and shivered. 'Wasn't sure if you would.'

It was a new experience to go out with someone who

thought she was an unknown quantity. Jack knew every-thing about her, which was usually comforting, but lately it made Hope wonder if she was boring and predictable. At least to Wilson, she still had novelty value. 'There was nothing on telly,' she explained with a grin, then held up the menu. 'I was thinking we should be really decadent and have champagne cocktails.'

Wilson raised his eyebrows. 'Why? Are we celebrating something?'

Tonight was absolutely not a celebration of anything. It was simply a drink between two sort-of friends, but Hope was determined to keep the mood light. 'I just want to get you in a really good mood before I hit you up for a colossal favour,' she said.

'Can you afford champagne on a teacher's salary?' Wilson asked, and he didn't even sound as if he was being rude, just doubtful that her credit was that good.

'That's why God invented overdrafts,' Hope said, and Wilson laughed. It was the first time she'd heard him really properly laugh, apart from at Latitude when they'd seen someone offering phone-charging services for ten quid a pop, which he'd found absolutely hysterical. For about half a minute he stopped looking stern and had a glint in his eye and a mischievous cast to his features.

'I'll let you buy me one glass of champagne, the cheapest one,' he said magnanimously. 'Then I'm switching to whisky and I'm buying. End of.'

Hope, and her bank balance, were in no position to argue. She'd imagined that she'd get the big issue of the Winter Pageant photos out of the way immediately, but an hour and one champagne cocktail, two glasses of Sauvignon Blanc and half a Rustic pizza later, she still hadn't managed to spit it out.

For the first time in their short but fraught relationship, the conversation was flowing as easily as the alcohol. Wilson told her about his latest job, which involved photographing sewage stations for a magazine, until Hope begged him to stop because she hurt from laughing at his impersonation of Alfie getting out of the car and catching his first whiff of raw sewage.

'Thought I'd become a photographer and it would be all glamour and shooting models in their undies and I end up driving to Didcot to photograph a sewage plant.' Wilson shook his head. 'Never told me about that at college. I bet your week hasn't been as exciting as mine.'

That should have been Hope's cue to ask about the photos, but then Wilson would say no and the evening might come to an abrupt end, so she found herself telling him about Blue Class's plans for an *X Factor*-style judging panel to decide who'd perform their Lady Gaga medley.

'So I told them that everyone would be performing, irrespective of their ability to bust a move.' Hope rolled her eyes. 'That's what they call it. "But Miss, Stuart can't bust a single move, and he's going to ruin it for everyone, Miss."'

'Are they terrified you're going to snatch back their stickers if they miss a step or fall behind the beat?' Wilson asked.

By now, there was a huge expanse of sofa on either side of them and they were sitting at a slight angle to each other so they could make eye contact without getting a crick in the neck, their knees bumping and Wilson's arm slung over the back of the sofa so his fingers could brush against Hope's shoulder. They were the slightest and most incidental of touches, but each time it happened, Hope had to catch her breath and squeeze her thighs tight together to stop that pulse of longing, which was wrong – because Hope loved Jack and she was only just starting to like Wilson.

'I think it's safe to say that I'm on the way to being half cut, so it's probably the right time to ask me to lend you a million quid,' Wilson flicked the end of her plait. 'Such an extraordinary colour,' he said softly, as if he was talking to himself. 'Have you ever thought of being a hair model?'

Things had been heading to a vaguely inappropriate place with the knee-bumping and the shoulder-brushing, but as soon as the words left Wilson's mouth, Hope slapped his hand away from her hair and started to giggle.

It was the kind of thing that she imagined photographers said all the time to get into girls' pants. Except Wilson had said 'hair model' as if it was really pushing the limits of all credibility to imply that Hope had the potential to be a proper model.

'Does that line ever work?' she asked, twisting away from him so she could flop back on the sofa cushions.

'It wasn't a line,' Wilson protested. 'Your hair's almost the exact same shade as a . . . a . . . what is it?' He clicked his fingers. 'That's it! A red setter.'

He sounded so proud of himself for comparing Hope to a dog that instead of being mortally offended, she shrieked with mirth. 'A red setter?' she repeated between giggles. 'God, I should sue you for slander.'

'Red setters are a beautiful colour. Seriously, I'd love to backlight you and then take some shots. What? What? Why are you laughing? I'm not trying to be funny.'

Hope flapped a hand at him. 'Nice hair, shame about the face,' she snorted. 'Way to kick a girl when she's down.'

'I didn't mean it like that,' Wilson said as he tilted his head so he could give Hope one those intense looks that he'd probably copyrighted. 'Actually, I suppose you are quite pretty even though your face is very asymmetrical.'

'Oh God, please stop,' Hope begged him, clutching her aching sides. 'Everything you say is worse than the last thing you said.'

Wilson settled back down with an aggrieved sigh. 'I'm never, ever going to pay you another compliment.'

'Oh, you must. It really cheered me up,' Hope told him, running the pads of her thumbs under her eyes to wipe away what was left of her mascara. And now that she'd stopped laughing and got Wilson to stop with the accidental

296

touches and stroking, she really should get down to business. 'So, this favour, well, compared to lending me a huge sum of money, it's actually a really teensy favour,' she began. 'And I won't be mad if you say no. In fact, feel free to say no.'

'Believe me, if I want to say no, then I won't have any problem with saying no.' Wilson smiled when Hope scowled at him. 'Come on, love, spit it out.'

'It's this stupid pageant. Mr Gonzales, the head, and Dorothy, who's head of the infant school and a grade-one pain in my arse, seem to think you have nothing better to do with your time than take photos of the whole shebang and do it for absolutely no charge.' Hope tipped her head back in annoyance and felt Wilson's hand warm against the back of her neck again. 'So, anyway, I can honestly say that I've asked you now. It was really cheeky of them.'

'All right, I think I can muster up enough indignation on my own without you doing it for me,' Wilson said. 'When is it?'

'Seventeenth of December. I know!' Hope added, because once she was indignant it was very hard to rein it in. 'Like you don't have enough things to do the week before Christmas.'

'Think I *am* going to be working every night that week,' Wilson said, and bless him, he managed to make it seem as if he'd like nothing more than to photograph the Red Class doing an interpretive dance to 'Jingle Bells'. 'I could ask one of my assistants.'

'Alfie?'

'Christ, no! He's not my assistant. He's a minion,' Wilson said in disgust. 'But Dylan might be up for it. His girlfriend's pregnant and he should probably see what he's got to look forward to in a few years' time.' He shrugged. 'You will have to bung him fifty quid, though.'

Hope did feel the tiniest bit disappointed that she wouldn't have an excuse to see Wilson after tonight, but she was just being silly. She couldn't have her cake and eat it too; besides, she was meant to be swearing off cake. 'I'm sure I can squeeze fifty pounds out of Mr Gonzales, if Dylan's up for it.' She folded her hands in her lap. 'Thanks, I really appreciate that.'

'Bet you wish you hadn't wasted champagne on me now.' Wilson nudged her leg with his. 'If I could, I would. Any time. You know that.'

Hope hadn't known that and just three terse sentences from Wilson moved her far more than she thought possible. Enough that she was nudging him back. 'I'm still glad we met up tonight,' she said rashly. 'It's been . . . you've been . . . it's been fun.'

'Doesn't have to end now,' Wilson said. 'We could have one more for the road and then . . .'

He didn't say what would happen after 'and then', but Hope had a pretty good idea and 'and then' wasn't ever going to happen. Not when Jack was the only person she wanted to 'and then' with, and her parents had just chipped in £250 towards six sessions with a relationship counsellor. 'I'm up for one more for the road but the other . . . I can't. It's not right, because even though technically Jack and I aren't together right at this very moment, it would still be cheating on him.'

She hated herself for mentioning Jack's name because it would break the spell. But then Wilson's hand was on the back of her neck again and this time it was deliberate because he leaned in to whisper in her ear, 'Remember what I said about options? What about keeping yours open?'

'What do you mean?'

'You know exactly what I mean,' Wilson said, and she closed her eyes as she felt his teeth lightly graze her earlobe. She squeezed her thighs even tighter together. 'Shouldn't put all your eggs in one basket, so to speak.'

What Wilson was suggesting violated the whole spirit of

starting over and having counselling and putting in the hard work to make their relationship stronger. But it sounded like a lot more fun than all of that. Except . . .

'I still love Jack,' Hope insisted. 'Maybe I love him a little bit less than I used to, but I do still love him with all my heart. And don't you think you deserve something more than being just a friend with benefits?'

'Right now, I'm not in the mood for anything more than being a friend with benefits.' Wilson picked up her hand and traced the heartline. 'You're so obsessed with doing the right thing. Doing the right thing never gets you anywhere in life.'

'But it's still the right thing to do,' Hope said, then scrunched up her face in irritation when Wilson softly chuckled because she'd just proved his point. 'I mean, you can't just ride roughshod over other people's lives because it suits you. If more people exercised a bit of self-control . . .'

Deep, deep down she knew Wilson was right. Jack and Susie had done exactly what they wanted without caring about the consequences. It was the same with her mother – what Hope wanted was immaterial if it got in the way of what her mother wanted. Even Justine, who'd taught the Red Class last year and had done a pretty poor job of it, was currently teaching in Sydney and sending Hope emails 'from Bondi Beach. Finished teaching the little shits and now I'm working on my tan.'

'The meek don't inherit the earth,' Wilson said, his fingers now sliding under the cuff of Hope's dress so the sudden caress against the underside of her forearm felt shocking and wonderful at the same time. 'They inherit sweet FA.'

His mouth was so close to her ear that technically he was kissing it, and Hope couldn't believe the havoc Wilson could cause just from stroking a patch of skin that couldn't measure more than two square centimetres at most. All she had to do was turn her head ever so slightly and they wouldn't be able *not* to kiss. 'I couldn't have a one-night stand,' she whispered. 'I'm just not like that.'

'Doesn't have to be a one-night stand,' Wilson said, but even though his hand was still on her arm, he was the one who moved his head so he was no longer murmuring sweet words of temptation into her ear. 'Could be for however many nights we want, but if you really want to do the right thing by a bloke who's treated you appallingly, well, more fool you. You say that you still love him, but surely love can't be *that* blind.'

Hope shook Wilson's hand off her arm. 'We were having a really nice time, please don't spoil it.'

Wilson didn't say anything but looked at Hope as if she was the main exhibit on a Guess My Weight stall at a summer fête, then he signalled the waiter to bring the bill.

Of course, then they had to quibble over who was paying for what, but much sooner than she would have liked, Hope was wrapped up, not in Wilson's arms, but in winter woollies and her tatty faux-fur coat, and standing shivering on the pavement.

She felt as if she might cry. Surely doing the right thing shouldn't make her feel so wretched, she thought, as Wilson stepped out on to the street and braced himself against the sharp wind that was whipping around them. And if she loved Jack . . . No! There was no *if*. She *did* love Jack, so why was she having feelings for Wilson that she had no business to be having, when he'd made it plain that all he wanted was a brief affair, and Hope wasn't made for no-strings-attached lack of commitment?

'Well, it was nice to see you again,' Hope said bravely, though her bottom lip felt very unsteady. 'If you wouldn't mind, can you pass my details on to your assistant?'

'Hope?'

She ignored him in favour of folding her arms for added protection against the wind and staring pensively at her feet.

Wilson adjusted his scarf and sighed in exasperation. 'Forget for one moment that I'd like to have sex with you – let's just push that to one side and focus on the fact that we're mates, and I'm trying to save you from making a terrible mistake. In the same way, I'd try to stop any of my mates from rushing into a burning building or playing with a loaded gun.'

'OK, for starters, getting back with Jack is *nothing* like playing with a loaded gun and secondly, I don't need you, or anyone else, to save me. I can save myself.'

'Can you, though?' Wilson obviously didn't seem to think so. 'When I first knew you I didn't like you, because I thought you were a bolshie cow with more volume than sense.'

Hope was incapable of doing anything other than opening and shutting her mouth but nothing came out, except a tiny, 'Oh, you . . .'

'When we went to that all-dayer in Stoke Newington and I queued up with you to get fish and chips and they'd run out of tartare sauce, you shouted at the woman about false advertising until she agreed to give you a quid back and some extra ketchup.'

'I did *not* shout at her. I merely pointed out that she shouldn't be charging a tenner for a tiny piece of cod and soggy chips when she didn't have any tartare sauce left, and that lemon wedge she tried to fob me off with was so dry, it was practically petrified and . . .'

'See! Where's that fire when you're dealing with Jack? You've turned into a lightweight. You've let him treat you like shit and now you're going back for more,' Wilson said and he tried to cup Hope's chin, but she pulled away.

'I'm not just rolling over and playing dead. I'm fighting for him because I think what we had is worth fighting for.' In her head there was still that picture-perfect memory of Jack coming through the front door and smiling when Hope said, 'Hard day at the office, dear?' like she did every evening, even though it had ceased to be funny the second time she'd said it, and had turned into just a habit that neither of them was inclined to break. That was what she wanted back; to feel safe and comfortable, and like everything in her world was where it was meant to be – not this crazy, chaotic state where she was alone, without Jack, and her stomach was constantly churning and she could taste fear at the back of her throat.

'What you *had*, as in the past,' Wilson pointed out, and he wasn't even trying to be a little bit gentle with her any more. 'You deserve better than him.'

'You're telling me to throw half my life away and I can't do that,' Hope said, and now the tears that she was brushing away with gloved fingers weren't happy tears. 'What he did . . . I can get over that, I know I can. He's not the first man to have an affair, and if we can figure out where we were going wrong, if I can learn to trust him again, then our relationship might be stronger than it ever was.'

Wilson opened his mouth to – Hope was sure of this – argue the point, but she put her hand on his lips. 'No more,' she begged. 'Please. There's no point in discussing it. My mind is made up and there's nothing you can say that will make a difference.'

They stood there for a long moment, Hope sniffing and wiping away each treacherous tear that threatened to run down her cheek. Wilson was illuminated in the street lights so when she looked up she could see the flecks of grey in his sideburns, and that he seemed resigned rather than angry or disappointed.

'I think you're a bloody idiot,' he said at last, and just as Hope was bristling all over again, he added, 'I'll wait with you until you find a cab.'

'I'm getting the bus,' Hope argued, as she turned away from him and prepared to limp down Parkway in boots that she longed to take off and hurl into the nearest bin.

'Fine, I'll walk you to the bus stop, then,' Wilson said, and he tucked his arm into hers. Hope wasn't in a position to argue because their fight had left her feeling weak and shaky, and now at least she could lean against him and take some of the pressure off her poor feet, and he was shielding her from the worst of the gale-force wind. 'For someone who's decided to do the decent thing and stick with her childhood sweetheart, you don't seem very happy.'

'I thought we weren't talking about it,' Hope pleaded, which would have sounded more effective if she wasn't burrowing deeper into Wilson and using him as a human windshield. 'We've only got about ten minutes left in each other's company so let's not have another argument.'

'Has Jack forbidden you from seeing me, then? When did we go back to Victorian times?'

No, I've forbidden myself from seeing you. Jack doesn't care if I see you or not. 'I said that I didn't want to talk about it,' Hope reminded Wilson, as they walked past a crowd of people shivering in the queue outside the Jazz Café, then turned the corner into Camden High Street.

Hope was just about to tell Wilson that she could manage the last fifty metres to the bus stop on her own when two tramps suddenly lunged at each other and fell to the ground in a tangle of stained clothes and matted hair. One of them tried to bite the other one, and Hope decided, as Wilson adroitly steered her past them, that it probably was better if he stayed with her until she was safely on the bus.

The countdown board at the stop informed her that there was a 29 due in two minutes. Hope reluctantly unthreaded her arm from Wilson's. 'Well, I suppose this is goodbye,' she said with a brightness that she didn't feel.

'You're only going to Holloway,' he said. 'Not off to war.'

The dazzle of car headlights and neon shop signs reflected off his glasses so it was hard to read his expression. Hope tried again. 'Well, then, I'll see you around, I guess.'

'I'm not going to wait for you . . .'

'I never asked you to!'

'I'm not going to wait for you,' Wilson repeated with heavy emphasis. 'But if you wise up to what a terrible mistake you're making sometime in the not too distant future then you know where to find me.'

'That's mean,' Hope said, because his words hurt like a thousand little paper cuts. 'And if I was making a mistake, which I'm 99.9 per cent sure I'm not, then there's no way that I'd want to jump straight in to a relationship.'

'Who said anything about a relationship? I thought we already discussed a consecutive string of one-night stands, during which time we probably wouldn't see other people.' Wilson was giving her that flared-nostril, superior look of old. 'How is that a relationship?'

'You're not funny! In fact, none of this is funny.' To show Wilson just how unfunny it was, Hope clonked him in the chest with her handbag.

'You're right. It's not funny. It's sad. In fact, it's tragic.'

Really the only way to shut him up was to kiss him. Or Hope could have got on the 29, which had just pulled into the stop, but she only had to take half a step to kiss Wilson and her feet *were* killing her.

As Hope pressed her lips against his, she felt Wilson's jerk of surprise, his mouth open on a gasp that never happened because she was there to silence it. And then he seemed to get over his shock, because his hands were on her and Hope could have died from the sheer relief of Wilson touching her again. No, not Wilson. Just someone touching her like they meant it.

Wilson cupped her face in his gloved hands and kissed her gently and he kissed her slowly, as Hope closed her eyes and tried to commit the feel and the taste and the Wilson-ness of him to memory because this would be the very last time she ever kissed a man who wasn't Jack.

The thought of that filled her with panic, and Hope struggled to get even closer to Wilson, almost biting at his mouth, as people brushed and barged past them in their hurry to board the bus. It was probably just as well that they were in such a public space, standing in the middle of the

304

pavement outside the remainder bookshop, because Wilson was fumbling to undo her coat so he could touch her breasts with glove-muffled hands, while his tongue danced in her mouth and, once again, Hope was rubbing and arching against him like a kitten on a catnip high.

If she'd been able to think clearly, then Hope would definitely have been reconsidering her rash decision to do the honourable thing and save her body for the exclusive pleasure of one man. But all she could think was, *Don't stop. Please don't stop. God, just haul me into that little alley by the side of Pret A Manger and fuck me.*

It took Hope some time to realise that they weren't devouring each other any more, her coat was neatly buttoned up and Wilson was cupping her face in his hands again so he could lightly press a kiss on the tip of her nose. 'You shouldn't be out this late on a school night,' he said a little breathlessly. 'You'd better jump on the bus.'

Hope stared at him in disbelief. 'But what about . . .' she started to say, but Wilson was already walking away.

'Like you said, I'll see you around,' he called over his shoulder.

Chapter Twenty-seven

The next day, Friday, may well have been one of the worst days of Hope's life. It was definitely in the top-five.

She'd started the day off despondently, which was only to be expected. The hangover didn't help, but neither did the feeling that she might never see Wilson again, unless she made a special trip to the organic butcher in Kentish Town, then marched up and down the high street until she just happened to bump into him. It wasn't just that she'd never see Wilson again, but also that she was saying goodbye to her last chance to have a different life, which had Hope feeling so gloomy as she trudged to school in a torrential downpour and fierce wind that had her almost horizontal.

She wanted her and Jack to be all right again, like she'd never wanted anything else in her life, but now Hope realised that if Jack came to his senses and came back to her, she was saying goodbye to the chance to spend the night in seedy bars flirting with louche men. To jetting off to Paris or Prague or New York at a moment's notice. To having wild, passionate affairs. Hope might not have necessarily wanted to do any of those things, certainly not on a school night anyway, but maybe she wanted to know that doing these things might still be possible.

Blue Class could sense that Hope's mind was not on them or their lettering skills as she sat at her desk with her chin in her hands and her head filled with intrigue and sex in expensive hotel rooms. She only came to when there was

306

an anguished shriek from the furthest corner of the classroom where Stuart had Timothy in a headlock. There were
also two incontinence incidents, which meant that Hope
had to spend half an hour going through the school's toilet
procedure. 'You need to try and save your pennies up for
break time,' she reminded them, as she did several times
each week. 'But if you really have to go in a lesson, then put
your hand up and ask to go to the bathroom.'

As if the day couldn't get any worse than sitting in a classroom that smelt of urine and disinfectant, Hope was
summoned to Mr Gonzales' office at lunchtime to find
Dorothy and Sarah, who taught Year Six, waiting for her.
Sarah was overseeing the junior-school portion of the
Winter Pageant, but just as Hope was steeling herself for a
very boring half hour discussing the dearth of parental
volunteers, she was informed that Sarah was suffering from
nervous exhaustion and had a doctor's letter excusing her
from all extra-curricular activities.

As far as Hope could tell, the only nervous exhaustion
that Sarah suffered from was when her lawyer husband
forgot to go to the off-licence on his way home from work.
She managed not to share this, and she even managed not
to burst into tears when the entire responsibility for the
Winter Pageant was dumped in her lap. However, she did
manage to lose her temper and tell a sobbing Sarah that she
was 'a bloody malingerer', and Mr Gonzales had to have a
quiet word with Hope in the corridor about 'being a team
player and taking one for the team'.

Hope was still seething at the injustice of it all at afternoon break, but as she sat in the staffroom with Elaine, her
anger slowly receded to be replaced by a grim sense of fore-
boding at the thought of couples counselling.

It wasn't as if the counsellor would make Jack sign a
sworn affidavit to say that he would never cheat on Hope
again, and Hope would promise to forgive him for cheating
and to never bring it up whenever they had a row, and they

could then be on their merry way. It would be an hour of dredging up all the unpleasant events that had led them to the counsellor's door. 'There'll be probing questions,' she grumbled to Elaine. 'I hate probing questions.'

'Yes, but they'll be questions that you know the answers to. It's not like she's going to ask you the square root of anything, is it?' Elaine took a sip of her tea. 'What kind of therapy is it? Cognitive, NLP, behavioural?'

Hope stared at her blankly. 'It's the kind that costs ninety quid a session. Jack's friend at work said that she was a really good counsellor.'

'The thing about therapy is that you only get out of it what you put into it,' Elaine said, with just the mildest hint of censure to her voice. 'But it can't fix things that are irrevocably broken.'

'I *am* going to put everything into it,' Hope protested. 'I'm just well . . . scared that it won't work, especially when I can't help thinking that Jack only agreed to go to get our parents off his case.'

The bell for lessons rang and reluctantly they got up and left the staffroom. 'You don't have to get back with Jack if you don't want to,' Elaine suddenly said as they reached her classroom. 'I mean, it's not like someone's holding a gun to your head.'

For a moment, Hope thought about the antique duelling pistols that her father had bought at a car-boot sale, then came to her senses. Her dad became incensed if her mother even dared to approach them with a feather duster. 'Apart from our parents and, well, me, it seems like no one wants us to get back together,' Hope said crossly. 'When Jack and I are *on* and things are going well, we are an amazing couple. We're in perfect harmony. We're like Fred Astaire and Ginger Rogers, so I get that you're just looking out for me, but you could try and be a bit more supportive.'

'You do know that when they weren't soft-shoe-shuffling on the silver screen, Fred and Ginger loathed the very sight of each other?' Elaine asked dryly as they heard a large thump and a bellow from her classroom and she had to hurry inside.

Jack was waiting for Hope at Finchley Road tube station with a fixed smile, and a bulging holdall as if he was all ready to move back in with her, which Hope took as a good sign.

'How was your week?' he asked, as they didn't kiss each other, not even on the cheek, but stood there with a respectable amount of pavement between them.

'It was bloody awful, if you must know,' Hope said, because she was still furious about the Winter Pageant and had spent the entire journey from Highbury to Finchley Road perfecting the blistering invective due to Sarah when Mr Gonzales and Dorothy were off the premises. She really should have let it go by now and cleared her mind free of negative energy in order to be more receptive to the healing properties of relationship counselling.

Jack didn't seem to mind, though. He nodded and said, 'I hear you,' with great fervour as they began to walk. 'The fucking production department expect us to produce the February issue in two weeks, because they need to pull forward on our deadlines for the ten days we have off over Christmas. Wankers!'

Hope remembered exactly the same scenario happening last year. Jack had ended up doing sixteen-hour days and she'd had to do all his Christmas shopping for him. 'Don't tell me that the Production Editor's been standing over your desk again demanding to know why it takes you more than two hours to design a double-page spread?'

'She has. Now it's all-out war between the art department and the production desk,' Jack exclaimed, looking at Hope in surprise like he couldn't believe she'd remembered. 'So, what's been going down at The Bull Pen?'

They spent an enjoyable ten minutes walking to the

consulting rooms in Frognal and bitching about their respective employers, and by the time they were sitting in the front room of a very large terraced house, they were still happily bitching, this time about the Monet on the wall.

After five minutes, they saw a man scurry down the hall, head lowered. 'Do you think he's crying?' Jack asked in a stage whisper. 'Do you think our therapist has made him cry?'

'Maybe she probed him too deeply about his mummy issues and he had to confess that at the age of forty-seven, he still wets the bed.' She was spouting nonsense because she was nervous, but Jack giggled and then Hope giggled, and every time it seemed as if they might stop and get themselves into a serious, therapy-type place, one of them would hiss, 'Bed-wetter,' and the giggles would start all over again.

They were still giggling and nudging each other when they realised there was a sallow-faced, middle-aged woman standing in the doorway of the waiting room and watching them with a mixture of expectation and dread.

'Hope? Jack?' she queried, as they both flushed guiltily. Hope gathered up her handbag, tote, *Evening Standard* and her hat, gloves and scarf, and wondered if they'd already violated the therapist–patient code before even making it as far as the consulting room.

'I'm Angela,' the woman said. She led them down a draughty corridor to a room that was just as cold and had big French windows, which looked out on to an overgrown garden. Angela sat in a chintz-upholstered armchair and directed Hope and Jack to the matching sofa.

Hope sank down into the sofa depths and cautiously looked around. There was no raffia or batik or dream-catchers, but there was a box of tissues on the coffee table in front of her, and Angela was definitely a cat lady. Arranged on a sideboard were several framed pictures of the same tabby cat and, Hope made a mental note to discuss this with Jack at a later date, a cross-stitched sampler of said cat with an extremely malcontent expression on his furry face.

'. . . discussion, solution and ultimately resolution.' Hope realised that Angela had been talking for quite some time and that she hadn't been paying the slightest bit of attention, even though she was committed to couples counselling and raring to go. She also noted that Angela's left eye wandered to the side, and her mousy hair, streaked through with salt and pepper, could really do with some intensive conditioning – well, Hope could empathise with that. She nodded earnestly like she'd been listening to every single word and agreed with each one of them.

'Yeah, that sounds cool,' Jack mumbled when he realised that Hope wasn't going to do anything other than nod manically. 'Right, Hopey?'

'Really cool,' she agreed, her voice all squeaky because this was a little bit terrifying and Angela didn't seem like the sort of person you could really confide in. She had a pinched, almost haunted look to her face like her life had turned out to be a series of big disappointments and she wasn't entirely sure why.

'So, I spoke to Hope briefly on the phone, but why don't you both tell me what you'd like to achieve from our sessions?' Angela asked.

Hope knew the answer to this one. 'He cheated on me with my best friend, even though he promised that there was nothing going on,' she began in a garbled rush because Angela needed to know the plain, unvarnished truth before Jack could put some spin on it.

'Well, yeah, I did,' Jack admitted calmly, as Hope felt herself sink a little further into the chintz-covered cavern that was the sofa. She'd bought a new notebook so she could jot down the key points of each session to read them back afterwards, but now Hope wasn't entirely sure that she wanted to make notes so that she'd have to relive what had gone wrong all over again. 'But we were having big problems way before that. Like, our relationship had bottomed out. And we could either get married like everyone expected, or break up. But I guess we'd been together for so long that I was scared of not being together, and when I started seeing someone else, it was because it was the only way I knew how to change us, me and Hope, y'know? At first, that's what was going on, but then I realised that I was falling in love with the other girl, Susie.'

Hope was utterly dumbfounded by this incoherent explanation of why they were here. 'What are you talking about?' she demanded of Jack, who moved away from her so he was almost sitting on the arm of the sofa. 'I thought we were here because even though you're supposedly in love with her, there's an outside chance that you might want to stay with me. Or is that not the case? Are you not even willing to make an effort?'

Jack shook his head. 'You're not getting it. *Why* did I shag someone else?'

Hope still wasn't entirely sure of the answer to this one. 'You keep telling me that you're in the grip of this sexual obsession, which I don't really buy. Usually you're the king of self-control. You can stop after only one bowl of ice-cream.'

'We just got so boring, Hopey. You tried to schedule our sex-lives so we only had a shag on Sunday mornings!'

'That's not fair! It wasn't like that at all. You were too tired in the evening and I didn't have time in the morning, so I thought it would be nice to really make it special and something to look forward to.' Hope couldn't help but gasp at the unjustness of Jack's accusation. 'I even bought croissants and the really expensive filter coffee for afterwards.'

'And that's another thing: the way you go through money like you're single-handedly trying to spend Britain out of the recession.' Jack wagged an angry finger at Hope. 'Every month, the joint account goes into the red by the fifteenth because you buy a whole load of crap that we don't need, which just makes the flat even more of a tip, because you're physically incapable of keeping a room tidy for more than five minutes.'

'At least I'm not completely anally retentive. Sometimes I think you get out a ruler so all the stuff on the bathroom shelf is perfectly aligned. And anyway, this is not the issue. You cheated. You lied. For *months*.'

'You're not hearing me, Hope!' Jack snapped. 'Yeah, I hold up my hands up. I did lie and I did cheat, and I am more sorry than you will ever know about the way I've treated you, but we need to talk about why it happened in the first place.'

Hope was all ready to snap something right back, but then she heard the scratch of pen on paper and turned her head to see Angela scribbling away on a notepad, and whatever the point of therapy was, it probably wasn't about sniping at each other in front of a paying audience. Or rather an audience paid for by their parents.

She sighed. God, they hadn't even touched on the heavy weight of their parents' expectations and their pathological need for a grandchild.

Jack had lapsed into silence too, and Angela lifted her head. 'Well, yes, this is all very illuminating,' she murmured, but didn't seem keen to explain any further. 'Now, why don't you tell me when you can last remember feeling excited about your relationship?'

Hope forced herself to look at Jack, who looked back at her, and she was frantically trying to think of a particularly happy time, but it was hard when what she really wanted to do was slap him. 'You go first,' she said with saccharine sweetness so she'd have more time to think.

It seemed as if Jack was struggling with the same problem. 'Well, um, it's hard to pick just one,' he said, which was hedging, plain and simple. He wrinkled his nose. 'I suppose it was when I was doing my degree in London and Hope would come and spend the weekend with me.

That was cool. I wouldn't see you for a few weeks . . .'

'Oh. My. God!' Hope gasped. 'The last time you actually got some joy from our relationship was nine years ago when we were living 170 miles apart and I didn't see you for weeks. Bloody great, Jack. Thanks for that.'

'OK then, Miss Snappypants. When was the last time that you felt buzzed about being with me? Or can't you remember that far back?'

Actually, the answer wasn't that difficult when Hope stopped being angry and took a second to think about it. 'When I came down to London to do my SCITT and we moved into that studio flat in Whitechapel.' She was all ready to wax lyrical about having no money and living on Pot Noodles and cider and yes, there had been an awful lot of unscheduled shagging, but Jack snorted.

'Yeah, the dingy bedsit in Whitechapel with the rats,' he said flatly. Then he leaned forward, elbows on his knees. 'So, what do you think?' he asked Angela, who looked quite taken aback. 'Any chance of a cure, or should we just quit while we're ahead?'

'So much for taking this seriously,' Hope muttered under her breath, as Angela put down her pad and clasped her hands against her bony chest.

'I don't like to use words like "cure",' she said in her reedy voice. 'It's about working together to resolve your issues. I assume because you're both here that you think these issues are worth resolving?'

That was the question Hope had been 100 per cent sure about until ten minutes ago. Now she glared at Jack until he grunted his assent, and she matched it with a grudging, 'Well, I suppose so.'

Jack cleared his throat. 'We're kind of not living together right now, because, well, we're not really together at the moment. Do you think I should move back in or . . .'

'Certainly,' Angela said with a smile. Even when she was smiling, she looked as if she was reliving the agonies of major dental work. 'If you both think that moving in together will be a resolution rather than a source of more conflict.'

'What do you think?' Jack asked Hope.

She shrugged. 'Well, it's up to you.' No, that wasn't what she meant. Counselling wasn't about taking offence every time Jack said something she didn't want to hear; it was about making Jack realise that they still belonged together. 'Of course I want you to come home. I'd love it if you did, but if you feel like you're being rushed and you're not in that place yet, I'll understand.' Hope shot Jack a pleading look and he nodded, almost imperceptibly – as if he was finally ready to throw her a bone.

'I'll sleep on the sofa,' he said, and Hope felt that they'd just taken at least ten steps backwards.

'You don't have to do that,' she whispered. 'I mean, I don't expect . . .'

'I do think that for the time being you need to concentrate on experiencing intimacy without having . . .' Angela swallowed and seemed to be having immense difficulty in finishing her sentence, '. . . sexual intimacy. Maybe you could take up a hobby together. Try something that you've never done before, like, say, bungee jumping or pottery.'

This time the look that Hope and Jack exchanged was conspiratorial and said everything that they couldn't say, because if either of them opened their mouth, it was inevitable that the only thing that would come out would be hearty guffaws.

Now as Angela again asked them what they'd like to achieve at the end of their counselling, and Jack again reiterated that he wasn't sure if they had a future together, Hope didn't automatically set her phasers to stun.

It was the reason why *they* were both there, after all. Although it was disheartening that Jack needed the guidance of a trained professional to help him make a decision that would affect them both, at least he was here, sitting next to her on the chintzy sofa, *participating*. That had to count for something. So, when Angela repeated the question to her, Hope nodded. 'Well, we seem to have reached a crossroads or a stalemate or, like, we're stuck in this holding pattern, so I think we need to see if we can commit to a future together.'

There was no point in dissembling or being vague. 'And by future together, I mean becoming properly engaged and then getting properly married,' Hope continued. 'I *have* to know you really mean it if you decide to come back.' For a moment, Hope thought she'd blown it, but Jack was nodding again rather than running for the hills.

As soon as Angela dismissed them, ten minutes before their hour was officially up, Jack and Hope scrambled for the door, and within seconds they were racing down the road and turning the corner so they could collapse against each other and laugh.

'Did you see the cross-stitch sampler of that evil cat?'

'Bungee jumping. Fucking bungee jumping. Do we look like we would ever go bungee jumping?'

Hope was still giggling as they retraced their steps to the tube station. She was pleasantly surprised when Jack took her hand. It had been a long, long time since they'd walked down the street holding hands.

'Hopey?' he said tentatively, and she tried not to stiffen in anticipation.

'What's up?'

'Can we make a pact that what happens in therapy, stays in therapy?'

'Doesn't that sort of defeat the purpose of being in therapy, Jack?' Hope looked up in time to see the conflict crease his face. She was getting really tired of seeing that expression.

'I think we should treat Angela's chintz consulting room as a safe place to talk about our problems, and I totally think we should do the homework and think of a hobby to do together, as long as it doesn't involve jumping from high platforms or throwing pots, but I don't think we should take all the bad shit we're having to wade through home with us.'

'But do you think fifty minutes a week is enough time to wade through all the bad shit?'

Jack pulled her into the glow of a lamp-post so she could look up to see him gazing down at her solemnly. 'I don't think either of us can be trusted to start talking about our problems on our own. It just leads to shouting and arguments, and I'm sick of them.'

'I am too,' Hope said. 'And I suppose she has set us tasks, hasn't she? You moving back in, finding ways to be intimate without being naked.' It all sounded good and feasible, but one thing was bothering Hope. 'You have been happy being with me during the last few years, Jack, haven't you? Because if you haven't, then what's the point?'

'Shhh, shhh. Of course I've been happy,' Jack insisted, cupping Hope's face in his gloved hands, which made her think of Wilson doing that when he kissed her, not even twenty-four hours before. She wanted to pull away, sickened by her own deceit, but forced herself to stay still. 'You can't measure a relationship's success on a scale of one to ten. Generally, being with you for pretty much half my life has made me happy.'

'And then all of a sudden it didn't,' Hope said sadly.

Jack tweaked her nose. 'That's why we're seeing the blessed Angela once a week.' He did, in fact, look happier. Finally all the conflict and confusion was gone from his face and he suddenly grinned at her. 'Come on, let's walk up to Swiss Cottage and get the bus to Camden and have dinner at the cheesy Italian.'

Maybe their parents were right, which a mind-boggling concept, and therapy was the answer to everything, even though Angela and her creepy cat obsession didn't exactly inspire confidence. Hope's smile was a little shaky to start with, but then she was out of practice. 'The cheesy Italian that has pepper grinders so huge that I'm sure the waiters are over-compensating?'

'That's the one,' Jack said, wrapping his arm around Hope's waist as they started walking again. 'Now, have you any ideas about hobbies that we could try? I was thinking that we should start playing *Bodycount*.'

'Is that some sort of computer game, or do you want us to take up serial killing?' Hope enquired drily. 'I was thinking more along the lines of kick-boxing or going jogging together so we can work on our interpersonal skills *and* I can lose all the weight I've put on.'

'You haven't put on *that* much weight,' Jack insisted somewhat unconvincingly. 'Still, I'm up for a jog as long as it's in the evening and it doesn't involve having to get up early.'

That was precisely what Hope had been going to suggest, but she instantly closed her mouth before she could plead the case for exercising in the morning when she was vaguely energised. They had to start compromising more, otherwise they'd stay stuck in the same place, and Hope hated the place where they were currently stuck. 'OK,' she agreed. 'And when we get back, if it's not too late, then maybe we could play a few levels of *Bodycount*.'

Chapter Twenty-eight

Hope didn't like to tempt fate, because that never turned out well, but over the next two weeks, she and Jack settled back into their groove. Except this time, it was a new groove. Not better or worse than the old groove, but different. At least, she hoped so, but it was still too soon to ask Jack if he'd reached any major, life-changing decisions.

It was easier when Hope was at work because she didn't have time to think about Jack, or worry about where their relationship was going, or if he was meeting Susie in his lunch break for a quickie. There was no time to think about anything but making sure Blue Class were ever so slightly ahead of the National Curriculum, as Dorothy had got a tip-off that the Council was planning a spot-inspection. It was all Hope could do to get her charges through her intensive lesson plans with the incentive of extended Golden Time on a Friday afternoon. She'd also managed to crowbar in another trip to Camley Street Natural Park on a day when it had rained solidly, and she now had Stuart's mother threatening to sue Hope, the school and the Board of Governors because his chesty cough had returned, and there had been five reported cases of TB in Islington in the last week, according to the local paper.

When she wasn't drumming knowledge into over-taxed little brains, Hope doled out stickers, filled in reports, and spent every break and at least an hour after school working on the Winter Pageant. She had started rehearsing the junior school two afternoons a week, sweet-talked a local club-owner into lending her his PA system, and persuaded the local traders' association into providing raffle prizes. She'd even found a rabbi to come in and explain the Chanukah story to Yellow Class. Then she'd had to field a reporter from the local paper who'd heard about her ambitious plan for a human menorah and thought she was setting nine seven-year-olds on fire. The journalist was very disappointed when Hope icily explained that they'd be wearing woolly hats with red, yellow and orange streamers sewn to them as a substitute for living flame.

Hope had imagined that after every stress-filled day, she'd dread coming home to work on her intimacy skills with Jack, but, much to her surprise, they'd stuck to their agreement to run in the evenings. Though he was barely able to leave work before eight, as soon as he got home, Jack and Hope would get into their running gear, complete with reflective tabards that she'd found tucked away in a staffroom cupboard, and would pound the cold, wet pavements of Holloway together.

The actual running, or jogging, wasn't much fun but at least the cold meant that Hope didn't sweat like a woolly mammoth in a sauna, and instead of checking the pedometer app on her iPhone to see how long she'd been running and, more importantly, how many calories she'd burnt, they talked. Jack had read somewhere that in order to run effectively, you shouldn't be so out of breath that you couldn't talk. Whenever Hope started panting heavily and was on the verge of calling it quits and limping home, he'd say, 'OK, you have to tell me the three things that happened at work today that pissed you off the most.'

Despite the lack of oxygen getting through to her lungs, it was a request that Hope could never ignore. Then she'd ask Jack the same question, and by the end of the third week of their rapprochement, they were managing an hour's run every other night as they complained and whined and generally bellyached about their jobs, their colleagues and the big mistake they'd made in choosing their respective careers.

Then, when they got home, they very democratically took it in turns to have the first shower and not use up all the hot water. They also took turns to sleep on the sofa, though Hope suspected that if they were sharing a bed sex would be the very last thing that either of them felt like, not when she stank of Deep Heat spray and Jack insisted on having a round of toast and Marmite just before he turned out the light.

Maybe the reconciliation wouldn't be going so well if their jobs were humming along and they weren't both so stressed. Still, Hope comforted herself with the knowledge that not so long ago, they'd have taken the stress out on each other, but at least now they were communicating and she could almost get back into her jeans again.

The only thing that was coming between them was Jack's iPhone. It started ringing in the morning, before he'd even got up, but Hope had learned her lesson and didn't go near it. Or she went near enough that she could see 'Blocked Number' flash up on the screen. The phantom caller would ring three times, then hang up. Ring three times and hang up, until Jack grunted his permission for Hope to turn the phone off.

Jack claimed that it was 'just someone playing silly buggers', but obviously it was Susie. Hope hadn't given much thought to how Jack had ended things with Susie, but it appeared she'd been cut off in a fairly brutal fashion. The end justified the means, as far as Hope was concerned, but one Thursday evening, when they'd come back from their run and it was her turn to grab the first shower, she was forced to reconsider her position.

The bathroom was the one room in the flat that always got toasty-warm and stayed free of arctic draughts. In fact, it became so steamy that condensation ran down the walls and they had to keep one of the window flaps open while they were having a shower. Then it was a tricky job to stand in the bath just near enough to still be able to hold the shower hose without yanking it off the bath taps, but far enough not be assaulted by icy blasts of air from the open window. That night, just as Hope turned off the taps and dived for a towel, she heard Jack on the phone.

He was standing outside the kitchen door, where she'd seen him and Susie kissing, and talking to someone who could only be Susie.

'Look, I told you, I need some time to think,' he was saying fiercely and quietly, so Hope had to climb back into the tub and press her face right up against the frosted-glass window in order to hear better. The window was freezing cold and she was worried that her skin might stick to it, but well, it would serve her right for eavesdropping. 'You *have* to stop this.'

Hope watched her breath puff out in little clouds until Jack gave a bitten-off groan of frustration. 'There's nothing to talk about. I can't see you right now, you have to respect that.'

Silence.

Hope hadn't known goose pimples could be so painful, and she was on the verge of giving up and scuttling for the warmth of her fleecy pyjamas, when Jack suddenly snapped, 'For fuck's sake, Suze, I owe her that much.'

Hope didn't want to hear any more. She yanked herself away from the open window so quickly that she almost slid over. It was one thing to believe that Susie was her arch-nemesis who occupied the number-one place on her shit-list of people who'd done her wrong and would get their come-uppance one day, it was quite another to have a ringside seat to the utter humiliation of someone who used to be your best friend. Hope had also been the victim of one of Jack's sudden changes of heart, and it hurt like a sucking chest wound, just like it hurt that Jack seemed to think that counselling was a penance that he had to endure, rather than the cement that would help them rebuild their foundations.

She pulled her pyjamas on then opened the bathroom door. One glance at the knowing yet defiant look on Jack's face meant Hope didn't have to confess that she'd been ear-wigging.

'I don't want to talk about it,' Jack said sharply as he brushed past her.

'But we have to!'

'We can talk about it tomorrow with Angela there,' Jack said, shutting the bathroom door in Hope's face.

They didn't talk about the phone calls in their therapy session the next evening, because Angela insisted that she wanted them to go on a trip down memory lane, to the very first halcyon days of their relationship.

'How you *start* a relationship is very often an indication of how you behave in a relationship,' she told them. 'It can even be a useful therapy tool in diagnosing and fixing the problems in your relationship.' She sat back and steepled her fingers, so she could peer anxiously over the top of them. 'So, how did you two start dating? Jack, you go first.'

Hope didn't know why he was frowning when the question was a no-brainer. Chaste snog after Youth Club disco, first date the following Saturday at . . .

'Well, I don't know,' Jack said. 'I mean, we'd lived next door to each other all our lives in a small village. There were only about ten teenagers in the place, so we all knocked about together and everyone just expected me and Hopey to get together, and so we just did. It wasn't like I sent her a bunch of red roses and asked her to go steady, it was a gradual process, and—'

'What are you—'

'Hope, we've talked about impulse control,' Angela cut in

and reminded her sharply. 'We have a rule that we don't interrupt when the other person is talking, don't we?'

Having been chastised, Hope sank back down. It was the cardinal rule that she was always drilling into Blue Class, except *her* sharp voice could put the fear of God into them.

Even Jack had the nerve to shoot Hope a resentful look, as he picked up his thread. 'As I was saying, it wasn't like I asked her out and we started dating. We'd sometimes pair up at parties and get off with each other, and we just ended up dating.'

'Hope?' Angela queried.

'My God, have you got rocks in your head?' Hope demanded, which was a contravention of another of Angela's rules, to respect what the other person said. 'That's not at all how we started dating. You asked if you could kiss me on the way home from Youth Club on the thirtieth of November, 1998 at approximately ten to ten and then you asked me to go to the cinema with you. Just me. No one else.'

'But that's—'

'Don't interrupt!' Hope barked at him. 'And we went to see the sequel to *Babe* on the fifth of December, and you paid extra for the superior-comfort seats, and because it was a film about a talking bloody pig and neither of us had any interest in watching it, we started snogging as soon as it began.' Hope pushed back a stray lock of hair with an angry hand. 'The fifth of December, Jack! Making tomorrow our thirteenth anniversary.'

'To tell you the truth, I thought you picked that date at random because you didn't know when we started dating either,' Jack muttered apologetically as Hope turned to Angela, who visibly shrank back in her chair. 'Anyway, I thought we'd already had our anniversary. You're *always* going on about how we've been together for thirteen years.'

Hope rolled her eyes. 'I was rounding up. That's how it

works. Everyone knows that.' She sighed. 'Well, if any of that is indicative of the state of our relationship, then I'd say our relationship is FUBAR, wouldn't you?'

'Um, what's "FUBAR"?'

'Fucked up beyond all recognition,' Hope replied. She rubbed the tips of her fingers over her temples. 'Jesus, Jack, that was one of the most important moments in my entire life and you can't even remember it!'

'I do remember going to see *Babe: Pig in the bloody City*,' Jack said sulkily. 'Look, so I don't have total recall of every single last hour of our relationship, but that doesn't mean I don't care about you. I love you. I've loved you for so long that I can't remember a time when I didn't love you.'

Angela beamed at them both, but mostly at Jack. Hope suspected that she much preferred Jack, who never had to be told off for poor impulse control, which was ironic, considering that it was his poor impulse control that had led them here in the first place. 'Well, you've both done some very good work in this session. I think that's all we've got time for.'

Hope could have sworn that their sessions were getting shorter as the weeks went by. They hadn't even had a chance to discuss Susie's phone-bombing and how Jack was totally not dealing with it. 'I think that's only been forty-five minutes, actually, Angela,' she insisted.

'Oh God, just stop it,' Jack hissed at her, as Angela squirmed in exactly the same way as Sorcha did when she needed a wee and was too scared to put her hand up.

'No, no, I think that's all for today,' Angela squeaked, brandishing her pad as if she was trying to ward off evil spirits, or deflect all the negative energy that Hope was sending her way. 'Your homework for this week. I'd like both of you to think of your five big relationship milestones.'

Jack practically dragged Hope up from the sofa, though she had been prepared to stay there and argue that they had at least another five minutes of the session to go. Ninety quid for forty-five minutes. Angela had to be minted.

'You're unbelievable,' Hope exploded as Jack was still pushing her out of the front door. 'You act like life is something that happens to you, rather than you being an active participant in it.'

'No, I don't!'

'And you knew I wanted to talk about Susie and the phone calls. You can't just keep avoiding stuff.'

'I hate it when you're like this. You get all angry and you won't let things go and your face stays red for hours.'

'You need to sort things out properly with Susie,' Hope said, even though she couldn't believe she was actually saying it. 'I'm not saying that I want you to choose between us yet, not when we still have another two weeks of counselling, but you need to let her know where she stands. Firmly but fairly.'

'I've tried, I really have, but she won't give me any space.' They were just about to turn the corner into the street that led up to the Finchley Road when Jack came to a halt and sank down on the kerb. 'I can't take this. I feel like everyone keeps trying to pull me in a different direction.'

'Don't sit down on the ground. It's cold and you'll get haemorrhoids,' Hope said worriedly, placing her hand on Jack's bowed head. He looked so lost, and all of a sudden, she wasn't sure that she knew how to find him. 'Come on, we're in therapy. Of course it's going to bring up things that are painful but it's all part of the healing process, right?'

'If you say so.'

The ground was glittering with the promise of frost and she really, really didn't want haemorrhoids either, but Hope sat down next to Jack and put her arm around him. 'I do say so. It's like when you hurt yourself and as the wound is healing, it itches something terrible. I guess our souls or our hearts are itching, or whatever.'

'I can't do anything right,' Jack mumbled. 'Even when I

think I've done the decent thing, it turns out I haven't.'

Hope wasn't sure exactly which of his women Jack was talking about – her or Susie – and she also wasn't sure that she really wanted to know. 'I thought we had a rule that what happened in therapy, stayed in therapy?' she asked teasingly, even though she thought it was a stupid rule and yet another avoidance tactic on Jack's part. 'We've been out of therapy for ten minutes and, technically, you're still psychobabbling.'

'I am *not*! I don't do psychobabble,' Jack said but he lifted his head and smiled weakly as if he was up for Hope trying to jolly him out of his existential despair. 'Well, I try not to.'

'We can talk about it next week with Angela,' Hope said firmly, because she was bloody sure it was going to be the very first thing they talked about as soon as they plopped their arses down on her sofa. 'I mean, this business with Susie, but until then we won't worry about it.'

Unless she keeps calling, Hope thought, but she'd cross that bridge when she came to it, and hopefully she'd cross it calmly without losing her temper. Anyway, it seemed to have Jack's vote and he was looking happier.

'Well, at least we only have two more sessions to go,' he said brightly and with evident relief, though Hope wasn't sure that he was any closer to reaching a decision on whether he should stay or go. Therapy didn't seem to be helping – Jack regarded it in the same way as the Delafields' cat, Charlton, regarded a trip to the vet to get shots and a thermometer shoved up his fundament.

It was getting to the stage where Hope knew she couldn't delude herself for much longer. The odds were stacked against her. Jack was with her in body, but his heart was somewhere else, about three miles away in Highgate by her reckoning, and she wondered what would happen if she called his bluff, because she didn't know how much longer she could put up with Jack's prevarication, especially as his prevarication was beginning to look a lot like cowardice. If she said, 'Fine, I give in. Go to her. I just don't care any more,' would Jack be gone faster than she could blink?

But Hope wasn't that brave, and, God help her, she did care. 'Come on, you're not a bad person. You've made bad decisions and you've acted like a dick, sure, but you haven't done anything so terrible that it's killed my love for you,' she said. 'I'm not even saying that as yet another ploy to get you to choose me, I'm just stating it for the record.'

Jack glanced over at her with a look so tender it made Hope wish that she didn't love him as much as she did, because these days that love was more pain than pleasure. 'I don't deserve you,' he said.

'No, you really don't, but you've got me,' she said, and Jack was still gazing at her like his eyes could say all the things that he refused to, and panic swept over Hope in an icy, shuddering wave, because it felt as if that soft, penetrating look might be the warm-up before Jack told her that Susie *did* deserve him. Hope stood up so quickly that she got a headrush. 'This is silly, just sitting here like this. Your arse must have gone numb by now. I think your penance for psychobabbling should be paying for dinner at the cheesy Italian in Camden. No splitting the bill.'

Going to the cheesy Italian in Camden for a debrief on Angela's thrilling choice of one taupe ensemble after another, and to speculate on her private life, had become a tradition.

Jack staggered to his feet and stamped up and down to try and coax the feeling back in his legs. 'You know what?'

'What?'

'Just because it's you, and I kinda love you, I'll even throw in a slice of tiramisu,' he said, his arm settling around her shoulders like it belonged there again.

'Are you feeling all right now?' Hope asked, as they once again set off for Finchley Road.

Jack didn't answer at first, and just as Hope was about to repeat the question, he nodded. 'I know I'm being a total pain in the arse right now. In fact, I've been a total pain in the arse for months, but I'm starting to feel all right. And, I'm beginning to think you and me are going to be all right, too. Better than all right. I think we're going to be just fine, Hopita.'

Chapter Twenty-nine

Jack had been an absolute textbook boyfriend for the rest of the evening, telling Hope scurrilous stories about celebrities that *Skirt* had shot recently, and even asking the waiter for a doggy bag because her stomach was still tied up in knots and she could only manage half her lasagne, though normally he hated to do that. Then when they'd got home, and she'd realised that she'd come on, he'd given her a back rub and made her up a hot-water bottle, without even being asked.

These were all splendid acts of boyfriendliness, but now it was Saturday morning and Hope wondered what kind of mood Jack would be in today. She rolled over with a groan because she had cramps and a nagging ache in her lower back, and saw that it was an unbelievable ten thirty. She'd set the alarm for nine, which counted as a decadent lie-in, so she could go to the gym. Though she hated to admit that Miss Hill, her old PE teacher, had been right, Hope found that exercise really was the best thing for period pain. Once she could actually will her body out of bed.

If she got a wiggle on, she could still make the spinning class at noon, Hope thought, as she made no effort to even sit up. She was just *thinking* of maybe at least pushing her hair out of her face because it was tickling her when the bedroom door was gently nudged open and Jack walked in with a laden tray.

'Happy thirteenth anniversary, sleepyhead,' he said

cheerfully and a little smugly, as Hope finally sat up and pushed her hair out of her eyes.

'What's this?' she gasped, though she could see what this was. On the tray was her favourite breakfast of a lightly toasted bagel with softly scrambled eggs and smoked salmon. There was a glass of orange juice, and her nose twitched before she even took note of the cafetière, because Jack had made proper coffee, even though they both agreed that it was usually too much of a faff and made do with bulk-buying Kenco when it was on special offer.

It was unexpected and thoughtful and unutterably lovely, but what made a tear leak out of one sleep-encrusted eye was the single white rose, bobbing gently in a plastic champagne flute.

Hope opened her mouth to speak but all that came out was a very ineffectual, 'Oh, Jack . . .'

Jack carefully placed the tray on her knees and sat down on the edge of the bed. 'I realised that I'd been rubbish at our anniversary for the last twelve years, what with not knowing that it really was our anniversary.'

'It must have taken you *hours* . . .'

'I had to get up at eight on a Saturday to go to Waitrose. There's proof right there that I love you,' Jack sniffed. 'I don't get up eight on a Saturday for just anyone and I remembered to turn off your alarm . . .'

'This is the sweetest thing that anyone has ever done for me,' Hope said truthfully. She looked down at the tray with a face full of shame. 'I haven't got you anything. Everything's been so up in the air, and you always say that anniversaries don't count unless you're married.'

For one giddy, head-spinning moment she wondered if Jack might have reached a decision that weighed heavily in her favour and bought her an engagement ring on his way back from Waitrose, though his options would have been severely limited and it would probably have had to come from Argos. And Jack *was* pulling something from the pocket of his jeans, and giddy and head-spinning were replaced by panic and a dry mouth.

'Well, it is our thirteenth anniversary, which could be unlucky, but I think we should reclaim thirteen as our lucky number, make it feel special, the way I want you to feel special,' Jack said, his hand closed around something that Hope couldn't see.

And if Jack did love her, really loved her, then yes, actually, he needed to put a ring on it, and now Hope was calm and ready to meet her destiny – and also curious to see if Argos did anything tasteful in the way of princess-cut diamonds in a white-gold setting. 'Well, I feel pretty special,' Hope murmured, and she'd have sworn that all she wanted was to be properly engaged, just that, but she could already see herself dieted to the bone and willow-thin as she gracefully glided up the aisle in a bias-cut, 1930s-style ivory wedding dress, her father smiling proudly down at her as he patted her hand . . .

'Aw, Hopey, I know you feel rotten because the only special thing going on is your special lady-time, so I got you this,' Jack said as he placed a box of Feminax on the tray next to her white rose. 'I even remembered to get you some raspberry-leaf tea.'

Hope wasn't quite prepared for the crushing tsunami of disappointment that engulfed her. If Jack was going to propose, then this would have been the perfect time to do it, what with the talk they'd had on the icy pavement last night, and the hand-holding between courses at the Italian restaurant, and even letting her have the bed, though it was her turn to sleep on the sofa. Maybe she was getting ahead of herself, though. 'We're going to be fine' didn't necessarily translate as 'Let's make things official' – they did still have to sort out the small print, and right now with her tummy cramping and her back aching, she needed Feminax more than she needed a solitaire on the third finger of her left hand. 'I think this has to be the best thirteenth anniversary anyone has ever had,' she said effusively, leaning forward carefully so she could kiss Jack's cheek. 'And I'm making your absolute favourite tea tonight, and I'll even tidy up as I go along.'

Despite the almost crippling period pain, their thirteenth anniversary was a rousing success. It was one of those December days when the clear blue skies made up for the fact that it was so cold that even though she was wearing a pair of fleece-lined gloves, and thick socks with her Uggs, Hope was losing all sensation in her fingers and toes as she and Jack embarked on a mammoth walk.

If they weren't in North London and taking regular rest breaks in chichi coffee shops, it might even have been a trek. They walked up the massive hill to Highgate Village to browse the bookshops, then they walked down a massive hill to Parliament Hill Fields, walked across the Heath to Hampstead, pausing to stare in shop windows at things they couldn't afford, then walked down another steep hill to Camden and the huge Sainsbury's where Hope bought the ingredients for her famous three-hour chilli.

Hope couldn't remember the last time she and Jack had spent so many hours in each other's company. The conversation was easy and relaxed in a way that it hadn't been since the summer. Or maybe even before then, because things had already been going horribly wrong with them last summer, though Hope hadn't known it at the time.

It certainly felt like everything was different now. They teased each other, without taking offence, and they talked about the future. A vague, blurry future, but Jack was happy to ask Hope where she'd like to go if they could manage a mini-break during spring half-term, and they played their favourite game, where they both got significant pay rises and five numbers and the bonus ball on the lottery (they both agreed that getting all six numbers showed a lack of imagination) and they could move into a proper house. 'In Muswell Hill,' Hope insisted, because she could get the

43 bus into work and there was a Whistles, a Space NK and more cake shops per head of the population than any place she'd ever been to.

Jack was more inclined towards Stoke Newington, but they agreed to compromise by moving to Primrose Hill instead.

'When we're living in Primrose Hill, you could convert one of the spare bedrooms into a studio,' Hope said, when they were finally home and she was slowly pouring a whole bottle of Barolo into her chilli. 'You always used to sketch and paint. Don't you miss it?'

Jack was about to open the second of the three bottles of Barolo they'd bought, but he looked up in surprise. 'Well, I suppose,' he said. 'I've been mucking around a bit on the computer with this illustration program I've got. Never seems to be much time for that kind of thing.'

'Maybe you should make the time, like with us running. Set aside an hour every evening when you do nothing but arty stuff,' Hope commented. 'Like I'm trying to do with the gym, so it just becomes routine.' She sighed. 'When this sodding Winter Pageant is over, I'll have so much free time I won't know what to do with myself.'

'Maybe you could take up knitting again?'

'Me and knitting never really got on, but I did read in *Skirt* that bunting is getting very popular.' Hope glanced around the kitchen, trying not to see the decaying worktop and the water damage around the sink but instead a string of bunting pinned to the shelves in a jaunty fashion. From the look of abject horror on Jack's face, he was imagining the exact same thing and his attempts to persuade Hope to live a sleeker, more minimalist life, where everything was brushed stainless steel and matt white with no retro floral prints, were going up in flames. 'I bet Blue Class would love to make bunting,' Hope mused.

'As long as it's only Blue Class,' Jack muttered. He stared around the kitchen with the same dissatisfied look that

Hope got when she stared around the kitchen. 'Maybe we should get started on the kitchen. IKEA's bound to have a sale, and even if we just got new cupboard doors, did something about the worktop, and painted, it would look better. I mean, it would really take some doing to make it look worse.'

Hope smiled at him. That was real commitment right there. 'As long as I don't have to climb on a ladder, or even a chair, I can paint and do things with screwdrivers. And I can change a plug,' she added proudly, because her father had once spent an excruciating Sunday afternoon teaching her life skills that he said everyone needed. Unfortunately, changing a plug had been the only life skill that had stuck.

'I'll take the plug off the kettle, just so you can put it back on again,' Jack promised, as Hope hefted her casserole dish into the oven. 'Shall we watch the first Woody Allen film while we're waiting the last two hours for the three-hour chilli to cook?'

Because it was their anniversary, and because Jack had put her to shame with breakfast in bed and the purchase of female-centric medication, Hope had acquiesced to Jack's pleas for a Woody Allen double-bill. Which was at least double the Woody Allen that she could handle, but he agreed that she could watch *The X Factor* in between screenings. They watched *Annie Hall* while they were waiting for the chilli to cook, and they were halfway through *The X Factor*, their empty plates and the second bottle of Barolo on the coffee table, when the doorbell rang.

Hope was stretched out the full length of the sofa, her socked feet resting on Jack's lap as she tried not to succumb to a food coma. This was what she'd fought so long and hard for, these quiet moments of domestic bliss when they were back to how they used to be, and now someone was trying to ruin it. 'Just leave it,' she told Jack, who hadn't stirred either. 'Anyone who rings the bell at nine on a Saturday night is not someone I want to talk to.'

'Yeah, it's probably God-botherers,' Jack agreed. 'To remind us to set our alarm clocks so we can go to church tomorrow.'

'Which is never going to happen.'

'Bloody right, it's not going to happen.'

The doorbell rang again and they both groaned. Hope nudged Jack with her foot. 'Usually the God Squad aren't so persistent. Maybe there's an emergency. It might be Alice from next door.'

Jack pulled a face. 'It's probably Alice from next door's babysitter.'

Alice from next door's babysitter was a nervy teenage girl who was no match for the combined force of Lottie and Nancy. Earlier that year, she'd come round because Lottie and Nancy had locked themselves in the kitchen and were eating raw cookie dough, and she was terrified that they were going to contract salmonella and die. Hope had had to go round there and use her scariest teacher voice to quell the rebellion.

But Alice from next door's babysitter would never have the stones to lean on the doorbell like that. 'Maybe Gary's forgotten his keys?' Hope suggested as she nudged Jack again. 'You go, he'll only leer at my tits, and I do actually have quite bad period pain.'

'Liar,' Jack said without any heat, because it wasn't true. The alcohol and the chilli had removed any last vestiges of menstrual cramps. 'You go, you always say that exercise is great for period pain.'

Hope glared at him, but she did need to go to the loo anyway, and she'd digested enough of the chilli that she could now put the apple crumble she'd made in the oven. With a put-upon sigh, she swung her legs off Jack's lap and made a great show of staggering to her feet. 'Don't you worry about me, I'll be fine,' she said in a wavery voice that made Jack roll his eyes.

There was no pause between the rings on the bell now. It

was just one long continuous peal, and as Hope opened the living-room door and hurried out into the frigid cold of the hall, she could see a shadowy figure through the frosted-glass panels. The shadowy figure could obviously see her too because it started hammering on the door.

'I know you're in there!' shouted a muffled voice, which sounded familiar, but not familiar enough that Hope could put a name and face to it.

Just to be on the safe side, she slipped on the security chain before she opened the door – and saw Susie standing there.

Chapter Thirty

'What are you doing here?' they both gasped in unison.

Then Hope remembered one important fact. 'I live here!' she snapped, and now that she'd identified Susie as their mystery caller, she couldn't actually look at her but stared at the little puffs of crystallised air that her breath was making instead.

'Jack,' was all Susie said. 'Jack.'

There were many ways that Hope could have replied, but she was too shocked to do anything other than stand there, staring at Susie and frowning because she wasn't meant to be standing on her doorstep. 'I'll go and get him,' was what she eventually said, then closed the door and padded back down the hall, the lino freezing her feet through her socks.

Hope took a deep breath before she opened the living-room door. Jack was sprawled on the sofa, remote control clamped to his chest. 'Who was it?' he asked lazily. 'Nervy babysitter, trick-or-treaters who are over a month late, evangelical Chr—'

'It's Susie,' Hope said, and the way that Jack went from nonchalant to bug-eyed in a nanosecond would have been funny at any other time.

'What does she want?' He was actually cowering, in the same way that Hope did when she was watching a scary film and hoped that the sofa would actually swallow her up so she didn't have to watch it any more.

Hope didn't feel an ounce of sympathy for Jack. He'd got

himself in this mess, and he had to get himself out of it, too. This wasn't a battle she could fight on his behalf. 'Well, she wants to see you. Obviously.'

Jack had other ideas. 'Tell her I'm not here,' he snapped, though he had no right to demand that of her. 'Please, Hopey, I'm begging you.'

'You want me to tell your ex-girlfriend to go away?' Hope clarified, but Jack didn't seem to understand the irony.

'She never takes no for an answer,' he insisted, and he was one panting breath away from Hope having to slap his face and tell him to get a grip. 'It will be better coming from you. I can't. I just can't!'

There was a series of short, sharp rings on the doorbell, and it was clear that the only way that Jack was moving from the sofa was if Hope dragged him from it by the scruff of the neck.

'You really are unbelievable sometimes,' Hope snarled, and slammed the lounge door behind her as she left the room.

'He's too scared to face your wrath,' she told Susie, whose finger was once again poised on the doorbell. 'Sorry and all that.'

'You've got to be fucking kidding me!' Susie looked as if she was about to storm the parapets, but then she thought better of it. 'He can't just decide he wants a time-out and not even fucking discuss it with me first.'

'I think you'll find he can,' Hope said without any malice, because a few weeks ago, she'd been standing in Susie's shoes. Not literally, 'cause Susie had size-three feet and could walk in a six-inch heel and besides, at least Hope had had enough dignity to phone Jack rather than hotfoot it to Susie's front door and demand entry, but she still had a horrible sense of déjà eeew. 'Not exactly made of the brave stuff, is he?'

It felt weirdly disloyal to be slagging off her boyfriend to her ex-best friend who was also her boyfriend's ex-girlfriend. The whole incestuous mess made Hope feel as if she'd wandered into an *EastEnders* plotline.

'He really is a dick sometimes,' Susie said, but she sounded sad and contemplative rather than venomous. Hope raised her eyebrows as she pulled her thick cardigan a little tighter. 'Look,' Susie continued. 'I know I shouldn't have come round, but you know about us, it's not like it's a secret, and he won't talk to me, and I'm going fucking crazy.'

It was absolutely freezing. Hope was sure that it was cold enough to snow, and she was also sure that her extremities were turning blue, but Susie didn't look like she planned to give up her vigil, and Jack certainly wasn't going to move from the sofa. Should she invite Susie in and let her and Jack sort it out between them? But then she'd have to stay in the room with them because they couldn't be trusted on their own.

'You can't camp out on our doorstep like this,' Hope said to Susie. 'It's too cold, for one thing.'

Susie was wearing a big squashy faux-fur coat, but she was shivering – though that could have been from rage. 'Well, then make him come outside and talk to me.'

She darted off the doorstep to bang on the living-room windows. The curtains were drawn but there was a chink of light showing through the gap. And then there wasn't, because Jack obviously preferred to sit in the dark and pretend that this wasn't happening.

Hope sighed. 'Look, I'm not inviting you in but . . . well, do you want to go and get a drink?' She wasn't even sure why she was asking, and she wasn't sure why Susie was nodding in agreement.

'I suppose,' she said warily. 'As long as you promise not to throw this drink in my face.'

It wasn't worth dignifying *that* with a response. Hope pointed at the pub on the other side of the square. 'I'll meet you in there in five. And I'll have a glass of something red.'

'If you're not there in five minutes, I'm coming back,' Susie threatened. Hope didn't doubt it.

She closed the front door and went into the bedroom to pull on another pair of socks and her trusty Uggs. If she'd known Susie was coming round, Hope would at least have made an effort to look a little more alluring. She was wearing jeans – at least she was back in her skinnies – and a leopard-print twinset, which was meant to be arch and ironic, but probably just made her look as if she was trying too hard, Hope thought as she touched up her mascara and tinted lip-gloss.

Jack stuck his head round the bedroom door, just as Hope was buttoning her own fake fur, which wasn't half as plush as Susie's. 'Has she gone?' he mouthed, as if he feared that Susie was still lurking outside and the sound of his voice would set her off again.

'She's in the Lord Palmerston, I'm meeting her for a drink,' Hope said tersely. 'You're welcome to join us.'

'What? Why would you even do that?'

'Because it was either that or invite her in for a cuppa. She wasn't going to budge.' Hope stepped right up to the door, but Jack also refused to budge. 'Look, she was my best friend and you and her . . . it's so messed up, and now she's going through exactly what I went through, and you're behaving in exactly the same way with both of—'

'I forbid you to go!' Jack cut right through Hope's explanation, then actually plastered himself against the bedroom door. 'You are not going for a drink with her!'

'Since when do you have the right to forbid me to do any-thing?' Hope tried to yank open the door. 'And, hello, are you *ten*?'

'I'm not having you go to the pub with Susie and talk about me!' Jack spluttered. 'Bitching about me. I know what you two are like.'

'Compared to what you've done with her and what she's done with you, me and Susie having a drink together hardly compares, does it?' Hope succeeded in simultaneously shoving Jack and yanking at the door, so he was left in the bedroom and she was standing in the hall. 'If you'd bothered to finish with her properly, then this wouldn't even be an issue.'

As soon as she walked into the Lord Palmerston, Hope was forced to tug off her winter gear as she was enveloped in a fierce heat from the roaring log fire, all the radiators going full blast, and everybody in the pub turning to glare at her until she shut the door.

Susie had grabbed a sofa in a little nook beyond the bar, and had a bottle of Pinot Noir and two glasses ready and waiting. 'Wasn't sure you were going to come,' she commented dryly when Hope sat down next to her. 'Bet Jack wasn't too happy about it.'

'What makes Jack happy isn't my biggest priority right now,' Hope said with matching dryness, until she remembered that it was their anniversary, they were in couples therapy, and what made Jack happy was actually her biggest priority at the moment. Unhappy people made bad decisions. 'Anyway, I don't want to talk about Jack with you.'

'What else are we going to talk about? Don't tell me you aren't *dying* for a debrief, because I know I am.' Susie chinked her glass gently against Hope's. 'You're the only person who knows what I'm going through.'

I went through it because you fucked my boyfriend sang the familiar refrain in Hope's head, and she was all set to shout and snap and maybe flounce out until she looked at Susie.

She was still the same beautiful Susie. Wearing exquisitely cut tweed flares, a sloppy silk blouse and a sloppier fine-knit cardigan, which would have made any other girl look like a hot sloppy mess, but made Susie look pulled together and elegant. Expertly made up: eyebrows in a perfect sweeping arch and wearing the careless smile that she did so well; but Hope knew Susie better than that, even if it had been a while. She could see how hard it was to blend in heavy concealer when the skin under your eyes was raw from crying. Could see the waxy, dull cast to Susie's face, and that her sleek, dark hair seemed to have lost a little of its glossiness. All in all, she was a little bit less than she used to be.

They sat there in silence. It was impossible to act as if nothing had happened, and that they could happily discuss the new season of *Glee*, what festivals they were planning to attend next summer and Jennifer Aniston's latest dating travails, because something *had* happened.

'The thing is, Hopey, I fucking love him,' Susie suddenly said. 'I knew it was wrong, and I knew that you were going to get hurt . . . I knew all three of us would get hurt, but I couldn't help myself.'

Hope was sick and tired of that same old tune. Love didn't sweep away everything in its path, including good reason and common decency. Not the love that she knew, anyway. 'Well, maybe you should have tried a little harder,' she said acidly.

Susie looked even more dejected. 'Doesn't matter anyway, does it? He came back to you, so you won in the end.'

As Hope's last sight of Jack had been him clumsily attempting to physically prevent her from leaving the flat, for the first time she had to acknowledge that maybe Jack wasn't such a prize. Or if he was, it was the kind of prize that came with four couples-therapy sessions and God knows how many weeks of no sex. She fidgeted uncomfortably. She wasn't being fair. Their relationship had improved immeasurably since they'd been having counselling: Jack was finally able to see that they had a future together, and today had been perfect until Susie had started leaning on the doorbell.

'You used to say that love was for losers,' she reminded

Susie. 'And you also said that you didn't even know what love felt like.'

'Now I am in love and it feels awful. I can't eat, I can't sleep, and if you and Jack had a pet rabbit, I'd have tried to boil it by now,' Susie spat, threading her hands through her hair. 'I don't know who I am any more, and I don't know why I love him when he's such a fucking coward.'

'We can't talk about him,' Hope said firmly. 'He's not up for discussion.'

'Oh, please,' Susie drawled. 'The reason you're sitting here is because you feel like you'll go mad if you don't talk about it. I mean, the way Jack has played us both; same shit, different girl. And do you want to know how he dumped me in the end?'

'No, I really don't,' Hope gasped.

'Well, I'm going to tell you anyway!' Susie almost shouted, shifting around until she and Hope were almost bumping noses. 'He waited until I'd gone to work, and then he packed up all his stuff, sent me five rambling text messages about his dad and your dad coming down for the weekend and how it was all complicated, blah blah blah, and then I get a text at one on a Monday morning, saying that he was going to have couples counselling with you and it was probably for the best if he didn't see me. Then the fucker turned his phone off.'

Oh Jack, what have you done? Hope thought sadly. 'So, he never called to explain things properly?' Hope asked, though she already knew the answer.

'Did he, fuck!' Susie supplied. 'And now I hate him and I love him and I've turned into one of those girls from a really cheesy rom-com. I even tried eating chocolate.'

'But you *hate* chocolate,' Hope said, because Susie normally couldn't stand the stuff. It had actually been a serious black mark against Susie, because a person who didn't like chocolate was obviously a person who was seriously flawed, until Susie had started shagging Jack and the black mark had become so big, it had obliterated every-thing in its path.

'I hate chocolate and I hate long, hot baths with scented candles and listening to Adele and shopping as retail therapy and all the other lame things you're meant to do to get over someone,' Susie ranted. 'None of them work, and I still feel like shit, and the worst thing of all is that I still want him – and I'm sorry, Hope, I really am, but I know he wants me too.'

'Wanting isn't the same as loving,' Hope countered, even as she tried to process that Jack – *Jack!* – could arouse such deep passion. But that kind of passion simply couldn't endure for thirteen years, not without both parties suffering from nervous exhaustion and frequent UTIs.

'You're frowning,' Susie noted. 'I've pissed you off, haven't I?'

'Of course I'm pissed off with you,' Hope insisted, and it was the truth, but she was only a little bit angry these days, which might have something to do with the counselling and Angela's attempts to encourage her impulse control, and because there was no need to be angry any more. Jack had said they were going to be fine, and it was the only thing he'd said in the last few months that Hope had believed. The soft, melting way he'd looked at her last night before he said it had cut through all her doubt and mistrust, so she could afford to be magnanimous. 'But it doesn't matter any more. I'm not glad it happened, and if I could erase what you did, I would, but Jack and I are closer than we've been in ages.'

'Yeah, but you're not very good at reading Jack, are you?' Susie pointed out belligerently.

'I can read him just fine,' Hope rapped back and actually she *was* starting to get angry now. 'I've known him my entire life. I've been his girlfriend for half that time so I understand Jack better than you ever could.'

'You're so good at understanding him that you didn't

even know he was cheating on you!' Susie shook her head as if she couldn't believe the depths of Hope's delusions.

'Well, I'm not going to make that mistake again, am I?'

'Ha! Ha!' Susie jabbed her finger in Hope's direction. 'So you *do* think that Jack will cheat on you again.'

'Who do you think you are? Judge bloody Judy?' Hope slammed down her glass, then folded her arms tightly so she wouldn't be tempted to use them for hurting. 'For fuck's sake, Susie! Just get over it. Get over Jack, because it's finished. If he wanted to be with you, he'd be with you. Find someone else. Go back to Wilson, if he'll have you, though I very much doubt it.'

'Yeah, right, like that's ever going to happen when Jack is the only man I want to be with,' Susie scoffed, and she seemed to be calming down now, almost as if she knew that she'd never be able to match Hope's rage, so there was no point in even trying. 'Actually, Wilson's been really understanding about the whole thing. Well, when he wasn't telling me what a selfish, home-wrecking bitch I was.'

The only reason that she wanted to talk about Wilson, Hope told herself, was because she couldn't bear to talk about Jack any longer. 'Wilson and I hung out a bit,' she said casually, making sure that she absolutely looked Susie in the eye. 'Before Jack and I started counselling. Y'know, hanging out as mates.'

From the searching look Susie gave Hope, it was obvious that her casual voice hadn't worked. 'Just mates? I wouldn't have expected that.'

'No, neither did I, but he's quite a nice bloke when you get to know him.'

'I can't believe I ever went out with him,' Susie said, and Hope waited for her to follow through with her usual comments about Wilson's prowess between the sheets. And right on cue: 'We had nothing in common, except we both liked it when I sat on his dick—'

'Please, shut up,' Hope said, closing her eyes and trying to scrub her brain of the image that Susie had just conjured up. 'So, listen, I don't want to argue with you any more. This whole thing, it's over, and you need to move on and you need to let Jack and me move on . . . together.'

Susie's lips twisted. 'How long is this going to go on for, Hopey? Have you got some sort of timetable in place to decide whether or not it's working? Or are you going to keep letting Jack walk out, then come back, for the next twenty years?'

'It's going to work. It *is* working! We've only had four counselling sessions and we're back together and everything's great.'

'So, what? Like, you're properly engaged now, are you? Have you set a date?' Susie asked, looking pointedly at the three silver rings on Hope's right hand.

'When we do, you'll be the first to know,' Hope said, scowling because that little dig had wormed its way right through to her heart. 'Actually, you'll be the last to know because this is it, Susie. It's so over between you and Jack that he doesn't want anything to do with you, which is why I'm sitting here having this conversation with you.'

'But he can't just end things without even saying goodbye properly,' Susie protested. 'I can't believe that you and him are settling back into bland domesticity, not when he said that . . .'

'What? What did he say?' Hope challenged, her eyes flashing.

The other girl shrugged. 'I don't like to kiss and tell.'

Hope counted to ten. Then twenty. It wasn't until she got to twenty-five that she was calm enough to say, 'Stop trying to wind me up.' She was even calm enough to pick up her glass again without worrying that she'd snap the stem. 'This is so silly. We're both grown women and we're fighting over a guy like we're still at school.'

Susie smiled slyly. It was a look that Hope knew only too well. A look that had led to both of them getting up to all

347

kinds of no good, from buying skunk from a dodgy bloke in a pub to going skinny-dipping on a Cornwall beach at three in the morning. It was a look that Hope had really missed. 'I'll tell you what would be really funny,' she said, gently nudging Hope's elbow. 'What would Jack do if we both decided to kick him to the kerb?'

Hope didn't even have to think about it. 'He'd have another steady girlfriend within a fortnight,' she said, 'A month, tops.'

'Nah, he'd go wild chasing after anything in a skirt. No way would he settle down so quickly.'

'He totally would,' Hope argued with absolute certainty. 'He might jaw on about how he's too young to settle down, but he went straight from living with me to living with you. Didn't even think about getting his own place or establishing any kind of independence.' She smiled a little smugly at Susie, who was still giving Hope her sceptical face. 'Jack's a settler. He hates changes, hates taking risks, unless they're forced on him, and he'd hate the unpredictability of being with a different girl every week.'

'Maybe you're right,' Susie mused.

'No maybe about it,' Hope said, and suddenly it felt so right to be sitting in a pub with Susie. Men were meant to come and go, but best friends were meant to be there for ever.

'The crappy thing is that when this whole situation settles down, however it settles down, you and me, we're not . . .' Susie tucked a stray lock of hair behind Hope's ear. 'We're not going to be cool again, are we? Not like we were.'

'There's no way we can. Not after everything that's gone on . . .' Hope couldn't finish the sentence because Jack and Susie were over, and she was sick of having to acknowledge that they'd ever been together. 'It would be too weird. And how would it make you feel having to look at Facebook photos of romantic dinners and mini-breaks and stuff?'

'It might not be that weird,' Susie said. 'My nan was

engaged to my granddad's brother before she married my granddad.'

'Oh, right. Did your granddad's brother die in the Second World War or something?' Hope asked gently.

'No! He went to Margate for a week with his work, and my gran copped off with my granddad while he was gone.' Susie stuck out her chin. 'And they all got over it. Used to go down the pub every Friday and Saturday night with Great-uncle Arthur, who ended up marrying this divorcée called Brenda. She was a bit of a goer. Listen, shall we get another bottle, before they call last orders?'

'I'd better be getting back,' Hope said without much enthusiasm because it was inevitable that she and Jack were going to have a row. 'But I'm glad that we got to talk.'

'Me too. Wish it had been about happier stuff, like that horrible girl on *X Factor*.'

'The one who looks like she needs a good scrub with a bar of carbolic and some steel wool?' Hope clarified grimly.

'Urgh, yes, and why is she always rapping? Because she can't hold a fucking tune, that's why.'

Now Hope really wanted to stay for another bottle and a bitch about the current crop of *X Factor* finalists, but Susie and she didn't get to do that any more. She stood up, put on her coat and tried to ignore Susie's slightly injured air. 'Anyway, glad we've got it all sorted,' she said briskly.

'Yes, I'm glad we got a chance to chat things out,' Susie said. 'But you should know, if things don't work out with you and Jack, I'll have him back in a heartbeat. Just so we're clear.'

Hope still couldn't even begin to understand the thrall that they had over each other, but she would do everything in her power to make sure that Susie didn't welcome Jack back with open arms. And open legs, too. That charming little thought set Hope's face into hard, unforgiving lines. 'I can *not* make it any clearer, just leave us the fuck alone,' she said, as she picked up her bag. 'And if you come round and start hammering down the door again, I'm calling the police.'

As Hope walked back across the square she realised, when she tripped over a perfectly level piece of pavement and almost landed on her face, that she wasn't on first-name terms with sober. But she wasn't drunk enough to charge into the flat all riled up and ready for a row. She was clinging to the belief that they were fine, but she didn't want to risk her temper being responsible for Jack reverting to his new and disturbing habit of stuffing a week's worth of boxer shorts, socks and T-shirts into his holdall and storming off into the night.

Her mind made up, Hope vowed that she was going to keep herself and her temper in check, even rummaging in her handbag for an elastic band, which she slipped on to her wrist before turning her key in the lock.

All the lights in the flat were off when she opened the front door and, for a moment, Hope felt icy fingers walk down her spine because maybe Jack *had* changed his behaviour and this time he'd stormed off before they'd even had a row. Then she saw a faint sliver of light under the bedroom door. She took a deep breath and opened it.

'I'm back,' she said cheerfully to Jack, who was in bed with his laptop on his knees and glanced up warily when he heard her voice. 'I'm gasping for a cuppa. Do you want one too?'

Jack looked at her from under his lashes, and Hope knew he thought she was toying with him and that any minute now he was going to have the full wrath of Hope Delafield unleashed on him while he was half naked and utterly defenceless. It automatically made Hope want to snap at him that he could make his own bloody tea, because she didn't lose her temper *all* the time. She lost her temper when she was provoked; like when, for example, he acted like an emotionally tone-deaf idiot.

She gave him a perky smile. 'Tea? Or shall I make hot

chocolate? I think we've still got the Fortnum & Mason stuff I was given last Christmas.'

'Hot chocolate would be great,' Jack agreed, closing the lid of the laptop. 'I put the apple crumble back in the fridge.'

'Thanks,' Hope trilled. 'We can have it tomorrow.'

She had a moment on her own in the kitchen to twitch her limbs in sheer annoyance, before Jack appeared. He'd pulled on jeans and socks and was holding her hot-water bottle.

'I'll make this up for you while you're doing the hot chocolate,' Jack muttered. 'How's the period pain?'

'Red wine is a great anaesthetic,' she said dryly, and Jack smiled, then stopped smiling as it occurred to him that this too could be another trap. 'I'll just go and get into my jammies, then.'

It wasn't until they were both sitting on the sofa sipping from mugs of hot chocolate, with real chocolate melting at the bottom, that Jack voiced his concerns. 'I know you're going to yell at me, so can you just do it? I didn't think anything was worse than you yelling, but, actually, I think the anticipation of the yelling is worse than the yelling itself.'

Hope pursed her lips. 'You sure about that?' she enquired. Jack tensed up and she was sure he was going to bolt. 'Look, I'm not going to yell.'

'But you went to the pub with Susie and I *know* you must have talked about me, so why aren't you shouting?'

'Because I was friends with Susie for a long time . . . well, quite a few months before she became *your* special friend, and we needed to clear the air,' Hope told him. 'And yes, of course we talked about you. It's natural, just like you and Susie must have talked about me. It's only when it's just you and me that we don't talk about Susie.'

'We talk about Susie in therapy,' Jack insisted doggedly. 'We agreed.'

'But we haven't talked about Susie, we've just skirted

around the subject.' Hope put down her mug so she could pull up her legs and shift until she was facing Jack, rather than sitting alongside him. 'It's going better than I ever dared to think it would, but this therapy is only going to work if we use the sessions constructively, rather than as a plaster that we only pull off once a week to see how the wound is healing.'

Hope was quite proud of that little analogy, and there was no need for Jack to look as if he didn't understand what she was talking about. 'I don't know why you have to bring this up when I've already told you that everything's going to be fine.'

'Yeah, but then Susie shows up and you won't talk to her, and you won't talk to me, and I feel like if I want to talk to you about how you deal with this stuff, or how you *don't* deal with it, you're going to walk out rather than have a discussion about it,' Hope said in a calm and measured voice like she was trying to soothe a feral animal.

'That's because you yell.'

'I. Am. Not. Yelling. But I am telling you that the way you handled breaking up with Susie, and Susie trying to break down our door tonight, was pretty much the same way you handled me – and it's not cool.' Hope held up her hand when Jack opened his mouth to protest. 'It's not cool, and you need to know that it's not cool so it never happens again.'

'But I don't like confrontations. That doesn't make me a bad person,' Jack burst out. 'It's like, one moment everything was ticking along and I knew where my life was going was OK, and now I don't know what the hell I'm doing. It's fucking scary, Hope.'

Sudden and sweet relief swept over Hope because, yes, they were back together but, finally, Jack was opening up. He was being honest with her and she could begin to understand why he'd been behaving like such an insensitive arsehole. She could cut him some slack, instead of secretly resenting him. 'But you don't have to go through this alone,' she said, stroking her hand down his cheek and feeling ridiculously pleased when his hand held hers in place. 'I'm here. I want to help, don't shut me out.'

'But even when you don't yell, you want me to confront all the shitty things I've done, and I could say that I don't know why I did them, but maybe it's just because I'm a shitty person,' Jack said, nuzzling against Hope's hand. 'I knew what I was doing with Susie wasn't right, but I did it because it was easier than figuring out what was wrong with us.'

'What *was* wrong with us?' Hope asked, and Jack shrugged helplessly because there hadn't been one landmark day when their relationship had started to flounder, it had been a gradual drip-drip-drip that had suddenly turned into a tidal wave. 'We should have been having more sex, shouldn't we? Exciting, kinky sex with props and costumes.'

Jack blanched as if the idea of Hope in a French maid's outfit, complete with feather duster, wasn't what he had in mind. 'More sex, maybe,' he said. 'But nothing *too* kinky, and I'd never have dressed up in a Plushy costume no matter how much you begged.'

Now it was Hope's turn to blanch and swat Jack with a cushion. 'Ewwww! We can get better at sex,' she said earnestly. 'Look how good we got at running. I can do twenty continuous minutes now without feeling like I'm about to die.'

'Honestly, Hopey, the sex was OK, I just wish there'd been more of it,' Jack insisted as he put down his empty mug and stretched out so he could lie on the sofa with his head in Hope's lap, which wasn't the sign of a man about to disappear into the night with approximately one-tenth of all his worldly goods and chattels. 'It was more that I felt like life was passing me by, and that I was already settled down, and the only thing I had to look forward to was being even more settled down when I should be doing wild and exciting things.'

Hope knew *exactly* what he meant. Occasionally when she got an email from Justine extolling the virtues of living five minutes away from the beach, smaller class sizes and rippling surfer dudes on every street corner, she had an urge to empty her bank account, jump on a train to Heathrow and buy a ticket for the next available flight to Sydney. Maybe even stop over in Thailand for a month and tour the islands . . . 'Yeah, wild and exciting does sound good sometimes.' She stroked her fingers through Jack's thick, shiny hair. 'You know, there's nothing to stop us renting out the flat and spending two years somewhere else,' she ventured. 'If we wanted to mix things up a little.'

'What? Like Manchester or Brighton?' Jack asked, doubt wrapping around every syllable.

'No! Like Sydney or New York, or even working with a charity and going somewhere like Haiti or Tibet.'

'But we'd have to get shots and even then we might still get malaria, and what if the people we rented to trashed the place?' Jack demanded, his limbs going rigid. 'I'm a graphic designer. I don't have transferable skills. I'd be no use in the Third World.'

'It's just an idea,' Hope said in a soothing voice, though she really felt like making her voice extremely strident. Jack may have thought he was yearning for thrills and adventures, but actually he hated anything outside of his neatly aligned, alphabetised comfort zone. Whenever they went to a festival, he packed loads of anti-bacterial hand-wipes and moaned on about how it was absolutely guaranteed that every single food-stall employee didn't wash their hands after they'd been to the loo.

When they went to the beach, any beach, be it in Ibiza or Lancashire, Jack whinged about sand between his toes and freaked out if a seagull came within six feet of him. He wouldn't go ice-skating, had made Hope promise on Blue

Class's lives that she wouldn't try out for Roller Derby, and when she'd wanted to take part in a charity sky-dive, he'd told her mum who'd then spent a week emailing her stories about people who'd gone sky-diving and ended up paraplegics.

When it came to wild and exciting, Jack absolutely sucked. So, having an affair with Susie must have been the very zenith of wild and exciting for him. It was about as wild and exciting as he was ever likely to get.

'I'm just saying that being with someone for a long time doesn't have to be boring. Look at Elaine and Simon. They go to festivals and they still smoke dope, and in the school holidays, they load the teen witches into the camper van and drive to Europe,' Hope explained, as she began to check Jack's hair for headlice. 'You couldn't call Elaine and Simon boring.'

'I guess not,' Jack agreed. 'I just get scared that we're going to turn into our parents.'

'Take that back! The day you join a golf club is the day I bash your head in with a shovel,' Hope snapped, and she wasn't even joking.

'I do take it back. I never said it. I'm trying not to even think it.' Jack stilled. 'Are you checking me for nits? There hasn't been another outbreak, has there?'

Hope gently cuffed Jack's head when he tried to move. 'No! Just force of habit.' She continued to rake her fingers through his hair. 'I think you're OK and, well, do you think we're OK?'

'Yeah.' Jack sounded a little amazed. 'We can walk through our problems without anyone shouting . . .'

'. . . or having a snit and flouncing out,' Hope finished for him. She grinned down at Jack. 'If Angela was here, I think she'd say that we've just had a breakthrough.'

'Talking of breakthroughs . . . I figured something out while you were in the pub,' Jack said. His voice had suddenly become so strained, it sounded like forming words was painful for him. 'Can I be honest with you?'

Now it was Hope's turn to still and stop checking Jack for headlice. 'Gosh, that sounds ominous,' she said lightly, though her light voice wasn't working very well. 'But, yeah, sure, go ahead. And no, I won't shout or yell,' she added, because she knew Jack would want a firm disclaimer before he opened his heart.

'I promised I'd take the therapy seriously and not have any contact with Susie because ... well, I know it seems like I was being a right bastard about it but it's just ... it's why I couldn't see her tonight. Couldn't walk to the front door and tell her to go away. I couldn't because, well, because ...'

'Because what?' Hope prompted gently, and she didn't know if it was because of the rich hot chocolate and the vats of red wine she'd consumed, but all of a sudden she thought she might throw up. 'Because she's even more scary when she yells than I am?'

'It's not funny, Hopey. Not any of it, not when I have to tell you that if I'd seen Susie standing there, when just talking to her on the phone was torture, I'd have left with her. These last few weeks with you have been great, and I'm so glad we're all right and we're friends again ... but I love her ...'

'But you said you loved *me*,' Hope said, and she wasn't yelling because even talking was hard enough. 'You love *me*!'

'I love you but I'm not ...'

'Don't say *that*! Don't you dare say it,' Hope warned Jack, pushing his head off her lap so she could scramble to the other end of the sofa. 'Don't you fucking dare!'

'But it's the truth,' Jack insisted as he sat up, swallowed hard and set his face in resolute lines. 'I love you, but I'm not *in love* with you.'

'Then try harder!' Hope pleaded. 'What you and Susie have is a fantasy. It's sex and infatuation. As soon as you have to deal with real life, go to the supermarket together, set up a joint account, pick up her dirty knickers from the bedroom floor, it won't last, I promise you!'

'But what if it does last?' Jack asked, and Hope didn't know how he could stay so calm and unmoved when he was telling her that he *loved* Susie more than her. 'And even if it only lasted a couple of months, I'd be happy just to have those two months, but it's more than that. She gets me and when I'm with her, I'm a different person. I like being that person.'

'But what if it did only last two months? Do you want me to wait? Because I will.' Hope choked out and she was too shocked, lulled by the weeks when she thought they were finding their groove again, to yell or cry or show a little backbone. 'Please don't do this, not if you love me even a little bit.'

'But I do love you,' Jack insisted, trying to take Hope's hand then stopping when she shrank back from him. 'That's why I'm doing this – because it's not fair on you.'

'And it's fair to do this *now*, on our anniversary? You said you'd give us six weeks of counselling before you made your mind up, and we've still got two to go. A lot can happen in two weeks.'

Hope wasn't aware of moving, but she'd curled herself into a little ball, and she couldn't even get her hands free to ward Jack off as he slid down the couch so he was pressed up against her and began to stroke the rigid line of her spine with a steady, calming hand. 'I'll stay for another two weeks so we can use Angela to help us end things like grown-ups,' he conceded, though it wasn't much of a concession. 'I know you don't believe me, Hope, but I love you – and I don't want everything we've had together to be ruined because we have one of those really ugly break-ups. We're worth more than that.'

'But everything we've had together has been ruined because you fu—'

'No!' Jack bit out, even as he kept stroking her back gently. 'Don't start that again, Hope. It's already been said, and I know what I've done wasn't right, but going on about it all the time doesn't change things.'

Hope peered out through a tangle of hair. 'Please don't, Jack . . .' she whispered. 'I can change. I can be the person you need . . .' She could hear her rusty voice saying these things, and even as she said them, Hope knew that she couldn't change. Her personality was pretty much fixed, good bits and bad, and she was stuck with it, even if Jack didn't want to be stuck with it any longer.

'I'm a different person now, Hopey, but that doesn't mean I don't want you in my life, because I do . . . Like, today has been perfect – but not once did it feel like we were a couple. It just felt like you were my best friend again, and you always will be.'

That was when Hope started to cry, though she didn't know how she'd managed to hold the tears in that long. As soon as the first sob was wrenched from her, Jack's arms were around her and he held her so tightly, surrounded her with the familiar feel and smell of him, that Hope wished that she could die right then, because she'd never have him like this again. Never have *this* again with anybody. 'Will you promise me one thing?' she hiccupped between sobs. 'Promise me you won't see her until after our last session. Will you give me that at least?'

'Hopey . . .' Jack groaned.

'Can you just give me *that*? Just two more weeks where it's just you and me?' She didn't care that she was begging and pleading and clinging to him with shaky limbs, because she was entitled to beg and plead and cling for this one last time. 'Promise!'

'I promise,' Jack said, with what sounded like a sigh of relief, and Hope wondered how long he'd been building up to and dreading this moment, and now it was done and he'd got off relatively lightly. But she was ruined, and all she could do was cry so hard that for that night, at least, they slept together on the sofa that they'd never got round to pulling out into a bed, with Jack's arms around her as he kissed her hair and her damp cheeks, and told her not to cry because everything would be all right.

Chapter Thirty-one

Although she'd railed about it constantly for the last month, Hope was grateful during the next week to be stuck with the responsibility for Balls Pond Primary School's Winter Pageant. Knowing that everyone was relying on her, from the tiniest member of the Red Class right up to Mr Gonzales and Jenny Jenkinson-Smythe, the Chair of the Board of Governors, meant that Hope had to push her heartache and her utter wretched misery to one side and throw herself into her work. She was even grateful to Sarah, who taught Year Six, for being such a feeble slacker, because organising and rehearsing and having meeting after meeting to discuss props, music and raffle prizes was all that was keeping Hope sane.

Then there was the time she spent trying to pin down Dylan, Wilson's assistant. Every time Hope emailed him a definite plan of action, with times and logistics all clearly spelt out, Dylan would reply with a tepid, *Yeah, let me get back to you on that*. It was just as well every parent would turn up armed to the hilt with camcorders, cameras, phones and other recording devices even if there were no high-res official photos for sale.

There'd also been a leaking pipe over the weekend, which had drenched the book corner, and the classroom reeked of damp as Hope tried to save the least-sodden books by drying them on the radiators. Timothy had become so distraught about the soggy fate of *The Velveteen Rabbit* that Hope had had to send him to the school nurse.

On the Thursday, when the Council's school inspectors turned up to do the threatened spot-check, Hope wasn't the least bit surprised. It really was that kind of week: a week sent up from the very bowels of hell. Hope took the class through their two-times table and then decided that she might as well go for broke and bust out the ten-times table, which Blue Class managed, without prompting, for the first time ever. Hope suspected the look in her eyes, the look that promised no more stickers for the rest of their natural lives, might have had something to do with their stellar performance.

After Blue Class had aced their numeracy skills, they then had a heated debate about recycling, their hot-button topic, and it was hard to get them to stop ranting about 'people who totally disrespect the planet by chucking their Coke cans in normal bins'.

'It's like shouting *right in the planet's face,*' they chorused.

Hope wasn't sure that the two women from the Council agreed, but at least Blue Class had proved that they could grasp a concept and run with it, and the inspectors looked like two women whose ovaries were beating out an urgent tattoo when Sorcha formally introduced them to Herbert, the class hamster.

As far as Hope could tell, the spot-inspection had gone as well as could be expected. She was still gainfully employed at the end of the week, so she decided not to worry about it. There were so many other things to worry about instead. Like the kitchen cabinets she'd promised Jack she'd sand down while he was working late, which she hadn't, because all she wanted to do when she got home was crawl into bed and stay there until she mummified between the sheets. Jack, of course, now had an ulterior motive in getting the redecorating of the kitchen underway. He'd even been to see Gary from upstairs to ask whether slapping white paint over every surface would be enough to fool a surveyor.

But, mostly, Hope worried about going to see Angela,

because all too soon it was Friday evening again. She'd never noticed how quickly Friday evening rolled around each week, but here it was and here she was sitting on the chintz sofa, whose springs were becoming more unsprung with each session.

Jack was holding her hand, which was new. Or, rather, he was keeping it on his knee by placing his hand on top of it. Hope could see Angela looking at Jack's hand resting on top of hers with a faintly puzzled expression, as if she wasn't sure how her counselling sessions had helped them achieve such a rapprochement.

Maybe that was why she started scribbling furiously on her pad, before Hope could tell her that ever since Jack had decided that he didn't want to spend the rest of his life with her, he'd become very touchy-feely. She glanced over at Jack to see if he was going to tell Angela his good news, but he just smiled vaguely at Hope and patted her hand.

Eventually Angela looked up and gave them both a nervous but approving smile. 'So, how did you both get on with the homework?'

Hope looked at her blankly. Homework? As it was, every minute of her waking day was accounted for – *and* she was expected to remember to do Angela's homework?

'You were both going to tell me your five relationship milestones,' Angela prompted.

'There's no point,' Hope said, and as she heard herself speak she marvelled, as she had done all week, that she could talk and move her limbs and drink tea and brush her teeth, even though she was broken. 'There's no point to doing this any more, I mean. Jack's finished with me. He wants to be with Susie.'

'We both decided that it was the right thing to do,' Jack added, though Hope couldn't remember having a say in the decision.

Angela didn't look that surprised. 'Ah, I thought you were both on the verge of a breakthrough.'

'Well, I think it was more my breakthrough than Hope's,' Jack admitted. 'But I think we both know it was the right decision.'

Hope didn't know why Jack kept saying 'we'. There was no 'we'. Never would be again.

'And how do you both feel about this?'

'Well, sad, obviously,' Jack said, not even noticing when Hope removed her hand from his knee so she could fold her arms across her chest. 'Yeah, really sad, and a bit over-whelmed and relieved, I suppose. Not relieved that we're breaking up, but relieved that we don't have to pretend any more and that we're both being really civilised about it.'

'We' was now Hope's most hated word, knocking 'moist' right off the top spot. She stared down at her shoes, because she'd found that if she focused on just one thing then it stopped her from bursting into tears.

'And how do you feel, Hope?' Angela asked gently.

Rejected. Unloved. Unloveable. Wretched. Heartbroken. Inside out. In the very pits of despair. These were just words, adjectives, that didn't even come close to how Hope really felt. There were feelings that she couldn't even let herself feel, because she knew that she'd break, and she wasn't sure she could put herself back together again. So mostly she made herself feel numb. She lifted red-rimmed eyes to look at Angela who was peering over the edge of her pad at her.

'What Jack said,' Hope replied, and she knew she sounded glib, even though she certainly didn't feel it, but she couldn't help herself. 'And as an added bonus, I've com-pletely lost my appetite. Reckon I'll be back in my skinniest skinny jeans by the end of next week.'

Angela frowned. 'Sometimes we resort to humour when we're trying to divert attention away from what we're really feeling.'

'Believe me, if you knew what I was really feeling, you'd have me sectioned,' Hope said as Jack shifted uncomfortably next to her, but she was sick of 'we' and pretending to be on board the break-up train. It was all bullshit. Just like turning up here every Friday evening had been an exercise in bullshit. 'We didn't decide anything. Jack decided, not me, and the reason that he decided was because on Saturday night there was a ring at the doorbell . . .' she began, but Jack started fidgeting furiously.

'There's nothing to discuss,' he practically yelped. 'We both know it's over, so what's the point of dragging up stuff that doesn't matter any more?'

'But what attracted you to each other? It wasn't just the sex, was it? It was obviously stuff you weren't getting from me.'

'I think what Hope is trying to say, is that she really needs some closure in order to work through this transition in your relationship,' Angela summarised helpfully.

Although Hope didn't think 'transition' was really the right word to describe the way that Jack was intent on destroying everything they could have been, she still nodded in agreement. 'I have tortured myself every day this last week trying to understand what it is about Susie that you can't live without,' Hope snapped. 'You say that we were having problems – but why was it Susie? Why wasn't it one of those hot thin fashionistas from *Skirt*? Why was it *her*?'

'Why do you need to know?' he asked. 'It's not going to change anything.'

'Because not knowing is killing me, and if you were getting some kind of, I don't know, emotional nourishment from her that you weren't getting from me, as well as fun sexy times, then that's something I need to work on for next time.' Hope paused. 'Not that there's ever going to be a next time, because I'm done with relationships. I couldn't stand to feel this fucking terrible ever again.'

Jack looked up at the ceiling. 'If you really must know, well, Susie was always so enthusiastic about everything.

We'd talk about art and design, and she encouraged me to work on my own creative projects.' He looked a little sheepish. 'And well, we talk about stuff that doesn't involve what we're going to have for dinner, or what needs doing around the flat, or our parents. When I'm with her, everything we do is new and exciting.'

Well, wasn't that just lovely for him. 'You could have talked about art with me,' she said bitterly.

'But you never ask,' Jack said.

'That doesn't mean if you'd wanted to talk about it I'd have refused to listen.' She ran her fingers through her hair, which really needed another comb-out. 'You can't have it both ways, Jack. Being part of a long-term couple does mean having to do boring stuff like menu-planning and DIY, but that's not all it has to be.'

'It was more than that, Hopey, but you don't want to go there,' Jack warned, but she had to go there. No matter how much it hurt, not knowing hurt even more.

'Tell me,' she commanded. 'Just tell me.'

'OK, it was the sex.' The words burst out of Jack's mouth as if they were jet-propelled. 'It wasn't like I expected us to be hanging from the light fittings every night, but mostly it was just once a week, if that, during term-time – and I'm sorry, Hope, I don't think either of us was ever so up for it that we were literally ripping each other's clothes off in places where we were likely to get arrested for ripping each other's clothes off.'

Hope was all set to deny Jack's accusations in the most vehement way that she knew how, which involved a lot of shouting and swearing, she even opened her mouth, but all that came out was a ragged exhalation of breath, as she scrolled back through all the many different times and ways that she and Jack had had sex. How nervous and excited she was for the first year, when having actual sex seemed like the most shocking, transgressive thing you could ever do with another person, even though it had taken a good few months before she'd actually worked out how she was meant to have an orgasm.

Then the student years of having sex with Jack in bedrooms of shared houses or halls of residence, when they were both too drunk or stoned to really get down with their big bad selves, especially as they had housemates who loved to bang on the wall every time the bed squeaked.

Then there was setting up their first home together, the squalid studio flat in Whitechapel. By then sex had become familiar and without any mystery, but mostly sex had been fun. Hope had thought it was a measure of how close they were, that they could giggle and take the piss out of each other even when they were lying naked in bed, but apparently it meant that they'd been doing sex wrong.

And then she got to the time they'd been having sex on the sofa a couple of weeks before going to Barcelona. Or they'd started to have sex, because it had been a couple of weeks and as Jack put it, 'If we don't do it now, we might forget how to do it altogether.' Hope hadn't really been bothered either way, but she'd decided to take one for the team, and about halfway through, when she had the TV remote digging into her shoulder blade and Jack kept threatening to slide off the sofa on to the floor, they'd stopped.

'Look, I'm not really in the mood,' Hope remembered herself saying. 'Shall we just watch *MasterChef* instead?'

Jack hadn't even put up a fight. 'God, yes,' he'd said. 'Shall I put the kettle on?'

Hope liked sex. She liked having sex with Jack, but if someone said to her, 'For the sake of the future of the planet, you must never have sex again,' she'd cope. Though if they substituted alcohol or chocolate for sex, then as far as Hope was concerned the world could go up in flames.

'It wasn't just me,' she said after what seemed like hours, but couldn't have been that long, because there'd been no subtle prompts from Angela or pointed looks from Jack.

'You never, ever once said that you wanted us to be going at it 24/7, or having sex in public places or, like, dressing up in rubber, so it's a bit rich to make out like I'm completely devoid of passion.'

'Oh, I'm curious that you—' Angela started but Hope never discovered what she was curious about, because Jack was cutting right across her.

'Well, you were certainly passionate about getting engaged,' he said shortly, like he'd given her fair warning that he was going to get brutal, and now Hope would just have to deal with the consequences. 'You were *obsessed* with getting engaged even though there was no need to.'

'There was every need,' Hope argued. 'We'd already bought a flat together and getting engaged was the logical next step. I don't know why you had to turn it into a such a big deal.'

'You were the one who made it a big deal!' Jack shot back. 'Why were you so desperate to get engaged?'

'Why were you so desperate *not* to get engaged?' Hope demanded.

'Because we'd get engaged and then, a few months down the line, being engaged wouldn't be enough and you'd want to get married, and then it would be kids, and within three years, my life would be over,' Jack stated like it was an absolutely unassailable fact.

'But getting married and having kids doesn't mean that,' Hope said, as she shook her head. 'Sure, it's the end of certain aspects of your life, you can't really pull an all-nighter any more, but it's also the start of something really wonderful.'

'So, you do want to get married and have kids? I knew it!'

'Well, yeah, one day,' Hope said, and now she was confused and shot a helpless look at Angela, who gave her one of her encouraging smiles but didn't seem inclined to leap into the fray. 'Not right now. Yes, I wanted to get engaged. There's nothing terrible about that, considering how long we've been together. Why are you trying to make me feel guilty for wanting to get married and have children at some stage in our future? If people didn't have children, then the human race would die out.'

'But I don't want children. Not in a couple of years' time. Not *ever*!' Jack snapped as Hope and Angela both turned to stare at him. 'There are so many things I want to do in my life that don't involve children. Maybe I want to work in New York . . . why are you snorting at me?'

'I'm snorting at you because when I suggested moving to Brighton or Manchester you had a panic attack. You're never going to live in New York, Jack, so stop fooling yourself,' Hope shouted, because she'd got over her shock at having to listen to all the things she'd never wanted to hear, and now she was furious that Jack was implying that getting engaged was the first step in her masterplan to bind him to her for ever by podding out child after child, when he'd much prefer to ponce about lower Manhattan. 'That whole weekend we were in New York you did nothing but moan. You hated the subway. You said the whole city smelt and that it was impossible to get a decent cup of tea.'

'I was just using New York as an example,' Jack protested. 'It could be Berlin—'

'Huh! Berlin!'

'Or Boston. I'm just saying that we want different things in life—'

'No! This isn't about your career, or wanting to live in some hipster paradise – this is about you shagging Susie right after we got back from Barcelona and the big fight we'd had about getting engaged. And you can try and blame me for driving you away, but the truth is . . . the truth is you're just a selfish arsehole who doesn't think of anyone but yourself.'

'That's not fair, Hopey.' Jack turned and tried pat her arm but Hope slapped his hand away.

'Don't talk to me about being fair,' she said. 'The way you've acted is hardly fair.'

Jack nodded slowly. 'You're right. I know you're right.'

'But is Hope right, Jack?' Angela suddenly piped up, her eyes gleaming. 'I think a lot of this is due to the flawed dynamic in your relationship; I hear a lot of talking but no real communication. Hope shouts to get her point across, and Jack, you back down without listening because you have an aversion to confrontation.'

Hope couldn't believe what she was hearing. Was that all Angela had to say to them? 'I'm shouting because I'm angry and I have every right to be angry. I'd rather feel angry than feel as *vile* as I have done all week.'

'I don't see an angry person, I see a very scared and unhappy person,' Angela offered, her voice dying to a croaky whisper as Hope bared her teeth. 'Well, anyway, we need to wrap this up.' She scribbled something down. '*Really* excellent work in this session. Well done! I'm assuming that you won't want to book any more sessions together for the new year? Though I think you could benefit from coming to see me on your own, Hope, so we can work on some techniques for your anger management. I take it that the elastic band isn't that effective any more?'

Hope was all ready to shout that she'd rather gouge out her own internal organs with a fork and a pair of pliers before she booked any more sessions with Angela, but she didn't need to say anything because Jack could tell that she was one breath away from a full-blown temper tantrum. 'Let's talk about that next week,' he said, as he began to grab Hope's coat and bag as she sat there muttering and shaking her head. 'It's really important to both of us that we end our relationship on good terms.'

'Oh, that reminds me – homework. I'd like both of you to think about where you see yourselves in ten years' time,' Angela informed them, surreptitiously checking the clock on the wall. 'And Hope, we'll talk about what your next steps should be. I think you could really benefit from some meditation techniques so . . .'

Hope opened her mouth, then realised that she had no words and might have to start screaming instead, but Jack clamped his hand around her arm in a vice-like grip. 'We'll talk about that next week,' he repeated quickly, as he pulled an unresisting Hope up off the sofa. 'We have to go. We've got dinner plans.'

As soon as they were outside, Hope burst into tears, and Jack could also tell that when she cried with that much intensity and that much snot, it was because she was absolutely, utterly, murderously furious.

'Come on, Hopey,' he said softly, as he guided her down the road. 'Angela was only trying to help.'

'I only shout when I really have to.' She was shouting now, and a couple walking towards them suddenly veered off across the street. 'Is that why I drove you away? Because I shout all the time and I'm shit in bed?'

'You're not. I've been a selfish dickhead,' Jack said frantically, taking Hope in his arms so he could shower her tear-soaked face in kisses. 'Honestly, Hopey, I'm being harsh with you because I don't want you to think that there's a chance that I'll change my mind. I know you hate me for it, but you'll hate me more if I keep getting your hopes up like I've been doing. I think that's the cruellest thing I've done.'

'I just can't deal with this anymore,' Hope sobbed. 'It never gets better. It just keeps getting worse and worse.'

Jack pressed his lips to her clammy forehead. 'Look, I'll stay with you the next few days so we can go home for Christmas and tell the parents together.'

They were done. Over. Finished. Up to their ankles in the painful business of breaking up. She knew that. She did, but . . . Jack was giving her two more weeks, and anything could happen in those extra days. By the time the combined power of two sets of parents had wheedled, emotionally blackmailed and beaten Jack down, then maybe they wouldn't be so over. Sure, Jack might have long talks about art and design and hot sex with Susie whenever he wanted it, but those weren't the ties that bound two people together, not like a Christmas in Whitfield with two mothers who could bring pressure to bear like North Korea.

Hope wiped her wet snotty face with the ends of her scarf. 'Do you promise?' she asked between hiccups.

Jack looked down at her as if he was looking at the most beautiful woman in the world and not a girl who had a red, blotchy, scrunched-up face. 'Absolutely promise. I even promise to come to the Winter Pageant, and I wouldn't do that for just anyone.'

Chapter Thirty-two

In the end, when it felt as if everything she held dear was circling the drain, Hope decided it was easier to focus on simply getting to the end of the week. Or getting to approximately seven thirty on Thursday evening, when the Winter Pageant would be over and she'd be on her way to the Midnight Bell with Marta and Elaine (and respective partners) for their unofficial Christmas dinner.

Hope worked until eleven each night with only a brief respite from the never-ending Winter Pageant preparations on Wednesday evening, when she worked on Blue Class's school reports instead, but that was almost like fun. Apart from Sarah from Year Six, all the staff gathered in the staffroom with a huge quantity of pizza and wine and pooled their resources and their expertise in writing the passive-aggressive double-speak that Mr Gonzales expected from them, rather than the plain, unvarnished truth.

'How do I say that Stuart is a vicious bully who'd rather belch and fart than spend even five seconds paying attention to me?' Hope asked the room at large.

'Oh, just say, "Stuart continues to experience some challenges learning in a classroom environment but I'm confident that with the right home support, we'll see a distinct improvement in his knowledge retention and interaction with his classmates,"' said a laconic drawl from the corner of the room where Sunil, who taught Year Five, was leafing through his old reports so he could recycle his greatest work.

And then it was Thursday morning. Hope was up at six to bake fifty cupcakes, which she'd frost and ice when she got home, and present to Blue Class tomorrow. Then she packed frock, heels and make-up bag for the night's festivities before she approached the slumbering lump under the duvet, whom Hope assumed was her soon-to-be-ex-boyfriend.

Jack had also been working like a dog and getting home either just before or just after Hope. There had been the faintest niggling doubt lodged at the very back of her mind that Jack was up to no good, until a motorcycle courier had come round at midnight on Tuesday with a Cromalin that had to be re-checked and sent back to the repro house. She got it: he really was working late.

Last night, he'd arrived home at two a.m., but the February issue of *Skirt* had been put to bed, and Jack had no intention of going into the office this morning, but was heading straight to the art department Christmas lunch at St. John Bread & Wine, where they'd spend the afternoon drinking away the pain of all the late nights. Jack had promised not to get too drunk and embarrass Hope by rocking up to the Pageant completely rat-arsed. He'd also promised to pretend they were still together because Hope couldn't deal with telling Elaine and Marta the awful truth. Not tonight. Not when she'd most likely burst into tears and beg Jack not to leave her.

Hope quickly left Jack a scribbled note reminding him of his obligations, unpeeled the edge of the duvet so she could plant a kiss on his ear, because some old habits refused to die, then hurried out.

Blue Class were already so over-excited that Hope half-wondered if she needed to talk to the dinner ladies about cutting down their sugar intake at lunchtime. They spent the morning making Christmas cards for their parents, grandparents and primary care-givers, and after lunch, Hope shepherded them to the assembly hall for the dress rehearsal.

An hour later, Hope was sitting in the back row, rocking from side to side with her head in her hands.

'Buck up, Hopey,' Elaine said, patting her back. 'You know what they say about a bad dress rehearsal.'

'Yeah, it means an even worse opening night,' Hope whimpered. She lifted her head so she could stare mournfully at Elaine. 'I wrote left and right on everyone's hands in indelible marker pen, so why do they all still insist on going the wrong bloody way?'

'Frankly, you're a lightweight,' Elaine informed her. 'You organise this Pageant for five years on the trot, and then you can come moaning to me about how primary-school children can't take any direction. Five years!'

'But you never had to do the junior school as well,' Hope protested hotly. 'I swear, Sarah's right at the top of my list, and she's going to stay there for quite some time.'

Elaine actually chortled. 'I'm sure she's quaking in her Russell & Bromley boots.'

'You know, she's not the only one on my list,' Hope said pointedly. 'I'm pretty sure I saw your name on there too.'

'Am I on this famous list?' said a voice behind her, and Hope twisted round, almost giving herself whiplash in the process, to see Wilson standing there with his camera bag.

'What are you doing here?' Hope asked in surprise, her voice breathless against the sudden slam-dunk of her stomach at the completely unscripted sight of him. 'I was expecting Dylan.' She looked at her watch. 'About half an hour ago.'

Although Wilson always looked the same, right down to the old-fashioned camera slung around his neck, Hope was surprised that the way she felt about seeing him standing there was new and different. There was a nervy excitement bubbling up inside her, which was a welcome change from just feeling sick with stress and despair.

'Dylan couldn't make it. He had to go and see a man about a dog,' Wilson said vaguely.

'Nobody ever has to go and see a man about a dog.'

'Well, he had to see a man about a pushchair, Moses basket and sterilising unit that he'd just won on eBay,' Wilson explained. ' 'Fraid you're stuck with me.'

'Really?' She needed to stop sounding so squeaky. 'Are you sure that's OK? Because in the end I could only scrounge thirty quid out of the PTA. Well, thirty quid and a box of luxury Christmas crackers.'

Wilson smiled. It was a tricky, shifty smile. 'I suppose it will have to do.'

'You going to introduce me, Hope, or do you only do that for people who aren't on your list?' Elaine asked. Hope had completely forgotten that she was sitting there. She'd also forgotten that she'd left Blue Class to Andy's tender mercies, and he was probably boring them to tears with tales of deprived children in the Third World whose Christmas would be spent walking 20 miles to draw water from a rusty well. After the introductions were made, and Hope couldn't leave Wilson cooling his heels in the hall any longer, she took him along to get reacquainted with Blue Class.

It was bedlam in the classroom. The children were meant to be having yet another run-through of their Lady Gaga homage but were mostly running around and screaming, until Hope walked in and purposely dropped the big *World Atlas* on the floor.

Then there was a ten-minute bollocking, five minutes spent reminding them that when they came back at half five they all had to be wearing black tights – yes, even the boys – then fifteen minutes of story-time. Wilson sat on the floor with them as Hope read *How the Grinch Stole Christmas*. It was either the floor or a tiny chair meant for a tiny person.

'You're very scary when you're in teacher mode,' Wilson remarked, when the last child had left for the day and Hope was walking around the room to check that the chairs were all firmly on the desks and that Herbert had enough water to last the night.

'I'm not that scary,' Hope said in a hurt voice, because it would be nice to find someone who didn't think she was a belligerent bitch with a hair-trigger temper. 'Usually ten minutes after I tell them off, Blue Class go back to raising merry hell again.'

Wilson walked over to the corner where the worst of the water damage was evident. Apparently, though Hope doubted it very much, it would all be fixed by the new term. He picked up a copy of *The Cat in the Hat* and started flicking through it. 'So, how have you been? You look well. Very well.'

Hope didn't look well, she looked like a girl who'd been dumped by the love of her life. Her complexion was muddy, her eyes were dull, and she was wearing a pair of sagging tweed trousers, a black polo neck with a stretched-out collar and scuffed Uggs. She'd also spent most of the day trying to tear her hair out of its thick plait and now had a halo of frizzy red curls, and not a scrap of make-up on. She felt frumpy and lumpy, even though she'd lost over a stone since she'd last seen Wilson and was a couple of pounds lighter than the usual 9 stone, 9 pounds where her weight usually stuck when she dieted and refused to budge any further.

'Thanks,' she mumbled and gestured jerkily at him. 'So do you.' He looked the same as he ever did, but that wasn't necessarily to say that he looked bad. 'Shall we go back to the hall and I can talk you through the horror that awaits you?'

Wilson didn't say anything. He put down the book and walked towards Hope, not stopping even when he was a foot away and she felt as if she should take a step back, if only for appearances' sake, but she stayed where she was until he was standing so close that she could feel the wonderful comforting warmth of him. Though Hope knew she was far too battle-worn for Wilson's brand of comfort to have much effect. Yes, she could remember what it felt like to be held by him, have his mouth on hers, but all she could really think about these days was that she'd never feel Jack's arms around her or Jack's lips on hers ever again.

'So, is there anything you want to tell me?' Wilson asked, right on cue.

'I'm not sure I know what you mean,' Hope said, screwing up her face in mock confusion, even though she knew exactly what he meant. But just as she hadn't told Elaine or Marta yet, she certainly wasn't going to tell Wilson. Not just because she knew she wouldn't be able to get more than five words into her sorry tale without turning into a weeping mess, but because she couldn't cope with him saying, 'I told you so,' or calling her a 'bloody fool' in that fondly exasperated way that he did – or worse, trying to kiss the hurt away. Right now, his kisses and his kindness would kill her. 'You mean about the Winter Pageant?'

'Hope?' Wilson's voice was a throaty murmur that made Hope take a teeny, tiny tiptoe of a step forwards, even though she'd sworn to herself that she wouldn't, until it would have been impossible to slide a sheet of tissue paper (left over from making fake snow) between them.

She dropped her eyes to the polished tips of his brogues. 'What?'

'Don't fuck with me.' It was a warning, but it sounded like a promise, even when Wilson took a step back. 'So, where's this set-list you were talking about?'

Chapter Thirty-three

The next three hours were both the longest and shortest of Hope's life. She'd left a taciturn Wilson to set up the lights, but before she could fret about their tense encounter, volunteers started arriving.

Hope became the annoying person rushing around with a clipboard and issuing orders. She even heard herself say to two dads who were mithering about the dicky PA system, 'Don't bring me problems, bring me solutions!' A little power was a very scary thing, but Hope felt as if she was in her element for the first time in ages. Maybe a little too much in her element, because an hour before curtain-up, when she'd changed out of her saggy work clothes into heels and her vintage bottle-green velvet wiggle dress that she'd only ever been able to get into on two previous occasions, she was grabbed by Polly, Sorcha's mum, who owned her own beauty salon and was in charge of hair and make-up.

'You're doing everyone's heads in,' she told Hope, as she forced her to sit down at one of the makeshift make-up stations in the junior-school cloakroom. She also forced her to accept a glass of mulled wine. 'Now sit down, stop getting in the way, and let me take the shine off your face.'

Hope had only planned to sit there for five minutes, but half an hour later, she had an even skintone plus winged liquid eyeliner (which she'd never been able to master on her own), her hair was in an elegant updo, and she was calm enough to marshal both her thoughts and her volunteers.

Wilson was busy doing things with lights and cameras and didn't even look up when Hope asked if he had everything he needed, and maybe he'd like a mince pie. The dads were all assembled around the sound desk with screwdrivers held aloft and didn't want any advice, but at least Blue Class were pleased to see her when Hope assembled them in a junior classroom. She looked like 'a princess, Miss' or 'Cheryl Cole, Miss, when she was a ginger, Miss', and they all wanted to know if her heels hurt, which they did, even though Hope had only been wearing them for forty minutes. And then it was ten minutes before show-time, and she had many things to cross off her checklist, and there were many people who were standing about doing nothing who needed to be given precise instructions.

The Winter Pageant started eleven minutes late, which was the least late it had ever started. Hope thrust a microphone at Mr Gonzales, then shoved him up the three steps on to the stage so he could introduce the Pageant. He made a very poor job of it as far as Hope was concerned, and next time, *not that there was going to be a next time*, she'd definitely write him a script and insist that he stuck to it.

Hope stayed rooted to her post at the side of the stage, pulling and pushing people on and off it, prompting, miming and glaring at children waiting to go on who refused to wait quietly.

There were many, many things that went wrong. The Red Class's interpretative dance to 'Jingle Bells' was a disaster. They forgot most of the words, so made up for it in the chorus with a lot of enthusiastic shouting, and a good three-quarters of them still couldn't tell their left from their right. There was also a problem with the living-flame hats for Yellow Class's human menorah, and Shona from Year Six, wearing a metric tonne of glittery body powder, was hopelessly miscast as the Virgin Mary.

It didn't seem to matter, though, to an indulgent, doting audience who laughed and clapped and whooped, and when the entire school wriggled on to the stage to sing 'God Only Knows' as the closing number, there were muffled sobs from all corners of the hall. Hope cried all over Marta, who kept telling her to pull herself together, and it wasn't just because if she did ever get married, she planned to walk down the aisle to 'God Only Knows', it was from relief and exhaustion and because on so many levels she *was* scared and unhappy, just like Angela had said.

Hope was trying to repair the damage done to her eyeliner and wasn't listening to Mr Gonzales thank the PTA and announce the raffle winners, so she gave an alarmed shriek when Javan suddenly took her sweaty hand and yanked her up on stage.

It was one thing to be backstage bossing people about, quite another to suddenly be on stage and blinking uncertainly at a sea of faces.

'And can we have a big round of applause for our very own Simon Cowell, Ms Delafield, who's been responsible for our wonderful Winter Pageant,' Mr Gonzales said, which was a back-handed compliment if ever Hope had heard one. 'I'm sure the PTA will rest easy tonight knowing that she won't be phoning them up to demand they sell more raffle tickets.'

That wasn't a back-handed compliment, it was an outright slating. Hope came forward, and to her horror, she could feel more tears welling up and she was going to cry on stage in front of the whole school. She looked down to make sure that she was actually wearing clothes, because she was sure she'd had this nightmare several times.

Mr Gonzales handed her the microphone and she stumbled her way through a long list of thank yous, from the dinner ladies who'd finished the lunch service and then started making mince pies, to Saeed, the caretaker, and his trusty glue gun, to the PTA and Rabbi Rosenberg. The only two people she didn't thank were her mother for giving birth to her, and Sarah, who had been telling people backstage that she'd been heavily involved in the Pageant until medical problems had forced her to step down unwillingly. Since when did a skimpy list full of question marks rather than hard information, on two pieces of double-spaced A4, count as 'heavily involved'? Since never.

Hope finished with a heartfelt plea for any unwanted books to replace Blue Class's water-logged collection, then handed back the microphone to Mr Gonzales, who gingerly put an arm around her shoulders in a way that couldn't be deemed as sexual harassment and said, 'But joking aside, there wouldn't have been a Winter Pageant without Ms Delafield, who's worked tirelessly on it for weeks. Now, can we have Blue Class up on stage?'

Blue Class bounded on stage like thirty very excitable puppies, with much shoving and pushing, and Hope would have stopped them in their tracks with a significant look and a muttered aside about stickers, but Caitlin and Maryam were presenting her with a huge bouquet of roses and lilies, followed by Timothy with a small Selfridges bag, and bringing up the rear was Luca with a big box of chocolates that looked as if several small hands had been trying to rip off the shrink wrap. Then every member of the class came forward to give Hope an enthusiastic hug – even Stuart, though Hope tensed every bone in her body and prayed that he didn't try and wipe his nose on her dress.

As Hope helped them off stage, Sorcha burst into tears because, 'Now nothing nice is going to happen for ages and it's still eight sleeps until Christmas.' Then the girly girls decided to cry too, and there were long moments until mothers were fetched and coats and shoes were found and finally all the pupils were off the premises, all the mince pies had been eaten, and Saeed was pointedly jangling his big bunch of keys because he wanted to lock up.

Jack was nowhere to be seen, and Hope wondered if he'd gone to the Midnight Bell with Simon as soon as the last shepherd had trooped off the stage, though she hoped he hadn't and had been there to see that some people adored her, even if they were aged seven and under. She retrieved her iPhone from her desk and saw, with dismay, that she had ten missed calls, five texts and three voice messages from Jack. She knew exactly what they'd say.

He was drunk. He was drunker. He was drunkest. 'Oh, Hopey, Hopey, Hopey, don't be mad at me,' he slurred on the final voicemail. 'I'm at Shoreditch House, I've been drinking for hours, and now the fashion and beauty girls have turned up and it's cold and you wouldn't be so mean as to make me leave and come to your carol concert, would you? It's only a carol concert, and I'll buy you an extra special present to make up for it.'

Hope was all set to call him back and shout, 'Only a carol concert? Only a bloody carol concert? You have got to be fucking kidding me! How could you let me down? Again?' Then she'd segue seamlessly into a huge list of his faults and be angry and confrontational and probably bring up the fact that he'd screwed Susie – and repeat to fade.

In the end Hope settled for stubbing her fingers on her touch screen as she sent him a text message: *It wasn't a carol concert. It was a WINTER PAGEANT, which you'd have known if you'd bothered to turn up. Lots of love, Hope*

She looked around the empty classroom and wondered how, after tomorrow, she'd get through three weeks without the distraction of work. Normally she loved Christmas, well, she didn't love going home, but she liked the food and presents part of it, and she loved coming back to London and visiting friends and raging so hard on New Year's Eve that it took her forty-eight hours to recover. This year Hope had a horrible feeling that on New Year's Eve the only raging she'd be doing was at the horrible mess she'd made of painting the kitchen skirting boards.

She heard a noise behind her and, startled, she turned round to see Wilson standing in the classroom doorway. 'Oh! Your money,' Hope said, inwardly cringing as she unlocked her desk drawer again to pull out an envelope containing six dog-eared five-pound notes and the box of crackers. 'I'm sorry it's not very much.'

Wilson stepped forward to take the envelope. He looked just as embarrassed, and suddenly thrust it back at Hope. 'Look, why don't you keep it? Put it towards some new books or hamster food or something.'

Hope couldn't even protest, because handing over thirty quid in used notes was far more insulting than keeping it. 'I'm sorry,' she said again. 'And thank you. Did everything go all right? I'm sorry that you got lumbered with it in the end, but thank you, I do really . . .'

'Are you going to say anything other than "sorry" and "thank you"?' Wilson asked with a small smile as Hope tucked the envelope away again.

'Sorry.' It popped out before Hope could pop it back in. 'You off, then?'

'Yeah, going to grab something to eat . . .' Wilson didn't finish the sentence but Hope was sure that he was looking at her meaningfully. Or maybe she just wanted him to be looking at her meaningfully.

'So am I,' Hope said slowly, as an idea began to form. 'I'm meeting Elaine and Marta, she teaches Reception, at a pub round the corner for our unofficial Christmas dinner. They do really good savoury pies.'

'Sounds nice.' It was the dictionary definition of non-committal.

Hope gathered up her handbag and coat, looked longingly at her Uggs but decided she could do another two hours in her heels if she got a cab home, then ushered Wilson out of the classroom. 'It's partners too,' she remarked casually. 'Except Jack is otherwise engaged.'

'Oh! Like that, is it?'

'It's not like anything,' Hope muttered. 'He's pickling his liver somewhere in Shoreditch. And well, I already paid for the meal in advance, and if you have to eat anyway . . .' Now it was Hope's turn to trail off, though she was sure that her look wasn't that meaningful. More like desperate because she'd missed hanging out with him, and having to sit around a table with Elaine and Marta and their life partners like a gigantic gooseberry was a punishment she didn't deserve. 'You'd like Elaine's husband, Simon. He used to be in a band and he has his own recording studio in their back garden.'

Hope didn't know if that was what sealed the deal but Wilson nodded. 'OK,' he said.

She waited for him to elaborate a little further but he just adjusted his camera bag and waited for her to start walking.

Chapter Thirty-four

The only thing more blissful than the sudden warmth and smell of home-cooking when Wilson pulled open the heavy wooden door of the Midnight Bell, was the bowl-sized glass of red wine waiting for Hope at the table where Elaine, Marta, Simon and Marta's boyfriend, Iban, were sitting.

She quickly introduced Wilson as she squeezed past Marta so she could sit down and pick up her glass. 'Cheers,' she said, then downed the contents in three swift swallows. 'Christ, I needed that.'

Wilson sat down next to Hope, opposite Simon, which was good, rather than opposite Elaine, which would have been really bad, because once she had a few drinks all discretion and reason disappeared. He immediately offered to get a round in.

'No! No! It's all paid for. We did a deal with Al, the landlord. Twenty-five quid a head for all the food and drink we can manage,' Hope clarified, as she poured herself another glass of wine.

'The rate you're drinking, he'll be bankrupt by the end of the night,' Wilson said.

'Nonsense. He makes a fortune out of us the rest of the year,' Elaine argued. 'But if you're going to the bar, can we have another bottle of red, a bottle of white, and what do you want? Lager, cider, champagne?'

By the time her steak and ale pie arrived and she fell on it with eager little cries, Hope was halfway to happy. It wasn't just the three large glasses of red wine, either – all the tension and the strain of the last week was ebbing away thanks to good company, good friends, good times. Which was rather hokey, but she was rather drunk.

Wilson and Simon had bonded over obscure indie bands of the 1980s and were happily discussing French New Wave cinema. Elaine was asking Iban deeply personal questions now it had been revealed that he and Marta were regulars at the Torture Garden, and that Iban had a piercing where no man in his right mind should have a piercing.

'But can you still pee standing up?' she kept asking him. 'Isn't there an issue with spray?'

And Hope was happily bitching with Marta about Dorothy and Sarah and the mothers that they couldn't stand. 'That child was still in nappies on the first day of school,' Marta complained bitterly. 'And when I told his mother that we expected all children to be toilet-trained, she said that they believed in child-led continence, and she wasn't going to hamper his emotional development to appease the Education Authority.'

'Poncey Islington mothers.' Hope pushed away her plate after a few mouthfuls, because if she was eating, then she couldn't be drinking.

'Eat,' Wilson ordered, pushing the plate back in front of Hope, who pouted at him. 'You need something to mop up the rivers of booze.'

'I had a mince pie earlier,' Hope protested.

'Eat your pastry and your potatoes,' Wilson said. He looked around the table at Marta and Elaine who were also in an advanced state of inebriation. 'Aren't you three meant to be working tomorrow?'

'Frankly, darling, I'm only going in to get the loot from parents grateful for my attempts to shape their children's tiny brains,' Elaine said grandly.

'Yes, I see a long day of colouring-in for Red Class,' Marta added. 'Very quiet, very hard colouring-in. What about you, Hope?'

'I know we sound like we're bad teachers, but we're really not,' she told Wilson earnestly, even though he seemed very amused by her earnestness. 'See, the thing about being a teacher is that you learn how to be a really good actress too. An Oscar-calibre actress. It doesn't matter if you've got a hangover or PMS or, like, you've just been dumped . . .' She swallowed hard, blinked a couple of times and when she realised that she was OK and not going to burst into tears, Hope took a fortifying chug of wine. 'Where was I?'

'Um, the bit where you'd just been dumped,' Marta said helpfully.

'Right, yeah, but like I was just using being dumped as a hypotheoritical, hypetet . . . that thing, what's it called?'

'Hypothetical,' Iban said, even though English wasn't even his first language. 'You mean hypothetical, yeah?'

Hope nodded. 'So, even if you have been dumped, hypothetically or otherwise, you can't bring all that bad shit into class with you. You just have to suck it up until three thirty.'

Elaine looked appalled, and for one moment Hope wondered if she'd read between the lines and was going to bawl her out in front of everybody for daring to keep her private life private. 'Do you mean to say, you're actually going to *teach* tomorrow?' she asked in scandalised tones. 'Have you done a lesson plan?'

'Oh no, I'm going to let Blue Class watch a DVD while I sit on the floor with them and let the girly girls stroke my hair.' Hope paused to ponder further. 'I was going to let them do some singing too, but I'm not sure the hangover I'm bound to have tomorrow could take it, but that's only because it's the day we break up. Normally I would never do that.'

Wilson looked aghast. Or rather, he looked slightly sterner than usual. 'But what was that your Head was saying about you being a credit to the school and your impressionable pupils?'

'I am! Except when it's the last day before the Christmas holidays,' Hope amended. 'Then I'm just there for the big tins of Quality Street and the Body Shop gift baskets foisted upon me.'

'I'm shocked and dismayed,' Wilson said, though he didn't look particularly either. 'Eat at least two of your potatoes or I'm cutting off your alcohol supply.'

It was a long time, or maybe the first time, that anyone had ever exhorted Hope to load up on carbs. And when Hope ordered and ate sticky toffee pudding with custard, Wilson shot her an approving smile and rested his arm on the back of her chair, so every time Hope leaned back, she could feel the little hairs on the back of her neck stand up to try and get his attention, and once Wilson absent-mindedly brushed her nape with his thumb, and really, she was acting like a thirteen-year-old girl who'd finally got to sit next to her crush object at the school disco and she needed to Get. A. Grip.

They were lingering over coffee and brandy when Elaine started making noises about going home. 'We left Lola and Abby to fend for themselves, and that never works out well.'

Hope should have been thinking about making tracks for Holloway too, but it wasn't like Jack was going to be home. Or if he was, he'd be stinking drunk. And she wouldn't be able to resist picking a fight with him. 'We might as well stay until they call last orders,' she reasoned, even though Al would be calling last orders in over an hour's time.

Marta and Iban had a whispered confab. 'We're going to see a band in Shoreditch,' she said. 'You can come, but there might be public nudity.'

'Are they a very shouty band?' Hope asked.

Iban nodded. 'The shoutiest.'

Hope wasn't in the mood for shouty. She looked at Wilson

pleadingly. 'You wouldn't make me drink on my own, would you?'

His thumb was stroking the back of her neck again, but he didn't say anything at first – though, over the strains of the Phil Spector *Christmas Album*, Hope could almost hear the cogs in his brain whirring. 'How do you fancy drinking somewhere else?'

'Like where?' Hope asked, mindful that she was wearing car-to-bar heels.

'I was planning to go to a Northern Soul night in Camden Town.' He dipped his hand. 'Do you fancy it?'

Hope did fancy it. She wasn't a Northern Soul aficionado but she'd liked what she'd heard, which was pretty much the original version of 'Tainted Love' and a compilation tape that her dad used to play on the way home from school on Friday afternoons.

'My parents swear that they once went to the Wigan Casino,' she told Wilson, 'though I very much doubt it.'

'Why would you doubt it?'

'You would, too, if you'd spent even five minutes with my mum and dad.'

'My parents – actually, my dad was a huge Northern Soul nut,' Wilson revealed. 'He used to go to the Wigan Casino, Blackpool Mecca, even the Golden Touch in Stoke-on-Trent. Hence my name.'

Hope frowned. 'You've lost me.'

'There seem to be a lot of Northern Soul artists called Wilson,' he grinned. 'Jackie Wilson, Al Wilson, Frank Wilson. He really wanted to name me after Garnet Mimms, but my mum put her foot down.'

'I'm not surprised,' Hope said. 'So, is your dad still into Northern Soul?'

'Till the day he dies. He travels all over to go to these Northern Soul weekenders, though his hip's a bit dicky these days.' Wilson twisted his finger around a lock of hair, which had inevitably escaped from Hope's updo. 'So you in or out?'

'I'm *so* in,' Hope said enthusiastically. It had been ages since she'd been to a club, and though she liked disco and soul and anything with a beat, the only music Jack ever put on her iPod was new albums by mopey boys playing guitars. 'Can we get a taxi?'

'Um, don't you have fifty cupcakes to ice?' Elaine asked sharply, as Hope turned to look at her in surprise, because she sounded so disapproving.

Hope waved an airy hand. 'Cupcakes, schmupcakes,' she said dismissively. 'I'll do them when I get in. It's not like I'm going to be *that* late.'

'But you said you had to frost and ice them.' Elaine was putting on her coat but paused so she could give Hope what was meant to be a deeply significant look. Hope gazed back at her with a 'who, me?' expression. 'Why don't you pop to the loo with me before I leave?' Elaine insisted.

'No, thanks, I don't need to go,' Hope said, because she knew that popping to the loo was not-very-secret code for, 'You're coming with me to a woman-only space where I can talk some bloody sense into you.' Then she'd have to tell Elaine what was really going on, and the lovely mellow drunk feeling would exit stage left. Besides, Hope didn't need anyone else's common sense, she knew what she was doing and she wasn't doing anything wrong. She was going with Wilson to a club where there would be lots of other people, and she would drink and dance and then go home. She'd probably be home before Jack, because once he was drunk, all bets were off – that reminded Hope that she needed to do something.

Ignoring Elaine, who was now standing over her with hands on hips, Hope yanked out her phone. There was a text message on it from Jack: *Why are you in such a mood with me?* which Hope also ignored as she texted: *If you get home before me DO NOT EAT ANY OF MY CUPCAKES!!!!! I know exactly how many there are and I will kill you.* She put her phone back in her bag and smiled at Wilson, who didn't even attempt to hide the fact that he'd been reading the text over her shoulder.

'Shall we get going, then?'

He stood up. 'Thought you'd never ask.'

Hope and Wilson said goodbye to the others outside the pub, and began to walk towards Highbury Corner to find a cab with its light on. She could have sworn that things had been getting a little charged between them back in the Midnight Bell, but now that it was just the two of them walking along the road, then in the back of a taxi, the atmosphere went back to being not charged. Wilson was positively garrulous as he volunteered the information that he wasn't going back to Preston for Christmas because he and all his siblings had clubbed together to buy his mum and step-dad plane tickets to San Francisco, so they could spend the holiday with his little sister who lived there.

'It was a joint Christmas and silver anniversary present,' he explained, as the cab weaved its way through the back streets of Islington. 'I've been ordered over to my other sister Melanie's for Christmas dinner. She's Alfie's mum. Lives in Highgate. My dad's coming down, too, with Maureen, his girlfriend. What about you? Are you going back home?'

'Yeah,' Hope said, without much enthusiasm.

'So, do you go to Jack's for Christmas dinner or does he come to you?' Wilson asked, and hearing him say Jack's name sounded wrong and weird and very unsettling.

'Jack and his parents and one set of his grandparents come to ours,' Hope explained. 'And Marge, his mum, and my mum cook the dinner together, and I'm meant to help them, while the menfolk go to the pub, but I usually storm off after ten minutes because I get shouted at for not peeling potatoes in an ergonomic and economic fashion.'

'Do you not get on with your mum?'

That sounded more like a question that Angela would ask, and Hope tried to shrug, but her shoulders were too slumped to be able to pull it off. 'Well, I do on one level, and then I don't on another much bigger level.' She sighed. 'I shouldn't wind her up as much as I do.'

'You're really down on yourself today, aren't you?' Wilson tapped her knee in an avuncular fashion. 'Tell you what, we'll get inside, do a couple of shots of something to get us in the mood, and then we'll have a dance. It's impossible to be in a bad mood when you're dancing.'

Wilson didn't dance, Hope was certain of that. He was too big and bulky, and didn't like to put himself in situations where he'd stand out or make a fool of himself. Still, if the shots worked their alcoholic magic, Hope quite fancied having a bit of a shimmy.

An hour of dancing and then she'd get a cab and she'd be home by midnight. Half past midnight tops, she decided.

Chapter Thirty-five

Hope was still on the dancefloor at two in the morning when the music suddenly stopped and the lights came on.

She put her hands to her mouth so she could catcall and boo more effectively, until Wilson pulled her away. 'Come on, Cinderella. Let's go and find your glass slippers.'

Hope had kicked off her heels hours ago, at around the time that the third shot of tequila had taken effect and she'd discovered that Wilson *could* dance. Like, really dance. Twisting, turning, spinning on the dancefloor, which had been dusted with talcum powder, and doing nifty things with his size-eleven feet that she wouldn't have thought possible.

She'd looked over at a wiry boy who'd leapt gracefully in the air in a star jump and landed in the splits before arching his back and spinning on his shoulders. 'Can you do that?' she'd asked Wilson, who'd shaken his head.

'Not even in my younger, skinnier days,' he'd said, taking her hands and modifying his footwork so Hope could follow. And that had been when she'd kicked off her shoes because they were getting in the way, and it had been ages since she'd danced, and then it had only been with her friends and never with Jack, because Jack had absolutely no sense of rhythm and was almost as terrified of dancing as Hope was of heights.

As the night wore on and the music had got faster and louder, with all those smoky-voiced men and women singing about love and loss set to a beat that matched the excited thrum of Hope's heart, the dancefloor had got more and more crowded. People had stopped doing the really fancy stuff and Wilson had taken Hope in his arms. Occasionally he'd whirled her round or spun her under his arm, but mostly he'd held Hope close as they'd danced. They'd only stop dancing to grab another drink, then find an empty patch on the dancefloor again and start swaying again.

With the lights back on, everyone looked a little lost and bewildered. Hope realised that the tight skirt of her wiggle dress was rucked up almost to her hips. She pulled it down and dropped to her knees so she could start crawling under chairs and tables in the hunt for her missing shoes and bag. She was very, very drunk. Tequila-drunk, which was a more messy and dishevelled kind of drunk than the drunk that Hope was normally used to.

She found one of her shoes in the furthest corner of the room and decided to put it on before she lost it, then limped forlornly across the floor, trying in vain to spot her other shoe and her huge handbag.

'It's your lucky night,' said Wilson behind her, and Hope turned round, nearly landing flat on her face in the process, to see him standing there with her shoe and bag in his hands.

'Oh God, I don't know how to thank you!' Hope cried, cradling her bag to her chest and looking inside. Everything seemed present and correct. She looked up in time to catch the leer on Wilson's face, like he had a really good idea of a way she could thank him. It was only there for one blink of her eyes, then his face settled back into its usual austere lines. 'I'm so on to you now, Wilson. That grumpy thing doesn't cut it any more.'

'I don't know what you mean,' Wilson snapped. 'I was born grumpy and you . . . You're very drunk, aren't you?'

Hope didn't know why he sounded so surprised. 'How

come you're not drunk? You matched me shot for shot.'

Wilson held up his index finger and slowly brought it towards his nose. If he hadn't been wearing glasses, he'd have poked himself in the eye. 'I might not seem drunk to the casual observer, but on the inside I'm absolutely spannered.'

'Good.' Hope nodded in satisfaction, then grabbed his arm to keep herself upright as she put on her other shoe. Her tights and the hem of her dress were covered in talcum powder. 'Shall we get gone?'

'Taxi?'

'Hell, yes!' It seemed perfectly natural, though rather impractical, to cling to Wilson as they tottered down the narrow, twisty stairs that led to the side entrance of the pub. There was a little crowd gathered in the doorway, shivering and not showing any inclination to move, so Hope and Wilson were forced to push through them and came to a grinding halt as they stared out on to a world that was heaped with mounds of snow. Yet more big, fat flakes were falling from the sky and turning Eversholt Street, usually a soulless thoroughfare that roared with traffic, into a scene from a Christmas card.

Hope stepped out and tipped her head back to try and catch a snowflake on the tip of her tongue. Within a few seconds even her eyelashes were so thickly coated with snow that she couldn't see, and she gave an excited little shriek and surged forward, not even caring that the snow was seeping through the thin soles of her party shoes.

She loved the snow, and not just because it made her think of snow days and missing school. Snow made everything look white and magical. It hid all the grey, all the rough edges, and always gave Hope the same kind of satisfaction she got from putting freshly laundered linen on the bed, or achieving a perfect glossy smoothness when she was icing a cake. Oh God, she didn't even want to think about icing cakes, or frosting then icing fifty cupcakes, to be more specific.

'You're not really wearing the right footwear for frolicking in five inches of snow,' Wilson said, coming up behind her. 'You'll get chilblains.'

'Do people still get chilblains?' Hope wondered aloud, as she skidded precariously along the street. 'You know, I think the cold air has sobered me up.'

Then she promptly fell over.

Wilson was laughing so hard that it was a while before he could help Hope to her feet. She realised that her hair was soaked because she hadn't put her hat on, and she was so cold that her teeth were chattering and her bones were aching, and, actually, she didn't like the snow half as much as she remembered.

Camden High Street was snowed-in, only a few cars were inching slowly down the road. Hope's heart sank as they approached a bus stop and saw a miserable huddle of people standing there like they were waiting to buy bread in an Eastern Bloc country some time in the 1970s.

'Been waiting long?' Wilson asked as Hope glanced up at the countdown board to see when the next bus was due. It was annoyingly, unhelpfully devoid of all information.

'For ever,' someone said glumly.

'At least half an hour,' someone else clarified.

Wilson turned to Hope with a resigned expression. 'We'll have to walk.'

Hope had walked home from Camden before, but that was on a balmy Saturday night when it had taken just under an hour and had included a mercy dash to the garage on Camden Road where she'd spent ten minutes begging and pleading with the staff to use their loo. But walking home in a fricking blizzard in high heels was quite another matter.

'Let's walk up to the station and see if we can get a dodgy minicab,' she said, and although Wilson looked disapproving he also looked as if he wasn't relishing the thought of walking home either.

It was the only night in living memory when even the dodgy minicab drivers were tucked up indoors. 'I'm not walking home,' Hope insisted. 'I can't. I'll die of frostbite. There must be a hotel somewhere near here.'

'I thought you were a hardy North Country lass, not a poncey Southerner,' Wilson scoffed, and it was all right for him in his brogues with the thick soles and a T-shirt and a jumper and a thick, lined woollen coat and scarf and hat.

'But when it snowed in Whitfield, my Mum made me wear wellies and thermal underwear,' Hope all but wailed.

'Look, it's ten minutes to mine . . .'

'More like half an hour in these conditions!'

'Twenty minutes to mine, and you can crash there or at least warm up.'

It was as good an idea as any. Though as they began to walk again, she didn't know whether she could manage even one single minute. Her feet were wet and cold. In fact, they were so cold that the word 'cold' ceased to have any real meaning any more. Same with the word 'frozen'. Her face, contorted in agony as it was, must have given her away even though she was trying to be a brave little soldier.

'Can you really not walk any more?' Wilson asked.

'I'm all right,' Hope said in a tiny, uncertain voice.

Wilson stopped and looked at Hope and her face, which was scrunched up in pain and discomfort. 'Well, I could carry you,' he offered.

'Don't be daft! It's really slippery, and we've got at least a mile to walk, and I'm not exactly a featherweight.'

He was already squatting down. 'Come on, I'll give you a piggyback,' he said. 'I'm used to hefting around heavy pieces of equipment.'

'Gosh, thanks for that,' Hope said, and she thought that Wilson must also still be quite drunk to volunteer for such a kamikaze mission, and maybe she was too because she was hitching up her skirt, giggling wildly as she did so, and climbing on to Wilson's back. He wrapped his arms around her thighs and rose slowly to his full height. 'Don't drop me!' she squealed.

'Then don't make any sudden movements,' he warned her as he set off slowly through the snow.

Hope wasn't cold any more. Well, she was, her feet were like size-six blocks of ice and she had a draught of arctic air whistling around her legs, but the rest of her, pressed up against Wilson as he trudged up Kentish Town Road, was toasty. Positively sizzling, in fact.

There wasn't much Hope could do to help him, short of losing a couple of stone within the next five seconds, so she decided to keep talking so Wilson didn't suddenly keel over from over-exertion and go to sleep in a snow drift, never to wake up again.

'I think that I could really love Northern Soul,' she said. 'But isn't it all on little seven-inch records? I don't even have a turntable.'

'Well, luckily for you, I have lots of little seven-inch Northern Soul records that I've converted to MP3s,' Wilson panted. 'You can put them on your iPod while you're thawing out.'

'That would be great, except you'll have to do it for me. I don't know how to put songs on to my iPod. Someone else always does it for me.' She didn't want to say Jack's name, even though Jack was probably snoring away under their 14-tog duvet, unaware that his only-just-ex-girlfriend had her legs wrapped around another man, and might actually die from hypothermia before the night was out.

She heard Wilson suck in a breath and thought that his keeling over was imminent until he exclaimed sharply, 'That's *pathetic*. It's not difficult to put songs on an iPod, even my seven-year-old niece can do it.'

'I've never got round to figuring out how to do it myself.' Hope wrapped her arms tighter around Wilson and rested her chin on the top of his head. 'I can change a plug but don't ever ask me to change a lightbulb.'

'Changing a lightbulb is much easier than changing a plug.'

'Not when you have severe vertigo.' Hope decided that Wilson didn't need to know that often she needed to hold someone's hand when she was going down stairs if she wasn't in the right, very focused headspace to master them unaided.

Wilson grunted as he took a left so they were off the main road and not that far from his loft. Hope really didn't want to walk, but she could hear his laboured breathing increasing with every step he took, so she dug her knees into him.

'Stop. Stop!' she said again, when he ignored her. 'I can do the last bit.'

'Are you sure?' Wilson asked, but he was letting Hope slide down and missed the agonised expression on her face as her feet made contact with the ground – or the thick snow that covered the ground. 'Let's just go as fast as we can.'

He tucked his arm tightly around her and they hurried through the narrow streets, without even the track of someone else's footsteps to make it easier. Hope went as fast as she could, feet trying to slip from under her, but even though she wasn't on his back any more, Wilson was still holding her up and she didn't doubt that if she did fall, he'd catch her before she could hit the ground.

Chapter Thirty-six

It only took three minutes to reach Wilson's building but they were the longest three minutes of Hope's life. The ten seconds it took Wilson to tap in the security code to open the door were longer still, and walking up the four flights of stairs on cold, unrelenting concrete hurt even more than tramping through virgin snow in paper-thin shoes.

As soon as the door was open, Hope scurried across the studio floor. 'Sorry to make myself at home, but can I put the kettle on?' she called over her shoulder as she hobbled up the spiral staircase that led to Wilson's bachelor pad, the metal steps adding insult to severe injury.

Wilson caught up with Hope before she'd even had time to locate the kettle and fill it with water.

'Bath,' he said firmly. 'It's the only way you're going to warm up and not contract pneumonia. I'll make tea and find you something to wear while you're in the tub.' Wilson took Hope's elbow and steered her to the bathroom, which was more of an alcove, but at least it had a door.

It took a couple of minutes to fill the claw-foot, roll-top bath with steaming-hot water, and then Hope was quickly stripping off her clothes. Getting naked in another man's home felt like a betrayal, especially when she could hear the other man pottering about on the other side of the door. Especially when Hope knew that if the other man knocked on the door and asked if he could come in, she wasn't entirely sure that she'd refuse him permission. God, what was wrong with her? Her and Jack were barely over, and as it was, Hope still wasn't 100 per cent convinced they were over until Jack looked their parents in the eye and told them it was over. Or he moved out and left his key. Or changed his Facebook Relationship Status to Single. Until then, they weren't properly broken up, which was why it felt so wrong to currently be naked in Wilson's bathroom, but she could hardly have a medicinal bath with her clothes on.

Hope slid into the bath and knew a moment of perfect bliss as her chilled, goose-pimpled flesh met silky-hot water. Then her flesh turned from an unattractive bluey-white to bright red, and she had to bite her lip hard to stop herself from crying out in pain when her feet suddenly felt as if they were under attack from millions of razor-toothed beasties.

Hope sat there with a fist wedged into her mouth as her icy flesh stung its way back to full working order, hardly daring to move because even wiggling her toes caused untold agonies.

There was a gentle tap on the door. 'I can't hear any splashing. You haven't drowned, have you?'

'No,' Hope called out in a voice that trembled a little. 'I'll be out in a minute.'

'I've left you some stuff outside and there's a robe on the back of the door.'

God, talking to Wilson while she was naked felt even worse than betrayal. But not so bad that Hope stopped wondering what would happen if she emerged from the bathroom absolutely starkers and slippery wet. The wave of lust that hit her, as she imagined pressing her naked body against black cashmere and dark-blue denim and feeling Wilson hard and getting harder through his clothes, was a warning that she needed to pull herself together. She still loved Jack and unlike Jack, Hope did have some semblance of self-control. Still, it was no wonder that when she stepped out of the bath and caught sight of herself in the mirror that took up one wall, all of her was flushed a rosy pink that owed more to her feverish imagination than to the hot bath.

Wilson didn't have much in the way of products, so Hope used baby lotion in lieu of body moisturiser, and then realised that there was absolutely nothing she could do about her hair, which had the consistency of a kitchen mop that had seen better days.

Then, safely swathed in a plush towelling robe the colour of clotted cream, Hope opened the bathroom door a crack to grab the neatly folded pile of clothes Wilson had left for her. The plaid pyjamas were far, far too big for her. Hope had to roll up the bottoms and yank in the drawstring around the waist as far as it would go, and the jacket came down to mid-thigh. She looked incredibly waif-like, which was a first.

Leaving her own clothes draped over the heated towel rail, Hope took a deep breath and opened the bathroom door. Now the wooden floorboards felt smooth and warm under her bare feet as she padded out into the huge living space.

'Go and sit down,' Wilson said from the galley kitchen. 'Just pouring the tea. Milk and one sugar, right?'

'Right,' she agreed. She sat down on the sofa, her legs tucked up under her, and looked around the room and remembered the last time that she'd sat here. How Wilson had made her tea then, too, and she'd fallen asleep on his shoulder.

It was strange how the circumstances could be the same and yet utterly different. Somehow, Hope didn't think that she was going to be doing much sleeping or actually . . . *Stop it! Just stop it right now*, she told herself sternly.

'What time is it?' she asked Wilson as he placed a mug of tea and a plate of biscuits down on the coffee table in front of her.

'It's nearly four,' Wilson said heavily. 'I've got an eight a.m. shoot.'

'I have to be at school at eight thirty,' Hope countered.

'And don't forget that you've got fifty cupcakes to frost,' Wilson reminded Hope, and when she rolled her eyes and groaned in not-so-mock despair, he smiled. 'I've just drunk an entire pot of coffee so I'll be sober enough to drive you home.'

Hope felt something inside her, it might have been her weary old heart, melt. 'You didn't have to do that,' she murmured, though if he hadn't done that, she didn't know how she would get home. Home, where Jack was passed out in an alcohol-induced slumber and might not even realise that Hope was AWOL. She thought about digging her phone out of her bag, which Wilson had placed in front of her, but decided if there were missed calls or crabby voice messages they could wait. She turned back to Wilson, who'd sat down next to her and was demolishing a chocolate Hobnob in three decisive bites. 'Apart from nearly being snowed in on Camden High Street, I had a really good time tonight.'

'You wouldn't be saying that if we'd had to bed down at the bus stop.'

'No, because you carried me on your back like I was Tiny Tim.' Hope shot him a sideways look. 'It was very heroic of you.'

'I carry random people around on my back all the time . . .'

Hope could sense him pulling back from her emotionally, could tell that he wanted to be quiet and wanted her to be quiet, too. Most likely, the pot of coffee had sobered him up, and all the flirting and teasing of earlier now seemed like a bad idea. It was best if she just gulped down her tea so he could take her back to Holloway to deal with her un-frosted cupcakes.

She felt Wilson looking at her but she kept her eyes on

her mug of tea, only shifting her focus when Wilson cleared his throat. 'Hope? Can I ask you something?'

'Course you can,' she said lightly, though he sounded so serious that she was dreading what his next words might be. 'You know me, I'm an open book.'

'I'd hardly call you that.' Wilson reached for another biscuit, then thought better of it. 'So . . . you and Jack, you've broken up, haven't you?'

'Well, I wouldn't say that. Not exactly.' Hope paused as she thought about how exactly she would say it, because there was still an outside chance that Jack would choose her. Choose them. Because they'd been together thirteen years and he said he still loved her and OK, it wasn't the same as being *in* love with her, but he cared for her, which was why he . . . hadn't even bothered to come to the Winter Pageant when he knew how much it meant to her. 'Scratch that,' she heard herself say. 'We are broken up. He doesn't want to be with me; he wants to be with *her*. We were four weeks into our horrible, painful counselling that was supposed to get things back on track, and all Susie had to do was turn up on the doorstep and, well . . .' She shook her head. 'We're over.'

'How are you doing?' Wilson wanted to know, and he didn't make any attempt to touch her or comfort her, but that was a good thing, because she was one fingertip away from coming undone.

'I don't know,' Hope said, finally turning to look at Wilson, who seemed curious rather than concerned. 'This is the first time I've admitted it to anyone else. Actually, this is the first time I've admitted it to myself, instead of pretending that Jack's going to have a change of heart. He's not. We're done.'

Wilson put down his mug and sat still, elbows resting on his knees as he cupped his chin. 'But you still love him, right?'

Hope sighed. 'I don't know. I've always loved Jack but I wonder if loving Jack is more a habit than something

I really *feel.*' Wilson bombarding her with questions had brought Hope's mood crashing down, though maybe that was the hangover kicking in early, or the prospect of having to go home. 'It all sucks, and I'm pretty wretched. I mean, getting drunk tonight and hanging out with you has been great, but generally I feel like I want to crawl into bed and stay there until they carry me out in a coffin.'

She knew that when they had conversations like this, and they'd had a lot of conversations over the last few weeks about how crappy Hope felt, Wilson would dole out some devastating home truths, but it was still easier to talk to him about it than to, say, Angela. For one thing, Jack wasn't sitting next to her on the sofa, and also Wilson was a lot easier on the eye than Angela, who didn't provide tea, Hobnobs or something comfortable to sit on. Which was a pity – she was really missing a trick, Hope thought, as she sipped the last of her tea. And unlike Angela, Wilson instinctively seemed to know that she was just gathering her thoughts and hadn't finished yet.

'I know you think I'm a total drama queen, but I don't know how I'll ever get over this or feel normal again. It's like I don't even know what normal is without Jack. He's been at the centre of my life for so long that if he's not there then I'm just going to be half a person.' Hope put down her mug so she could hug her knees. 'I don't want to be half a person.'

'Now that I've got to know you properly, I don't think you're a total drama queen,' Wilson said. He shot her a lazy grin. 'Not all the time, anyway.'

'Well, that's progress of a sort, I suppose,' Hope said, and she could have smiled too, but instead she sighed.

'I know it seems impossible now, but you won't always feel this way,' Wilson said softly. 'Not going to happen overnight, but you'll get over it and when you think about Jack, you won't want to cry or take a contract out on him. You might even end up being friends.'

Now it was Hope's turn not to say anything because she couldn't ever imagine a point in the future when she and Jack could be friends. Not when she loved him as much as she did and not after what he'd done to her ... why would she want a friend like that?

'You know I was engaged, right?' Wilson suddenly asked her.

Hope turned to him. 'Well, no, I didn't.'

'I was. We were together for five years. Loved her to pieces, went through loads of stuff together. Not just the good stuff.' Wilson was staring off into the middle distance as if he was lost in memories. 'Her dad dying, the magazine I was working on closing, even a miscarriage. We were solid, then three weeks before the wedding, she left me for another woman.'

'Oh my God,' Hope breathed. 'That's awful. Did you have any idea?'

'Not really – which was why I was planning to spend the rest of my life with her,' Wilson said dryly.

'How on earth did you cope?'

She expected Wilson to tell her that he put on his best stiff upper lip and soldiered on, but he shook his head. 'I didn't. Went on a six-month bender, if you must know, but I did get over it eventually. Mind you, not sure that my liver has ever fully recovered.'

'I wonder whether anyone gets over this kind of thing?' Hope mused.

'If it doesn't change you, then you were never in love,' Wilson pointed out. 'No one gets through life scot-free. Shit happens. It's how you deal with it that shapes you, not the actual event itself.'

Wilson was actually pretty good at giving advice. It wasn't anything tangible that Hope could do tomorrow and know that she'd instantly feel better, but it was still good to know that she might come through this alive. 'So, your ex ... is she still on your Christmas-card list?' she asked, because surely it was easier to have no contact at all, to not be reminded of her, but Wilson was nodding.

'Yeah, I was even best man at her civil partnership.'

'Wow. Even though she ended it three weeks before you were due to get married?'

'But when she asked me if I'd donate some of my sperm, I told her to bugger off,' Wilson said, and he sounded so disgruntled about the temerity of his ex that Hope wanted to giggle. She managed to school her features into something more sympathetic. 'So, anyway. Remember that this isn't going to destroy you.' He paused. 'It just feels like it will for a while.'

Lauren always insisted that it took a week for every month you dated, or a month for every year that you were in a relationship, to heal your broken heart. Hope realised she was in for a long, painful thirteen months, and then she realised that since she'd been sitting on Wilson's sofa, she hadn't once entertained the idea that she and Jack would get back together. At last that had finally sunk in, and while she still wasn't happy about it, not even a little bit, Hope was accepting it. It was one tiny step on a very, very long road . . .

'You know what's weird?' Wilson suddenly nudged Hope and disproved her theory that he knew when she wasn't in the mood for talking any more.

She frowned. 'No. What?'

'That I'm meant to be giving you advice and a shoulder if you want to cry on it, but you're sitting there in my pyjamas and smelling of my bubble bath, neither of which are that alluring, and all I can think about is how you . . .' Wilson swallowed hard and Hope could hardly breathe as she waited for him to finish his sentence. 'You're warm and naked inside my clothes and I don't think I've ever wanted anyone as much as I want you right now.'

Hope hadn't been feeling alluring sitting there with frizzy hair and wearing baggy pyjamas, but now she was conscious that she was naked underneath the brushed cotton, which suddenly felt like a caress on her bare breasts, and when she shifted restlessly she could feel herself growing heavy and damp.

She didn't know what to say. There wasn't much that she could say either, except that she was meant to be broken and blue and crying on Wilson's shoulder but, actually, that wasn't what she wanted from him right then. She wanted his big heavy body on her, in her, and saying the words out loud would be yet another betrayal, but not as much as uncoiling her legs in an unsteady movement so she could rise up on her knees, take off Wilson's glasses, place them carefully on the coffee table and fling her arms around his neck.

Hope imagined that she could taste Wilson's shock, but she chased it away with her lips and her tongue, her hands on either side of his head to keep him still while she kissed him. Because he was always kissing her, and that seemed terribly unfair and one-sided.

Wilson's arms had been hanging limply by his sides, but as he started to kiss her back with a ferocity that was a little bit frightening but mostly thrilling, his hands clasped her hips and he lifted Hope as she scooched over so she was straddling him and God, yes, she could feel the hard nudge of his cock rubbing against her clit, which felt like it might detonate inside its brushed-cotton prison.

It was obvious that Hope wasn't going anywhere, was happy to stay right where she was, arching against the delicious promise of his dick, but Wilson pulled away from her voracious mouth so he could start to unbutton her pyjama top. He sighed as he slowly uncovered her breasts, sliding his hands into the jacket to shape their swollen fullness, thumbs pressing against her peaked and aching nipples.

'You're beautiful,' he said softly, reverently, and no one had ever said that to Hope before. No one. Not even the one person who should have said it to her many times and sounded like he meant it. 'Your freckles,' Wilson continued, tracing the freckles that dusted her skin, before Hope could think herself to another place, a place where she shouldn't be half-naked with someone who wasn't Jack. 'If we had enough time, I'd kiss every single one. How far down do they go?'

'All the way down,' Hope said, as she slipped the pyjama top down her arms so Wilson could see the mass of brown blotches on her shoulders, where they were at their most prolific. 'Got them everywhere but my palms and the soles of my feet.'

Hope had never thought of her freckles as sexy before, until Wilson quirked an eyebrow, one hand hovering over the drawstring knot that was holding up her pyjama bottoms.

'Everywhere?' he asked with interest.

Hope thought about slapping his hand away because she wasn't sure how far she wanted this to go, but she decided that there was no harm in giving him a visual demonstration if he really, really wanted one. 'Everywhere.'

'Well, that's something to bear in mind,' Wilson murmured just before he kissed her again.

They kissed for long moments, hands exploring, clothing pushed impatiently out of the way. And then they'd stop, and Wilson's hands would still be on the curve of Hope's hips, and she'd rest her forehead on his shoulder and try to catch her breath.

The next time they stopped, it was so Hope could tug Wilson's jumper and T-shirt over his head and as he sprawled back on the sofa sideways, she snuggled against him. The drawstring knot on her pyjama bottoms had been loosened and Wilson's hand rested just inside the waistband so his thumb could stroke against the jut of her hipbone.

'Why are you doing this?' Hope asked as she traced her finger around one hard, flat nipple. Without his clothes, Wilson was solid and firm, but not as bulky as Hope had imagined. He wasn't rock-hard like he lifted weights for hours every day, but obviously there were benefits to lugging around heavy pieces of photographic equipment. 'I mean, why me?'

'You really want to talk about this now?' Wilson sighed and shifted around so he could get more comfortable and Hope could slip into the little valley between his body and the sofa cushions. 'Why not you? You're smart and funny, and I never could resist a damsel in distress.'

'I'm not a damsel and I'm not in distress,' Hope pointed out, because being heartbroken wasn't the same as being distressed. 'It's just before this all happened, well, I thought that you didn't even like me that much.'

'I didn't. Bolshie cow, remember? You and Susie brought out the worst in each other,' Wilson said, and if this was his sexy talk then he was failing miserably, although Hope had been the one to raise the subject, but he was right. Together, she and Susie had been loud and obnoxious and invariably drunk. 'But since then, you've grown on me and I have a weakness for girls who I can't have.'

'Isn't that kind of a moot point at the moment?'

'I suppose it is,' Wilson agreed, dipping his head to catch a rosy nipple between his teeth and give it a hard suck so for one moment Hope forgot what they'd been talking about as she gasped and arched against him, the pyjama bottoms slipping a little further down so Wilson could place the shocking warmth of his hand on her bottom. He lifted his head and, in the dim light, the gleam in his eyes was unmistakable. 'You going to let me have you then, are you, Hope?'

The way he said it . . . his voice still gruff and stern, but in the right context, gruff and stern became wickedly, dangerously sexy. Still, there was no way that Hope could give Wilson the answer that he wanted (though God, she wanted it too) so she bit her lip instead.

'Is this just about revenge?' Now Wilson's voice sounded

hurt, and Hope tried to take away the pain by scattering kisses across his chest.

'No! Of course it isn't,' she said. 'It never was. It might have been about being comforted once, but now it's about wanting you. It's just that . . . well, am I just on the rebound? Because if I am, then it's not right, is it? To use you like this. And is it too soon? I mean, we only split up last week.'

'I'm really quite happy if you are on the rebound,' Wilson's hand tightened on her arse meaningfully. 'Are you saying this is all happening too soon?'

'I don't know.' Hope burrowed against Wilson and his arm wrapped around her even as he grunted like she was really testing his limits and his patience. 'It's not like life comes with big flashing lights above the doors that you're meant to go through.'

'You're half-naked in my arms. I'd say that was as good as a big flashing light.'

'Please don't take this the wrong way,' Hope begged and she sat up, which meant digging her elbow into Wilson's ribs so she could brush the tangle of hair out of her eyes and pull together the gaping edges of his pyjama top. 'It's not to say that this isn't special or that I don't want to be here, but until you I'd never even kissed another man except Jack . . .'

'You must have! At university . . .'

'I didn't! We'd been together five years by then and why would I throw that away on a few drunken gropes with sweaty Electronic Engineering students and I really thought Jack and I had a for ever and ever kind of deal – and now you're right, I'm half-naked in your arms . . . Oh, fuck!'

Hope was suddenly filled with shame and self-loathing. She was an awful, terrible, horrible person. She was meant to be out of her mind with grief, but she knew exactly what she was doing, and what she was doing was wrong. According to Lauren and those 'How to Get Over a Broken

411

Heart' articles in all the magazines, it was going to take her at least thirteen months to be a fully functioning human being again, but here she was already in another man's arms. It didn't say much about the depth of her love for Jack that she was aching and wet for another man. For Wilson, who hadn't moved, hadn't said a word to condemn her, but Hope was trying to scramble away from him, which was hard when she was wedged between him and the back of the sofa. 'Let me up!'

Wilson didn't let her up, but took her wrists in a firm hold. 'Listen, Dylan didn't have to see a man about a pushchair tonight. I told him that I'd take the photos because I wanted to see you again,' he said. 'I even gave him a hundred quid when he kept bitching at me that he really needed the money with a baby on the way.'

'Oh.' Hope stopped struggling, until she decided that Wilson's subterfuge, though flattering, didn't even begin to compare to her treachery. 'But that doesn't make it right me using you like this and . . .'

'What if I'm OK with being used? God, Hope, you've only been with one man your entire life. Aren't you even a little bit curious to see what it would be like with someone else?' Wilson asked Hope urgently. 'You're a free agent. You can do whatever the hell you like.'

And when he put it like that, it didn't seem so awful in the grand scheme of things, but maybe she was letting herself be convinced because she wanted to be, Hope thought as Wilson let go of her wrists, and slid his hands down the length of her spine so he could delve into the pyjama bottoms and cup her arse.

'Enough talking, more kissing,' he said.

'But it is still wrong,' Hope mumbled, and she wished that she could just shut the hell up. It was already wrong, what with the kissing and being bare chest to bare chest. Any other wrongness that occurred was just gravy. 'Don't you think?'

Wilson kissed her then, sliding his tongue possessively into her mouth so Hope couldn't speak, but she didn't really want to do anything other than kiss him back, and this time when they stopped kissing, she had managed to unbuckle his belt and undo his jeans, and the pyjama bottoms had slipped so far down her hips that she might just as well have not been wearing them. Wilson obviously thought so because he pushed them slowly down so they were tangled around her knees.

Here we go, Hope thought to herself, all ready to slip her hands inside Wilson's jeans, but then she wasn't able to do anything but gasp as his mouth grazed the tip of one swollen breast before sucking it into the warm heat of his mouth.

He lavished attention on her breasts for long, long minutes until they were gleaming damply and so sensitive that when he moved back Hope wanted to cry out as she felt the air stir against them.

Wilson's chest slowly coming back into view distracted Hope from the clamorous demands of her own body. Jack was so wiry and thin, that Hope always felt too fleshy in comparison. But Wilson wasn't like that all over, she thought as she pressed her palm against his stomach and felt the hard ridge of muscle just beneath the skin. Wilson also had a faint smattering of hair across his chest, not foliage by any means, but Jack didn't and again it was different.

Hope knew she shouldn't be comparing and contrasting as much as she was, but it seemed to her that Jack was still a boy and Wilson was very much a man. Looked like a man, talked like a man and acted like a man as he lowered her back down on to the sofa so he could kiss her again.

And when his hand slid up her thigh, he didn't falter or fumble or negotiate like Jack would have ('I'll let you go first if you promise to give me a blow job afterwards'), he just cupped her damp pussy and looked her right in the eye.

'I'm not going to fuck you but I am going to make you

413

come,' he told Hope and it should have been scary because this was Wilson (*Wilson!*) but Hope trusted him implicitly. Wilson didn't go in for double-speak or bullshit and if he said he was going to make her come, then he'd exhaust every possible avenue until her heart was racing, her eyes were rolling back in her head and her brain had short-circuited.

Hope dipped her head to give Wilson her tacit approval and wriggled to get more comfortable. They ended up side by side, facing each other, so they could still kiss as Wilson parted her thighs and explored her wet swollen pussy with the tip of one finger, while his tongue slipped into her mouth.

The finger stroked and pressed and teased but never exactly where she wanted it, so in the end Hope was forced to wrench her mouth away from Wilson's so she could give him directions. 'You're about two centimetres out,' she said breathlessly. 'Just to the left a bit.'

'I know exactly where it is,' Wilson snapped, resting his thumb on her clit for one fleeting second, before going back to the same ticklish teasing that he'd been doing for what felt like hours – thumb slipping around her clit but never properly making contact, while a finger traced the edge of her cunt without slipping inside.

Hope ground her teeth in frustration. 'I need more stimulation than that to come,' she tried to explain. 'A lot more.'

'I could do without a running commentary from the cheap seats,' Wilson said. 'We do it my way, or we don't do it at all.'

For a moment, a long moment, Hope was tempted to snap her legs shut and tell him to forget it. She always gave Jack detailed instructions, otherwise it would have taken them all night to do what could be done in twenty minutes, which included a little bit of snuggle-time afterwards.

Maybe that was what Jack had meant when he'd dissed

their sex life, but after ten years you fell into a routine and oh! . . . Hope arched back against the sofa as Wilson rubbed his thumb against her clit and slipped a finger inside her just long enough for her to think that they were finally starting to get somewhere – and then he was just circling around her clit again with a maddening, featherlight touch.

Hope huffed in annoyance. 'I was just saying . . .'

'I have done this before, you know,' Wilson said, biting down on her earlobe. 'Quite a few times, as it goes.'

Was that why Susie had gone for Jack? Or Jack had gone for Susie? Because Wilson's technique left a lot to be desired, and Hope was bossy and always told Jack exactly what she expected from him before she'd even dropped her knickers?

'Give me your hand,' Wilson suddenly said, and Hope stopped frowning so she could blink at him warily.

'Why?'

'Well, I'd quite like to come too,' Wilson said, taking her hand which had been resting limply on her hip and pulling it towards him and down, down until it was resting on his cock, hard and pulsing, even through his jeans, which she hadn't managed to completely unzip. Hope's first instinct was to snatch her hand back and maybe freak out a little bit, but then Wilson took his hand away and her own fingers were shaping him and curiosity was taking over. Curiosity was making her unzip his Levis all the way down and slip her hand into his shorts because the whole time she could hear Susie's smug voice echoing in her head: *'he's got a big dick and he knows what to do with it.'*

Was it bigger than Jack's? Hope couldn't tell, but as her fingers explored, Wilson felt a tiny bit longer maybe, definitely thicker, and just wrapping her hand around another man's cock should have been the very definition of wicked, but if it was, then it was wicked in a very good way. Feeling someone up was so teenage and reminded Hope of those long-ago evenings in her bedroom, door ajar because she was forbidden to close it when Jack was on the premises, something loud on her stereo to drown out the sound of the little moans and gasps they both made as they went to third base, dry-humped, heavy petted and all the other things they did that weren't full-on, penetrative sex.

Truth be told, Hope missed the hours that she and Jack used to spend snogging and groping and becoming familiar with the workings of a body that wasn't their own. Once they'd started to have sex, all the snogging and groping had fallen away because snogging and groping weren't enough by themselves, they were simply a means to an end, and the end was always sex.

Wilson murmured something indistinct and throaty when Hope thumbed the head of his cock, and she realised that she'd been absent-mindedly stroking him as she took a detour down memory lane. She'd obviously been doing the stroking with some measure of success because finally, *finally* his finger stopped circling and plunged deep inside her and it was her turn to voice her approval with a greedy little moan.

There was something ridiculous about the two of them squirming on a sofa barely wide enough to contain them, hands down each other's pants. The skin on Hope's wrist chafed against the zip of Wilson's jeans, and his pyjama bottoms were looped around her ankles and she didn't even have room to kick them off, but it didn't feel ridiculous to be kissing Wilson while he finger-fucked her slowly and deeply, thumb working her clit as she jacked him off.

Hope strained to get closer to Wilson, not even kissing him now, but simply breathing heavily against his open mouth as his fingers moved faster, went deeper, echoed in the touch of her own hand as she rubbed his wet-tipped cock.

Then he crooked his fingers inside her to hit a spot that Hope had only read about in magazine features titled '10

Ways to Spice up Your Love Life' and 'The Sex Trick Guaranteed to Give You an Orgasm Every Time'.

Her free hand gripped Wilson's quiff, trying to hold him still as she stiffened against him, toes curling, muscles clenching, her fingers involuntarily tightening around his cock so that when her brain was able to fire on all cylinders again, she realised that Wilson had come too. She also realised that his fingers were still moving on her, inside her to catch every last flutter.

Hope waited for the shame and the embarrassment to kick in, but they were nowhere to be found. But yes, she blushed a little when Wilson finally released her, then sucked her juices from his fingers with the same look of quiet appreciation he usually showed for ancient malt whisky.

'Thank you,' he said, dropping a kiss on each one of her drooping eyelids.

Chapter Thirty-seven

At six thirty the world outside was dark and muffled by a blanket of heavy snow. Wearing thick socks and with socks stuffed into the toes of a pair of Wilson's boots so she could walk in them, Hope made it to his car unaided.

Then it was a slow, perilous drive to Holloway, Wilson's ancient Saab protesting loudly with every metre. When they turned into the square where Hope lived, the car skidded and she gripped hold of the dashboard as Wilson swore loudly but managed to keep them on the slippery road.

'You will be careful driving back,' Hope said, as he walked her the last few steps home, even though she'd told him that she could manage. 'Promise me you'll take it slow.'

'Yes, Mum,' Wilson said with a frozen grin as they reached her door. All the lights seemed to be off, so Hope reckoned she could sneak in very quietly and Jack would be none the wiser. It would be a secret between her and Wilson, which was wrong, but she also liked the idea that she and Wilson shared a secret. 'So, what happens next?'

'I don't know,' Hope said, because she really didn't. She'd been fixated on the idea that she could somehow trick Jack into staying with her for so long now that, apart from making lists, she hadn't really thought about what her life would be like without him. She probably wasn't ready for another relationship right away, but the thought of spending more time with Wilson was a pleasing one. 'What do *you* want to happen next?'

'I want you not to answer a question with another question,' Wilson said, but he smiled at her. 'I'm up for seeing you again, maybe having some of those one-night stands we talked about a while ago. There's absolutely no reason why we can't hang out now, is there?'

Hope bent down to tug off Wilson's boots. 'No reason at all,' she agreed. 'Unless I have another emotional freak-out and decide to join a nunnery instead.'

'They'd kick you out within minutes for having impure thoughts.' They were both talking in whispers now. 'You're going to have emotional freak-outs. It's all part of the process. Anyway, love, you were having emotional freak-outs long before you broke up with him indoors.'

Hope tried to scowl but her heart wasn't in it. The sky was lightening from a dark, dense navy to a Wedgewood blue; a reminder that the night was almost over and it was the dawning of a brand-new day and brand-new resolutions.

'I do also have moments of great calm,' Hope insisted, but Wilson didn't look as if he believed her, and both of them were shivering now. 'I'd better get inside and you should go. I don't want you freezing to death before you even make it back to your car.'

'Well, give us a kiss first, then.' Wilson already had his hands on her hips to bring her closer and was this the worst betrayal of all, passionately kissing Wilson on her own doorstep while Jack was sleeping just a few feet away?

'Jesus! What the *actual* fuck?'

Except Jack wasn't sleeping, because he'd appeared there on the doorstep, grey with tiredness like he hadn't slept, and was staring at Hope, still in Wilson's arms, with equal parts horror and disbelief.

Hope stared back at Jack as Wilson's arms fell away, and then she turned to look at Wilson instead. Whatever final niggling doubts she might have had about Wilson exacting a painstakingly planned revenge were swept away by the discomfited expression on his face.

'What the fuck?' Jack said again. 'I thought you were dead or stranded somewhere, and all the time . . . what the fuck have you been doing?'

'Well, we went for our Christmas meal, then we went on to this club . . .'

'We? Who's *we*? I know you weren't with Elaine because I phoned her,' Jack barked.

'I was with Wilson,' Hope explained rather pointlessly.

'Who you said you weren't going to see again!'

'But you were the one who said I could!' Hope bit her lip so hard that she almost drew blood rather than remind Jack that he'd said he didn't have a problem with her hanging out with Wilson, because he trusted her. 'But I haven't been, until last night.'

'Yeah, well, you more than made up for it, didn't you?' Jack was in jeans and a jumper, so Hope didn't know if he'd been to bed yet. Normally he didn't even know what the morning looked like much before eight and it wasn't even seven. He had his hands on his hips as he glared at her, and all he needed was a rolling pin to complete the picture of the wronged spouse. 'So, again, what the fuck have you been up to?'

'Maybe now isn't the time, when Hope's standing in her socks in the freezing cold,' Wilson pointed out from where he stood behind her.

Jack drew himself up until he was at least 5 inches taller, and showed all his teeth in a fair approximation of a snarl at the inference that he didn't care about Hope's physical well-being like Wilson did.

'It's got nothing to do with you,' Jack said belligerently. Hope heard Wilson snort, and she wasn't sure if Jack had too, but she put one frozen foot forward.

'Shall we not do this on the doorstep?' she suggested, trying to push Jack's rigid body aside so she could get through the door. But then she turned back to Wilson, and this wasn't how their goodbye was meant to go. It was meant to be far more *Brief Encounter* than this excruciating, embarrassing scene. 'Look, I'll . . . well, I'm sorry. I'll call you, OK?'

'No, you bloody won't!' Jack exploded and he grabbed Hope's hand and yanked her into the hall.

'Are you going to be all right?' Wilson asked quietly, but it was the kind of forceful quiet that would have made all the hairs on the back of Hope's neck rise up if they weren't already vertical. 'I can come in if you want.'

If possible, Jack became even more furious. Hope had never seen him like this, with fists and jaw clenched so tight, his face bright red with anger. 'Of course she's going to be all right,' he hissed, as if he was too angry to even shout any more. 'I'm not going to hit her because I would never, ever do that, and you don't know anything about me, and I'll tell you something else, you know fuck all about Hope, too.'

That wasn't even a little bit true. Yes, Jack would win every time if they went on a *Mr and Mrs*-style gameshow and he had to answer questions on her favourite food and what side of the bed she slept on, but Hope knew that when it came down to it, after all those years, he didn't have a clue about what was really going on in her head or her heart, whereas Wilson already seemed to have a grasp on the basics.

'You sure about that, are you?' Wilson asked in the same scarily quiet voice, because he might have the inside track on Hope but he didn't seem to realise that he was deliberately goading Jack. Or maybe he did.

Jack started to say something, but it was mostly 'fucking' and 'wanker' with a few other swear words thrown in at random.

'That's enough!' Hope shouted in her most teacherly voice. She pushed Jack down the hall, turned to give Wilson

421

one last helpless, hapless shrug, and shut the door in his face.

'You fucked him, didn't you?' Jack demanded, as Hope brushed past him and walked into the kitchen. 'Didn't you?'

'Of course I didn't,' Hope said immediately, and it was the truth. The right answer – except Jack was asking the wrong question. She hadn't fucked Wilson, but she'd still cheated on Jack.

'But you spent the night with him?' His voice was quietening down at last. 'You slept with him.'

She hadn't done that either, and unless Jack kept playing Twenty Questions and eventually managed to stumble on the exact truth of what she'd been doing with Wilson, Hope could get away with it. Because all he'd actually seen was a kiss on a doorstep.

'Look, he came to dinner with us and then the two of us went to a club in Camden,' she hurriedly clarified. 'And I was only going to stay for an hour but I started doing tequila shots . . .'

Jack moaned like he was in pain. 'You're an animal when you drink tequila!'

Hope decided to ignore that little aside. 'So I stayed longer than I meant to, and when we left at two, it had been snowing and we couldn't get a cab or a bus, so we had to walk to Wilson's. I mean, I couldn't walk home in these, could I?' She produced her ruined shoes, which she'd stuffed into her handbag. They were still soaking wet and the soles had curled up like medieval jesters' shoes. 'And yes, I was with Wilson and . . . well . . .'

She could just say that nothing had happened. She could. Already she'd given Jack far more explanation than he'd given her about spending night after night and lunchtime after lunchtime and snatched hours here and there with Susie, but the words were stuck in her throat. Because something had happened and to deny it, even to save her

own skin, was like admitting it hadn't meant anything –
when it had.

'I didn't shag him,' she said. 'We sort of fooled around,
but I don't really want to talk about it.'

Jack had been leaning against the kitchen door but now
he slid down until he was sitting on the floor, knees drawn
up to his chest. 'I can't believe that you'd do this after all
that we've gone through. After all the things you've said . . .
why? Because you were mad at me for not coming to your
carol concert?'

When was Jack going to get it into his head that it hadn't
been a carol concert? It had been a flaming Winter Pageant,
that she'd put her heart and soul into – it really wasn't the
issue right then, but still . . . 'You knew how much
the Winter Pageant meant to me, and you couldn't even be
bothered to stop drinking for long enough to see the last
half-hour, so yeah, I was pissed off with you, but it had
nothing to do with that,' Hope said, and she didn't even
dare snap at Jack. Getting angry with him when he was so
obviously upset would be like chucking petrol on a
barbecue. Instead, she opened the fridge and started taking
out the Tupperware boxes containing her cupcakes

'So, why? To get back at me because of Susie?'

Hope looked up in surprise. 'Of course not,' she said, and
she thought it was the most truthful thing she'd said so far.
'Not everything is about you and Susie.'

'Then why? You can't fancy him! He's such a pretentious
wanker.' Derision curled itself around every word. 'That's
what you used to say.'

It had been a long time since Hope had seen Wilson as
nothing more than a retro hairstyle and a permanent sneer.
She could hardly even recognise Wilson from Jack's
description, because he wasn't like that at all. He was kind
and considerate and funny, and yeah, still a little intimidating but it was a very, very sexy kind of intimidating – and
she couldn't tell Jack that so Hope got the butter from the

fridge, pulled out a mixing bowl and the special jar of sugar with vanilla pods in it that she used for baking. 'You know I've been hanging out with him a bit,' she said at last, as she doggedly creamed butter and sugar to make frosting. 'I got to know him better.'

'Do you hate me so much that you'd do this to me?' Jack asked, and she could hear his voice thickening and if he cried, then Hope would cry too.

'Jack,' she said, her eyes fixed on the bowl. 'I really don't mean to be nasty, but this wasn't about you. It was about me and Wilson, and well, you don't really have any right to be giving me a hard time about this. You don't want to be with me, you want Susie, so what I do with other people really isn't your business any more . . .'

'I can't believe that you'd throw that back in my face.' Jack wiped the face in question, and if he wasn't crying then it was only through a superhuman effort. 'What I did with Susie was completely different.'

The only way that Hope could see that it was different was that at least she'd resisted that wicked little voice in her head egging her on. And she might have finally given in, but that was only because in the deepest, darkest part of her heart, she knew that Jack was never coming back to her. She could have had sex with Wilson weeks ago, for that matter, but she hadn't because she'd wanted to do the decent thing by Jack. Whereas Jack hadn't even considered doing the decent thing. He'd met up with Susie to buy Hope's birthday present and ended up getting his rocks off like a free gift with purchase of a pair of Stella McCartney shoes, which Hope had now given to the local Cancer Research shop. That was how it was different.

But she wasn't going to drag this up all over again, because there was no point any more. Jack had already chosen his future and Hope . . . well, her future was shadowy and un-defined but least she had *options*. Even so, she didn't want it to end like this, with rows and recriminations and bucketloads of regret. 'I'm sorry,' she said, and she meant it. 'I am so sorry that I've hurt you. It wasn't my intention.'

'Well, it sounds like I was the last person you were worrying about,' Jack said, dragging himself to his feet. 'And your "sorry" means fuck all. You can't just say sorry and think it's all squared away. It isn't.'

Hope began manically chopping chocolate. 'I know that, but I am sorry, Jack. And yeah, I suppose my timing was a bit off.'

'You went out and threw yourself at the first bloke you could find,' Jack said savagely. 'And I've spent all bloody night worried sick about you.'

'It wasn't like that,' Hope said and she was crying now, tears plopping into the bowl of chocolate that she was trying to melt over a bain-marie. The plan had been that after she'd made the frosting, she was going to make icing so she could put everyone's initials on a cupcake, but fuck that. Why did she always have to make everything so complicated? 'I've been really selfish and thoughtless and I'm sorry.'

She dropped her wooden spoon, even though she was meant to be frantically stirring the melted chocolate so it wouldn't go lumpy, to go over to Jack standing in the doorway, because he was hurting and Hope still loved him, which was why she wanted to take the hurt away.

'I'm sorry,' she said again, because if she kept saying it, then eventually he'd believe her. 'I'm so sorry.'

She went to touch his arm, but he flinched and it wasn't because her fingers were sticky with butter, sugar and chocolate. 'Don't,' he bit out. 'I don't want you near me right now. I can hardly bear to look at you.'

Hope shut her eyes, and when she opened them she wished she hadn't, because Jack had never looked at her like that before, like she was a dog turd that he'd found smeared to the sole of his favourite pair of limited-edition Converses. 'I forgave you,' she said in a low voice. 'And I agreed to let you go.'

'No, you didn't. You'd never have done this if you really had forgiven me. What were you thinking? That you could go out and shag someone else and we'd be even?'

'We can get past this,' she insisted. 'We got through everything else. We both know that we'll still be friends when this has all blown over, so will you *please* stop looking at me like that?'

'Fine! That I can do,' Jack said and strode out of the kitchen and down the hall.

The front door closing behind him had an awful note of finality in its loud thud.

Chapter Thirty-eight

Hope wasn't quite sure how she made it through the day without bursting into tears.

She was sleep-deprived, that was a given, and the hangover kicked in as she walked into school with her cupcakes and their lumpy frosting – only to bump into Elaine who proceeded to give Hope a tongue-lashing that rivalled anything that Caroline Delafield had ever come up with. She was 'selfish, feckless and any fool, even Marta, could see that you're self-sabotaging your relationship with Jack because you don't have the guts to break up with him', Elaine told Hope, after she'd frogmarched her into the staff toilets.

'It's not like that,' Hope said, although she could see that to someone who hadn't been told that Hope had been dumped by Jack a fortnight before, it might look that way.

'And what about poor Wilson? Lovely bloke. Doesn't deserve to be treated like that,' Elaine continued, shaking her head and tutting. 'I have to say, I'm seeing a whole new side of you, and I don't like it very much.'

There wasn't much that Hope could say in her defence, not even that Wilson had been very happy to be treated like that, but the bell rang while she was stuttering her way through a half-hearted defence of her reprehensible actions and she had to scurry off to her classroom.

Blue Class refused to be quiet in deference to Hope's fragile state. They had three and a half hours before they were done with school for three weeks, and they wanted to tell Hope exactly what they were getting from Father Christmas, at great length and in excruciating detail. They also wanted to discuss how much they'd rocked the Winter Pageant, and what on earth Timothy meant when he said it was statistically impossible for Father Christmas to deliver presents to every child in the world – even allowing for different time zones, and the fact that Santa could change reindeer every hour. 'And, Miss, how do reindeer even fly, anyway? How do they get up in the sky and stay there?'

If Hope hadn't had a headache before they started on the never-ending questions about reindeers and aerodynamics, then she definitely had one now. Eventually she could take no more, and stuck *Kiki's Delivery Service* in the DVD player, and within five minutes there wasn't a sound coming from anybody and Hope could get on with writing out Christmas cards.

Rather than brave the staffroom and Elaine's wrath at break-time, Hope went out into the blistering cold, this time in wellington boots and two pairs of socks, to wander around aimlessly and try to decide what she was going to do with the rest of her life, now she'd finally accepted that Jack wasn't coming back.

Now she'd have to figure out who Hope Delafield was, when she wasn't one half of Hope and Jack. Or HopeandJack, which was what everyone called them, like their names were just one word and that they were one being, instead of two separate people.

Being single was hard work, and Hope wasn't even thinking of Lauren and Allison's tales from the dating frontline. She was thinking of having to go back to living in a shared house, like she'd done when she was a student. And deciding who'd get custody of the car and the washing machine in the split, and winding up their joint bank accounts, and cooking meagre meals for one, and living every single day without someone who was sunk into the very marrow of her bones. Who knew what mood she was in before she even opened her mouth. Who'd shared every bad thing and every good thing that had happened to her in the last thirteen years. Who communicated with her in their own private language of in-jokes and looks and hand gestures.

It wasn't just about finally letting Jack go. It was about letting a part of herself go with him, and maybe she wouldn't be on her own for ever, and maybe she'd even fall deep in love again, but it would never be the same. Jack had had the best of her, and whoever Hope might love in the future would love a woman who was a little bit less than what she used to be.

Remarkably all her soul-searching had only taken fifteen minutes. Hope trudged back to school, inwardly dreading the last ninety minutes of term, when Blue Class would give out their cards and presents and, as a special treat, perform their Lady Gaga medley all over again. As she walked through the playground, sticking to the edges so she wouldn't be spotted and immediately have several small children clinging to her, her phone beeped.

It was a message from Wilson. *Is everything OK? Even if it isn't, you'll get through this. You're made of strong stuff.*

It was sweet of Wilson to think so, because Hope felt as if she was made from something weak and insubstantial like blancmange or bubble wrap. She didn't know what was going to happen between them, and she didn't want to be one of those pathetic girls who couldn't be on their own and *had* to be in a relationship, but Hope was curious to see what Wilson and her could be. Even just 'a series of consecutive one-night stands' might be fun, judging from his performance a few hours ago.

I am OK, she texted back. *Apart from a demonic hangover. Thanks for everything you did last night. All of it. I'll be in touch once the dust settles.*

And that was all Hope could write, because there wasn't anything else to say, but just as she got to her classroom, her phone beeped again and her heart did an unexpected little skip and a jump – until Hope saw that she had a message from Jack. *I'll see you at counselling tonight. Don't be late.*

Her heart stopped skipping and jumping in favour of plummeting to the floor. It wasn't just Jack's uncompromising prose style, which told Hope in no uncertain terms that he was still furious with her, and likely to stay that way for quite some time. She also didn't want Angela there to witness Jack's fury and listen to all the gory details, her eyes darting back and forth behind her smeary glasses as she judged Hope. Or judged Hope even more than she already had.

The incipient dread cast a gloom over the rest of the day, even though it was spent with Blue Class exchanging cards and gifts. Hope hadn't been left out either. She received many home-made cards – her favourite was Javan's, which featured Father Christmas being slaughtered by a squad of ninja assassins – and soon her desk was obscured by a huge pile of presents. As well as several tins of Quality Street, Roses and Celebrations, there were gift baskets from Boots and the Body Shop, mugs, teapots, cookery books and scented candles, and Stuart's mum, Saskia, had gone all out with a bottle of Moët and a hamper from Carluccio's, which didn't make Hope like Stuart more, but she did feel even more guilty about not liking him. However, her favourite present was the hat, scarf and gloves commissioned by Sorcha and Luca's mums and knitted by Timothy's mother, who usually sold her woollies in a very posh boutique in Camden Passage.

Her cupcakes and cards seemed like a paltry offering compared to the generosity of their parents, but Blue Class received them with rapturous delight, apart from Stuart, who apparently was now dairy- and gluten-intolerant and had a nut allergy, too.

By the time the bell rang at one, Hope was exhausted, mentally, physically and emotionally, and it was a miracle on the level of the Virgin Birth, which all of Blue Class were intrigued and confused by, that she'd managed not to burst into tears.

She did almost cry when Elaine presented her with a crate of home-made elderflower vodka and the offer of a lift home. Although the lift home meant that Elaine could give her a stern talking-to both in the car and after Hope had half-heartedly invited her in for coffee and cupcakes.

'So, are you regretting the way you behaved last night?' Elaine asked, once Hope had presented her with a mug of black coffee and two misshapen cupcakes that hadn't passed her stringent quality control. It was a welcome change of subject. On the way home, Elaine hadn't stopped telling Hope that she was having a mid-twenties crisis.

'Elaine, you don't understand.' Hope was sitting bolt upright in the uncomfortable armchair that had a spring loose where her left buttock cheek liked to rest. She knew that if she sat as she usually did in a slouch/sprawl combo, she'd be fast asleep within minutes. 'Jack and I had a talk the weekend before last, well, mostly he talked, and he's chosen Susie. He loves her and he wants to be with her, so I don't know why he's quite so angry with me. Yeah, I stayed out all night and I should probably have called him, and he caught me kissing Wilson on the doorstep this morning. But, really, he needs to lay off the wronged-lover routine because he's not my lover any more.'

'Kissing? This morning? Did you spend the night with Wilson? What have you been doing?' Somehow Elaine managed to sound both disapproving and as if she'd die if Hope didn't confess everything at once.

Hope didn't confess everything. She confessed right up to the kissing and then faded to black, because no matter how ashamed she was of her duplicity of the night before, she wasn't ashamed of what had happened on Wilson's sofa, because, as she'd told Jack that morning, it had nothing to do with anyone but her and Wilson.

By the time Elaine left, with the rest of the non-standardised cupcakes and a tin of Roses, which she'd swapped with Hope for a large box of Ferrero Rocher, they were friends again.

'We're having people over for Christmas Eve,' she said to Hope as she stood shivering on the pavement and waiting to wave Elaine off. 'If you fancy it.'

'We're going up North on the twenty-second,' Hope said, and she literally had to bite her tongue so she didn't add a 'just kill me now' on to the end of the sentence. 'Have to tell the parents the bad news in person.'

Elaine gave Hope a quick but fierce hug. 'I'm so sorry about you and Jack, sweetie. Is there no chance that you might get back together?'

Hope shook her head. 'Seriously? I think he'd made up his mind weeks ago, and agreeing to counselling, well, he was just going through the motions.' She squirmed unhappily on the doorstep. 'It's taken me a while to get my head round it; it's why I never told you. I thought that I could persuade Jack to stay, especially once the parents became involved, but I was just deluding myself.'

'So, was that why you copped off with Wilson?' Elaine asked. 'To convince yourself, or was it one last attempt to make Jack jealous so he'd realise you were his one true love?'

'God, no! I mean, Jack's angry, but I think it's more self-defensive anger because now he has a vague idea of what he put me through and he feels guilty,' Hope said. 'The thing with Wilson happened because I wanted it to. I wanted it very much. Does that make me a bad person?'

'Of course it doesn't. You deserve a bit of fun,' Elaine insisted vehemently. 'So, I guess I won't see you until the New Year, then?'

''Fraid not, but if I was around, you know I'd love to

come to yours for Christmas Eve. You have the wildest parties,' Hope added wistfully, as she remembered the time Simon had bought canisters of laughing gas off the internet and decanted it into party balloons so his guests could huff it down and spend the rest of the night giggling like loons.

'Like I say, if you do happen to be around, you know where we'll be,' Elaine said, and she shrugged and did a weird, starey thing with her eyes that Hope couldn't decipher, but then again she was so sleep-deprived that she could barely see straight as it was.

Three hours later, Hope was at the wired, teeth-chattering, about-to-start-hallucinating-little-green-men stage of tiredness. She sat in Angela's waiting room and wondered if Jack was going to be a no-show. She'd already seen the patient who had the appointment before them rush out with his head down as was his wont, and Jack should have been here by now. Hope prayed that it wouldn't just be her and Angela.

A minute before their session started, Jack arrived, red-faced and out of breath. 'Sorry, I'm la . . .' he began, then Hope saw him mentally check himself, because he was still angry with her and didn't owe her an apology for being late. 'Christ, you could have made a bit more of an effort, couldn't you?'

He was also going to pick on everything she said and did, because it was what Jack did when he was in a bad mood, especially when Hope was the cause of it. 'I'm sorry,' she said in a conciliatory fashion, because she'd decided to take Jack's anger as her due and she simply didn't have the energy to get angry too. Hope gestured at her sloppy sweater, leggings and Uggs ensemble. 'It was the closest I could come to wearing pyjamas, without actually wearing pyjamas.'

'Yeah well, if you hadn't been out all hours shagging that pretentious wanker, then you wouldn't be so tired,' Jack snapped.

'I told you, there was no actual shagging,' Hope sighed, like that really mattered. It still counted as cheating even if there hadn't been a penis entering a vagina, but before she could get into specifics, Hope realised that Angela was standing in the doorway and looking as if her eyeballs might hurl themselves out of their sockets.

'Right, well, best to get started right away,' she said, as she hustled the pair of them down the corridor that led to her room. Hope had a horrible feeling that this evening their session wouldn't be cut short by fifteen minutes. 'So, how *are* you two?' Angela asked before their bottoms had even made contact with the sofa.

'Oh, so-so,' Hope prevaricated, but she could feel the full weight of Jack's glare, even though she was staring resolutely ahead at a spot 5 centimetres to the left of Angela's left ear. 'You know how it is.'

'Why don't you tell Angela how it is?' Jack demanded, before directly addressing Angela, who was quivering where she sat. 'She went out last night and shagged Susie's ex to get back at me, or because she's pissed off that I don't want to stay with her and get married and have babies. I don't know. Hope's not exactly been forthcoming on the details, even though I practically caught them at it on the doorstep this morning.'

There were so many half-truths and untruths in Jack's statement that Hope wasn't sure how to defend herself. 'We were kissing,' she told Angela, because for once it was easier to talk to Angela than to Jack. 'This morning. It was just kissing.'

When the man you were kissing wasn't the man you'd been in a relationship with for the last thirteen years, it was always a lot more than 'just kissing', but Angela nodded as if she understood. Maybe she did have hidden depths after all.

'And spending the night with another man?' Angela queried, her voice almost breaking on the last word. 'When

434

Jack was seeing someone else it altered the equilibrium in the relationship; by mirroring Jack's behaviour, were you hoping to shift it the other way?'

You *what*? 'It wasn't like that,' she protested weakly. 'Jack and I aren't in a relationship any more, so technically I didn't do anything wrong, even if my timing was lousy. But, the thing is, Jack, that I get it. I get what happened with you and Susie now. About wanting someone so badly that even though there's a million good reasons why you shouldn't, that one selfish reason cancels them all out.'

Jack sneered, as if he'd never been in that position and didn't have even the vaguest idea of what Hope was talking about. 'Did you even think about what it might do to me?'

'I didn't really see how it would affect you one way or another,' Hope admitted. 'So I tried not to think about you at all.'

It sounded so callous when she tried to be honest, Hope thought despairingly. Jack obviously thought so too. 'Not good enough,' he stated bluntly. 'I think you owe me an explanation.'

'Why should I?' Hope asked, wishing that they weren't doing this when she'd had no sleep for thirty-six hours, was still in the grip of a tequila hangover and felt so vulnerable that it seemed as if her skin had been stripped off and her nerve endings had come to the surface. 'There are some things that you're better off not knowing, and there are some things that are none of your business. You absolutely refused to talk about your affair with Susie even though you knew I was in utter hell about it.'

'Ha! You see?' Jack crowed triumphantly. 'I knew this was about Susie. I knew it was about revenge.'

'God, you haven't listened to a single word I've said, have you? Jack, you're my *ex*-boyfriend, you don't have a say in who I see or what I get up to any more.' And she knew she was being childish, but Hope curled her legs up under her, tucked her arms into her chest and bowed her head, to show that she was absenting herself from the proceedings, because between Jack and Jack's ego there really wasn't any room left for her.

There was silence. The kind of silence that had teeth and claws, so Hope tried to focus on the sound of her own breathing, making it deep and even and regular, so that despite all the emotional distress, she was close to falling asleep when Angela cleared her throat timidly.

'Well, this is all rather . . . well . . .' Hope lifted her head in time to see the utter helplessness on Angela's face as she struggled to summarise the shit that Hope and Jack were in. 'So, did you have a chance to do the homework?' Angela asked a little desperately.

Jack cleared his throat. 'You really want us to go through our homework assignment? Really?'

Hope had to agree with him. What did it matter where they were going to be in ten years' time? It certainly wasn't going to be with each other.

'Well, I do think it's a very useful exercise,' Angela insisted, and she looked so woebegone that Hope started to feel sorry for her, and even Jack sighed in capitulation.

'Right, so I had a definite plan of where I'd be ten years from now, and it was in a live/work space in Hoxton where I ran my own design company, and I got to travel a lot and had all this interesting work, and the latest gadgets, and that was great, just what I wanted, even if it did feel a little shallow – but somehow, no matter how hard I tried, I couldn't see Susie in the picture.'

Hope cautiously raised her head out of the crook of her arms, only to see Jack giving her the evil eye. Then he shrugged. 'I tried so hard to put Susie into my future, then Hope didn't come home last night and when she did rock up she was with *him*, and I could have killed them both.'

Angela actually gasped at Jack's display of un-characteristic machismo, though Hope was less than impressed. 'Well, I could have told you that Susie wasn't cut out for a life of domestic bliss, even if it was in a live/work space in Hoxton,' she said, and she sounded bitter but she'd earned the right to be bitter.

'It's not that,' Jack said sharply. 'It's that I was only thinking about one part of my life, the professional part, and I've spent all day being mad at you because when I think about the future, I don't really want the minimalist designer loft, it's just something that I think I *should* want. Really, when I look into the future, all I can see is you and me and we're living somewhere like Brighton, 'cause I could still commute to London from there, or I might freelance or have my own studio or what have you . . .' Hope could see him relax, the rigidity slowly ease out of him as he began to describe the Jack and Hope of the future. Because it turned out that *she* was in Jack's future.

Apparently, ten years from now, they had three children, two boys and a girl, but they were trying for another baby because they didn't want an odd number of children and, besides, Hope came from a large family and Jack had hated being an only child. They lived in a house five minutes' walk from the beach and in the catchment area for the best local schools.

Jack wasn't exactly sure if Hope was still working as a teacher, or had decided to stay at home and go back to work once their youngest child that hadn't even been born yet started primary school, but she baked a lot of cakes, and they kept chickens in their back garden as well as having an allotment where Hope grew their own vegetables. She was also a stalwart of the local Preservation Society.

Basically, in the space of ten years filled with child-rearing and gardening, Hope had turned into her mother. And, quite frankly, Hope wasn't on board with the idea that Jack got to do something he loved while she spent all her time barefoot and pregnant. Well, not barefoot – if she was raising chickens and growing spuds, she'd spend most of the time in her wellies.

But despite her disbelief at Jack's sudden change of heart, there was a part of Hope that liked the sound of this vaguely bucolic existence. With two children, certainly not four. And maybe, instead of chickens, they could have a couple of mini-pigs, and before all this happened, they'd have travelled, seen a bit of the world on at least two other continents, not including Europe.

Hope stuck her head out from beneath the cradle of her arms again. 'That's really how you see our future?'

'Kind of. Though right now I'm still so angry with you I'm not even sure if I'll get the bus home with you.'

Hope felt her face begin to slacken, as if the tears were all set to fall, but aware of Angela's beady eyes fixed on her, she willed her muscles to behave. 'OK, well, I suppose I deserve that.'

Jack had gone back to not looking at her again. 'Yeah, I guess you do.'

But for all his talk of ten-year plans, Hope refused to let herself get sucked into Jack's little domestic fantasy. It was just Jack smarting from the night before because he'd never had to think about Hope existing in a world without him, a world where there were men who might actually want her. Besides, Hope couldn't see further than three months into their future, where Jack would still be pissed off at her and she'd have nothing to listen to but the disapproving voice of her own conscience and his passive-aggressive asides . . .

'Hope?'

She realised that Angela was saying something. To her. 'Sorry. What?'

'I asked where you saw yourself in ten years' time,' Angela repeated. Hope's eyes drifted to the clock. They only had another fifteen minutes left. Why, oh why, was Angela determined to make them sit through the whole hour? Because she was a sadist who got off on other people's misery and got paid for it. 'Well, Hope?'

This time the silence didn't just have claws and teeth, it

also had a stun-gun and a machete. Hope could hear the hand of the clock mark off every second that she sat there without answering. She couldn't even think of some happy-families bullshit because there didn't seem any point in pretending any more.

'You couldn't even be bothered to do the homework, could you?' Jack suddenly said. 'Shows how committed you are to making this work.'

'But we'd already agreed, or you had, that this wasn't working, so there was no point imagining you and me together ten years from now when I knew that wasn't going to happen,' Hope said. 'But I did try to think about where I'd be in ten years' time, but I just couldn't get a definite picture in my head. Like, maybe I want to be living abroad, and I probably will have children or maybe I won't, not after spending all day looking after other people's . . . it's all just a big blank, really.' The big blank wasn't as scary as Hope thought it might be. It actually felt a tiny bit thrilling, like she could do what she wanted, be whoever she wanted to be. Nothing was mapped out. Nothing was planned. It was all possibility.

'Maybe you couldn't think what ten years from now would look like, because you've always thought about a future that had me in it,' Jack suggested softly.

'Well, of course I always pictured you in my future. It's going to take a while to adjust to the idea that we're going to have separate lives . . . but the thing is . . .' Hope paused, because she had a horrible suspicion that she was about to do what she'd spent the last three months trying not to do. To articulate the unspeakable truth that was actually the reason why he'd slept with Susie, and she wanted to shag Wilson, without the air-quotes. As Angela would have said, if she hadn't been staring at them avidly with her mouth hanging open, Hope knew she was about to have her light-bulb moment. 'The thing is, Jack, you were right all along. I thought if we went home for Christmas that I could get the parents to talk you round, but I finally see that we don't have another ten days in us, let alone a future.'

The tears began to fall quite unexpectedly. One moment Hope had been able to deliver her epitaph on their relationship with a clear head and a clear voice, the next she was sobbing. She was crying for them, for what they'd had and what they might have been, but she was also crying because she was tired and headachy, and she felt dirty in the way she always did when she'd stayed up all night. And if she was crying, then at least she didn't have to talk any more.

'Oh, Hope, don't say stuff like that,' she heard Jack murmur throatily as if he was pretty close to tears himself, and then unbelievably she felt his arm around her so he could pull her in.

She was happy to be pulled so she could awkwardly wrap both arms around him and get tears and snot on the shoulder of his Lazy Days hoodie. Jack's hand tried to smooth back her hair, but he was fighting a losing battle. 'Don't you want to be with me, then?' he asked.

She'd said it once already, but now that Jack was holding her and he was real and solid and not a sneering facsimile of himself at the other end of the sofa, Hope didn't have the guts to say it again. 'But you don't want to be with me! You're angry with me and you hate me and you want Susie. And maybe you can't see her in your future yet, but that's because you and her are still so new and when . . .'

'I don't hate you, Hopey.'

'Yes, you do, because you think I did a hateful thing.' The end of the sentence was swallowed up in an anguished wail, and then Hope was crying again and Jack was soothing her again and she didn't have to talk.

'Well, this is very exciting. I never thought you'd have such a breakthrough, Hope,' Angela said. Then she had the audacity to rustle a tissue box enticingly in Hope's face, but Hope was damned if she was going to give Angela the satisfaction of taking one of her tissues.

Instead she sat up, wiped her wet face with the sleeve of her jumper and took a couple of deep, centring breaths. 'I am sorry, Jack,' she breathed. 'But you're going to have to get used to the idea that I'm probably not going to spend the rest of my life being celibate.'

'What if I can't?' Jack asked. 'What if I don't want to?'

Hope smiled through the tears. 'Well, I'm hardly going to take a vow of chastity, am I?'

'No, of course you're not, but what I'm trying to say is that I love you,' Jack said, leaning forward so he could give Hope a sideways look from under his lashes. 'I really love you, Hopey.'

She nodded. 'Yeah, I love you too,' she muttered quietly, because Angela had seen and heard quite enough and surely their hour was up by now. 'Doesn't change anything though, does it?'

'But it's a pretty good basis to start again, if we both agree that we still love each other,' Jack said, and this time he was the one to turn and glare at Angela when she gasped. Then he turned the full weight of his big blue stare back to Hope. 'I don't think I love Susie, not the way I love you. It's not love, it's infatuation, and what we have is deeper, it's in my blood.'

It was exactly what Hope had wanted Jack to realise. These were the words that her heart and her head, and all the other bits of her, had longed to hear. So, why wasn't she roused from her lethargy and hangover, she wondered. Why wasn't she jumping up to do a victory lap of the room and punch the air in triumph a few times, instead of staying on the sofa and frowning? 'But you're still mad at me, aren't you?'

'I'd rather be mad at you, Hopey, than be without you,' Jack said earnestly. 'We could do this, we could start again. I love you.'

'You've told me that so many times these last few weeks that it's stopped meaning anything,' Hope confessed, her voice thickening with the threat of more tears. 'You can't keep doing this. You make promises and then in a few days, or a few weeks from now, you'll have changed your mind and I'll have to deal with all the hurt and pain again. It never gets any easier.'

'But, Hopey . . .'

'I can't. I'm exhausted. I'm done. I'm not doing this any more,' she insisted. 'You say you love me, you say you want to try again, but what's going to be different this time?'

Hope could see the surprise on Jack's face, as if he hadn't expected to meet any resistance, but how could he blame her, given his track record? She didn't trust him any more, and she didn't trust his epiphany that they were meant to be together. He was jealous that she'd done things with Wilson that she'd only ever done with him, but he'd just have to get over it.

'Everything will be different,' Jack said fiercely, suddenly clamping his fingers around Hope's thigh. 'I'll be different, I swear.'

'I know you think you mean it, and right now you probably do, but it's not enough.' Hope patted his hand to take the sting out of her words, and she thought that if her heart wasn't already broken, then it was broken now, because hadn't this been her goal all along, ever since they started counselling? For Jack to see the wrong he'd done and vow to put it right? But when it really came down to it, they were just empty words coming from a man that she used to love, that she'd always love, but who wasn't worthy of her love any more. 'You won't feel like this in a few days, not after you've spoken to Susie.'

'We'll have more counselling,' Jack said. 'And we'll both take it seriously and really work on it, and well, we'll get properly engaged. Like, I'll go out and buy you a ring tomorrow.'

It was the shock that made her giggle. The shock and the intent look on Jack's face, the same look he got when he was making a list, or working on a layout, or debating which of his vast collection of T-shirts he was going to wear. 'Now you're just being silly.'

'I'm serious. Serious like a heart attack. Serious like a fucking nuclear strike.' Jack was smiling too, nudging her with his arm, because he was still convinced that Hope was about to cave. 'Serious like Celine Dion singing a power ballad.'

'Oh God, don't start doing one of your joke raps. I'm not getting back with you, and I'm not getting properly engaged to you,' Hope said between giggles. 'You're just upset about last night. You'll feel differently tomorrow.'

'No, I won't, and you're the one who wanted to be properly engaged!'

'I think I was obsessed with getting engaged because, on some level, I could tell you were pulling away from me, but now I know that an engagement ring isn't going to bring us back together again,' Hope explained, giggles quietening down. 'I'm not saying that I'm agreeing to this, to any of this, because you're not right in the head at the moment, but I think we need a major break from each other and if, *if* you still felt the same six months from now, then we could start again by taking things very slowly.'

She sounded so rational, Hope thought to herself, proudly, and if the last few months had done any good, then at least they'd made her grow up a bit and lose the Pollyanna attitude.

'But we still love each other,' Jack said again, as if those words were a mantra that would wipe out the past and bring HopeandJack back. 'You do still love me, don't you?'

Hope sighed. 'I do, but there have been times lately when I haven't liked you at all, and I don't trust you any more. I don't suppose you trust me, either.'

'But you promise you didn't actually fuck him?' Jack had turned his face away from Hope again, and seeing the way the tips of his ears were now carmine, she prayed that it was out of embarrassment, rather than any residual anger.

'I didn't, but I suppose we did stuff that constitutes cheating, though as far as I knew I was single when I did this stuff,' Hope said, and she would never tell Jack, even if (and it was the biggest if in the world) they did reconcile and live happily ever after, that she was glad that she'd been single, even if it was only for a few days. Single enough that she'd spent an hour in Wilson's arms and, though there was plenty that she did regret, she didn't regret that. Still, it seemed politic to ask Jack, 'Do you think you can ever forgive me?'

'I can as long as you agree to forgive me,' Jack said tentatively, and Hope nodded, even though she knew it would take months, maybe even years, before she'd consider Jack exonerated of all his crimes. 'So, are you in, Hopey?'

'I wouldn't say I was in, not exactly. I think we should maybe start dating again, not living together, and see how it goes,' she clarified. 'But it's not going to be easy, Jack. We're not the people we used to be and we can't slip back into old hab—'

'I know. I know. But we'll have more counselling and I swear, Hopey, when I put a proper engagement ring on the proper finger, you'll feel more secure. Everything will fall into place.'

Hope was just about to remind Jack about the dangers of quick-fix solutions when Angela coughed and raised her hand timidly, as if she was requesting permission to speak, even though it was her consulting room and their session had already run twenty minutes over. 'I hate to interrupt, when it's all going so well, but I think we need to start wrapping things up.' She smiled awkwardly, showing two neat rows of beige teeth. 'It really *was* a useful exercise,' she added in a surprised voice.

'I'm sorry that we've been banging on for so long,' Hope said, because she was starting to wonder if there had actually been solid scientific reasoning behind all the home-work and exercises Angela had made them do. Certainly, a miracle had occurred in the last hour, though Hope wasn't entirely sure who was responsible for it. 'But, well, thank you.'

'Do you really want us to live apart, Hopey?' Jack asked. 'Because I don't see why we can't take things slowly but still live together. I'll even take the sofa bed every night. But don't you think it'd be nice to be close again? Even if we only cuddled to start off with.'

Once again, Jack wasn't listening to a single word Hope was saying. 'Yeah, well, let's get Christmas out of the way and then talk about our living arrangements. And at the moment, all I'm up for is cuddling. Fully clothed cuddling.'

'Oh!' Angela gasped. 'Do you mean . . . ? Well, that's quite unexpected.'

'What is?' they asked in unison.

Angela tugged unhappily at the neck of her blouse. 'At our first session, I asked you not to um, have, err, intimate relations,' she actually whispered the last two words as if they were far too shocking to say out loud. 'The subject of physical lovemaking did come up in our previous session, but I didn't want to interrupt your flow by asking how abstinence had worked out for you.'

Hope and Jack shared a look of utter bemusement, then Jack shrugged. 'Well, it worked out fine. We took turns to sleep on the sofa; besides, we were both working late every night, then going for a run together after we got home, and we were too tired to even think about intimate relations.'

'Yeah, especially when I kept pulling that muscle in my thigh,' Hope added, relieved that the conversation was on safer ground.

Now it was Angela's turn to look bemused. 'Oh,' she said again, her pointed chin wobbling. 'Oh. That's rather unusual.'

'Is it?'

'Well, yes, yes it is.' Angela glared at Hope as if it was all her fault. 'Whenever I do couples counselling, I always advise them to desist from relations, and they always report back that they didn't desist and that actually by not desisting, they'd rediscovered their spark and felt much closer. It's reverse psychology!'

Well, we didn't know that, Hope wanted to say, but she just tried to look concerned instead.

'So, we *should* have been having relations, then?' Jack's concern sounded genuine. 'What does it mean that we haven't? Should we have? Is it really bad that we haven't?'

Angela cast her eyes downwards and shook her head. Hope could have sworn she heard her faintly tut. 'I think we have a lot of ground to cover and now that you've made a commitment to continuing with your couples therapy, I strongly advise that you book *at least* another six sessions with me for the New Year. You've made good progress, don't get me wrong, but there's still a huge amount of work we need to do.'

'Yeah, couldn't agree more,' Jack said to Hope's horror, because although she'd committed *provisionally* to more counselling, she'd been planning to tell Jack that she wanted the counselling to come from someone who wasn't Angela. She and Angela just hadn't bonded. 'We've barely scratched the surface.'

'Or maybe we should see where we are in the New Year,' Hope prevaricated.

'What's the problem?' Jack asked Hope. 'I'm sure the folks will pay for it, or we could probably scrape the money together.'

'Why don't we talk about this over Christmas?' Hope suggested, imperceptibly nodding her head in the direction of Angela who was flicking through her diary.

'Ah, I hate to bring pressure to bear, but it's best to book now,' Angela said, then gave them an almost playful, conspiratorial look. 'January is my busiest time. You wouldn't believe how many relationships break down over

the Christmas holidays when families are forced into prolonged contact with each other.'

Hope could believe it only too easily.

'We're definitely coming back in the New Year,' Jack said,
turning to glare at Hope, so she decided to forbear. She
could even put up with, say, six more sessions with Angela
if she had to. 'We really need this, Hopey.'

'OK, fine,' she agreed. 'If you think it's for the best.'

'I'm so pleased.' Angela beamed. 'I'd really like to work
with you as you rebuild your relationship. You've both
made such a good start that it would be a great shame to let
all that hard work go to waste.'

Jack was nodding again. 'That's what we think.'

'You're really learning to open up and communicate your
needs and desires, Jack,' Angela said warmly. 'And, well,
Hope, let's make a commitment to *really* tackle those anger-
management issues in the New Year.'

Hope could feel her hackles and her blood pressure start
to rise, even though Jack now had his hand on her knee.
'Easy, tiger,' he whispered. 'Easy . . .'

She gave Angela a tight, thin smile as the other woman
looked at them both thoughtfully. 'I'm sure this decision to
reconcile is very exciting—'

'We're not reconciling. We're thinking about reconciling,'
Hope interrupted, because no one seemed to be getting the
message that she wanted to take this very slowly. Glacially
slowly.

'Hope, we need to do so much work on that impulse
control of yours,' Angela said reproachfully. She rearranged
her cardigan. 'As I was saying, it's very exciting, but I advise
caution. You both need to be certain that your relationship
can evolve and take into account the changes that you've
both gone through, so I'm going to set you some homework
for the holidays. Why don't you each write a list of the
things you love about each other and exchange them on
Christmas Day?'

Hope was tempted to make gagging noises, but then she felt guilty. She owed it to Jack to at least try and make a go of things, instead of snarking and bitching. She sat up straight and tried to look on board with Angela's idea. Then she risked a glance at Jack, who pulled a face at her.

'I think it will be very romantic.' Angela was all but simpering now. 'And I'll let you decide how you wish to progress with your intimate relations . . .'

'It's OK,' Hope said hurriedly, because intimate relations wouldn't be happening. Not for months, and she had visions of a red-faced Angela handing over a series of instructional booklets complete with flowcharts and diagrams. 'We're all over it.'

'Yeah, we can take it from here.'

Angela clasped her hands together and looked up at the ceiling as if she was asking for divine assistance. 'In that case, I'll just wish you both a Happy Christmas and *bonne chance, mes braves.*'

Chapter Thirty-nine

'You wait till you see your Christmas present, Hopey,' Jack crowed for the umpteenth time that day, as they walked up to Highbury Corner and the little bar where Allison's band, The Fuck Puppets, were having their Christmas party. 'It's going to blow your brain right out of your ears.'

'I hope you haven't spent a lot of money,' Hope said carefully. 'What with us being kind of broke.'

'Money, schmoney. Anyway, you can't put a price tag on happiness.'

Hope was pretty sure that you could, but she didn't want to dent his buoyant mood. Jack had been stuffed full of good cheer ever since their counselling session three days before. He'd nod and smile every time Hope reminded him that they were taking things slow, but the words didn't seem to be sinking in. He was constantly dropping hints about sleeping together 'just so we can cuddle all night long', and the evening before, when Hope was trying to wrap her Christmas presents, Jack had decided that the sofa could be put to much better use for an impromptu snogging session.

It was very hard not to be swept up in Jack's optimism, and the more she resisted, the more Hope was aware that she had to cut Jack huge amounts of slack. He was trying to prove his love, and though Hope doubted his motives and his staying power, she had to let him try. Just like Jack had let her try to win him back, though if she'd been as annoying as he was, with his constant attempts to give her backrubs and gaze soulfully into her eyes when she was trying to read or watch TV or do the washing-up, even when she was putting the bins out, Hope was beginning to understand why she hadn't been successful. All she wanted was time and space to marshal her scattered thoughts. She'd even had to write a hurried and apologetic Christmas card to Wilson while she was sitting on the loo, because it was the only time that Jack left her alone. And now she was back to feeling like an ungrateful bitch again.

'You really don't need to get me anything special. A hand-made certificate saying that you'll do the washing-up for a year would make me ecstatically happy,' she said, and Jack laughed even as Hope frowned and wondered if all his good resolutions and promises to change would last for another year.

To banish these dark thoughts, in fact so she wouldn't have to think at all, as soon as they reached the basement bar next to Highbury and Islington tube station, Hope set out on a single-minded mission to get as drunk as she could.

'You're caning it a bit hard, aren't you?' Jack remarked when Hope exhorted him to match her drink for drink. 'If I kept up with you, I'd still be way over the limit for the drive back home tomorrow morning.'

'Well, let's go up the day after, then,' Hope shouted over the cacophonous racket of The Fuck Puppets' support act, an all-girl Sex Pistols tribute band.

Jack shook his head. 'Hopita! That's crazy talk. My mother would write me out of the will, and Caroline would probably banish you to the garden shed for the duration of our stay.'

'Oh well, sod it. I'm going to get another drink,' Hope decided, pushing past Jack so she wouldn't have to look at his happy face for a second longer, because she should be happy too. But maybe she'd been unhappy for so long that she'd got out of the habit.

Still, drinking made Hope happy, even if it was a

temporary fix, and hanging out with Lauren and Allison made her happy too, because she hadn't seen either of them in ages. Lauren was all loved up and in the first throes of romance after the success of the first date, and all the subsequent dates after that, with the man she'd been eyeing up on her morning bus for *months*. Allison, however, was not loved up, and consequently was annoyed with both of them. 'I've almost forgotten what the pair of you look like,' Allison complained, just before she disappeared backstage to get into her stage outfit. 'But at least Lauren replies to texts and Facebook messages – unlike a certain person with red hair who, unbelievably, seems to be back with the guy who shagged around behind her back.'

These were all fair points and serious obstacles to Hope getting happy. She tried to explain about the Winter Pageant and the counselling, and that working through their relationship issues had taken quite a bit of time, but Lauren and Allison were both unimpressed.

'Love Jack, I really do,' Lauren said, once Allison had gone to get ready. 'But I have a zero-tolerance policy on cheating. How on earth do you come back from your bloke fucking another girl? He *lied* to you for months. That night that you had the dinner party, he looked me right in the eye and swore there was nothing going on between him and Floozie. I'll never feel the same way about him now, and I've known him since I was three. I just don't understand how you could take him back.'

'It's not as black and white as that,' Hope argued. 'He thought he was in love with Susie, and no matter how much it hurts, you can't really blame him for falling in love with someone who isn't me. It's one of those things that no one has any control over.'

'Don't they?' Lauren folded her arms. 'How about keeping your dick in your jeans? It's not that difficult to do. It's what separates us from the animals.'

'Yeah, but things weren't that good between us, we were

having problems, and anyway, maybe I've done some things I shouldn't have, too.'

Lauren's elfin face was all eyes. 'What kind of things? Things with someone else? With someone else's penis?' Hope would have thought it wasn't even possible, but Lauren's eyes widened even further. 'It wasn't Floozie's boyfriend, was it? The snarky one with the glasses? What was his name again?'

Hope had to down her vodka and cranberry in one before she could answer. 'Wilson?' she answered, which was as much as she could say without incriminating herself. She made her own eyes go wide. 'Why would you think that?'

'I don't know. Just that he always used to stare at you without blinking. Was never sure if that was creepy or sexy.' Lauren tried to stare at Hope without blinking but it ended up as more of a squint, and Hope realised that Lauren was somewhere between tipsy and squiffy, and if she could distract her with drink, then Lauren would forget what they'd been talking about altogether. She always phoned Hope after a night on the sauce to have the blanks filled in. 'Have you ever touched a penis that didn't belong to Jack, Hopey? It would be kind of weird if you hadn't.'

'Yeah, but it would be kind of weird to just randomly touch random penises, or penii. Whatever. Shall I go to the bar?' Hope asked a little desperately. 'Come on, let's do some shots.'

'I swore off shots after the time I ended up in Theydon Bois at three in the morning.' Lauren was wavering. 'But it *is* nearly Christmas.'

'And there's no school in the morning.' Hope nudged Lauren. 'Tequila, vodka, Sambuca, all of the above?'

'Let's start with vodka and see how we get on.'

Despite the night's shaky start, the addition of vodka shots meant that by the time The Fuck Puppets took to the stage dressed as slutty Christmas trees, both Hope and Lauren were long past squiffy and heading straight for good, old-fashioned drunk, and needed very little encouragement to get on stage for the encore and shout their way through 'Winter Wonderland' and 'Jingle Bell Rock'.

Usually when Hope was this drunk, Jack disowned her. Or kept warning her that she 'was making a right show of herself', but this night, he didn't seem to mind at all. On the contrary, he was complicit in keeping Hope's alcohol levels topped up, even though he switched to root beer so he'd be able to handle the long drive back to the mother country in the morning. After the bands had finished, Hope persuaded the DJ to play 'Twist and Shout' and Jack even took to the dancefloor with her. He didn't dance so much as shuffle from one foot to the other with his arms tight around Hope, but he was dancing. More than that, he was trying really, really hard to get them back to a happier place.

Hope knew she'd been putting up walls, but she felt something inside her come tumbling down when she glanced up at Jack's face and saw it pitted with effort, hair falling into his eyes, his bottom lip caught between his teeth as he jerkily propelled them around the tiny dancefloor.

'I do love you, Jack,' Hope murmured, but he couldn't hear her over the music so she had to bellow it, which wasn't very romantic, but Jack's eyes lit up and he gave her a goofy, elastic grin that she hadn't seen for a long, long time. Hope hadn't realised how much she'd missed it, how much she'd missed Jack when he was being loving and silly and not trying to be cool. Looking up at him now, Hope was sure she could see the boy she fell in love with. She just needed to find a way back to him.

Even having to wait for the bus home while it tipped down with rain couldn't dent Hope's newfound sanguinity or the effect of all the spirits she'd drunk. Once they were home, she was going to throw herself heart, body and soul into reconciling them. She was going to show Jack that she was in. She was *so* in. They were going to have intimate relations tonight, if it killed her.

'Put the kettle on and make me a cuppa, there's a love,' she begged Jack, as soon as they got through the front door and were still dripping on the hall lino. 'I'm going to put on my black lace knickers.'

'Does that mean what I think it means?' Jack asked, snuggling up behind Hope and nuzzling through damp hair until he could kiss her neck. 'And why put them on if they're going to be taken off after five minutes?'

Hope started as Jack's hand closed over her breast and gave it a quick friendly squeeze. 'Ten minutes,' she insisted. 'At least ten minutes of foreplay before the knickers come down.'

'Is that before or after you drink your tea?' Jack's hand crept down because it was the turn of her left buttock to get a squeeze.

'I'm excellent at multi-tasking,' Hope reminded him as she twisted out of range of his hands. 'Right, I'm on knicker duty, you get on with the tea-making.'

It was all clear to Hope now. Intimate relations would have sorted them out weeks ago if Angela hadn't tried to get all smart and reverse psychology on them. If they'd been having sex, then *obviously* everything would have been better, and there would have been none of that business with Wilson. She couldn't feel guilty about the night because it had been wonderful and Wilson had been wonderful, but maybe it had been nothing more than finding solace with another man because she was skin-starved and desperate to be wanted by someone and Jack wasn't there any more.

But Jack was right there in the kitchen now and tunelessly whistling as he waited for the kettle to boil and if they had sex now and set the alarm for ten, they could probably have sex again in the morning and still make it back to Whitfield in plenty of time for dinner.

Taking off her sopping leopard faux-fur coat was a step in the right direction, especially as it smelt of wet dog. Or maybe it smelt of wet leopard. A fake wet leopard, Hope decided as she tugged off her black knee-high boots without unzipping them first and nearly fell over.

Hope kept all her sexy stuff in the bottom drawer of her nightstand, even though her sexy stuff consisted of one pair of black lace knickers, a copy of *The Story of O*, which squicked her out rather than turned her on, a Rabbit, which Jack had brought her with the ridiculous idea that she'd let him watch while she used it, and a pair of pink fun-fur handcuffs, which were far more tacky than they were sexy.

Really her collection of sexy stuff was pitiful, Hope thought, as she yanked off her tights and boring white cotton pants and threaded one foot through her seductive black lace boy-cut shorts, which chafed her unmentionables if she wore them for too long. Putting them on standing up proved to be far more complicated than Hope had expected, so she lay down on the bed.

The room whirled around her once she was horizontal, and Hope had to shut her eyes for a second so everything stopped whirling and stayed still like it was meant to. It was so comfy that ten more seconds couldn't hurt, and Hope thought about sitting up to put her knickers on but that would have required a Herculean effort on her part, and when Jack came in with her tea not two minutes later, she was naked from the waist down, the knickers clutched in her hand, and snoring gently.

Chapter Forty

'Honestly, Hopey, you don't have to keep apologising,' Jack said the next morning, when he got behind the wheel of their Nissan Micra, which spent most of its days parked several streets away and covered in a tarpaulin. 'The first ten times was enough.'

'But I am sorry,' Hope croaked. 'Not just for falling asleep when I promised you intimate relations, but for throwing up all over the bathroom floor an hour later.'

'Yeah, well I am still kind of pissed off about that,' Jack admitted, as he pulled away from the kerb. 'Usually you're really good about being sick in disposable containers or on easy-wipe surfaces, but I'll let it go just this once if you promise to stop calling it "intimate relations".'

Hope glanced at Jack suspiciously. He'd have been well within his rights to be seething, even though she had already walked down to Marks & Spencer to stock up on snacks for the journey as an act of contrition. Well, contrition and a futile attempt to clear her pounding head.

She unscrewed the top from her bottle of Diet Coke and swallowed another two paracetamol. They really needed to start working soon. 'I can't take music right now, shall we listen to Radio 4 instead?'

'Radio 4 is for old people,' Jack said indignantly, but the ready smile of the last few days was hovering on his lips, and Hope was relieved that going to sleep on the job, or before the job had even got started, hadn't undone days of goodwill. 'What about a podcast?'

They were becoming experts at compromising, Hope thought to herself a little smugly, as she nixed the idea of listening to a whole load of musos waffle on about the recording of some classic rock album and agreed to a *Doctor Who* podcast. Soon they were heading through North London to join the M1. Jack didn't even get angry when the satnav directed him to Brent Cross Shopping Centre, and it took them half an hour to get out of the car park.

'This good mood of yours, how long is it going to last?' Hope asked, once they were on the motorway. 'It's starting to freak me out a bit. You are allowed to be grumpy if you want.'

'But I don't feel grumpy. I feel really happy,' Jack said simply, turning his head ever so slightly so that he could smile at Hope, before quickly averting his gaze. He didn't like driving on the motorway and preferred to give the road ahead his full attention, but he liked being driven by Hope even less because she crunched the gears and didn't give the road ahead enough of her attention. 'You're going to be really happy, too, when you open your Christmas present. Ecstatic, in fact. Pity that we're expected to stay in our respective houses, because you'll be wanting to give me some serious intimate relations as a thank you.'

'I thought we weren't going to call it that any more?' Hope folded her arms and tried not to think about the ordeal that lay ahead, including the separate bedrooms in separate houses, which was more about Caroline and Marge not being able to agree who should host the golden couple than for reasons of propriety. It was much, much nicer to think about the Christmas present that Jack had been bigging up all week. 'So, what is it, then? Give me a clue.'

'It's vintage, and I think it might make your mum even happier than it makes you,' Jack said obliquely.

'My mum hates anything vintage. She says it's just second-hand, and somebody probably died while they were wearing it.' Hope ripped open a bag of Percy Pigs and shoved one in the direction of Jack's mouth, which he opened obediently. 'So, is it something I can wear?'

'Yeah, but it's not clothing.'

'Hmm, is it an accessory?'

'Kind of.'

'It either is, or it isn't.'

Jack shook his head. 'It's not so much about what it is, but what it symbolises.'

'So, what does it symbolise?'

'Well, how much I love you, for a start,' Jack said with the same direct, matter-of-factness that made Hope feel a bit teary. 'Shall we stop at Scratchwood Services for the first cup of coffee of our trek to the ancestral homeland?'

'Like you even have to ask.' They always stopped for a coffee at every other service station, which also meant stopping for a pee at every other service station. It broke up the journey. 'I didn't think we'd get here again.'

'We always get to Scratchwood. It's inevitable when you join the M1 at Brent Cross.'

'No, I meant a metaphysical here,' Hope said. 'You and me together again. I mean, it was less than a week ago that I—'

'Don't say it,' Jack said a little sharply. 'I don't ever want to think about that, about you and him, the fact that there was a you and him, even if it was just for one night.'

Hope sighed. 'I've said I'm sorry. Repeatedly.'

'I know you are, and I don't want to get into all that again either.' Jack quickly patted her knee, then put his hands back in the ten to two position on the steering wheel, before he could lose control of the car and have them hurtling into the path of a juggernaut. 'But I'll tell you one thing: the fear of losing you really made me get my shit together.'

She wasn't sure exactly how she was meant to respond to

that. It made her feel rather like a toy that Jack had outgrown, until he'd seen how much fun someone else was having with it. But maybe Jack's reasoning wasn't the issue here so much as the end result, especially as the end result involved Jack finding everything about her, including her hangover, endearing and saying stuff like, 'You know, I could give you your present early, if you like. Because this present is so amazing that I think when the mums see it they'll completely cave on the whole issue of us sharing a bedroom.'

'This present sounds miraculous,' Hope said with a giggle. 'Does it also cure cancer?'

'Well, it's not *quite* that good.' Jack turned into the slip road that led to Scratchwood. 'Actually, your present is in two parts. You have to read the first part while I go and get our coffee, and then you can have the second part.'

'It has parts? And one of the parts is readable?' Hope was intrigued. Maybe the readable part was actually a ticket to a fairytale country cottage with full amenities and absolutely no Caroline Delafield in it.

'That's what I said.' Jack parked the car. Then he pulled a crumpled sheet of paper out of the glove compartment, even as he unbuckled his seatbelt. 'Just read it and then you can have the rest of your present.'

Hope reminded Jack that she wanted an extra shot of espresso in her coffee before he closed the car door, then glanced at the piece of paper. She'd seen it before. In fact, she'd ripped it out of the A4 pad she used for her lesson plans and given it to Jack last Sunday morning, when they'd gone to the Landsdowne Arms in Primrose Hill for lunch, and had agreed to sit there and take an hour to do their homework for Angela. Not rushing through it. Not doing it at the last moment. Not snarking about it. But giving it due care and attention.

She smoothed out the paper and began to read:

REASONS WHY I LOVE HOPE DELAFIELD

1. She's my best friend.
2. I can't imagine life without her.
3. But when I do try to imagine life without Hope it's a lot less fun.
4. Her smile, especially when I'm not expecting it, still takes me by surprise.
5. She's funny ha ha.
6. Also, she's funny peculiar. Hopey freaking out about even *looking* up at a really tall building, let alone climbing a ladder, always cracks me up, and I'm sure she thinks little magical pixies put the music on her iPod for her.
7. She's going to be an amazing mother. The kind of mother who bakes cakes and does arts and crafts projects and won't care when mud gets tramped over her clean kitchen floor. (Well, she won't mind too much.)
8. My mum and dad love her too. Maybe even more than they love me.
9. The thought of her with another man fills me with rage like I've never felt before, but it also makes me really, really sad.
10. How she eats yogurt off the back of her spoon. Can't explain it any better than that.
11. She never complains when I make her listen to three different versions of a song and ask her to guess which one has been digitally remastered.
12. I want to grow old with her. I can see us forty years from now, side by side on our mobility scooters, still taking the piss out of each other, still able to make each other laugh.
13. Great tits! (They really are, Hope.)
14. She makes the best roast potatoes in the world.
15. I was fucking terrified of the idea of settling down, until I realised I was more terrified about the thought of losing Hope.

Hope read the list twice and she knew for certain that Jack really did love her. No matter how he felt about Susie, his love for her hadn't disappeared. It had gone through some changes, but it was still there. He loved her and that was the important thing, it would keep them together, even though Hope wasn't entirely sure that she recognised the Hope that Jack was in love with. His Hope seemed flaky and unsure of herself unless she was in the kitchen. Also, though he claimed he didn't want any, he seemed awfully fixated on the subject of children lately.

Her phone beeped with a text from Jack. *Stuck in a monster queue. Might be some time. Do you want a muffin?*

While she was waiting, there was no harm in reading her own list to see how it compared, although hers was very much a work in progress. She'd thought she'd have no problem coming up with at least fifty reasons why she loved Jack, but last Sunday there had actually been a lot of pen-chewing and wondering if they should have done their lists after lunch, because she'd been finding it hard to concentrate while surreptitiously glancing at the menu written on the blackboard on the wall behind him. Still, she'd kept at it for the allotted hour with the idea that she'd revise and rewrite her list at a later date, and as Jack was probably going to be ages, now was the perfect time.

Why I love Jack

1. Because the sex is quite good and we DO have the potential to have really good sex, if we both work harder at it.
2. When I've had a bad day at work, he always cheers me up by doing his Cartman from *South Park* impression, and it's still funny and it still makes me spit out my tea.
3. He always gives me backrubs when I have my period and goes out to buy me Green & Black's chocolate even if it's raining.

4. There's so much stuff I don't know how to do because he always does it for me, not just putting the songs on my iPod and taking them off, and changing lightbulbs because I start sweating if I even look at a ladder, but loads of other things too. Like, working the satnav and adjusting the time on the DVD recorder and the oven and changing the oil in the car . . . the list is endless.

5. Oh God, our mothers! The recriminations, the tears and the endless rounds of: 'You don't just bail out when things get a little tough, and this is going to kill your grandmother.'

6. Nobody else but Jack will ever call me Hopita Bonita. Nobody else would even be able to come close to thinking up a pet name like Hopita Bonita.

7. If we did split up then there's no way we can sell the flat without taking up the tatty carpets and re-painting the walls and getting the dodgy living-room lights rewired and doing something about the oven smoking.

8. But I can't imagine waking up and not seeing Jack lying there next to me, and it's been thirteen years. How can I turn my back on thirteen years? Maybe this is just a phase we're meant to go through and our relationship will be stronger and better for it.

9. I'm pretty sure he won't cheat again, and I don't think that he'll ever see her, Susie, again.

It was only a rough first draft, but even so Hope was horrified. These weren't reasons why she loved Jack; they were reasons for them to stay together against all the odds. Because the odds were saying very clearly that she didn't love him. Not really. They were good friends. They were loving friends, even, and it was all too much of a faff to split up.

It was such a deep secret that she could barely form the thought, but Hope had always felt like the junior partner in their relationship. Jack was the cool one, the prettier one, the talented one, and the only way in which Hope was more than Jack was in the amount of love she had for him. She loved him more than he loved her, and that was just the way it was.

Love wasn't a thing that could be measured out, but Hope knew that if she could weigh it on her kitchen scales, all the devotion, the regard, the passion and the need she had for Jack would always outweigh what he felt for her. Until now.

They'd both admitted that there had been problems in their relationship, problems that had crept up on them when they weren't looking, but now it occurred to Hope that their biggest problem was that she didn't love Jack *enough* any more.

Hope squinted her eyes and tried to see into the future, but no matter how hard she tried, she couldn't see Jack in it. If she was brutally honest with herself, then Hope had to admit that forty years from now, she still wouldn't trust Jack. Every time he said he was working late or didn't return a phone call in a timely fashion or he said he was going Crown Green Bowling with his pensioner mates, she'd be torturing herself by imagining him with other women.

She wanted to trust him, but wanting something wasn't enough to make it actually happen. And Hope knew that Jack didn't trust her now either, she couldn't expect him to, and without trust, there was no happy-ever-after. Not when her love was peeling at the edges, and was no longer the glue that kept them stuck together.

Her phone beeped again, and even the thought that it might be Jack with an update on the monster-queue situation made Hope feel sick. Thankfully, it was only a text from Jeremy.

FYI. Ma has invited Vicar 4 Crimbo lunch. Says U need arseload of spiritual guidance. (She didn't say arseload tho.) Jez x

Hope groaned out loud. She'd been dreading the visit back home as it was, without a guest appearance from the local vicar, an unmarried man in his late sixties who thought he was living in the nineteenth century. Hope still had cold sweats about the time he'd been drafted in by her mother when she'd realised that Hope and Jack were having sex out of wedlock. There had been a lot of talk about hellfire and Homes for Unmarried Mothers, even though he was meant to be United Reformed.

She'd have to get through the next week as best she could, Hope decided. Put a brave face on it. Smile through gritted teeth. Be vague and non-committal on the subject of marriage and babies, and when they got back to London, she'd talk to Jack. Definitely before December thirty-first, because she didn't want to start the New Year the same way that they'd spent the old year – with doubt and uncertainty and crossed wires.

It was going to be awful, but staying together for the wrong reasons was worse, and surely Jack would realise it was for the best. That he didn't love her like he thought he did, and that this sudden passionate love that he felt for her owed more to Hope spending the night with Wilson than anything else.

If they split up, or *when* they split up, Hope would be free to spend other nights with Wilson if she wanted to, or she'd be free to fall in love with someone else, or not get bogged down in all the trials and woes of another relationship but go on dates and have affairs and . . .

Hope nearly jumped out of her skin when there was a tap on the window and she saw Jack standing there with two Styrofoam cups of coffee and a huge grin on his face. She had a silly, childish urge to lock all the doors so he couldn't get in the car, slide over on to the driver's seat and leadfoot it until she ran out of motorway. But that was just stupid.

Still, she shuddered when Jack opened the door on the

driver's side, and it had nothing to do with the icy-cold air that whistled through the car.

'Here you go,' Jack said, handing over her coffee. 'Extra shot of espresso, warm milk, no foam.'

'Thanks . . .'

'So, did you read it, then?' Jack asked eagerly. 'What did you think?'

'It was really unexpected and very, very touching,' Hope was able to choke out truthfully. 'Not sure if I really live up to your PR, though.'

'Oh, I think you do,' Jack assured her and as Hope was wondering how she could steer the conversation on to a more general theme, he pulled something out of the pocket of his coat. 'I had the naff idea of stashing this in the bottom of your coffee cup, but it is vintage, used to be my grandmother's, and I was worried you might swallow it.'

'What is it?' It was obvious what it was, because only a ring would fit in the small, squat jewellery box, but maybe a ring was just a ring. 'I mean, is that what I think it is?'

'I also thought about trying to conceal it in a cracker for you to pull during Christmas dinner, but I had visions of it landing in the cranberry jelly. I suppose I could go down on one knee, but it's fucking freezing outside,' Jack said cheerily.

He opened the box with a grand flourish to reveal a simple diamond solitaire in an old-fashioned claw setting. 'So, hey, Hopita Bonita, after thirteen years, shall we finally make it official?'

'No! Oh God, no!' Hope burst out, and she couldn't be any kinder than that because the words didn't even come from her heart, but her gut. The thought of being engaged, or being properly engaged, had been an overriding theme of the last year, but now the sight of a diamond ring destined for the third finger of her left hand filled her with horror. She'd just made a monumental decision that they needed to break up for their greater good, but Jack was forging ahead with plans for them to spend the rest of their lives together.

Hope thrust the box back at Jack. 'Sorry, but no. I *told* you we should take things slowly, so why would you think this is what I want?'

Jack shook his head violently. 'What? What the fuck? This *is* what you wanted. I know you came out with all that stuff last Friday because it seemed like the sensible thing to say, but you can't deny it, Hopey, you've been *gagging* for me to propose.'

'Maybe once I was, but now . . . This would be the worst idea either of us have ever had,' Hope said. 'You're in love with the person who I used to be and an idea of the person you think I'm going to be, and neither of them is who I am any more.' She shut her eyes so she wouldn't have to see the bewildered look on Jack's face or the ring he was still holding towards her. 'I love you. I do, but I don't want to marry you.'

'Why the fuck not?' Jack demanded. 'Have you any idea how much I wrestled with this, and then you just throw it back in my face? It's about him, isn't it? I knew you'd fucked him.'

'OH, GOD!' Hope screamed in sheer frustration. 'It's not about him. It's about you and me. We're holding each other back. We will never be the people we need to be if we stay together.'

'What kind of person do you need to be? You are what you are, Hopey, and you can't change that,' Jack bit out. 'Like I can't change who I am. I came back to you. I *chose* you. Doesn't that count for anything?'

'You'd never have had to choose, because you'd never have had an affair if you'd been happy with me, or getting what you wanted from our relationship,' Hope said and she sounded and felt deathly calm now, because she knew that she was doing the right thing. One day – not now, because he honestly looked as if he might throw up – Jack would realise it too. He'd even thank her for it. 'We have nothing in common any more.'

Jack stared at her in bemusement. 'We have loads of things in common.'

'We have thirteen years of shared experiences, but really, Jack, if you met me at a party and we got talking, I wouldn't be the girl you'd end up taking home,' Hope said sadly, because she wasn't. Jack didn't have any friends from back home or university like she had Lauren or Allison. He hadn't done it callously or with any calculation, but he'd thrown them off as soon as he started working on *Skirt* and now he only hung out with other boys who worked as graphic designers and wore T-shirts with slogans printed on them in Helvetica type. They drank in Shoreditch, shopped at A.P.C. and American Apparel, and for all their urban edge, there was something confined and safe about their world.

Hope wasn't like that. Or she didn't want to be like that.

'I would want to take you home,' Jack insisted. 'I love you.'

'You love me like you love The Beatles,' Hope said as she impatiently wiped away the first inevitable tear. 'You grew up with their songs and you know everything about them and they're comforting. Like, you always listen to *Rubber Soul* or *Abbey Road* when you're in a good mood, and when you're feeling down, you put on *The White Album*, but they don't hold any surprises for you any more.'

'Don't do this, Hope,' Jack said quietly. 'You'll always regret this.'

'No, I'm going to be sad. I'm going to be really, really sad, but if I do this now before we go down a path that's hard to get off, then there's an outside chance that we might still be friends. I'd regret not having you in my life, but I don't want you to be at the centre of my life any more.'

'Are you in love with him?' Jack demanded, and Hope could only cover her face with her hands to stop herself

467

from screaming again. It was like a horrible metaphor for their relationship that they were trapped in a cramped stuffy space, arguing because neither of them understood where the other one was coming from.

'You're like a scratched record. Wilson's my friend and yes, I'm attracted to him, but I don't love him, I don't even know if I could love him and anyway, you said you loved Susie. Did you suddenly just stop loving her?'

'Don't start that all over again! Is that what this is all about?' Jack shouted, and he suddenly wrenched open the door of the car so he could hurl his cup of coffee as far as he could, which actually wasn't that far. 'How many times do I have to say I'm sorry?'

She hadn't wanted to do it like this. In fact, it had been merely minutes ago that Hope had even realised that she was going to do this, and now they were shouting at each other in a small car in the Scratchwood Services car park, and even though Jack had slammed his door shut again, people were walking past the car and peering at them curiously as it was obvious they were having the mother of all rows. 'Look,' Hope said, clinging on to the edge of her seat, like she was clinging on to her temper. 'Look, you did fall in love with Susie. You did sleep with her and it changed everything.'

'You think I don't know that,' Jack said bitterly, and he tossed the jewellery box on to the dashboard. 'I did one bad, stupid, horrible thing in thirteen years. Can you just give me a break?'

'You have no idea, do you?' Hope clutched her hands through her hair. 'It isn't just the cheating, you've put me through hell. You made me tell our mums that we were breaking up. You stormed out whenever you felt like it. I even took it in turns with you to sleep on the fucking sofa! Why did *I* have to sleep on the sofa?'

'You agreed. We agreed that it was fair to take turns,' Jack reminded her, but Hope shook her head.

'No, you decided and, as usual, I agreed with you, just like when you got struck by a lightning bolt and realised you were still in love with me and that we were all systems go, I eventually went along with that, too.' Hope placed her hand on Jack's arm, a gesture that she'd made maybe ten thousand times so that touching Jack was as familiar as brushing the hair out of her eyes or scratching her nose, but now, in this moment, touching Jack felt like something she wasn't allowed to do. But touching Jack also made him Jack again, and not just the man she was going to leave.

'You have to get over this, Hopey,' he said in a low voice.

'I can't, and for all my nagging and shouting, we both know that you drive this relationship. We always end up doing what you want – but not this time,' Hope said, her voice thrumming with resolve. 'We are not good for each other. Susie, for all her faults, and she has many, won't stand for your shit. Not like I do. It's over, Jack. We can't do this any more.'

'But we're on our way home!' Jack pointed out. 'Maybe I shouldn't have proposed, but we've got Christmas to get through, and then we'll come back to London and we'll have more counselling and . . .'

'No,' Hope said firmly. 'No.' She unbuckled her seatbelt. 'I'm not going home. I'm staying in London.'

Jack looked at her with a mixture of shock and awe. 'You can't. Your mum will kill you.'

'Just watch me.' Hope was just about to open the door, when Jack touched her arm. It was a light, tentative touch as if, like her, he already felt that he didn't have the right to touch her any more. 'You can't just make a decision like this in five seconds flat.'

Hope turned to him with troubled eyes. 'The thing is . . . this decision wasn't made in the last five seconds. I think I've been working up to it for the last three months.'

Jack bent his head. 'I'm so sorry,' he said, but it made no difference.

'It's OK,' Hope said, swallowing down her anger, because she was sick of being angry with Jack. 'I'm sorry, too.'

Jack scrambled out of the car to open the boot and help drag out her suitcase. 'I could drive you back to Holloway, if you like?' he offered, but Hope shook her head.

'I'll be fine. I mean, technically, I think I'm still in London.'

'This is so surreal. Like, fifteen minutes ago I was proposing, and now you're leaving me and I'm letting you go.' Jack looked baffled. 'This is all so fucked up. You're going to have to spend Christmas on your own.'

The thought of spending Christmas on her own, of being on her own, wasn't a horrifying one. 'I'll be fine,' Hope insisted. 'I could always go round to Elaine's or Alice from next door would probably have me.'

'But, it can't end like this, what about . . .' Hope was sure that Jack had more to say, but she couldn't bear to listen to it, so she rose up on tiptoe to press a last, lingering kiss on his mouth.

It was the saddest kiss in the world.

Chapter Forty-one

With the help of Google Maps, Hope was on a bus within thirty minutes of abandoning Jack in the car park like an unwanted puppy.

In an hour she was on a tube train, and not even an hour after that, she was home. She hadn't cried, although she felt as if she should be crying, but she had a tense quickening in her stomach as if a million tiny birds were flapping their wings against her abdominal walls. Hope couldn't tell if it was dread or exhilaration or a heady combination of both, but she knew she couldn't stay in the flat they'd bought together. Besides, she'd planned to spend the next six days in Whitfield and there was nothing to eat in the house, apart from several huge tins of chocolates and a couple of fancy biscuit-selection boxes.

Hope was determined not to wallow in chocolate and self-pity. Now wasn't the time for wallowing, it was the time for re-grouping, nursing her wounded soul and making some nourishing soup, while she painted the kitchen. As soon as she was back from the bloodbath that was people doing their Christmas food shopping in Morrisons, she turned round and went out again, this time to the big DIY store on Holloway Road, to buy paint and things to apply paint with.

The third time she walked through the front door, Hope's mind was already racing with options that would force her to go out again, but she ignored the clamouring voices and instead put on the ill-advised dungarees she'd bought a couple of years back, which could only be improved by a splattering of buttermilk-coloured paint, tied her hair up in a scarf and tried out a Rosie the Riveter pose in the bathroom mirror.

Then she got busy with masking tape and a paint-roller, and listened to Radio 4 as she painted all the kitchencupboard doors that she could reach without a ladder. But then there was nothing to do until tomorrow when the doors would be dry enough for a second coat, and now Hope couldn't even make a sandwich because she didn't want to smudge the paint.

She decided to run a hot bath so she could soak and scrub at the blobs of dry paint. Hope had only just carefully eased herself into the water when her phone rang. Mindful that she didn't want to compound her misery by dropping her phone in the water, she carefully picked it up with a damp hand.

Hope almost wished her phone had gone to a watery grave when her mother opened the conversation with, 'Well, you've really gone and done it now, haven't you, young lady?'

'I was going to call you,' Hope said weakly, although she hadn't been going to at all. 'I know it might have come as a bit of a shock, but not really, if you think about how things have been between Jack and I.'

'Jack and me,' her mother barked. 'The poor boy is in pieces, and what about your father and me? Or Marge and Roger? You've ruined Christmas for everyone. I hope you're happy!'

'Well, no, I'm not even a little bit happy.' Hope sank as far down in the water as she dared. 'I was going to wait until after Christmas, but then when Jack proposed . . .'

'He actually *proposed*?' her mother queried sharply. 'What *is* wrong with you, Hope?'

'We don't love each other. Not like we used to.'

'What's love got to do with it? You're not a teenager any

more, and you're throwing thirteen years out of the window because you have this silly notion that you need to find yourself. Well, all you'll find is a selfish, inconsiderate girl. You've let everyone down.'

'Oh, I think I'd have let them down more if me and Jack, sorry, Jack and I, had got married, then decided to get a divorce a few months later,' Hope snapped. 'And don't you dare call me selfish! You don't give a shit about what I want or what Jack really wants, it's all about you and Marge and this ridiculous idea that you've been peddling all our lives that we're perfect for each other. We're not!'

Her mother didn't say anything for a while, though Hope could hear her choked gasps like she was holding back her sobs.

'Mum,' she said in a much gentler voice. 'It's really not the end of the world. Couples break up all the time, but surely you can understand why I couldn't spend six days with Jack and both our families after telling him that we were over?'

'No, I don't understand at all. It's Christmas and you know that none of your grandparents are in good health,' her mother reminded her grimly. 'This could be the last Christmas that we all spend together, and now you won't be here. I hope you can live with that.'

It made Hope feel guilty, as it did every time her mother sang the same song, but both her grandfathers usually dozed between meals, her father's mother was always glued to the TV and made everyone take a vow of silence during the Queen's speech, and she'd call her other grandma in a couple of days to explain the situation, and she was sure she'd get a much more sympathetic reaction than she was currently getting from her own mother.

'There's not really much I can do about that, Mum,' Hope sighed.

'What you can do about it is to get off your bottom, make your way to Euston and buy a train ticket. There's no way that you'll get a seat at such short notice so you'll have to stand for the entire journey, but let that be a lesson to you.'

Hope ground her teeth and felt a shooting pain in her jaw. 'No,' she said simply. 'That's not going to happen.'

'Well . . . How . . . No? No?'

She gave her mother a lot of backchat and bad temper but rarely outright defiance. 'I'll call you in a couple of days,' Hope said with what she felt was great daring. 'Love to Dad.'

'Now just wait a minute. You will not call me in a couple of days, I want you home tomorrow, do you hear me?' Caroline Delafield was shouting so loudly that Hope was sure that even Alice from next door could hear her.

'Short of making Dad drive all the way down to London, physically restrain me and carry me to the car, you can't make me come home.' Hope kicked her legs out in frustration and sent a wave of water sloshing on to the bathroom floor. 'You might find it hard to believe, but I'm actually having a pretty crappy time, and you haven't even asked if I'm all right. Do you dislike me so much that you can only stand to be around me if Jack is there to sweeten the deal? Why can't you be on *my* side for once? Is that too much to ask?'

'That's not fair, Hopey!'

'Good, so you know what it feels like then, don't you?'

Then Hope did something that she'd never dared to do before and hung up on her mother, *then* switched off her phone so her mother couldn't call her back to harangue her. Both the phone call and the hanging-up rattled Hope so much that once she got out of the bath after a quick lather and rinse and not the long, luxurious soak she'd planned, she realised that she'd been going about this all wrong.

She needed to wallow for a little bit. Wallowing was all part of the grieving process. Her mind made up, Hope climbed into her cosiest, fleeciest pyjamas, made up a hot-water bottle, stuck the first season of *Sex and the City* into the DVD player (Jack had always refused to let her watch it

474

when he was around), then got a tub of pralines and cream ice-cream out of the freezer and a bottle of Baileys that had been a present from a grateful parent from the fridge.

Eating a whole tub of ice-cream drenched in Baileys and sobbing as soon as Mr Big appeared on the screen didn't make Hope feel even a little better. Inevitably, she had to suddenly scramble off the sofa and just made it to the bathroom in time to throw up the sickly concoction. She stayed on the bathroom floor, almost curled around the toilet bowl, and knew that the sobbing she'd done on the settee had just been a little warm-up for these tears. She was crying because of Jack, that was a given, and because she had a terrible relationship with her mother, and because she'd just been sick, and because now her future was a blank page. She could be who she wanted to be, go anywhere in the world, do anything she wanted, and that kind of unfettered freedom was utterly terrifying. So terrifying that Hope found herself rising to her knees to throw up again, although there was nothing left in her stomach but bile.

As she crawled into bed with nothing but a hot-water bottle for comfort, Hope had never felt so alone. Lauren had gone up to Manchester today to see her sister before she ended her journey in Whitfield. Allison had flown out to Mauritius as she had no truck with her mother insisting that she came home for Christmas. There was Elaine, but they didn't have the kind of friendship that could stand tearful phone calls at almost midnight, unless all of Blue Class had suddenly been wiped out in a freak accident. Hope could only think of one person that she could call, and knew that they'd drop everything to come round and make her toast and tea – and that was Wilson. He'd be sure to tell her in no uncertain terms what he thought of her unreasonable demands, but he'd still do it. And it was a tempting thought, but God knows, she'd made enough unreasonable demands on him to last several lifetimes.

Instead she lay in the darkness, and every time she fought

her way to a place of relative calm so she might be able to go to sleep, a fresh wave of panic and regret and horrible, bone-aching, heart-rending sadness washed over her, and she cried until the tears trickled across her cheeks and into her ears and she had to keep shifting position.

The twenty-third of December was a brand-new day, heralded by bright winter sun pouring down on Hope as she slowly and carefully uncurled her limbs and stretched so she could assess how her wounds, both physical and emotional, were faring. She ached from the excesses of the night before, head faintly pounding, stomach slightly bruised, and she still felt miserable, but she didn't feel as if the end of the world was quite so nigh.

Hope lay there for a while, contemplating the rest of her life and how she'd never again wake up with Jack curled around her and snuffling soggily against her neck, his hold tightening as she made a bid for freedom. People always said that being on your own wasn't the same as being lonely, but Hope knew it would be a while before she could tell the difference. Especially as right now there was no one to moan at until he got out of bed and put the kettle on.

She didn't have a renewed sense of purpose, but Hope managed to paint a second coat on the lower kitchen cupboards, and she even managed to stand on the second rung of the stepladder for, ooooh, five whole seconds as she contemplated the feasibility of painting the cupboards above the worktop. Five seconds was all it took for her heart to start racing and beads of sweat to pop out along her forehead. Still, there were lots of other bits of wood she could paint, like the windowsill and the skirting boards, and she could even paint halfway up the walls. It wasn't like she was *completely* useless.

She was just giving the skirting board a second coat of the duck-egg blue she'd chosen as an accent colour when Hope heard the satisfying thud of the post being dropped through the letterbox. It was just the distraction she needed, but the handful of stiff envelopes containing Christmas cards addressed to 'Jack and Hope' threatened to derail her, until she came to a large white Jiffy bag with only her name on it.

As far as Hope could remember all the Christmas presents she'd ordered on the internet had arrived, been wrapped and sent off, or were currently in Jack's custody, so she couldn't imagine what it was.

She sat cross-legged on the hall floor and tore into the parcel without any thought of carefully unpicking the flap so she could reuse the padded envelope. When she pulled out the card, it was obvious who'd sent it, because instead of a winter scene or a couple of fat robins in Santa outfits or even the Nativity tableaux favoured by her parents' friends, the card featured Blue Class all wearing Santa hats and smiling goofily at the camera. Even though he'd been in a mood with her the evening of the Pageant, Wilson had still taken the time and effort to arrange this little photographic surprise for her. God, he'd even magicked up thirty Santa hats out of thin air or, rather, he'd sweet-talked them out of Dorothy who'd taken charge of the keys to the prop cupboard and had been very reluctant to let them out of her sight.

DEAR HOPE

HAPPY HOLIDAYS. HOPE (I WISH YOU HAD A
DIFFERENT FIRST NAME, BECAUSE IT MAKES WRITING
MESSAGES IN CARDS VERY TRICKY, BUT ONLY THE
WORD 'HOPE' WILL DO) THAT THE COMING YEAR
BRINGS YOU THE HUGE AMOUNTS OF LUCK AND
HAPPINESS YOU DESERVE.

BEST WISHES
WILSON

As well as the card, there were also three CDs in the Jiffy bag with a typewritten note.

Hope
I asked the DJ at the Northern Soul Night to send me
over a copy of his setlist so I could burn you a CD. I
also burnt some other tracks that I thought you might
like.
   More importantly, here are detailed and, dare I say,
foolproof instructions on how to put the songs on your
iPod.

Wilson

He'd written out a bullet-point list that didn't seem too onerous, and had even provided a couple of links to online video tutorials that Hope could watch if she didn't understand a set of clear and concise instructions that even some of Blue Class could follow. Still, for now she could listen to the CDs on the DVD player in the lounge, and she'd be able to hear the music in the kitchen if she really cranked up the volume.

So, the second day after she left Jack turned out to be a good day after all. There was one minor wobble and a weep when she heard Irma Thomas sing 'It's Starting to Get to Me Now' on one of Wilson's mix CDs, but she managed to steer clear of all alcohol and tins of chocolates. And if she couldn't get back to sleep after waking up for a pee at three in the morning, because she started to agonise that she'd made a terrible mistake and that Jack was probably at that very moment in a tacky Rochdale nightclub chatting up a nubile eighteen-year-old who was home from university for the Christmas break, that was only to be expected.

Then it was the third day after she left Jack, and there were lots of reasons to be cheerful. There was Elaine's Christmas Eve party that evening, and when Hope bumped into Alice from next door on her way to buy yet more masking tape and white spirit, she invited Hope to join them for Christmas dinner, so she'd have someone to talk to who wasn't aged twelve or under, or her husband Robert, or related to Robert.

Hope set off down the Holloway Road at a jaunty pace, ridiculously pleased when the staff at the DIY shop greeted her like an old friend. Then she stopped off at Waitrose to buy some nice bottles of wine for Elaine and Alice, and some posh treats for herself for tomorrow night and Boxing Day. Spending Christmas in London and flitting from one social engagement to another was a much better option than being stuck at home and having to peel Brussels sprouts under her mother's exacting eye. In fact, Christmas Eve was shaping up very nicely until Hope wandered past the hairdresser's in the shopping arcade. The fact that it was Christmas Eve and the salon had empty chairs should have been an indication that maybe it wasn't a very good hairdressing salon, but Hope caught sight of her tangled, paint-splattered hair in one of the salon's mirrors, and it was such a pain to have to tie it up in a scarf and it always got soaked with sweat when she was running, and if it was shorter and more manageable then she'd probably never have to have another comb-out for as long as she lived. Her thought process took less than five seconds, then she was pushing open the salon door and asking if they had any appointments free.

At least Hope hadn't burst into tears in the salon. At least she'd spared herself that humiliation. No, she'd lied and said that she loved her new haircut, which was meant to have been layered and shoulder-length, but had ended up as an uneven jaw-line bob because the girl who'd been cutting her hair had been more interested in telling Hope what a complete bitch the salon owner was, and how she expected her staff to work until nine on New Year's Eve, and that she and her husband were fiddling their tax return. Hope even tipped her ten pounds and wished her a Happy Christmas before she hurried out, felt the cold air rush to meet the newly exposed back of her neck, and *then* she burst into tears.

Back home, she did all the stupid irrational things that anyone does when they've had a terrible haircut, though as Hope understood it, terrible haircuts were a rite of passage that should have been over and done with by your sixteenth birthday. If only she'd listened to her mother who'd actually been right when she'd told her, repeatedly, to leave her hair alone, Hope thought, as she dunked her head under the cold tap and applied serums and mousses and straighteners. All her efforts amounted to nothing. There was no escaping the fact that she had a wonky bob that was shorter on the right side than it was on the left. Also now that she didn't have so much hair, what she did have left looked more ginger than auburn or red or Titian. And Hope had never noticed how much her ears stuck out, or how weak her jaw was.

It was barely worth wrapping a scarf around her head so she could get on with the painting, because some buttermilk matt emulsion could only improve her coif, Hope thought as she dipped the roller into the paint tray, and then the day went from bad to much, much worse as the bulb in the kitchen light blew and tripped the fuse at the same time. Sorting out the fuse was a simple matter of flipping a switch, but the lightbulb was another matter entirely.

It was only just past lunchtime but the vague promise of daylight was already fading. There was no question of painting, or even making a cup of tea without electric light. Hope went as far as taking a new lightbulb out of the drawer and fetching the stepladder from the little lean-to by the back door. Then she eyed the lightbulb and the top step of the ladder on to which she'd have to climb to change it. The top step, which meant there'd be nothing to hold on to as she extended her arms up towards the light fitting.

Hope's first instinct was always going to be to call Jack, but as soon as he answered the phone with a weary, 'Hey, what's up, Hope?' she wished that she'd waited for her second instinct to come along.

'The lightbulb's blown in the kitchen,' she explained, again realising too late that she should probably have started the proceedings with a gentle enquiry about his emotional health. 'And it tripped the fuse, which I sorted out, but I can't change the lightbulb. But, anyway, how are you?'

'How do you think I am?' Jack demanded. 'And you know what? You're the one who fucking turned me down when I proposed, so you don't get to phone and ask how I am, and you don't get to call me just because you need help changing a sodding lightbulb.'

He was right. And Hope was wrong, and flushed with shame and mortification. 'Jack, I'm sorry. I didn't think. It's just I'm so used to calling you and I know I started wittering on about the lightbulb, but I've been thinking about you a lot.' Hope sighed. 'I pretty much think about you all the time. How are you holding up?'

'Oh, I'm just *great*. I feel like I'm on top of the fucking world, especially after I found your list on the floor of the car and the only reason you supposedly loved me was because I was good at doing stuff,' Jack sniped. 'It comes to something when the love of your life is only with you because you put songs on her iPod and go to the shops for ice-cream.'

'It was only a first draft,' Hope protested. 'It was a shitty first draft, and if I'd written it six months ago, it would have been a completely different list, you . . .'

'What the fuck ever!'

Jack was furious with her, and Hope knew that he was well within his rights to feel like that, though she wondered if it wasn't his pride that hurt as much as his heart, because nothing he was spitting at her was inclined to make her change her mind. 'I'm really not the love of your life,' she reminded him softly but with just a soupçon of acid to go with it. 'If I had been, you wouldn't have shagged someone else.'

'I might have known you'd bring that up. We've been on the phone for what? Three minutes. Great restraint there, Hopey.'

Hope stopped feeling guilty or sorry for Jack, because he was forgetting some very important details about why she'd broken up with him. Instead of blaming her, Jack should have been ruminating on all the pain he'd caused her so he never made the same mistakes again with the next girl who was supposed to be the love of his life. 'Just for the fucking record, Jack, I don't need you any more!' Hope shrieked. 'I can do stuff by myself. In fact, I'm getting off the phone because I can't stand talking to you for a second longer, and I'm going to change the bloody lightbulb on my own!'

Hope ended the call without bothering to find out if Jack had got the message, but as she'd been yelling, she was sure he'd picked up the highlights and then, while her blood was still up (and currently rushing to her head) she grabbed the lightbulb, marched over to the ladder and was on the top step before she even realised what she was doing.

Don't look down, Hope told herself, as she firmly planted both feet on the step, sucked in her tummy muscles and reached up to unscrew the duff bulb. She could hear her frantic breaths as she dithered, wondered if she might actually throw up, and finally took stock of the fact that she was on top of the ladder. She froze, all her limbs stiffening, because she had a bulb in each hand and if she came down the ladder to get rid of the old one, Hope knew that she'd never be able to climb back up.

Right on cue, she felt the sweat breaking out, her hands going clammy as she wobbled for one alarming second, but then managed to right herself.

You can do this. You can do this. You can do this. Except she couldn't do this, and now she couldn't get down either, because she was paralysed at the top of the ladder, both hands occupied, so she couldn't even go down a step and grip the bar at the top.

Hope tried to rationalise the situation. She was on top of a six-foot ladder, and what would be the worst thing that would happen if she fell off? OK, she might bang her head and die. That would be very bad, but it would be much worse if she fell off, broke several limbs so she was unable to reach her phone, and had to lie in her own urine on the kitchen floor until Jack came home on or around the twenty-eighth of December. Though maybe Alice from next door might realise that something wasn't right when Hope didn't turn up for Christmas dinner and come round to check that everything was OK.

Of course, there was another option. Maybe Hope didn't fall off the ladder but stayed on it long enough to change the bloody lightbulb. Because it wasn't just a lightbulb, it was a metaphor for her life, her future, for not being with Jack but being single and taking charge of her own destiny.

This time the voice in her head was a lot more forceful. *If you can't change a simple bloody lightbulb, then you are screwed. How are you going to lead a normal, fulfilled and independent life if you can't even get up a ladder to perform a simple act of household maintenance? So, stop being such a big baby, suck it up and change the fucking lightbulb, Hopey! Change it right this fucking minute!*

The voice in her head was so terrifying that Hope ignored the sweat that was dripping into her eyes and making them sting, she even ignored her phone, which had suddenly started to ring, the shock making the ladder wobble again. She ignored everything but the message her brain was passing on to her hands to reach up and screw in the lightbulb.

Once she was done, Hope couldn't believe that she was done. Instead of scrambling to safety, she actually stayed where she was to check that she had just done the unthinkable and changed the lightbulb all by herself. And then she stayed up the ladder for the time it took to clasp her hands over her head in victory, which made the ladder teeter alarmingly and Hope scramble down to safety in record time.

When her feet were firmly planted back on the kitchen floor Hope hugged her sweaty self in triumph. She felt utterly elated, as if she'd just run a marathon, and she wished that there was someone to hand who understood the enormity of what she'd just achieved. It wasn't three rungs on a ladder but one giant step for Hope. Her phone rang again just as she was contemplating whether she could climb the ladder again to paint the upper cupboards, *just because she could*.

As she picked up her phone, she saw she had a missed call from Jack and he was calling her again. She really didn't want to segue into the next instalment of their ongoing fight, or to hear all the horrible things he'd had half an hour to work on. Hope even thought about not answering, but then she decided that if she could get up a ladder to change a lightbulb then she could take Jack's call.

Even so, her 'Hello?' was extremely cautious.

'Hopey! Thank God, you're all right,' Jack gasped. 'When you didn't answer before, I thought you'd broken your neck and were lying dead on the kitchen floor.'

'Well, I'm not,' Hope sniffed.

'Look, I'm sorry about earlier. I've just been getting it from all sides, and every time I see your mum, she gets tearful and starts going on about how much you hate her.'

Hope sighed. 'I don't hate her. Don't particularly like her very much at the moment, but I don't hate her.'

'Well, do you think you could ring her and tell her that?'

She could, but she wasn't going to. 'Did you not hear the part where I said that she was way down on my list of favourite people?' If her mother was that racked with remorse, she could change the habits of a lifetime and ring her only daughter to apologise, which would happen the day that the apocalypse began. 'So, now we've established that I'm not dead, is there anything else?'

She sounded cold, Hope knew that, but maybe cold was the way to go. When she forgot and treated Jack like her friend, or her boyfriend, it was confusing for both of them.

'I'm sorry about before, about snapping at you,' Jack said. 'And I could ring Otto, he's around, he might be able to come and change the bulb.'

Hope sucked at being cold. 'That's really sweet of you,' she said. 'I'm sorry too. I shouldn't have rung you, but I'm used to ringing you. It's going to be a hard habit to break.'

'So, this isn't just a temporary break or a trial separation, and then when I come back we'll start counselling ag—'

'No, Jack, no. It's real,' Hope told him, all her glee and exhilaration gone, and now she was on the verge of tears. 'I shouldn't have called you. It was thoughtless and selfish and . . . and I think we need to not talk until after Christmas, because this isn't helping either of us.'

There was silence and Hope began to wonder if they'd been cut off until she heard Jack swallow. 'Is that what you really want?'

Hope wasn't sure that she even knew what she really wanted, but she knew what she didn't want. 'Yes, yes it is.'

'But what about the lightbulb?'

'Oh, that? Actually, I did it myself,' Hope said.

'You climbed up on the ladder?' Jack sounded incredulous.

'Yeah, that's why I didn't answer the first time you called. I was frozen with terror, and I knew that if I got down to answer the phone, I'd never get back up again.'

'You climbed up a ladder,' Jack repeated. 'Oh, Hopita Bonita, you don't need me any more, do you?'

'Please don't think that. Just so you know, I loved you for a lot more reasons than what I wrote on that stupid list. Not just because you were handy to have about the place.' Hope tried to laugh but it was entirely without mirth.

'Though you can wield a screwdriver like no one else.'

'You're not to worry, you're going to be fine on your own. Don't think you're going to be on your own for long, though. Someone will snap you up in no time at all,' Jack said, and he sounded misty-eyed and wistful. 'You just see if they don't.'

'You're just saying that to be kind, but thank you.'

'No, I'm really not. It's the truth,' Jack said sadly. 'So, I guess I'll see you after Christmas. Am I allowed to text you with my ETA?'

'Of course you are!'

There was nothing left to talk about after that except to stammer their way through a goodbye that felt as if it was the last thing they'd ever say to each other.

Hope was in despair for ten long minutes after she got off the phone. Unhappy enough to break into one of the tubs of Celebrations and root through to find the giant Maltesers. Just as she was stuffing the last one into her mouth, she caught sight of the ladder and, still masticating honeycomb, she climbed up it. It was still scary. It was still not one of her favourite things in the world, but she could do it.

It made Hope wonder what else she could do if she put her mind to it. She took that thought and ran with it, gathering up the CDs and the sheet of instructions Wilson had sent her, and hurrying into the bedroom. After a few false tries and a rummage under the bed to locate the right lead, Hope managed to hook up iPhone and computer.

The rest was easy. Hope was almost incandescent with rage when she realised that putting songs on to the iPod was child's play. Quite literally. Most of Blue Class would have been able to do it, and then she was angry at Jack for never letting her do it herself and controlling what she could play, in some patriarchal plot to force her to listen to The Beatles ad nauseam and lots of scruffy-haired, guitar-led indie bands who all sounded the same. The nerve! Hope bristled as she discovered a folder in iTunes labelled 'Hope's crappy music', and in it were all the beloved shouty riot-grrrl bands that she'd adored in her shouty teen years, and her show tunes! Oh, and Gloria Gaynor!

Hope had to stop right there, cue up 'I Will Survive', grab a hairbrush and let rip. On the second round of 'Go on now, go!' she even jumped on the bed, until she caught sight of herself in the mirror and saw that she was the living embodiment of every wronged-woman, rom-com cliché, and stopped immediately.

She spent a happy hour deleting everything on her iPod, and creating new playlists for the gym and walking to work, and for her sad moments and her happy moments. She even made a playlist for when she had a bad day at work, which ended with 'Everything's Coming up Roses' sung by Ethel Merman. It was only when she started squinting at the computer screen that Hope looked out of the window to discover that it was pitch dark and she was due at Elaine's in less than an hour.

There wasn't time to do anything but put a couple of sparkly clips in her raggedy hair, which matched her silver skinny-knit jumper, which she wore with her skinniest skinny jeans – thankfully she could still get into them despite her Celebrations binge. Because she was only going to Elaine's, who lived a good ten minutes' walk from the nearest bus stop, and it was freezing outside, Hope shoved her feet in her Uggs.

It wasn't until she was on the bus heading towards Hackney and she'd got over the novelty of having an iPod full of songs that she actually wanted to listen to, that Hope switched from iPod to iPhone and wondered if calling Wilson would ever be a habit that she got into.

Maybe it would, if he always sounded so pleased to see her number flash up on his phone. 'Hello, stranger,' he said. 'How are you?'

'I'm fine. Really fine.' As soon as she said it, Hope knew that it was true. Or, at least, she was going to be fine. There might be times when she stepped backwards instead of moving towards the light, but she was on the right path.

It turned out that Wilson was fine, too. He'd just finished his last job of the year and was heading over to a little gastropub near Parliament Hill Fields, where his staff were waiting for him to pay for a slap-up meal and all the alcohol they could pour down their throats before the landlord called last orders.

'And what about you? Are you oop North?' Wilson asked, exaggerating his Lancashire accent.

'Down South, and on my way to Hackney for Elaine's annual Christmas Eve bash. Simon makes a pretty lethal elderflower vodka,' Hope said.

She heard Wilson suck in his breath. 'So the two of you decided to stay in London?'

'No, just me. Jack's in Whitfield because, y'know, we're not . . .' At the last moment, she couldn't get the words out because it seemed so desperate, so obvious, and that wasn't why she was calling him. Well, Hope had thought it wasn't. 'Listen, I wanted to thank you for the CDs, and guess what? I put them on my iPod. It was so easy!'

'I did tell you that,' Wilson said, but he sounded distracted as if this wasn't the conversation that he wanted to have.

'And I climbed up a ladder to change a lightbulb,' Hope told him, and finally it was all right to be unbearably smug about that major achievement. 'It took me about half an hour and most of that was spent imagining myself falling off and breaking every bone in my body, but still . . .'

'Oh God, I expect you to be running the world by the end of the week,' Wilson drawled, and even the gaggle of teenage girls surreptitiously swigging from a bottle of cider and shrieking at the back of the bus couldn't dent Hope's good mood, or stop her stomach curling in on itself when his voice got all low and drawly like that. 'Are you disgustingly proud of yourself?'

'I am. I even went back up the ladder just for kicks.'

'Course you did – but can we skip back to the part where you're in London and he's not? Anything significant about the fact that you're not spending Christmas together? Like, you're still broken up?' Wilson asked, and he made it sound like just an idle enquiry but Hope was sure that she could hear the catch in his voice.

Talk about leading questions. 'Well, we sort of got back together,' Hope admitted. 'And then we broke up again.'

'Again?' Wilson didn't seem that impressed with her statement, and Hope wondered if she'd been getting ahead of herself, if it had been arrogant to think that Wilson might be interested in her news. 'I can't keep track, Hope. You're always breaking up, then getting back together for the sake of the house plants and the fact that you've been together for decades.'

'Well, for starters, we don't have any house plants, and also thirteen years hardly counts as decades and . . . and . . . this time it's for good.' Hope lowered her voice as she realised the couple sitting behind her were now leaning forward so they could eavesdrop more effectively on her conversation. 'This time it's different because, well, I was the one who broke us up, and it's over. It's *so* over. No regrets. No going back. It's the best thing for both of us,' Hope said, and it didn't matter how many times she said it, it was still difficult to say, and it still made her throat ache as the words squeezed their way out. 'So, Jack drew the short straw and had to go back home for Christmas while I stay here.'

Wilson let out a long, low whistle. 'How are you doing?'

'Up and down,' Hope said truthfully. 'I've been through every emotion it's possible to go through in the last forty-eight hours, but I absolutely know it was the best thing to do – and I think, deep down, he does too.'

'You're not spending Christmas Day on your own, are you? 'Cause you're welcome to come round to my sister's. She's got enough food in to feed the five thousand and still have leftovers to last until New Year's Day,' Wilson said.

'Alice from next door has invited me round for Christmas lunch,' Hope replied, and she tried to sound as if she was fine with that, though she'd heard Alice and Robert through the party wall having many tense conversations about everything from their free-range organic turkey to just what Alice intended to say to Robert's mother if she went off on one about Alice's stuffing. 'Should be fun.'

'You know what else might be fun?' Wilson asked, and Hope was sure that it wasn't just her imagination and that he was drawling again.

'What would that be?'

'If we got together later in the evening. I mean, I could come to yours, if you wanted.'

It was too soon for Wilson to be asking Hope stuff like that in the same purry voice he'd used when he was bringing her off. And far, far too soon to come round to the flat she jointly owned with Jack if there was an outside chance that there might be a repeat performance.

'Or I could come round to yours?' Hope heard herself suggest. 'If you wanted.'

'Oh, I want,' Wilson said, and Hope felt as if every millimetre of her skin was blushing. 'Say, around eight? Shall I come and pick you up?'

'No, I can walk, though getting home might be a problem, unless I want to pay about a gazillion quid for a taxi.' Everything Hope said seemed to indicate that she was primed and good to go.

Wilson obviously thought so. 'You'd better bring your toothbrush just in case, then.'

Hope thought he might mention the possibility of one of them sleeping on the sofa, but he didn't, and before she could broach the topic herself, he said, 'I'll see you tomorrow, then. Enjoy the elderflower vodka.'

He rung off and Hope turned round to glare at the couple behind her, who were so up in her phone call that she was almost wearing them as earrings; then she folded her arms and tried to look prim and slightly despondent, as was appropriate for a woman who'd recently come out of a long-standing relationship.

It would have been more convincing if she could only wipe the sappy smile off her face.

Chapter Forty-two

It was the oddest Christmas Day Hope had ever experienced. It was also the first one she'd ever started with a hangover, which would never have happened on her mother's watch.

When Elaine had opened her front door to see Hope standing there with two bottles of Cava, a huge bag of tortilla chips and a brave smile, she'd looked rather put out. 'But what on earth are you doing here, Hopey?' she'd demanded. 'You're meant to be up North. And where's Jack?'

Though she could have sworn that she'd been fine, Hope's face had collapsed in on itself, and Elaine had let her cry all over her very expensive Vivienne Westwood Anglomania dress, and had insisted that she didn't have to have any elderflower vodka, but unearthed a bottle of Stolichnaya and proceeded to get Hope good and drunk.

Little Sorcha's mum, Polly, had arrived just in time to back Elaine up when she'd tried in vain to tell Hope that she'd be fine on her own and that it would be the making of her. Hope hadn't been convinced, but at least Polly hadn't begun drinking yet and had neatened up the ends of Hope's crooked bob. After that it had all been a bit of a blur; Hope knew that she'd cheered up because she distinctly remembered Singstar being switched on and singing 'The Winner Takes it All' with Marta, and talking about breeding poodles with the drummer of a minor indie band who'd been recording their second album in Simon's studio, but apart from that she wasn't even sure how she'd got home.

Still, it was nice to come to at her own pace, without her mother pounding on her bedroom door at five-minute intervals to make sure she was ready to go to church. It was even nicer not to have to go to church, or try to explain to her mother that she was an apathetic agnostic.

At a very civilised one o'clock, Hope hopped over the garden wall with yet more bottles of Cava and huge chocolate Santas for Lottie and Nancy, who were appalled that she'd broken up with Jack, but had obviously been told not to mention it by Alice. Still, they made up for it by shooting Hope evil looks every time she caught their eye.

Apart from that, it was actually rather lovely to be a guest and not a beleaguered daughter who was only good enough to peel potatoes and de-vein prawns. Hope offered to help, but Alice asked her, through gritted teeth, to entertain her mother-in-law. Hope was expecting a battle-axe with a blue rinse, but instead Sophia was a dyed-in-the-wool leftie who'd marched at Aldermaston, camped out at Greenham Common, and had recently been kettled in Whitehall. They spent a pleasant hour drinking Cava with pomegranate juice and getting very angry about education cuts, library cuts, NHS cuts, and any other cuts they could think of.

Soon it was time to sit down for Christmas dinner, and it seemed that every family groaned at the jokes in the crackers and insisted that everyone wore their paper hats, and were more interested in eating the stuffing and the pigs-in-blankets than the actual turkey. Normally Hope loved Christmas dinner, she even loved Brussels sprouts, but she was too churned up to eat. It wasn't just about Jack or her hangover, but also a lot to do with seeing Wilson in a few short hours, with toothbrush, which could only mean one thing. It was a thing that terrified and thrilled Hope in equal measure. Not that it was a thing that she could actively participate in, because it would be wrong and tacky when she and Jack had only just split up. But just the thought of the thing was enough to have her toes curling in her shoes, because having sex with only one person, for the entirety of your adult life, made the mere thought of a thing with someone else a little bit frightening.

'You've barely touched your sticky toffee pudding,' Hope heard Alice exclaim, as Lottie muttered to Nancy, 'She doesn't even deserve any pudding after what she did to Jack.'

Hope pushed her bowl away with a rueful smile. 'Sorry, I'm absolutely stuffed from your roast potatoes,' she said, even though she'd only been able to manage one, with was five less than she usually shovelled into her mouth. 'Shall I make a start on loading the dishwasher?'

'You will not,' Sophia said with great force. 'You're a guest in this house and, anyway, it doesn't take long to load a dishwasher. Not like doing the washing-up, which wastes far less water.'

It was another two hours and a viewing of *It's a Wonderful Life* before Hope was allowed to leave, after she promised that she'd take half the turkey and a completely intact chocolate yule log with her.

It was six o'clock by the time she was safely back on her side of the garden wall, and all the panic and anticipation that she'd had to tamp down reared up again, and Hope found herself doing a complete circuit of the flat with arms flailing in all directions, which accomplished precisely nothing, when she had much to accomplish. Although she'd had a bath that morning, Hope felt the need to shower and shave off every extraneous hair on her body. It was also very important that she slathered herself in a fig-scented body moisturiser that she'd bought herself, rather than use any products Jack had liberated from the *Skirt* beauty cupboard.

Hope wasted ten minutes hunting for the knickers that matched her black and white polka-dot bra, not that Wilson was going to be seeing them, so it didn't really matter whether they matched or not, and then she stood in front of her open wardrobe and steeled herself for the style dilemma that lay ahead. It was important she looked vaguely on trend but not especially sexy, as that would only send out the wrong message. Then again, Hope didn't want to look as if she'd made no effort. After all, a girl had her pride.

Eventually, she wriggled into a teal-blue lace shift dress, with long sleeves and a high neckline, even if the hem hovered at mid-thigh. Still, thick woolly tights made the short skirt look a lot less come-hither, and she went easy on her eye make-up – just a quick up and down with her mascara wand, before dusting her face with powder and applying some Rose Salve lip balm.

Hope was now running late. She zipped herself into her black knee-boots with the sensible heel and quickly packed a bag with toothbrush, vitamins, pyjamas and a spare pair of pants, only because she *might* have to stay over. If it got really late and Wilson was drinking and she couldn't get a cab without taking out a second mortgage. Then she grabbed the two bags she'd packed with yummy treats and alcohol, and headed out into the frozen, deserted streets of N7.

The frost made everything glitter like the Christmas decorations Hope could see when she glanced idly in at people's windows. She turned off to walk past Holloway Prison, where she hoped the inmates were having a nice Christmas (apart from the serial killers, obviously), then wended her way through the back roads to get to Kentish Town. It was usually a good forty-minute walk, but she was striding along at great speed, and not just because the sooner she arrived, the sooner she could get indoors where there was central heating, but because the fizz of anticipation was quickening both her blood and her step.

As she hit Kentish Town Road, which was deserted apart from a gang of teenagers gathered outside the one convenience store that was open and trying to persuade people to buy them alcohol, Hope's phone beeped. She reached for it with bumbling, gloved fingers, the fizz fizzling out as she braced herself for a text from Jack or, worse, her mother, which would make all her good cheer evaporate and her conscience kick in, so she'd be forced into an abrupt U-turn and a cold walk home.

Hello, Miss Delafield. You still coming? Shall I meet you halfway? Wilson

Hope's good cheer returned in full force as she pondered why the thought of meeting Wilson halfway seemed rather saucy and suggestive. The fast walk had upped her heart rate, and Hope suspected that she wasn't filled with good cheer so much as raging horniness. Not that there was anywhere open at quarter past eight on Christmas night where she could buy a quick dose of bromide. She really must remember not to drink too much, because that was when all her best intentions fell flat, Hope decided, as she adjusted the strap of one of her jute bags.

No need, she texted back. *Only five minutes away. Please crank up the central heating.*

It didn't seem like five minutes, but no time at all before she was standing outside Wilson's building and pressing the buzzer.

'Is it you?' asked Wilson.

'No, it's burglars,' Hope replied. 'Burglars whose fingers and toes are turning into little icicles.'

Wilson laughed in the split second before he buzzed her in. She began the long trek up the stairs and as she reached the third-floor landing, she heard a door above open and when she rounded the next corner, Wilson was heading down the stairs to meet her.

'Happy Christmas,' he said. 'Kettle's on.'

'I have half a turkey, a whole chocolate yule log, cashew nuts and a tin of Quality Street,' Hope informed him, and she was sure that it wasn't the long march from Holloway and the stair-climbing that made her sound so out of breath. 'And posh bubbly and cheap bubbly.'

They came face to face on the fourth landing and Wilson didn't say anything, just stood one step above her – and all of a sudden, Hope felt ridiculously shy. She also felt like quite the brazen hussy, with her toothbrush and a spare pair of knickers stowed away in her handbag.

'Hey,' she croaked and raised her eyes timidly to see Wilson smiling down at her. Wilson wasn't given to smiling much, which was a pity, because when he did, he looked almost silver-screen handsome, and Hope felt her frozen limbs begin to thaw out. 'Have you had a nice day?'

'Well, I discovered that Brussels sprouts taste much better when they're fried in bacon fat. Here, let me take some of this stuff,' he added, relieving Hope of both of her jute bags. 'And I was forced to play football on the Heath with a gang of under-sixteen-year-olds who had no respect for the off-side rule.'

'Well, at least you worked off some of the bacon fat,' Hope said, as she followed him up the last flight of stairs, and found herself in the perfect position to ogle – no, not ogle – appreciate Wilson's long legs and the firmness of his arse. Christ, she needed to nip the appreciating in the bud, because they were just two friends having a Christmas drink. Though could you really be friends with someone when you'd already given each other an orgasm and had a nagging suspicion that a Christmas drink might lead to more of the same?

'How about you? What kind of day did you have?' Wilson asked as he shouldered open the door to his studio and ushered Hope through.

'Mostly I talked about political protest with Alice from next door's mother-in-law,' Hope said, as they walked across the room together. Then she walked up the spiral staircase first and wondered whether Wilson was staring at her legs and what he could make out of her arse through her bulky winter coat. 'I wish our Brussels had been done in bacon fat 'cause they tasted a little swampy.'

She was finally on Wilson's home turf, where it was cosy and warm, and all the lights had been dimmed. He'd even lit tealights in votive candle-holders and lined them up in rows on the windowsills. Hope couldn't decide if it was festive or seductive.

Wilson was unpacking the gourmet treats she'd brought with her, as Hope slowly unbuttoned her coat. It felt like she was performing a striptease, especially when Wilson lifted his head, looked straight at her and began to walk over from the galley kitchen to where she was still standing by the door. He held out his arms for her coat, then waited as she unwound her scarf and pulled off her hat.

'Oh, Hope, you cut your hair,' he said sadly. 'Why would you do that?'

Her hand shot up and kept going, because each time she went to touch it, her hair was so much shorter than she remembered. After Polly's repair job, Hope didn't think it looked so bad – there was something of a flapper vibe to it, and it had a slight wave now it wasn't weighted down by its own length. But maybe she'd just been kidding herself, because Wilson had angled his head so he could see her new do from all sides and was looking distinctly underwhelmed.

'It tangles really easily,' she explained. 'And I thought it would be easier to manage and I fancied a change. You hate it, don't you?'

'I don't,' Wilson protested. 'It suits you. It's just a bit of a shock.'

'Do you think it looks more ginger?' Hope couldn't help asking. 'It just seems more *orange* now.'

'What? No! It looks gorgeous, you're all eyes and cheekbones,' Wilson said gamely, lightly touching the ends, and as Hope turned her head his warm fingers brushed against her cold cheek.

Hope thought she might have gasped, because she'd been agonising about that first touch, and she saw Wilson's eyes widen and darken, and she couldn't say which one of them stepped closer, but she heard the soft thud of her coat fall to the floor, and then she was in Wilson's arms and they were kissing.

Chapter Forty-three

Not tentative, polite kisses. Not at all. Wilson's tongue was fucking her mouth as Hope coiled herself around him, one hand sliding down his back to grab his arse and haul him closer.

Just when Hope thought she might actually swoon in Wilson's arms, he tore his mouth away to place ferocious, hungry kisses on her neck as he tugged ineffectually at her dress, the dress that was never meant to come off, which was why Hope was already trying to tug down the zip.

'No,' Wilson said hoarsely. 'I want . . . I've thought about undressing you. I've imagined it for so long.'

This should have been the point when Hope told Wilson sternly that they could kiss and only kiss, but it was to go no further than that. Instead she was leaning against the back of the sofa and running her hand up his chest so she could feel the frantic thud of his heart under black cashmere. 'What else have you imagined?' she asked.

Wilson stepped between her thighs so Hope could feel the prod of his hard cock against her belly. 'I told you that I wanted to kiss every single one of your freckles. I want to see where they stop, and I'll kiss you there too, but mostly I've thought about fucking you.'

Hope hung her head and tried to catch each panting breath that came out of her mouth. 'I've thought about that too,' she admitted. 'I shouldn't have, but I did.'

'You're going to say it's too soon, aren't you?' Wilson's

voice was resigned as he took a step back. 'You've only just got out of a long, difficult relationship, and you're not ready to jump into bed with the first guy who asks.' He sighed. 'Why did I have to fall for a nice girl?'

'I'm not a nice girl!' Hope said indignantly. 'But it *is* too soon. I was worried that this would happen if I came round, and I swore to myself that we'd just have a little drink and a laugh, and if I did have to stay the night, it would all be respectable and above board.'

'You're right.' Wilson smiled tightly. It wasn't a fraction as beguiling as his earlier smile. 'Tea or champagne? Or should we not risk alcohol?'

'It *is* too soon,' Hope repeated. 'And if we have sex it will make everything really complicated . . .'

'Yeah, I think you already mentioned that.'

'. . . but I don't care that it's too soon, I don't care about complicated, and I really don't care about being respectable and above board,' Hope said, bracing her arms against the back of the sofa so her heaving breasts under teal-coloured lace were thrust forward. Wilson's eyes were immediately drawn to them. 'I've had it up to here with doing the right thing. I want to do all sorts of bad things, and I want to do them with you.'

'You absolutely sure about that?' Wilson clarified, but he wasn't making any kind of move, even if his eyes were still fixed on her tits.

Hope wanted to stamp her foot, but she settled for a fervent 'Yes!' and then, thank God, Wilson had closed the distance between them and his mouth was on hers again, and he was half lifting her so he could stagger towards the slatted staircase that led to his bedroom.

He even attempted the first step, which was sweet of him, but if Wilson carried on like this, he'd either drop her or give himself a hernia, which would curtail the evening's agenda of all sorts of bad things before they'd begun. Instead Hope stood on her own two feet, took Wilson's hand, her fingers twining around his, and led him up the stairs to his bed-room.

It was a long, low room under the eaves, lit only by the candles downstairs, so they were half in shadow, until Wilson snapped on the bedside lamp and Hope could see his huge bed, with an old-fashioned iron bedstead, dressed in crisp white linen. In fact, she couldn't tear her eyes away from the bed.

'Turn round,' Wilson said.

'Why?' she asked, even as she turned round, then shivered as she felt Wilson's lips press against the back of her neck, that sensitive patch of skin which had always been hidden by her hair.

'Because I'm going to undress you,' Wilson replied, and he started to slowly inch down the zip of her dress, kissing each millimetre of skin that was gradually exposed.

When the dress got stuck on her hips, Hope worked the fabric loose and kicked it away, then pushed down her woolly tights, while Wilson stared at her, his tongue moistening dry lips, as if Hope was seductively unrolling a pair of silk stockings.

Then she was standing in another man's bedroom in her underwear, and Hope suddenly realised the enormity of what she was about to do with this other man who wasn't Jack.

It was someone else looking at her body, running his eyes over the freckles that dusted her breasts, and along the slope of her belly and the curve of her hips and on to her thighs, which would never be long and lean even if she took up marathon-running. That didn't seem to matter so much with Jack, because Hope's body was as familiar to Jack as his own, but Wilson might have higher standards.

He'd been with Susie after all, and before Susie there had been other women, and he was a photographer so some of those other women must have been models – and she'd been with no one else but Jack. Just Jack.

'You look like a Vargas girl,' Wilson suddenly breathed, his hand gently and tentatively stroking her hip as if he was scared to touch her. 'I could just picture you painted on the side of a Second World War bomber plane.'

'You could?' Hope asked doubtfully.

'Absolutely,' he said, and then he dropped to his knees so he could kiss the big splodgy freckle on Hope's left knee, because she even had freckles on her kneecaps. It was the first time a man, or anyone, had bowed down before her and though that felt weird and vaguely wrong, it also made Hope feel less self-conscious about standing there in her M&S knickers and bra.

Wilson was now investigating the freckles behind her knee, which tickled. Hope touched the top of his head, careful not to dislodge his quiff, which was still vertical despite the earlier, frantic kisses. 'I'm feeling a bit under-dressed,' she pointed out. 'Maybe you should lose some clothes too?'

'I suppose I could, while you're arranging yourself on the bed,' Wilson agreed, as he slowly got to his feet and grimaced slightly when he straightened up. 'Yeah, this might work better if you were lying down, because I think I pulled something when I was playing football.'

'I could massage it, if you wanted,' Hope offered as Wilson nudged her nearer to his huge bed. 'I am a trained first-aider.'

'Later,' Wilson said, and then he pulled his jumper and T-shirt over his head, and the view was so good that Hope stopped worrying about the most flattering position to lie in and decided to concentrate on the floor show, as Wilson toed off his shoes and pulled off his socks. Hope propped herself up on her elbows, all the better to see, and because it flattened her tummy and perked up her boobs. Wilson raised his eyebrows at her. 'Seen anything you like?'

Hope nodded. 'Quite a lot of things, actually,' she said, and she'd never been good at the sexy talk, but Wilson seemed so relaxed and unfreaked out that it made her feel relaxed and, well, about 50 per cent less freaked out than she had been.

Eyes fixed on hers, Wilson unbuckled his belt and pulled it slowly through the loops on his jeans, then he began to unbutton them with what looked like great difficulty. Up until then, Hope's gaze had drifted across the firmly muscled planes of Wilson's chest, resting appreciatively on his biceps and the way his pecs rippled as he moved. He was solid without being flabby, and it was going to feel so good when he was on top of her, or when she was on top of him and not worrying that she was going to crush his ribs. But then Wilson pushed down his jeans and his boxers and kicked them off, and Hope could see exactly why he'd had difficulty in unbuttoning, and now she knew that it hadn't been false advertising when Susie had said that Wilson had a big dick.

Of course, she'd already touched it, but that time Wilson had only unzipped his jeans, and Hope hadn't even glanced down, but now she had a perfect view of his cock and it was big and beautiful, though Hope had never thought of cocks in that way. He was already lovely and hard, his dick straining upwards so it was almost touching his belly, and Wilson stroked it almost absent-mindedly as he smiled at Hope. It was a smile full of promise and she couldn't help but smile back.

'You should probably roll over so I can get to work on those freckles,' he told Hope as he moved towards her.

'But then I won't be able to see you,' she complained, but Wilson's hand was already on her hip and she was turning over to lie on her front on his bed, her hands shaking slightly as she rested her head on her folded arms.

She felt the bed shift as Wilson kneeled on it, then his fingers curled around her left ankle, and she smothered a shriek as he licked a path along the arch of her foot. 'I don't have any freckles there!'

'Just checking,' Wilson said, and he began to place kisses

along her calves. It tickled, and she wriggled on his duvet cover, breath catching in her throat as he reached her upper thighs. But though his fingers hooked into the waistband of her briefs, he began to kiss his way up her spine, unclipping her bra so he could trail his tongue along the red marks it had left, until he arrived at her shoulders, where the freckles reached critical mass. 'I think this might take some time.'

It seemed to take for ever, with Wilson alternating between butterfly brushes against Hope's skin and hot open-mouthed kisses that had her scrunching handfuls of quilt between her fingers. Then he was on the move downwards again, slowly tugging her panties down with a little tut, as if he was annoyed with them for hiding Hope's arse from him. Still, she tensed up as her bum was displayed in all its rounded glory.

She tensed up even further when she felt Wilson's mouth rain kisses down on her buttocks, and his hand slipped between her legs to keep her still, the tips of his fingers centimetres away from where she was already wet and aching for him.

His fingers shifted higher and Hope thought she might have stopped breathing altogether as she felt them graze against her pussy, but then he was moving away and she wanted to cry, just a little.

'Turn over,' he said with a commanding edge to his voice so Hope didn't think of refusing, even though as she rolled over and fidgeted until she was lying on her back, pillows propped up behind her, she felt ridiculously shy and naked in a way that wasn't about not having a stitch on.

Wilson didn't even disguise the fact that he was running his eyes over her body with an intensity that bordered on obsessive, so nothing would escape his scrutiny, not her pot belly, or her splayed thighs, or the way that her breasts were too small to balance out her wide hips.

'God, you're so fucking sexy,' he said in a thick, treacly

voice, and he was touching his cock again, but when Hope's hand crept over so she could join in, because it felt as if they'd been doing this for hours and she hadn't even got to touch him yet, he slapped her hand away. 'Not yet. I'm only halfway through my task.'

'Maybe you could finish it later,' Hope suggested, but Wilson just smiled and shook his head.

He started with her feet again and as he travelled up her legs, biting softly now and again, Hope started squirming, thighs parted so Wilson would have to be blind not see how much she wanted him, but he simply placed a hundred tiny kisses on her neatly trimmed mound and continued upwards.

'I can't take much more of this,' Hope gasped. She felt as if it wouldn't be too long before she began to cry from pure, unrelenting frustration. 'I want you so much that it hurts.'

Wilson lifted his head from where he'd been dipping his tongue into her belly button. 'Promise I'll kiss that better in a bit, too,' he drawled, and Hope was just about to hit him or kick him, she hadn't decided which, when his hands closed around her breasts.

She lifted her arms so she could wrap her fingers around the bars of the bedstead as Wilson's mouth worked furiously on one pouting nipple, sucking it hard, while his fingers teased her other breast. Then he switched over.

When Hope let go of the bedstead in favour of grabbing Wilson by the quiff, he stopped. Finally, she thought, relaxing her limbs and getting ready to take him in her arms, but he was sliding back down the bed and settling himself between her thighs.

'Now where exactly does it hurt?' he asked and before Hope could answer, he decided to find out for himself.

In Hope's limited, one-man-only experience, oral sex wasn't something that happened the first time. In fact, the only time it happened was when she absolutely begged Jack to reciprocate after she'd given him a lengthy blow job.

Even then, he did it with a put-upon air and not much enthusiasm. But then Hope stopped thinking about what Jack did and didn't do, because all she could concentrate on was what Wilson was doing: two fingers gently thrusting inside her, grazing a little spot that made her buck her hips, as he caught her clit gently between his teeth and sucked on it.

She was coming before she even knew that she was coming, twisting and turning against Wilson's clever mouth, so he had to put his hands on her hips to hold her down and make sure that she didn't decapitate him with her thighs. Hope reached down to push him away and pull him up so he was lying next to her as she tried to catch her breath.

'Was that all right?' he asked, and Hope could hear his hesitation, as if he wasn't confident of his performance.

'God, it was more than all right,' Hope sighed. She ran the back of her hand along his flushed cheek. 'If you give me a moment to recover, I'll return the favour.'

'I'd rather fuck you,' Wilson said, and his gruff, plain way of speaking might be kind of scary and annoying sometimes, but when Hope was naked on his bed, it was wonderfully arousing, even though she'd been sure that she needed at least half an hour to get her second wind. 'Can we bank the blow job?'

'I think that can be arranged,' Hope said with a giggle, turning on to her side so she could smoosh against Wilson and kiss him slowly and wetly as her hand reached for his cock. This time Wilson didn't stop her, and she closed her fingers around him, mentally comparing him to Jack because she couldn't not. She wasn't a size-queen, but his cock was big and solid like the rest of him, and even as they kissed, Hope's mind was racing with the possibilities of what it would feel like when they were fucking.

The kisses had started off slow and languid, but as Wilson shifted so he was lying over her and she could feel the head of his cock nudging against her inner thigh, the kisses became fiercer, hands started wandering and she was canting her hips, trying to get just an inch of him inside her.

'What are you doing?' Hope hissed, when Wilson lifted himself up so she was suddenly cold and untouched. 'Did I do something wrong?'

'No, you were doing things exactly right.' Wilson nodded his head in the direction of the nightstand. 'Could you grab a condom?'

That was something else that Hope hadn't had much experience of before. She'd been taking the pill ever since she'd turned sixteen and had gone on a stealth mission to the family-planning clinic in Rochdale, and had been on it ever since because she knew where Jack had been – although when they'd been having make-up sex, she hadn't known that he and Susie were really shagging, which was another thing she should hate him for . . .

'Hey, hey! Where did you go?' Wilson asked softly, and as Hope brushed the hair out of her eyes, she pushed the bad thoughts away.

'Sorry,' she said, scrambling to her knees and opening the drawer. 'One condom coming up. Shall I do the honours?'

As Hope leaned over to put the condom on, curiosity got the better of her. Besides, it seemed rude not to when his cock was so hard and so near that it was a simple matter to take him in her mouth. Wilson tasted clean and salty. Hope swirled her tongue over the tip of his dick, her eyes on him as he threw his head back and caught his lip between his teeth. She was all set to suck, hard, when he actually lifted her off him and practically threw her back down on the bed.

'Not helping,' he said through gritted teeth, snatching the condom out of her sweaty hand and prising it out of its foil wrapper. 'Obviously you can't be trusted.'

'Obviously,' Hope agreed, parting her legs once Wilson was safely suited up, and coaxing him back down. 'But I just couldn't help myself.'

Wilson lowered his head and nipped her neck, and they

were right back where they'd been a moment ago, except now Hope was worming her hand between their bodies to take hold of his dick again and guide him into her. He pushed in slowly, an inch at a time, then retreating, before pressing home a little further so Hope could feel him filling her, stretching her, and when his cock was deep inside her, she wrapped her arms and legs tightly around him.

They hardly knew each other, not really, but they were as close as two people could possibly be, and though it felt right, in fact it felt really good with the walls of her pussy gripping him tight and the base of his cock rubbing against her clit, it was also a little sad. Because in that moment, Hope knew that she and Jack were really over, there was no going back now. And she didn't want to go back, but to not have that option any more was a little frightening.

'Stop thinking,' Wilson whispered in her ear. 'No thinking, just feeling.'

And then he moved, pulling out of her, to thrust back in, harder and faster than he had before, and Hope was scoring her nails down his back to urge him to go even harder and faster. She lifted herself up so she was almost sitting on his lap, revelling in the slap of flesh on flesh, the bedstead banging against the wall and Wilson's voice telling her how beautiful she was, how tight she was, how he could become addicted to fucking her. Then she was almost there, almost but not quite, just needed Wilson's hand suddenly dipping down, thumb rubbing hard against her clit, and she was biting down hard on his shoulder, urging him on with eager little cries, as his rhythm faltered and he was coming too.

'That was the best Christmas present I ever had,' he said later, when they were both lying flat and spread-eagled on the bed, only their little fingers hooked together. 'Even better than when I got a Scalextric.'

Hope still wasn't capable of rational thought, much less speaking, so she just smiled and hmmed her agreement.

'Are you all right?' Wilson tried to prop himself up but

Hope refused to relinquish her grip on his little finger. 'No second thoughts?'

Surely if she was having second thoughts, she wouldn't be sprawled in a state of post-coital bliss with her mind resembling mush? 'No, I'm good,' she murmured. 'Really good.' Except, there was one thing. 'Don't take this the wrong way . . .'

Wilson tensed up. 'So you *are* having regrets?' He stopped tensing, in favour of slumping. 'I knew this would happen. You didn't do anything wrong and there's no point in beating yourself up over someone who—'

'Don't!' It took great effort, but Hope sat up. 'Don't you dare bring *that* up when all I was going to say was that I'm really hungry.'

'Oh, right. Sorry.' Wilson curled his fingers around hers again. 'I'm hungry too. Starving, to be more accurate. I was so nervous about you coming over that I could hardly eat a thing all day.'

'I could only manage one roast potato,' Hope volunteered.

Wilson sniffed. 'I didn't even have any pigs-in-blankets.'

Hope rolled over so Wilson would get the full benefit of her plaintive expression. She pulled her hand free of his so she could fashion herself two little paws. 'Please will you go and make me a turkey sandwich?'

Chapter Forty-four

They spent the next three days in bed, so that Hope wasn't sure when it was day and when it was night, though she didn't much care. Her mind was a hot red blur of what they'd done, what they were going to do, all the things she'd ever wanted to try, but had never had the courage to suggest in case Jack thought she was some kind of freak.

But if Hope was a freak, then Wilson was too, because whenever she managed to falteringly describe a scenario that had provided her with fantasy fodder for years, Wilson would quirk an eyebrow and murmur, 'Hmm, sounds interesting.' Then he'd pause and get a faraway look in his eyes. 'So, if you're up for that, then how would you feel about embellishing it a little?' Wilson's embellishments always seemed to lead to things that Hope wouldn't have thought were anatomically possible, or had to be illegal in at least five countries, not that she minded when she was screaming herself hoarse and clawing at the bedsheets.

It wasn't all about sex, though. It was also about eating turkey sandwiches the size of bricks and drinking tea or wine as they chatted. The kind of inconsequential chatter that meandered through childhood pets and films that made them cry, to their all-time favourite midnight snacks, to the most drunk they'd ever been. It was the unimportant stuff that really defined who you were, and that you shared when you were starting to really get to know someone. Because although, technically, they'd known each other for months, it had been months of not liking each other very much, then months of *Sturm und Drang*, and it was only now that they were really figuring out the meat and bones of each other.

Hope now knew that Wilson hated pickles, couldn't sleep until he hoovered the sandwich crumbs off the bedsheets with a dustbuster, and had been thinking about getting a cat for years, but didn't know if he was ready to assume responsibility for another living creature. 'I have to check that Alfie has washed his hands after he's had a leak, so having to deal with litter boxes would just be too much,' he'd complained.

Hope had thought that she might go home to get some fresh clothes or to give Wilson some time and space. But as she spent most of the time either naked or in one of Wilson's shirts, and when she got back into bed after foraging for food and drinks in the kitchen, he'd wrap his arms around her and insist that she'd been gone too long, fresh clothes and giving Wilson some time and space weren't really an issue.

She didn't know where this was going. If it was just a few days of the wild, uninhibited, no-strings sex that Hope had always imagined single girls had, or if it was something more permanent, more meaningful. But after years of no surprises, her life all planned out, not knowing was an exhilarating white-knuckle ride.

On the fourth day of their confinement, after they'd bathed together in Wilson's claw-footed, roll-topped bath, sipping the champagne that they'd only just got round to opening, legs entwined, Hope decided that she couldn't stay here for ever. For one thing, they were running desperately short of milk, they'd finished the last of the bread the night before, and Quality Street and slightly stale mince pies weren't a nutritionally balanced diet. Besides, Jack was due back any day and there were things that needed to be sorted out.

'Oh dear,' Wilson said, when Hope tripped down the stairs

from his bedroom wearing her lace dress and clutching her iPhone. 'You have this look that makes me think you're dressed for more than a trip to Tesco's.'

'What kind of look?' Hope asked as she switched her phone back on.

'Mulish,' Wilson explained. 'Determined. Not particularly happy.'

'He's back,' Hope said, as she skimmed through her messages. 'In fact, he's been back since yesterday, and he wants to know if I've run off to join the Foreign Legion.'

Wilson got down the last two clean mugs. Due to the lack of milk, they'd both resigned themselves to choking down camomile tea. 'I suppose it's not the kind of situation that's going to take just a phone call?'

Oh, how Hope wished that it was, but . . . 'I have to see him. Hanging around a tiny flat, waiting on someone else, when you don't know where they are or if they're coming back, is horrible.' She hoisted herself up on one of Wilson's kitchen stools and rested her elbows on the breakfast bar. 'Anyway, I can't stay here for ever.'

'Well, no, not for ever,' Wilson conceded, and Hope felt her heart sink. She'd had enough of for ever to last a life-time, but four days was hardly any time at all. 'But I was going to cook an actual meal for tea. A meal that includes these green things called vegetables.'

Not knowing where she stood or how to negotiate these first hesitant steps didn't seem quite so exhilarating after all. It seemed like very hard work. 'So, do you want me to come back, then?'

'I don't know. Are you planning to come back?' Wilson asked, but all his attention was fixed on pouring hot water on to herbal tea bags. 'You might go home, and he's there and he wants to give it another go, and you might think that it's a good idea. It wouldn't be the first time.'

Hope tried to picture Jack at his most beguiling, his most persuasive, but she couldn't think of anything that he could say that would make her want to give it another go. Probably, whatever he had to say would lead to yet another row and at least one of them in tears, but Hope wouldn't know until she went home.

Wilson put a steaming mug down in front of her and for just one moment his hand rested on her shoulder, fingers squeezing gently. It was comforting, but it didn't make what Hope had to do any easier. 'I'll text you in a couple of hours, shall I?'

'You don't owe me anything,' Wilson suddenly said. 'If you are walking away from a long-term relationship, then you shouldn't jump straight into another one. I wouldn't expect you to and, let's face it, Hope, it's too soon for you to have any idea of what you really want.'

'I like you, though. I like you a lot.' Hope tried to run her fingers through her hair, but it was thoroughly unsatisfying now that there wasn't much of it. 'But you're right, I need to figure out who I am when I'm not one half of a couple.'

'I don't know where this is going, and I won't make you any promises. It's not my style.' Wilson leaned over so he could cover Hope's hand with his. 'But I can offer you dinner in a couple of hours.'

Hope nodded. 'With vegetables.'

'Damn bloody right, with vegetables.'

Going home took two buses and a slow, foot-dragging walk. As Hope unlatched the gate, she could see the light on in the lounge and her stomach clenched painfully as she hunted for her key.

She heard the sound of footsteps as she opened the door, but it was still a shock when Jack appeared. Her body gave a quick jerk of recognition. It was Jack, and Hope was still used to being pleased to see him.

'Shall I put the kettle on?' he asked, and she nodded and followed him into the flat.

Jack went into the kitchen, and Hope walked into the

bedroom to dump her stuff, then stood there, unsure of what to do next, because it didn't feel right to make herself at home and use the bathroom or help herself to something from the fridge without permission, which was stupid when her name was on the mortgage deeds, right next to Jack's.

There was no point in skulking, but forcing herself to walk into the kitchen was one of the hardest things she'd ever had to do. Hope leaned against the worktop, arms folded, and saw that Jack had finished painting the kitchen cupboards buttermilk and duck-egg blue.

'Kitchen looks nice. Very Shaker on a B&Q budget,' Hope remarked, as she gazed around the room. She could feel Jack watching her, but she couldn't bring herself to look him in the eye.

How had he been able to come home, after shagging Susie, and act like nothing had ever happened? How had he been able to do that?

'Here you go,' Jack said, handing her a mug of strong tea, sugar already in it, because he knew just how she liked it.

'Thanks.' Hope took a sip and she hated herself, because all she could think about was how long it would take her to drink her tea and gee herself up to start a conversation that she was dreading, so she could then pack a bag and leave.

'You've been with him, haven't you?' Jack asked hoarsely, and finally Hope had to turn and look at him.

'How can you tell?' she asked, because really there was no point in denying it. They were broken up. They were broken up, and objectively she was free to do what she wanted. Subjectively was another matter.

'I just know.' Jack waved a hand in Hope's general direction. 'You have this freshly fucked glow about you.'

'Please, can we not have an argument?' Hope pleaded, and then she looked at Jack's face, properly looked at him instead of making her eyes skitter away at the last moment because she was too much of a coward.

He looked like hell.

It had always been a sore point with Hope that Jack lost weight easily, but in a week, he'd become gaunt and drawn; there were purple shadows under his eyes and he had spots. Jack had never had spots, not even when he was a teenager, but now he had a bumper crop of zits along his forehead and chin. Hope took no pleasure in knowing that Jack was suffering, just like she'd suffered at his hands, although she'd got fatter rather than thinner.

'Oh, Jack,' she sighed and she put down her mug so she could wrap him up in the tightest, fiercest hug she was capable of.

Jack let her hug him, his arms enfolding her too. 'You cut all your hair off. Your mum's going to kill you.'

Hope choked on a giggle. 'What will she do with her time, now that she won't have to spend most of it nagging me to have a comb-out?'

It wasn't long before the hug felt awkward. They both realised that it was too prolonged at the exact same second, but disentangling themselves was even more awkward, and standing in the kitchen a foot apart from each other felt agonising, as if they'd suddenly found themselves on stage without a script.

'So . . .' Hope tried to smile brightly but it fell off her face as soon as it had appeared.

'So . . .' Jack repeated.

'So . . . you can stay here if you want . . .'

'So . . . have you spoken to Susie?'

They both stopped again and grinned sheepishly at each other. Jack nudged Hope with his hip. 'Does this mean that it's over, and for once we both agree that it's over?'

'I think it does,' Hope agreed, and she nudged him back, and he nudged her harder, so she had to grip on to the worktop to bump him really hard with her hip, so he lost his footing and was forced to move, and Hope had won. And they were both smiling at each other, and it was all stupid and ridiculous and nothing made sense any more, so they could drink their tea and even joke that if Hope's absence from a family Christmas hadn't killed any grandparents, then all their grandparents were likely to be around for years to come.

'So, you can have the car if you want,' Jack said, as she began to wash up their mugs. 'Do you want the car?'

'To tell you the truth, I'd rather have the washing machine,' Hope replied. 'And if you wanted to stay here, I could probably crash at Lauren's for a while.'

'I probably won't stay here, though,' Jack said, and he ducked his head and ran his finger along the edge of the worktop. 'I mean, I'll probably stay with Susie, if she'll have me.'

It wasn't the agony that it used to be when Hope imagined Susie and Jack together, but it still hurt. 'I think she will have you,' she said softly.

'And you and him? Is that serious, then?'

'No. Not right now.' Hope bit her lip. 'Not sure if it ever will be, but I can't deal with anything serious at the moment.'

'We'll still be friends, won't we, Hopey?' Jack sounded so panic-stricken that Hope looked at him in alarm. 'If I lost you as my best friend, it would be even worse than losing you as my girlfriend.'

It wasn't the most tactful way to phrase it, especially when Jack was already planning to move in with Susie, but Hope knew what he meant. 'Of course we'll still be best friends,' she insisted, taking Jack's hand so she could curl her fingers around his. 'I'll always, always love you. You ever need anything from me, whether it's cash or a shoulder to cry on or a kidney, I'm there for you.'

Hope didn't know how it happened, but they were kissing. Arms around each other, lips on lips, and they were desperate kisses that tasted of sadness and regret. Goodbye kisses. Then Jack took his mouth away from hers, pressed his lips against her forehead and stepped back.

'I'm going to go now,' he said gently. 'Is that all right?'

Hope nodded. 'Yeah, course it is.'

Jack was already backing out of the room. She hadn't even noticed his bags packed and in the hall. 'I meant it, Hopey. Best friends for ever.'

'Like I said, if you ever need a kidney,' Hope said and folded her arms as she watched him walk away.

The front door gently closed behind him.

Epilogue

Some months later . . .

Even though all the windows were open and a summer breeze wafted through the rooms, the flat reeked of paint.

Hope finished the bit of coving she was working on, put down her paintbrush and carefully climbed down the ladder. She was still a bit shaky on the dismount, and she still didn't appreciate the way Lauren and Allison gave her a round of applause. Yes, it had been funny the first time they did it, but the fifteenth time? Not so much.

'I'm getting a beer,' Hope announced. 'Anyone need a refill?'

Otto raised his hand. 'Me, please.'

Hope shook her head – there were already three empty Stella Artois bottles lined up next to the skirting board he was painting. 'I'm sorry, but you've reached the three-bottle limit,' she told him sadly. 'We all agreed. After three bottles, people start painting wonky.'

Otto didn't agree, but backed down after some fierce glaring on Hope's part. She wandered into the bedroom where Lottie and Nancy from next door were giggling every time Marvin lifted his paintbrush and his T-shirt rode up to display his spectacular abdominal muscles to their over-eager pre-pubescent eyes. Alice from next door and Elaine and Simon had nearly finished the bathroom, and as Hope stepped out of the back door into the garden, there was a text from Marta to say she and Iban were on their way over with pizza and another bottle of white spirit.

Hope snagged a beer from the plastic bucket full of ice and sat down on the sofa, which was currently masquerading as garden furniture. *Everyone I love is here*, Hope thought to herself, and for one blissful second she felt mellow and content, until reality reared its ugly little head and her mind was back on her monumental to-do list, and all the items on it that still had to be ticked off before she and Jack handed over the keys of the flat to Gary from upstairs.

There'd been no point in even trying to sell the flat in the current economic climate, so they'd decided to rent it out and keep paying the mortgage. It made sense, though Hope's mother had insisted that subconsciously it was a way for them to stay together.

'How are we staying together when Jack's moving to Brixton and I'm going to Australia?' Hope had asked, when her parents came down to ferry most of her worldly goods back to her old bedroom.

Caroline Delafield had just smiled tightly. 'You'll only be in Australia for a few months.'

'I'll be gone a whole year,' Hope had reminded her. 'You know I'm travelling around the Far East before I even get to Australia.'

'We'll see,' her mother had said. 'You won't like it there. It will be far too hot and you'll get sunburn, maybe even melanoma, and I've heard things about *their* National Curriculum.' She'd sniffed. 'You had your interview via Skype. Via Skype! That's not how civilised people do things.' Hope could have sworn that she'd then muttered something about 'convicts'.

But Hope had let it go, because her mother had only just about forgiven her for her Christmas no-show and for cutting her hair off and, anyway, she wasn't going to have to see her for twelve months.

When Justine had emailed Hope to ask if she fancied doing maternity cover for one of her colleagues, it had been in February when London was in the grip of an arctic cold front and there'd been sheet-ice on the streets of Holloway for weeks. Then Justine's headmaster had, yes, interviewed her via Skype, and once he'd realised that Hope had a better work ethic than Justine, he'd offered her five thousand more than she was currently earning, promised she wouldn't have to take responsibility for the school carol concert, and implied that all houses in Sydney came with a swimming pool and air conditioning as standard. Hope still hadn't been entirely sold, but when she'd mooted the idea to Mr Gonzales, he'd said that Dorothy was taking retirement at the end of the next school year and Elaine was primed for promotion, so he could guarantee her a job teaching Yellow Class when she came back to England.

It seemed to Hope that life rarely came with satnav, but just this once it was obvious which way she should go. She was heading for the unknown, for having adventures and seeing the world, but with safety wheels and a job to come back to. There was no earthly reason to stay in London . . . or rather there was only one reason not to go . . .

'Just so you know, I'm not waiting for you,' said a gruff voice behind her, and Hope turned round to see Wilson standing in the kitchen doorway. He had paint splattered in his quiff and little dots of emulsion on the lenses of his glasses, which might have been why he was looking so grumpy.

'I know,' Hope said, scooching along the sofa, so Wilson could sit down next to her. 'You have mentioned it once or twice.'

'Just so we're clear.' Wilson clinked his beer bottle against Hope's. 'Play your cards right, though, and I might come out for Christmas.'

'Unless you've fallen in love with a model.'

Wilson smiled. 'Or you're shacked up with a surfer.'

'But if I'm not and you're not, then you're going to be in a world of trouble if you don't come and spend Christmas with me.' Hope leaned back against the sofa cushions. 'Did you see me climb up the ladder with a pot of paint in one hand?'

Wilson nodded. 'Yeah, I did. Hard not to, when you were telling everyone that you were climbing up the ladder with a pot of paint in one hand.'

Hope stuck her tongue out at him and he grinned and reached out a lazy hand to ruffle her hair, which she'd decided to keep short.

They sat there in silence, sipping beer and watching the sun cast shadows on the garden, which had been Hope's pride and joy. If Wilson had taught her one thing, apart from how to check the air pressure in her car tyres and where to source the really good vintage, it was to enjoy being quiet without the need to fill the space with empty words. She rested her head on his shoulder and didn't feel even a little bit guilty that all her dearest friends were working like slaves to paint her flat.

It was perfect, and it lasted for three minutes, until there was a commotion behind them and Hope looked round to see Susie being carefully helped by Jack down the two steps that led to the garden.

'Is there room for a little one on that sofa?' Susie asked, and when Hope agreed that there was, she waddled over.

Even though she was only halfway through her second trimester, Susie had perfected the lumbering gait of the heavily pregnant and was now gingerly aligning her arse with the sofa as if she was eight months gone with triplets.

The sun glinted off Susie's rings: the engagement ring that was *not* the same ring that Jack had offered Hope, and the platinum band he'd put on Susie's finger when they were married the month before at the Dover Street Arts Club on a Wednesday afternoon during term time, so Hope could offer her excuses and an Alessi juicer from their wedding list. She hadn't quite got used to the bittersweet pang when she saw the rings, and yes, there had been some dark days and darker nights when she'd cried herself to sleep, but she was crying for a fantasy that had never been real. Jack had only offered her marriage and babies as a last resort, but he'd gone to Susie half an hour after kissing Hope goodbye, and within six months, he was married and whipping out photos of the ultrasound at every opportunity. It turned out that he did want to settle down after all; he just hadn't wanted to settle down with Hope, and that hurt. Or niggled when she thought about it too much, in the same way that the scar on her palm itched when she got angry.

'Mopey Hopey is back in the house,' Susie teased, as she smoothed her hands over her beautifully rounded belly. 'Sad to be leaving?'

'A little bit, I suppose,' Hope admitted, glancing over at her rosebushes that she'd nursed through greenfly and groundfrost. Their little basement flat hadn't felt like home ever since that Saturday night the previous September. She'd spent far too much time here huddled into her own misery, as her hopes and dreams had slipped away, like salt spilling through her fingers. 'But I won't miss the smoking oven, or the faulty wiring, or the sea-grass carpet.'

Jack had gone to get a bottle of beer but now he perched on the arm of the sofa next to Susie so he could stroke her hair. 'There must be a few things you'll miss,' he insisted.

Hope thought about it. 'I'll miss the Golden Lantern's crispy aromatic duck,' she said finally. 'That's about it.'

She expected Jack to get some crack in about how she always thought about food before anything else but, as so often happened these days, there was nothing left to say, and Jack and Susie started to have a murmured conversation between themselves.

Hope turned to Wilson, who rolled his eyes, but the effect was lost thanks to the splodges on his glasses. 'You're covered in paint,' Hope told him softly. 'Shall we see if Marta's turned up with the white spirit?'

Susie winced when they got up, as if the cushions shifting was bringing on the Braxton Hicks, and Jack placed his hand on her bump and Hope, who knew him so well, knew his face better than her own reflection in the mirror, had never seen him smile so sweetly. She'd loved Jack with all her heart, but she'd never made him as happy as Susie did.

'Remember to email me your details,' he muttered vaguely, as Hope brushed past him.

'I'm not leaving for another two weeks,' Hope said, but he was nuzzling Susie's neck, making her giggle as she pretended to squirm away.

'You all right?' Wilson asked, once they were in the shadowy cool of the kitchen.

Hope glanced out of the window at the golden couple now smooching on the sofa, then tore her eyes away to look at Wilson, so solid and still by comparison, his expression stern, until she reached up and, with the edge of her nail, dislodged a blob of paint from the corner of his mouth.

'Never better,' she assured him, as she continued to pick away at the paint flecks that covered his face. 'How did you manage to get paint in your sideburns? Even Blue Class don't get themselves into such a mess.'

'You're hurting me,' he growled, then smiled as Hope kissed each spot better. 'Think you missed a bit.'

Then she kissed his mouth, which was relatively emulsion-free, and it was only when they heard Marta and Iban come through the front door that they broke apart.

You Don't Have to Say You Love Me

Sarra Manning

Sweet, bookish Neve Slater always plays by the rules.

And the number one rule is that good-natured fat girls like her don't get guys like gorgeous William, heir to Neve's heart since university. But William's been in LA for three years, and Neve's been slimming down and reinventing herself so that when he returns, he'll fall head over heels in love with the new, improved her.

So she's not that interested in other men. Until her sister points out that if Neve wants William to think she's an experienced love-goddess and not the fumbling, awkward girl he left behind, then she'd better get some, well, experience.

What Neve needs is someone to show her the ropes, someone like Max. Wicked, shallow, *sexy* Max. And since he's such a man-slut, and so not Neve's type, she certainly won't fall for him. Because William is the man for her . . . right?

The Boy Who Fell to Earth

Kathy Lette

Meet Merlin. He's Lucy's bright, beautiful son – who just happens to be autistic.

Since Merlin's father left them in the lurch shortly after his diagnosis, Lucy has made Merlin the centre of her world. Struggling with the joys and tribulations of raising her eccentrically adorable yet challenging child (if only Merlin came with operating instructions), Lucy doesn't have room for any other man in her life.

By the time Merlin turns ten, Lucy is seriously worried that the Pope might start ringing her up for tips on celibacy, so resolves to dip a poorly pedicured toe back into the world of dating. Thanks to Merlin's candour and quirkiness, things don't go *quite* to plan . . . Then, just when Lucy's resigned to a life of singledom once more, Archie – the most imperfectly perfect man for her and her son – lands on her doorstep. But then, so does Merlin's father, begging for forgiveness and a second chance. Does Lucy need a real father for Merlin – or a real partner for herself?

Funny yet heartbreaking, witty and wise – this unputdownable, bittersweet novel about keeping your family together when your world is falling apart is the wonderful Kathy Lette at her very, very best.